Viking Fire

JUSTIN HILL

Little, Brown

LITTLE, BROWN

First published in Great Britain in 2016 by Little, Brown

1 3 5 7 9 10 8 6 4 2

A CIP catalogue record for this book
is available from the British Library.

Hardback ISBN 978-1-4087-0279-6
C-format ISBN 978-1-4087-0450-9

Typeset in Garamond by M Rules
Printed and bound in Great Britain by
Clays Ltd, St Ives plc

Papers used by Little, Brown are from well-managed forests
and other responsible sources.

MIX
Paper from
responsible sources
FSC® C104740

Little, Brown
An imprint of
Little, Brown Book Group
Carmelite House
50 Victoria Embankment
London EC4Y 0DZ

An Hachette UK Company
www.hachette.co.uk

www.littlebrown.co.uk

For Percy, Madison,
Issy and Teddy –
we're home

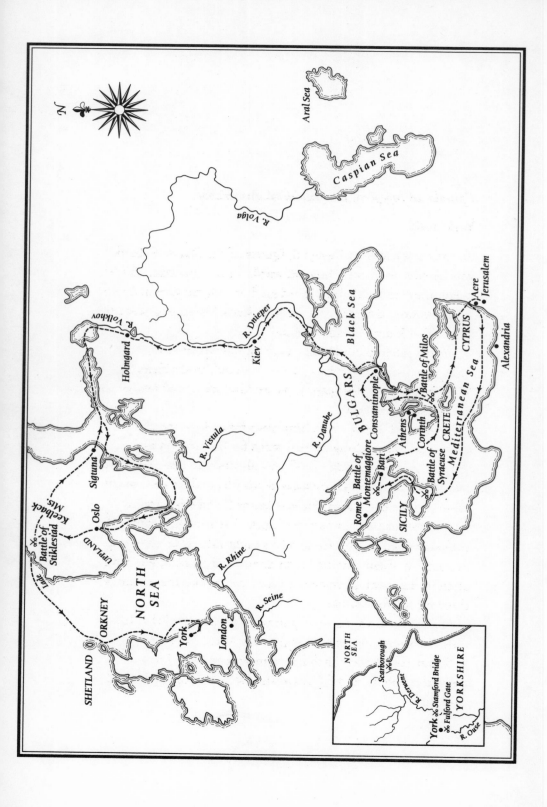

N

Aral Sea

Caspian Sea

R. Volga

R. Volkhov

Holmgard

R. Dnieper

Kiev

Black Sea

Battle of Milos

CYPRUS

Acre
Jerusalem

Constantinople

Athens

CRETE

Alexandria

Mediterranean Sea

Corinth

BULGARS

R. Danube

R. Vistula

Sigtuna

Battle of
Montemaggiore

Bari

Rome

Battle of
Syracuse

SICILY

Oslo

UPPLAND

Reedback
Mts

Battle of
Stiklestad

Lake

SHETLAND

ORKNEY

York

London

NORTH
SEA

R. Rhine

R. Seine

NORTH
SEA

Scarborough

R. Derwent

Stamford Bridge

Fulford Gate

York

YORKSHIRE

R. Ouse

Epistola ad Ingegerd, from Ealdred, Archbishop

York, 1069

To the most excellent Ingegerd, Queen of the Danes, I thank
you for your letter and the kind words for my brothers, which
meant more to me than polished gold or well-cut jewels. As to
your question, the answer is yes. I do know the resting place of
your father King Harald's bones.

We have kept them hidden, here, in our Minster, all
these years, since calamity came to our land, in the shape of
William, Duke of Normandy, whom God has raised over us to
punish us for our sins.

In the week I spent with him, your father kept me close
to his side. From a king more famous for his prowess as a
warrior, I was expecting a bluff and ill-educated man, but I was
surprised. He talked expansively of his life, and he was not the
brute that we had feared. He was learned, and wise, and had
not wasted his time among the Greeks. He missed, I think, the
company of educated men and he sought me out often in the
five days we spent together. Sometimes on a journey, but more
often in the evening, when the fires were lit, and the darkness
thrown back for a while.

He was not a young man, and perhaps suspected that his
time was short, and wanted to get everything said.

'I understand the Northumbrians well enough, but tell
me of the Saxons, and the Mercians. What are their laws and
customs?'

I answered his questions as honestly as I might, and even in a short time a brotherly feeling sprang up between us. He had travelled more widely than any man I know. Even as far as the Middle Sea, which the Ancients called the Mediterranean. He talked of founding a monastery at the city he had just founded.

'I want monks and a stone minster, and land to support it all. And a library!' he said. 'You must have a library here. How many books?'

'Twenty-seven,' I said.

I listed them, and halfway through he sat forward in wonder. 'You know, in Micklegard there are libraries which have hundreds of books.'

'I have seen the same,' I said. 'In Rome.'

'You have been to Rome?' He sat back. 'I was at Rome. And Micklegard. And Jerusalem.'

I was filled with wonder. 'You were at the Holy City?'

He nodded.

'What did you do there?'

He laughed. 'You would not believe me if I told you.'

We sat, each of us reliving the wonder that a room for books brought. He wanted a library and a scriptorium, and I volunteered the names of a few young monks who I thought would be interested in helping to bring the light of learning and God to the Norse. He asked questions about the amount of land needed, where the monks would come from, and whether they should follow the Eastern Church, or the Church of Rome.

I said that we were educated and honest and followed the Lord in all his ways.

'The Greek priests said the same,' he said.

'But we follow the Rule of St Benedict.'

'What is this rule?'

'*Quia tunc vere sanctimoniales sunt,*' I quoted. Whosoever

lives by the labour of their hands, as our fathers and the
apostles did, then are they truly monks.

'I too follow the Rule of St Benedict,' he said.

I was surprised, and I think it showed. He held out his
hands, crossed with old scars, other men's blood rimming his
nails. 'I have lived all my life by these.'

'I do not think St Benedict meant the labour of fighting,' I
said.

'No?'

'No. I mean, he wanted men to work and grow and heal.'

He sat forward and shook his head at me. 'If we were all
healers, who would protect the weak? Or punish the heathens?
Or uphold the law against wicked men?'

I said nothing, and he sat back.

'That is what I have done,' he said. 'All my life. My first
battle was against the Devil.'

'You mean temptation?'

'No,' he said, suddenly serious. 'Lucifer himself.'

'Did you win?' I asked.

He sat back and looked at me as if I was joking. 'No, of
course not. Only God can beat the Devil.'

In drawing up this History (by which I mean a true account)
I have been working from three sources: my own memories;
the memories of others (which were sometimes in conflict
with my own), and the notes that I took at the time when
your father and I started work on what we thought would be a
hagiography of his brother, St Olaf, and then quickly seemed
to point towards a secondary work, which would deal with his
life separately.

Over the last three months two of my best scribes have made
a complete copy of the original for your library. It was only in
the making of the work that I recalled some incidents which
needed more explanation or comment. Rather than scrape

the vellum clear, and delay the sending of this work for yet another season, I have added these as marginalia, or inserted extra leaves, whichever proved less troublesome. In a few cases, where it was impossible to know what had been thought or imagined at a certain time, I have followed the example of greater chronicallers, such as Herodotus, who furnished tales that seemed to fit.

The places I have invented, I hope these will do the work of history and that you will not find them too distracting.

PART I
Norway

CHAPTER ONE

The Battle of Fulford Gate

20th September 1066, outside the east gate of York.

Harald Hardrada: Here, man, give me your hand. I will not kill you.

Look men. See what we have found. An archbishop. What a thing to find on a battlefield, and untouched. God is with you, I see.

The Lord is not with your army though. See, your lord, Earl Edwin, has hitched up his skirts and is running for the gate. I do not think he will make it. The one leading the pursuit is Rolf the Bald. Great gangly legs. He never stops, that man. His father was the same. Not a patch of hair once they turned thirty.

Do you want to stay down there in that ditch? Someone will mistake you for a corpse. They will use your head as a stepping stone. That's it, take my hand. Come, it's only blood, and it's neither of ours.

Push old red-cloak off your legs. His hour has come and gone. Do you know him? Last night he probably sat on Earl Edwin's benches and bragged how he would throw us back into the sea, like fish. This morning he sat in Edwin's hall and broke his fast, marched along the Scarborough Road, stopped at this ford, and readied himself for battle. An hour ago he drove off his horse, far back from the battle, clenched his shield grip, crossed himself and taught the men next to him, bade them be not frightened.

And then I came.

Poor old red-cloak. He should have stayed abed. All these corpses should. They could have grown old and tiresome and bored their grandchildren with tales of their youth. Even now this man's wife stands a few leagues away. She stands at the door of her longhouse. The green acres of Northumbria stretch out before her. There is a chill in the wind. The wheat is in, but something troubles her. She does not know if the battle has happened or not. She sniffs, shuffles her worries: has the earl made peace, why are the pigs restless under the beech trees, where is that boy?

Her husband's seed has quickened in her womb, and she thinks of the last two children that they buried during Lent. This new child will be born with the lambs at Easter. Behind her his daughter is sitting in the light of the smoke hole, learning spindle-work. She cannot concentrate because of the two kittens that are pouncing from under her stool. The white-spotted one climbs up her skirts.

In the yard the slave girl picks a blade of dry summer grass from the milk bucket. It fell from her sleeve as she walked, the bucket slopping against her left leg. Watching her from down the field is this man's son. He is sitting with his back to a beech tree. He is angry because he thinks himself old enough to fight, and he resents his father for leaving him behind.

'Look after your mother,' was the last thing his father told him, and that son fumbles with those words, twists them in his mind, like the ends of a straw rope. He picks long grass stems to chew. The outer sheaths are dry, but the inside is still wet and green. The sap is bitter. He chews the ends flat. He tosses the grass like a javelin into the stabbing forest light about him. The first beech leaf falls. It drops at his foot, bright as a new-struck coin. He does not know it, but if that boy was here, he would be dead as well. Trodden three bodies deep into the mud. And here his father lies, mouth open to take his last breath.

Look! Your earl's huscarls still want to die for him. Three of them have drawn up a shieldwall to block the pursuit. They are young men. They have lost their spears. Their swords flash silver as they draw them. Two of them have steel helms. The other is dark. He lets his locks fall free. The wind catches them. They do not stand a chance of course. See the giant advancing on them? The one with the Russian shield? That is Grimketel. He was with me in Micklegard. He's a miserable bastard. I have seen him kill three and look for a fourth. Men think because he is so big he will rage at them, but see, he is as cunning as a fox. Just watch.

There.

It is done. I told you.

Kings are often right.

I hope they made peace with God.

It seems your earl has lived to see the sunset. Even Rolf has come to a halt. Much closer to the fences and the archers will feather him. He turns and sees behind him the others are stooping to pull off the gold armbands and pick silver-hilted swords from the hands of men who should have used them better.

I have been in his place many times. The battle is won and the fury abates and you find yourself standing in a field of treasure and lesser men who lagged behind are bent over like women at harvest time. Look, they're already at work cutting off rings, unwinding belts, strapping on dead men's swords. It is messy business. Your hands get much bloodier than this. Here, give me your cloak. It's wet enough.

There. Now my hands are clean. That is what Pontius Pilate said, did he not?

Do your sins weigh on you?

Mine do not weigh on me. But this mail coat does. Christ's balls! I used to wear it all day without thinking. I used to sleep in it. But fifty winters take their toll. Mail hangs heavy on old men's shoulders. See the silver here, I took that from Micklegard. The belt from Rome. This hem was woven by Sicilian nuns for me, because I saved them from the heathen. She is a fine coat of mail, is she not?

I call her Emma.

9

CHAPTER TWO

The Northern Way

My brother, Olaf, was king of Norway.

When I was a boy, and the winter nights were long and cold, and the storm would put its mouth to the smoke hole, and blow long mournful notes, then we would all gather close to the fire, shoulder to shoulder, our backs to the darkness, hands spread to the flames, as the tale-spinner spun.

I would sit on my mother's lap, wrapped inside her cloak, and dream-listen, half in this world, half in the world of gods and giants and matchless men who died rather than submit. Blue and purple flames would lick slowly at the seasoned, shadowed hearth-logs, rising amber into the darkness, and I always imagined myself grown-up to be my brother's war-hound, his shield in battle, his most loyal warrior.

In my mind's eye I could see it all. I would share the ale-horn with him, I would stand at his back when battle came; and when all about us were slain, I was the one who would stand back to back with him and take the blows that were meant for him in my own flesh, and I would die defending him, and my name would always be remembered as King Olaf's brother, Harald.

*

My country is Uppland, on the Northern Way.

Norveyr, we call it. Norway, in your tongue. My father was chief of Uppland. My brother Olaf gathered a great treasure from England and France in the years before my birth. My earliest memory of him was when I was five, or six. My brother Halfdan was carving runes into the church door with his eating knife. I was lookout, but I saw nothing because I was watching Halfdan work.

The note of the household had changed. Even Halfdan paused.

'What is it?' he said.

I did not know.

My mother was shouting. She was calling my name. 'Har-ald!'

I should not have helped Halfdan. I knew I would get a beating. Then she came around the hall by the pigsty and saw me standing as guilty as a sheep-thief.

'Harald!' she shouted. 'What are you doing?'

'Nothing,' I said.

She pointed across the fields to where my father was helping out with the farmhands. 'Olaf is coming!'

I did not understand at first.

'Quick!' she shouted. 'The king! Go fetch your father!'

Her orders rang out as she marched about the homestead. 'Saddle the horses with the gilded saddle. Scrub the benches. Scour the beakers. Bring the ale, woman!' She set us all into a fluster, and I ran to find our father, excited as a dog, or a spring lamb.

The dogs were barking by the time I found my father standing by the side of the field, looking at his pale mare. The north wind stirred her plaited mane and tail as she bent to tear the turf.

I called out 'Father!' and he turned in the way he had, of almost wondering who you were and why you were disturbing him, and went back to his farmhands.

'Lame again,' one my father's men said as I caught my breath. The man clearly thought she should be cut up and fed to the dogs, but my father was a kind man.

'Give her a week,' he said. 'And then keep her from cart work till the shearing is done.'

He looked up at the clouds, to see if this was a good time to shear. I tugged his sleeve. 'Father,' I said. 'Mother says that Olaf is coming! She says you must come. His ships are in the fjord.'

I tugged again, and when he turned to me I could see he was unhappy with being disturbed.

'Tell Mother I'm coming.'

I ran through the June grass. It was as tall as my waist. I was laughing, and shouting Olaf's name over and over, though it meant nothing to me then. Children are like puppies, they excite easily. It is all fresh to them, who have seen so little.

When I got back to the hall my mother had rolled up her sleeves and she was shouting at my eldest full-blood brother, Guttorm, to clean his shoes and brush the chaff from his hair.

Halfdan had slunk away, but she saw me and speared me with a shout. 'There you are!' She marched across and put both hands on my shoulders to steer me into the milk-yard where the maids were as noisy as hedge birds, as they brushed each other's hair.

'Inga!' she shouted. 'Dress him!'

Inga was my favourite of my mother's maids. She had soft, clean hands, green eyes and a small button nose, sprinkled with pale freckles. She spoke with a lisp, which I always thought was the most charming thing. She was light and fragile, like a netted sparrow that a farmyard boy holds in his cupped hands.

Inga led me to my mother's room, to the open wooden shutter, and stood me in the light and pulled spiked burrs from my kirtle and hair; brushed the moss from my elbows, then wrinkled her freckles and let out a sigh when she found a sheep-tick on my neck. 'What have you been doing?'

'Nothing,' I lied. She let out a breath. A casual pagan curse, that people did then, without thinking, and bent me over her knee to get me in the square of light from the open shutters.

I sniffed as she used her nails to work the tick's head free. As the sun came out it turned the floor-rushes to gold. A bumble bee's low hum drifted into the room and then out again. There are no flowers here, I thought, they're all outside, great banks of them, slipping down the mountainsides like an avalanche of yellow.

At last she was done, and rubbed the bite with beeswax and stood me up before her, pulled something out of my head and held it before my nose to let me see. 'Been bird nesting?'

'No,' I said, though that was not true. I tested myself as every hero did, though my tests were little things, like scaling the garth apple tree's tallest branch, daring to climb down into the damp dark well-mouth, walking home through the dark forest when the hag of evening was gathering her skirts about her, and you could feel her chill night breath, and all you wanted to do was run.

Inga dropped the twig on the ground. It was hung with green moss, thin and scraggly, like old man's beard, and there was a knotted clump of my own hairs too, silvery-gold in the wan light.

'There!' she said when she was done, and turned me round to see my clean blue kirtle, black trousers, and calfskin boots. She ran her fingers through the hair at my temples, and shook the locks out. We all wore it long, men and women alike. 'Very handsome!' she said. She bent down so her head was close to mine.

'Now! Run along with you. And don't get into trouble!'

That was my quest that day as I ran out to find my mother.

She flustered like a young maid. Light stabbed down through the smoke-hole like a finger of Jesus. It slanted and hit the side of the hearth. It gilded the freshly swept and dampened hearth stones with sunlight, lit the carved oak benches too, brought them vividly from the shadows.

'Good,' she said, and had all the English hangings shaken out and rehung along the hall walls till all the spades and hoes and scythes were hidden and the room was filled with shapes and colour of small embroidered men and women, performing great feats of courage and bravery and resolve.

13

I tried to keep out of the way as fresh straw was strewn on the hall floor, tables and benches were set with clean linen, drinking jugs and ale, and she saw me suddenly and stopped. 'Where's your father?'

I gaped for a moment, thinking I had forgotten to tell him, but then I remembered and I blurted out, 'He's coming!'

'Are you sure you told him?'

I nodded.

'Where is he?'

I ran to the hall mouth, but could not see him and began to panic.

But then my father came in the back door, where the livestock were kept in winter. He threw his broad-brimmed grey hat onto the high table, and took in the fuss with an air of well-worn tolerance.

'There you are!' she said, and looked at him in a way that told me that he was a disappointment to her.

He did not care for war, unless it was needed. He did not care so much for anything, but farming. 'So. Our king is here, is he?' he said, to me, as if she wasn't in the room with us. 'Well, I should go and dress or your mother will not be happy.'

'Yes, dress!' she called. 'And change your boots.'

My father stepped out half an hour later in his scarlet cloak, sword and helmet, but he was still wearing his blue woollen trousers, and his farming boots.

'They're covered in muck,' she said.

'Earth,' he said, 'not mud.'

'You're the chief of Uppland,' she told him, as if he had forgotten such a thing, but I heard the disappointment there too. My father enjoyed nothing more than to be inspecting his oxen, counting his lambs, picking up his girls, and carrying them on one arm, or showing his sons how to hitch an ox.

'I am,' he said, 'and I think I look the part.'

'From the boots up,' my mother said.

*

My father's name was Sigurd. Sigurd Sow men called him, but there was nothing of the pig about him as he took hold of his stallion's jewelled bridle and swung himself up. He was a fine horseman, and moved his mount about with casual ease as the yard filled with neighbours and their men. They were all dressed in their finery. He greeted them all. They shouted and laughed, and the air was full of drumming hoofs as more distant neighbours heard the news and rode down to join in.

'Let's go!' my father called, and swung his hand about his head, and led them off. The swirling mass of men and women began to follow him down to the shore to greet the longships, and Halfdan and I ran alongside them for a short way, as long as enthusiasm could last.

The world I grew up on was that little stretch of level ground between the hulk of the mountains, where the winds tortured the old trees into weird shapes, and the depths of the fjord, where monsters lurked and the middle was so deep that no fathom-weight could find the bottom. It was where the Midgard Serpent slept, men said, and waited till Ragnarok, when it would slither out onto the land, and battle Thor and the Old Gods for this Middle Earth, between the peaks and the shore.

I stood with my feet in mud, watching my father escort Olaf up from the shore.

'Are you excited?' Inga asked. Her quest, I guess, was to keep me out of trouble.

'Yes!' I shouted.

'Do you remember your brother?'

'No,' I shouted.

'You must,' she told me, but I didn't and so she lifted me up, and raised an arm to point. 'There he is! That's your brother! He's the king.'

I'd eaten stories of Olaf since before I could talk, sipped them from my mother's breasts, sprinkled them on my bread and porridge, supped them down when the skald stood up to chant his tales, and the oft-tilted ale-jug was passed from hand to hand. But he was shorter than I had made him in my mind's eye, stouter than a hero should be, with sandy hair and broad cheeks, scrubbed red by the sea-salt winds. There was something about him, like a beautiful girl, that drew your attention, and it took me a while before I realised that it was his eyes, which were palest blue with dark rims, as cold and shocking as winter meltwater.

He pulled his horse to a halt, swung one leg over, landed as heavily as a wheat sack before us.

The earth trembled as he landed. I felt it through my calfskin boots.

He spoke as loud as a hero. 'So, these are my brothers!' he roared, and we stood and stared. My mother had to prod my eldest brother forward.

He said, 'We are pleased to see you return safely from your battles, brother.'

'Thank you. You must be Guttorm.'

Guttorm blushed and bowed.

Olaf came along the line. 'You must be Halfdan.'

I stood up to Halfdan's shoulder, and watched my middle brother hang his head and nod slowly and silently, with his fingers at his mouth, like a thrall who fears to betray himself with words.

'And you must be Harald!'

Olaf bent down so that he was on my level, and pulled what he thought was an ugly scowl. I scowled back so he ruffled my freshly combed hair, that Inga had worked on, and I shoved his hand away – as I did to Halfdan and Guttorm when they bullied me.

From the pinch of her fingers on my shoulders I knew I was in for a beating. 'Greet the king properly,' she told me, but I refused. No one pushed me about. Little as I was.

Olaf reached out a hard, kingly hand and I shoved him off again.

'Harald!' my mother hissed.

Even my father stepped forward. 'Harald,' he said, and made a gesture with his head. 'Show some respect.'

I felt all their eyes upon me, pushing me forward, as the ox is goaded on with willow switches towards the butcher's axe. But then someone laughed.

It was one of Olaf's warriors.

'He got you there,' he said.

Olaf laughed as well, and ruffled my hair once more, harder this time, and gave me a shove that was not friendly.

My mother beat me. Halfdan and Guttorm shook their heads at me, and even my sisters gave me The Look. Only Inga came to find me as the feast started, and the fires were lit and stacked high with last year's logs.

'You alright?' she asked.

I was standing in the yard outside the hall, where the dogs and goats ran free. My father's white boar-hound was chewing on a pig's ear. Her fangs showed as the hard gristle crunched under her hind teeth. I sniffed and nodded, and wiped a snail-trail of snot onto my fresh kirtle.

'You'd better come in,' she said.

I folded my arms and put on the biggest pout I could manage. 'I don't want to.'

'Your mother will be angry.'

'I don't care.'

Inga put her arm about my shoulders. 'Come, Harald, sit on my knee.'

'No,' I said.

'If I give you a kiss?'

'No,' I said, but she bent to kiss me, and her breath was green mint and I squirmed away and she kept kissing me and at last I laughed.

The white boar-hound had finished by now, and was sniffing under the branch where the pig's body had been hung, lapping at the blood-drips. One of the dogs sniffed me. I did not fear them and gave them a hand to lick.

'Come!' she said and held out a hand. 'Or I'll kiss you more. I bet you could sit at the high table, if you promised to be good.'

I would be good, I thought, as she led me inside.

It seemed that I had been forgiven. My mother held a hand out to me, low under the high tables, a secret gesture that she saved for me. 'Off you go,' Inga said, and gave me a gentle shove, but my mother's face dropped when I ran past her.

I had seen a better seat, next to the king, on my father's broad lap. He was as surprised as she. 'Up you come!' he said and landed me on his lap. He and Olaf were talking of things I did not understand. The earls of Lathe. How to terrify a rebellious chieftain. Things I did not know my father cared about.

Olaf caught me looking at him a number of times, and as his cheeks grew redder, he turned to me and took my hand. I do not know what I thought a king's hands would be like, but his were dirty and engrained as a farmhand's.

Mine were clean and smooth, and he turned one over with a thumb, and took the other one as well.

'Do you farm?' he asked.

I shook my head.

His eyes were cold as winter sunlight. Sometimes they shocked you into silence.

'Do you fish?'

I shook my head. I was the youngest. I did what I pleased. I did not work in hall or farm or boat.

Olaf scowled. 'It does not do to spoil a child.'

'He is not spoilt,' my father said. There was a hint of tension in the exchange. He and Olaf had not lived happily together, as foster father and stepson.

'Is he not?'

'No. He is not spoilt. He's still young, that is all.'

'He's five,' Olaf said. 'When I was five you made me work.'

'I did not.'

'Yes,' Olaf said. 'You did.'

'Well, it did not harm you.'

'Nor will it harm him.'

As the meal was finished and the servants took away the bowls and plates, Olaf tipped his horn back and drank, and then stood up. 'This is good fishing weather,' he said, and took my arm high up, above the elbow, and half-dragged, half-carried me from my father's lap. 'Get the boat ready!'

There was a babble of voices and words thrown up to dissuade him – un-kingly, ungainly, dangerous, wet and inclement – but his fingers were tight about my arm.

He dragged me along the freshly strewn reeds, over the high threshold, and through the grass down to the Midgard Serpent, pebble-fjord-shore, as a thief is led to the hanging tree.

'Rognvald,' he called out. 'Otli. Spear-Hedin. Kalv.'

His retainers came forward and took the oars and he set me down and I could not flee, not with everyone's eyes on me.

The boat rocked and splashed as they climbed aboard and swung the oars overhead and set them into the oarlocks, then two of Olaf's men shoved the boat out into the water, and the six of us were afloat. Olaf breathed wine and ale on me as he showed me the craft he had learnt when he was a lad and I watched him and stayed silent and unwilling.

'You do it,' he said, and I made an effort.

'Good,' he told me and I liked him then. 'Here, take the end of the net. We'll throw it in when the water is deep. That is where the best shoals swim.'

We were less than a bowshot from the shore when my mother shouted Olaf's name.

He was bent over me, showing me how to untangle the net. He did not look up. My fingers were small. 'Yes,' he said. 'Good.'

My mother shouted again. 'O-laf!'

She waved and pointed but he took no notice until one of his men spoke.

'Olaf,' the one named Rognvald said. There was warning in his tone that stopped us both. Rognvald's face was looking along the fjord, where the mountain-towers stood watch on the restless waves of the shimmering-dark sea.

'Hunting whales,' he said.

The keel-less boat wobbled as Olaf turned to look, and I saw through his legs the black snakes of the whale-pack loping towards us through the grey water.

Olaf called for a spear but there was none, so they gave him an oar and he braced himself as if he was Thor waiting for the Midgard Serpent. There were shouts from the shore: advice, warning, caution. The rout came towards us so fast that he barely had time to raise the oar above his head, brace himself and hurl. If he landed a blow I do not know.

A whale rammed us hard and someone shouted in terror. It might have been me, I cannot say. I fell into the nets and clung to them as water slopped into the rocking boat. They were like the goldsmith's knotwork all about us. Whale breath was wet on my face. It smelt of herring and oyster water. A black fin brushed past. I saw black and white, and then an eye, dark as the well-mouth, which looked at me, and I could see thought there, malevolent, evil, unblinking thought.

The cold fjord water boiled as hundreds of silver herring leapt from the sea as if it were a kitchen cauldron, and the black-backed gulls screamed and dived and took their fill; and Olaf grabbed me from behind and lifted me.

The boat rocked violently, the rowers called out in fear, but I knew he would not drop me. He was my half-brother. We shared a womb. I will be his man, when I am full-grown. He would be a fool to drop me, and Olaf is no fool, everyone knows that.

'Are you afraid?' he whispered in my ear.

I shook my head. If I shivered it was because of the cold sea air, and the breeze that cuts through all. 'This is slaughter, Harald,' he hissed, and I took it all.

Gulls balanced on the breeze. They plucked stunned fish from the water. I shouted and laughed. There are no words for joy this pure.

'Never flee,' he hissed into my ear. 'Never fear! Do you understand?'

I opened my eyes wide to the roar of water and whale and desperate fish. I saw the slaughter of the herring, and was not afraid. I nodded and he held me up as the whales hemmed the herring into a smaller and smaller circle.

And then it was done. The slaughter was over, the water stilled like slow-settling dust after the army's horses have passed out of sight, and we were not dead.

Only a few herrings remained, floating prone on their sides. The chopping waves diminished, gulls landed and floated and bickered like fishwives, dipped back for one last stunned fish floating side-up among the ripples. They lapped as the water calmed and the wind blew from across the fjord, dulling the water like brushed steel, and I laughed. Even Olaf seemed thrilled and he turned me so that we were face to face. 'Good?' he roared.

'Again!' I shouted and he laughed and crushed me to his chest, and for a moment our bodies were joined. We were survivors; we were both kings; two half-brothers made one.

I was still small enough then for him to lift in his arms, small enough to believe all the tales I heard; small enough to believe like a child, in heroes.

CHAPTER THREE

Budli's Stallion

I was twelve when Olaf fled Norway.

It had been a normal September morning. The frost that had settled in the night was melting into thick white dew, on the high slopes the pine forests were salted with the first fall of snow, and over the low, harrowed fields, mist gathered like gossips.

It was the time of year we call Gormánath – the month of slaughtering livestock. I had helped bring the sheep herds down from the slopes. They stood nervously in their pens, while the pigs were still rooting for the last of the beech nuts, and across the fjord I heard the long, mournful call of a wolf, that set all the dogs' hackles on end, and they stood alert, straight, tails stiff, noses raised to the air.

I spent the morning with my bow, looking for hazel grouse, and loosing wild shots at a heron and a goose. Halfdan had taken a boat across to one of the wild islands to feather a seal or two, and I was already in a bad mood by the time I found the place I had tethered my horse, and swung myself up and turned her head for home.

I cannot remember who brought the news, but it had already arrived by the time I arrived. The stable lad's face could not hide it.

Something is coming, his eyes told me, before he took the bridle and led my horse to the paddock.

I thought someone dead. I felt everyone's eyes on me as I slipped the quiver off my shoulder and strode across to the hall.

I could hear shouting as I approached. It was my father. I did not have to bend under the threshold, but I remember that out of the sunlight the air was dark and cool as cave-breath, and at that moment my father slammed the door of his chamber at the head of the hall, slammed it again so hard the hall-timbers shook and motes of old grey ash hung in the air.

I stood looking about me. No one wanted to speak. There was speaking enough from my parents – loud, furious, recriminatory. It was like Thor's thunderstorm, but not high on the mountainside when you can count the moments between the flash and the boom, but here, inside the hall – anger and fury and volume, where there should be warmth and shelter and companionship.

The remaining servants fled outside, finding themselves jobs to do, to look busy, to not be noticed, to not have this storm turn its rage upon them. I stayed, despite my fears. I was twelve and thought myself man enough to hear it all.

When the anger subsided and silence fell I approached the split-oak planks of their door, and put my hand to the uneven wood and felt the tremble of my mother's grief-stricken words. 'He's fled! He's left us.'

There was silence. I did not believe it at first, but then I heard fear in her voice.

'They will come for us now! We will be next. All of us.'

I stood transfixed. Olaf could not have fled, I thought, not without me. His brother.

I put a hand out to steady myself, pictured my father walking over to where she stood – one hand on her chest-lid – knuckles pressed to her mouth. In my mind's eye he puts a hand on her shoulder. He isn't one for gestures of kindness, but I'd seen him do it when her favourite horse broke its leg, and it worked then.

'He fled,' she said again. Nothing more. I turned my back on their door as if I can unhear the words, as if knowledge is something that we can unlearn, as if I could stay childlike for a little longer, and refuse the wisdom that hurt can bring.

My father stormed out into the fields, banging every door on the way. The hall, the stable door, the smoke-house. I heard stifled sobs coming from my mother's room. I did not think I had ever heard her cry before. She was not that kind of woman.

My mother's door was open. Her maids sat by her door. Two of them were holding each other, Inga was sitting on a stool, staring at nothing.

Inga frowned and shook her head, but my mother was inside, and she was crying and I had to go to her.

I stepped through the doorway. The only light came from the two candles by her altar, where her silver cross stood, and the low hearth-fire. I stood in the doorway and I wanted to go to her. I wanted to tell her that I would not flee. I dragged my feet along. She was sitting on a stool, hands on her lap, still as a runestone. Her head was bowed; there were tears on her cheeks; she sniffed.

I moved as stiffly as a corpse. I had to clear my voice to speak.

'Mother?'

'Out!' she hissed.

My throat was tight with all the things I wanted to express, but she turned and looked at me and her eyes were red and swollen and inhuman with fury. 'Out!' she shouted and I stepped back in guilt and horror and no one caught my eye.

In the months that followed I put on cheerfulness as a traveller dons a cloak against winter's chill. The men of Norway were still not used to kings, I told myself. It was like trying to saddle a wild horse and sit upon it. Olaf had ridden Norway for thirteen winters. It was a fine gallop.

But beneath the garments I dressed my face with I felt betrayed.

I was his little brother and I loved him, and I would have done anything for him not to let me down like this.

I never spoke about Olaf's flight but once, when it was spring, and the evenings were growing longer, and the rook chicks were loud in their high twig nests, and my mother held out a hand towards me. She was sitting on her stool in the grass outside the hall, one of my father's black hounds stretched out at her feet. A coldness had fallen between us, like Olaf's shadow. I hesitated. I was a lone wolf, now, I thought, without pack or leader – but she beckoned to me again. Come, her expression said, and I took the hand and despite my stiffness she drew me in.

'I'm sorry,' she said and pressed me into her.

I tried to pull away but she would not let go and we did not need words, we both knew what she was trying to say and I thawed a little and stood as uneasily as a boy, with one foot in a man's boot and one in his own. 'I won't flee,' I said after a long pause.

She patted my back.

'Good,' she said, and her chest lifted with her breath and she looked into my eyes and said, 'Don't.'

There were raids, after that. Men who wanted revenge on Olaf's family for things he had done when he was king. Men who thought that he might have left treasure behind, and men who just wanted to test our watch, and the strength of our spirit.

My father was not a warrior, but he led the men of the valley and drove them off. Even Budli brought his sons, who were hard-looking men, rowing across the fjord to help us. We were all fair game now.

The raiders never took much more than a few sheep, but they were fearful times. We ate no more than was needed, said no more than was necessary, we did not feast. The hall's flames felt small and chilled and begrudging.

I was thirteen when my mother died. 'Keep practising your sword work,' she told me between the racking coughs. She held onto my hand as if I was a rope keeping her close to the shore. The sicker she grew the tighter her hand-grip. 'You're a fine boy. You'll be a handsome young man.'

I had no words to say to her, but took hers into me and let them settle.

Before the end she gave me a sword and a helmet, that I would grow into, and as she grew weaker she held a cloth to her mouth with one hand, and crushed my hand with the other. 'Olaf will come back,' she said. 'And then he will need you.'

I stood and nodded. I would be there.

At the end she could only whisper. Each breath came slowly, and the words hissed out like the air from a bellows. 'Be strong. Be brave. Do not be cowardly.'

I nodded and her words filled me up, and lay like leaf mulch in the hollows.

I had seen death many times, in cattle, sheep, and men. But I had not seen it in my mother before and I watched it with disbelief as day by day it consumed her.

I was curious, tired, dreading – and did not know what a day would be like which did not start with her straightening my collar, shooing me out of the door and hissing, 'Out with you now!', or licking her finger and wiping a smear on my cheek, or chanting our prayers together at night, and then letting out a sigh, and turning and wondering what she had to do before bed; then turning to me, and saying, 'Be a man worthy of honour, Harald,' and me shaking my head, and saying, I shall, Mother, and remembering the oyster-wet breath of whales on my cheeks.

But the next day, I knew. In one night it all changed. She was gone, her mouth bound closed to stop the soul returning.

I went through the whole wake alone.

She saw you through childhood, I told myself. A boy of thirteen does not need a mother any more.

At my mother's funeral the sun did not shine, and a chill wind blew from the north and we buried her near the wooden church my brother had built at the head of the fjord. We set her into the earth's grip and raised a modest mound over her. We set no stone there.

My father was not one for waste.

It was harvest-time and the first yellow leaves tumbled along the lane, rattling and crisp as old bones. Her maids wept, of course, and my father looked at us – especially me, the youngest, and my sister, Ingrid – and held out both hands to gather us in, and there was water in his eyes, like low clouds that threatened rain.

'Come lad,' my father said. He put his arm about us, and led us all away and I leant into him as we walked along and I remember clearly hearing the sound of wethers bleating on the hillside and thinking it was weeping for a moment, and felt my own sadness rise, and swallowed it back.

Boys of thirteen were almost full-grown. Grief was a doorway I had to pass through. On the other side, I thought, was manhood.

What was done was done. I did not hesitate, but stepped outside and smelt the wind.

It was troubled.

My sisters were weak and timid. My father found them good husbands, good farming men who would never achieve much in their lives beyond raising livestock and children, and who would treat them well.

He considered this a victory in life. That was my father's way. He did not need fame or glory.

I spoke little those years. Inga was married by then. Some men said she had given birth to Olaf's daughter. All I knew was that she had married a man from over the hill in Vestfold, and that she had lost her freckles at the same time.

There was talk at her betrothal feast of buying Budli's prize stallion, and that evening, after the meal had been cleared away, my father handed me a horn of ale and poured one for himself, and he said, 'So! Should we buy it or not?'

I shrugged. 'Whatever you like,' I said. His smile faded. I could see that I had hurt him, but I did not know what to say. I was my mother's child, even after death.

My father bought the stallion, sired it onto Guttorm's mare and almost a year later he was leading it out when it smelt a mare in season and kicked him in the gut. I was there, and I heard the low groan he let out as he fell slowly backwards.

'Christ!' he said. I had never heard him take the Lord's name with such grim passion. I helped carry him to his bed, and he lay down and he waved us off. 'I'm fine. Give me a short rest.'

He never stood up again. His belly turned black, and he sweated with the pain, gnashed his teeth together, and groaned.

Each morning he said he felt a little better, but when he tried to rise, he could not, and he said, 'Tomorrow' and we all agreed with him. He would rise on the morrow, and lead us out to inspect the lambs and the cow and the litter of seven piglets.

But he stopped saying that after a week, and then he barely spoke at all. He'd never been a talkative man, and by the end he seemed to have run out of things to say. The last words of his that I heard came as Guttorm and I sat by his bedside.

'Don't you have anything better to do?' he whispered.

We did. It was herring time, so we all got up and walked to the door.

By the time we came back, smelling of fish and sea and fresh boat pitch, he was dead.

Guttorm took over the farm, and the chieftaincy, and we argued straight away about Budli's stallion.

'Kill it,' I said, but he shook his head.

'Father would not want that.'

He was right, but that didn't make it any easier. Every time I saw the beast, black in the paddock, raising its head from the hay, or standing with the wind ruffling its mane, or lifting its head to smell the wind, I thought, 'There goes my father's killer, unavenged.'

I would have cut its throat, as the pagans still do, but I knew that Guttorm was right. My father would not want us to waste such a fine stallion.

'He's a fighter,' he'd have said. 'That's why we bought him. Don't punish him for being what he is. That makes no sense.'

In those years I was as restless as an unburied ghost. I grew taller and stronger than any of my brothers, with hair that was fairer than any girl's, and a thin boy's beard that was brown like a fox's tail.

'Look at you!' Thorgred said.

She had been my mother's maid. She was a short, practical woman with a strong grip and short fat forearms and would wring the chicken's neck in the kitchen yard when it was too old to lay, then wipe her hands on her apron and drop the kicking body into the steaming pot for plucking, slap her hands together to clean them, and then walk away.

After my mother died Thorgred grew kinder and liked to give me eggs that she boiled and carefully peeled with her dark nails, and she would wipe the last bits of shell onto her dark shawl and pass it to me, and I would bite into the warm golden egg yolk.

'You need to put some flesh on you,' she told me and handed me another egg.

I dipped them into the salt bowl and ate them, warm and firm and she would natter away, and from the grit there I sieved out a few details about my past, or my parents, that I had not known.

'Oh! Olaf used to drive your father to distraction,' she said. 'He sent him away in the end, when he was twelve. He was sick of being mocked.'

Or, 'Your mother never knew how lucky she was to be taken in with another man's child in her belly. She always acted as if she was the chieftain's son!'

Or, 'I think she cared for him in the end. She bore all seven of you, and none of you died, and that's a blessing in itself.'

Or, 'The treasure that Olaf brought back from England! My, you never saw such wealth.'

Or, 'They were almost sunk, gold and all. They were soaked,

all of them, and frozen to the marrow. Olaf looked like a drowned man as he came into the hall that night, but your father piled the fire high, and dressed all his men in dry clothes, and that night he promised to use his influence with the other great chieftains, to help Olaf become king.'

But I was most interested in stories about myself. About how I fought with Halfdan, or Guttorm. How I refused to be born, even though my time was due, and when I came I was a long and skinny thing, with hair so fair it looked like I was bald.

'And look at you now,' Thorgred said. 'You grow faster than the beans! Half a man indeed. Your mother always said, "Harald's a warrior. Mark my words. He will leave. He'll not stay here."'

I drank all this down, and waited for more. '"Do you know what he said to me?" your mother told me one day. You were down at the shore, playing with wood chips. "What are those?" she'd asked you. "Ships," you said. "What ships?" "Longships."' She laughed and winked. 'See. You are destined to be a warrior, Harald!'

These things were like treasures lifted from a locked casket. But the longer my mother had been dead, the more distant they became. They belonged to a time I did not well remember, as unknowable as the messages that old men see in the flight of birds, or the pattern the timbers of a wrecked ship make upon the shore.

I felt like the farmyard bean whose tendrils outgrow its poles and flail about in the morning breeze, with nothing left to grip onto.

That first year after Olaf's exile men had asked, 'Where has Olaf gone?'

The next they wondered, 'When will he return?'

But after the third year passed with no news, the question had got shorter and the loss of one word made all the difference. 'Will he return?' they asked, and I could not answer. I was thinking of my future now.

The greatest king was Knut, but I could not follow him: it was he who had bought the men of Lathe with English silver, and ordered them to rebel against Olaf.

But if not him, then who? There were no heroes I could think of now that Olaf was gone. The world that the tale-spinners had woven for me as a boy, as the hearth flames wound one over the other, had gone like a vivid night-dream whose images and details slip away with the dawn, leaving only the feeling and the sense of loss.

And then, on another of those unremarkable and undistinguishable days in my fifteenth year, when I sat on the mouldy stump of a half-rotten log and watched roe deer grazing on the forest's margins, a longship appeared at the end of the fjord.

It had twelve oars each side, a plain white sail, a figurehead of brass, perhaps, or maybe gold with the light of the sun upon it.

It was too small to be a raiding ship, but Guttorm shouted up to me to gather twenty men to greet it. 'Don't take Duthi or Ketil!' he shouted. 'I need them.'

He meant take weapons, of course, so I strode into the hall and took my father's best boar-spear from the wall, and stood on the threshold and blew a long low note on the horn.

I could only round up ten men.

Halfdan was sitting by the fire, whittling a stick.

'Come,' I told him. 'There's a ship.'

He did not look up. 'So?'

'Guttorm wants us to meet it.'

Halfdan rolled his eyes. 'It's not Viking weather.'

I left him behind. He was half in name and deed, but he taught me early on that there is no point in arguing with men who want to spend their time on earth whittling sticks. They whittle their own lives away, a knife stroke at a time, and end up with nothing but a stump of wood where their grave lies.

I had no one to copy then, except the men of the old tales, so I sent a lad with good eyesight on one of those ponies with short legs and an ambling gait that can go all day without trying, to ride along the shore and scout them out.

He came back after as long as it took the tree's shadow to move six paces round and slipped down and held onto the pony's mane to keep it.

'If they have mail they do not wear it,' he said. 'Nor helms.'

'Do they carry a banner or a sigil?'

'None that I saw. But they were dressed in bright colours, like a kingfisher, and none of them wore yellow.'

Dun yellow dye was made from the soil; it was the colour of thralls and farming men. It was the colour of old men's fingernails, the smoke-slime on hanging bacon, the serf's patched homespun. It was a colour of thieves and trespassers. Close up, you could mistake a man dressed in it for a tree or a bush, nothing of note; viewed from afar and he was invisible.

I was dressed in a fine cloak of poppy red with an amber brooch. I leant on the shaft of the boar-spear and tried to look like a warrior. I felt them all watching me. I had no idea what to do, except wait, so wait we did, and they lay out on the grass and went to sleep, and I looked at them and felt like Jesus at Gethsemane, when the retainers of the Pharisees come for him with sword and torch and spear, and only Peter stands up to defend him.

I stood alone and waited. I had no idea what was about to happen, or that the ship's arrival would be one of those moments that changed the course of my life. But for that day's events, I might have grown old and bitter as ale that has sat in the barrels too long.

As the ship turned towards us it was clear that it was going to beach on the shingle by the river mouth. I kicked the sleepers up and led them down to the shore.

The ship's captain climbed up onto the prow and hailed me across the water.

'I seek the hall of Sigurd Sow!'

'You have found it,' I called back. 'I am Harald, Sigurd's son. He is dead now. Two winters past.'

The man waved and jumped down, acknowledging my words, but I knew him, I realised. It came back to me in a moment.

I knew his face from among those who had sat with my brother and listened to the court poets tell their legends. I had seen it many times with the light of amber coals on his cheek, lit with the glow of ale, laughing and carefree. It was as if one of those dream heroes had sailed across the chasm of dawn to find me, trapped in this middling world. The closer he came the more I knew him – as if he were a long-lost brother whose mannerisms were mine own.

It was not Olaf, but it was one of his type, one of his men. I knew it from his golden armbands, silver-worked belt, his warrior's sword, rich with jewels, the weight of his tread, the power of his grip. And as he splashed ashore and took three great strides towards me, his name came to my lips. He was the one who had warned us about the hunting whales.

'Rognvald!' I called out, like the shipwrecked man who is plucked from the rock as the waves lick round his feet. He reached out for my hand and seized it, as a man does who pulls another from the mud.

'What news?' I asked him, and he laughed at me.

'What news indeed,' he said. 'Do I have news!'

With Rognvald's arrival it seemed he brought the firelight shadows alive again. Olaf was coming to reclaim his throne. He was crossing from Sweden with an army of his own and wanted us to raise the south for him. We were going to crush the men of Lathe who had betrayed him before. My only fear was that the battle would be done before I arrived. That I would not get to stand at Olaf's side and prove my mettle.

Looking back, I can feel that fifteen-year-old boy still deep inside me. We share the same skin, he and I. We have that much in common. He is the acorn that has dropped onto the forest floor. Small, hard, overlooked – entirely blind to the fact that the winter days are no longer getting shorter.

My spring had come.

The time of roots was done.

CHAPTER FOUR

The *Bjarkamál*

'We need to leave in three weeks,' Rognvald told me. It was late afternoon in May, Eggtide we call it, the time of lambs and the blue clusters of forget-me-nots, of melting snows, mountain streams tumbling headlong down the steep slopes to reach the fjord waters.

Rognvald was like a stone dropped into a still pool. The ripples spread out across Uppland and beyond. Everyone who remembered Olaf well wanted to join his cause.

'Remember the riches Olaf brought last time,' men said. 'You'd be a fool not to join him now. He has luck with him.' Just one look at Rognvald and they could see how much wealth Olaf might be bringing.

All of a sudden their talk was free of lambing and fox kills and next month's weather. They talked of war and deeds their grandsires performed, the raids they had been on to England and beyond. Everyone wanted a new spearhead for their son or husband, a new shield rim, dagger, boss, new rivets for a treasured mail shirt that has hung too long gathering dust on the hall wall. The dale rang to the sound of hammers and furnace bellows pumping one after the other till the fires inside were white as stars. All day the oxen brought in loads of charcoal and bog iron. Men and beasts were weary. You could hear it in the note of their hungry lowing as the teams were uncoupled, and the men led them to the ox-garth. As the gate swung shut behind them, the ploughmen's voices rose to calm them, until silence returned.

I alone did not care for Olaf's treasure. I would fight for him without contract or honour, I told myself. He was my brother and he was the king, and I had always been his most loyal follower.

So Olaf is returning, I thought, as if I needed to repeat the words just to believe them. Olaf is returning. We are to give battle, I will stand by my brother's side and . . .

Flames have a way of bewitching a man. The little flickers of light above the glowing embers were elf-lights, my mother always said. But now, with fresh logs of silver birch, the flames did not flicker, they roared and chomped and cracked, like a dog with a bone clamped in his hind teeth.

A spark flew, and I brushed it off my knee. It had not singed, but it had broken my daytime dream. I looked up, Rognvald was staring into the fire. He did not hear the noise. He was still caught in the flame-dance, absent-mindedly scratching the back of his lapdog.

It was the first time I ever saw such a thing. For me a dog was much like a man: either a thief, a coward, or a fine beast fit for baiting or bringing a wild pig to ground.

But his dog was something unknown to me. It was no larger than a cat, with black ears, sharp and alert, and ugly, bulging eyes. Why he kept it I could not tell. It looked like a boggle-eyed devil. Other men thought so too, and Thorhild, my mother's old maid, would mutter some warding spell whenever it looked her way.

He treated it like a favourite slavewoman, or pampered child. It was all the fashion in the south, he told us. This particular one came from Kiev, the whelp of one of Prince Jaroslav's bitches. An ugly thing to come from a royal house, I thought.

'Will more come, do you think?' Rognvald asked, referring to the muster.

'The men that come late are not worth having.'

He nodded, and turned back to the fire. The flames gleamed in his dog's eyes before they closed.

Two days later we picked our way up to the tops of the valleys, and out over the moors and purple heather, to the northern ends of Uppland. There was a vast blue sky above, snow-peaked mountains on the right, and to the left the land tumbled down to the sparkling summer sea. I breathed in the high mountain air, felt a touch of silk on my forehead and wiped it away. Let the Norns spin a fine pattern for me, I thought. Let it be bright and bold and colourful, like a well-dressed man seen from far across the valley.

Anything but dun yellow.

We threaded our way from valley to valley, over flat boggy moorland, hearing the call of the grouse and the curlew, that sings its own name, *coor-lee, coor-lee* to the listening heather.

After two weeks we came at last to the great valleys of the North, which run east to west, down from the mountains to the sea. It was here that we met with Olaf's army, tanned dark as calfskin from the high mountain crossing. I knew my brother the moment he appeared, riding a white horse at the top of the pass, his wind-stiffened banner flapping behind him. He gleamed out gold against the grassy slopes, with silk shirt, embroidered cloak, and thick gold bands on his arms.

We all stood and cheered and lifted our arms. 'That's Olaf!' I called out to Guttorm. 'Look.'

I wanted to be the first to greet him, and Guttorm let me take his horse. 'Go on!' he waved to me. 'Go meet your brother!' And I heeled her forward, bent low over the mane, the wind stinging tears of joy from my eyes.

'Is that you?' Olaf said to me as my horse thundered to a halt before him. 'Look at you!'

I laughed and looked at him instead. His face was three years unfamiliar: older, of course. He was stouter and thicker, and had aged more than three years, but his eyes were as clear and cold as I remembered.

'You're a man now.'

What I said I do not remember. My words were lost as the others caught up and crowded and jostled round, shoving, pushing, greeting.

I saw Guttorm at the back. The midsummer sun had turned his cheeks a little pink, his hair was thinning. He stood back and let others take his place. 'Everything in good measure,' he liked to say, and caught my eye and winked.

I felt that even though I was further from Uppland than I had ever been, I was now with Olaf, and at home.

Battle came at midsummer, when the summer days were at their longest, the night its narrowest; the year at its crux, the long slope to winter begun.

Olaf's captains all expected to be heard. Some thought that we should wait and see if more of the locals would come to our side; others said strike now, before the Lathe earls' strength increased. Olaf listened to their raucous noise, then closed his eyes as if listening for whispered words, and one by one the men fell silent. He sucked in a breath, and I felt a thrill on my back, as if a feather had brushed my nape, then he blinked open his eyes, and I saw that God had spoken to him. 'Tomorrow we march to meet them. It is God's will that we put their unworthy souls to the test.'

Olaf and God had spoken. The discussion ceased. There was nothing else to decide.

As the shadows lengthened behind us, Olaf and I stood on the ridge above the camp, looking down the wide valley towards the sunset and the sea. A king is always in demand, and that night was the first time we had been alone and the years dropped away from us and we talked of Uppland and the farm.

He remembered all the men who worked there, and their wives

and children, and questioned me about them all. I told him all I knew. Who was married, who had died, who had gone off a-Viking.

He surprised me. 'I thought you had forgotten about us,' I said.

'Not for one single day.' There was silence for a while. I watched the midge columns rise like smoke into the air, golden in the sunset light.

'How is Halfdan?'

Halfdan was the black sheep, the one the elves slipped into the cot at birth, the changeling. 'He did not want to come,' I said.

Olaf could tell from the tone in my voice what I thought of Halfdan. I had almost learnt how not to let my middle brother disappoint me. 'I'm not surprised. But you came.'

'Of course,' I said. 'And Guttorm.'

'Yes. Guttorm. He's solid.'

At the end Olaf nodded. The grasses were noisy with insects. They had to make the most of the short season. Neither of us spoke. Our breaths only heightened the stillness.

He drew in a deep breath. 'So,' he said at last. 'She died.'

I nodded.

'She did,' I said.

'Tell me how.'

'She was sick.'

'What sickness?'

I'd blamed Olaf so many times for my mother's death. I'd cursed him for his cowardice, blamed him for my life on an Uppland farmstead. I'd nurtured resentment over many things and named it 'Olaf', as a child will name a toy of twisted straw. But now I was standing with him, all I could say to him was, 'Grief. She died of grief.'

I could see Olaf's jaw set hard. He nodded.

His blue eyes were still evening water – quiet and thoughtful. I no longer blamed him. Guilt is like a raven. It always finds its way home.

'She was buried according to Christian ritual,' I said.

38

He looked up and nodded, and forced a smile. 'Good,' he said. 'Sigurd died too.'

'He did?'

My father was much easier to talk about. Olaf and I did not share his blood. We did not have that in common. It was as easy as talking of a cousin or an aunt that lives across the valley. I felt the weight lift from us both.

'He bought Budli's black stallion,' I said. 'It kicked him in the gut, and he never stood up again.'

'Was he in much pain?'

'Yes,' I said. 'But he did not let out a sound.'

'He took me in, you know. When I was an orphan babe, and raised me as his own. I was never good to him. He sent me out when I was twelve.'

I knew.

He laughed. 'He would have made a great warrior,' Olaf said. 'Guttorm takes after him.'

'He does,' I said, but both of them had the love of farm life in their marrow. They wanted dirt under their fingernails, the smell of newborn lambs, the view of well-tended fields and herds, multiplying with the summer. Their enemy was blight and hail. Their treasure a great stock of golden grain, rafter-hung hams, a well-fed folk.

Olaf and I were both our mother's sons. We wanted war, and fame, and adventure.

'You've grown,' he said. I puffed up like a blacksmith's bellows-skin. He pursed his lips. 'I should have taken you. I can see that now.'

'I was only twelve,' I said, though I'd always felt ill-used.

'Well,' he said. 'What is past is past. But tomorrow will you fight with me?'

I did not know why he should ask me this and spoke with passion. 'Of course,' I said.

'No, I mean, with my retainers. Mother's ghost will be happy, I think, to have us both together. Daring the Fates.'

I had not expected this. A thrill went through me. I had to cough to clear my throat. 'Yes,' I said. 'Of course!'

As we stood there was a burst of laughter at the far end of the camp. That was the end where the Swedes who had come over with Olaf were camped. It will be their captain, Egil, I thought. He was a great joker and had a pet bear cub that clapped its forepaws together in return for fish. The jest was passed along the campfires – to Olaf's retainers, to my Upplanders, and then at the end the camp of hill-men. Soon both fields were filled with laugher.

The veil of golden midges hanging over the camp, the thought of us being united again, the long blue evening skies. It all seemed good.

I thought of the Swedes. 'King Onund has done you well,' I said.

Olaf looked and nodded. 'Yes, they're a fine band. Though it was as much Astrid's work.'

Astrid was Olaf's wife. He had left her behind in Sweden with his daughter.

There was a long pause. A group of men were walking up to where we were standing.

I did not know them, but then I saw their leader, and realised they were the hillmen who had joined his cause.

'Have you met Dags?' he said.

I shook my head.

He led me forward. 'Dags!' he said and shook hands with the man, and each retainer.

They looked at me. 'This is my brother, Harald Sigurdsson.'

Dags wore a cloak lined with fox fur, and a kirtle so old and faded it was hard to make out the colour. He was so broad and thick he reminded me of an ancient yew. I took an instant dislike to the man. He had the manner of a horse-thief and looked me up and down as if he was wondering if I had anything worth stealing 'How old are you, lad?'

I was fifteen, but I felt older. 'Seventeen,' I lied.

He reckoned me up. 'Can you carry that sword?'

I prickled at the suggestion. 'Keep up with me and see.'

Dags laughed: a deep, rumbling sound, like a distant landslide, but he seemed entirely taken with me now, and chuckled as he turned down the valley to where the enemy army was camping for the evening. 'Yes, I shall keep up. I'll be right behind you, Harald.' He turned down the valley. As evening fell their bonfires blazed against the midsummer dusk. They gleamed in constellations, the men of Lathe, the men of Thord Hund, all the hoary northern chieftains, numerous as a sparrow-host when the seasons turn.

'There's more to battle than numbers,' Dags spat, then rubbed it into the grass with his toe. 'There's mettle, for one. And luck for another. And your brother has both by the cartload.'

You learn a lot about a man from how he spends his last night before battle. I watched the great warriors stand and brag, and felt tired and silent. I had not seen Guttorm since that afternoon, and made my way back through the camp – a cloaked and listening shadow – to where the pride of Upplanders were gathered.

It felt good to sit with neighbours and friends. The silences were filled by the noise from Dag's end of the camp. The main fire was near a stand of willows at the bend in the river. Guttorm was there, solid as ever, like an oak. As the evening drew its cloaks about us, he came and sat with me. Neither of us spoke. The flames crackled and gnawed, as a dog on a bone. The golden light was on our hands and faces and sparks flew up into the night-blue sky.

'How is Olaf?' he said at last.

'Confident,' I said. 'He is with all his captains.'

Guttorm nodded. He could see through the gaps in my words. 'They're a noisy bunch.'

I nodded slowly. The flames were low, the blue and yellow lights had caught my tongue, speech seemed like an effort. 'This is not how I imagined the night before battle,' I said at last.

Guttorm laughed. 'What did you think it would be like?'

'I thought we would be like Dag's men. Drinking. Feasting. Boasting. That's how the poets have it.'

He rubbed his hands together. 'Well. Make poems of your own.'

There was a sudden roar of laughter from Dag's fires. I wondered if Olaf was there. I pictured him in my mind's eye, bragging, golden with firelight, fearless before battle. The Swedes started up a new song, and they were belting it out as a challenge to the rest. No one beat them, I think. It all ended with laughter, and slapping of backs and vows about what each man would do in battle, on the morrow.

'Well, if I'm to meet the Maker tomorrow, it's time I slept,' Guttorm announced, and put his hands on his thighs and rose, and I followed, exhausted.

We lay down together, all the men of Uppland, our shields and spears beside us, cloaks thrown over us. I lay for a while, looking up at the stars through the leaves of the willow. The ground was damp and cool so close to the river. So tomorrow you fight your first battle, I thought, and tried to stay awake, but my eyes were heavy and I wanted to sleep and rest for a while. If sleep is just a foretaste of death, I thought, it cannot be too bad to die. You only have one death, what matters is not when but how you die.

Next morning as we broke our night's fast, Thormond, one of Olaf's skalds, put his horn to his mouth and blew a long note. He started among the Swedes, and strode through the camp, chanting the *Bjarkamál*, which told of the downfall of the great hero Hrolf Kraki, who was surprised in his lodging by treacherous hosts.

It had been Olaf's favourite poem as a lad, and I had heard it many times, but never like this. Or rather, it never felt as alive as then.

Thormond's voice sounded like a drum as he beat out the words; a blacksmith's hammer ringing loud and clear.

Awake, arise! Rally, fellows!
Not to wine nor wives' soft thighs,
But to hard Hilda's game of war
Rally your ranks as Hrólf us taught,
Alone in the strife I stand amongst slain
A bulwark builded of fallen bodies

I stood as Thormond strode along the shallow river.

The water was clear and foaming where it tumbled over rocks. In the east, behind the mountains, a red sky glowed like coals. We called the red sky 'Thor's Beard' and it was meant to be portentous of something, but what it was I didn't know.

When Guttorm saw my face he laughed. 'Everything's an omen, when you look back on it.'

Olaf was already on his horse, dressed for battle, the sun on his golden helm, his captains helping to organise the warbands.

Each man rose quickly after that, throwing on his war-gear, stuffing his things into a sack, and tossing them onto the backs of ponies. We were ready first.

'Do you want to lead us down?' Rognvald shouted to me. 'We're heading down to the farmstead. The one with the turf roof.'

I waved to show I'd understood and told Guttorm.

'Fetch the banner,' he told me, and I brought it from outside his tent: my forefathers' emblem of the White Boar on a field of black.

'Will you carry it today?' he said, and I felt a thrill go through me. It was a great honour.

'Yes,' I said, and looked about as if someone was about to take it from me. But no one did. They seemed to look with admiring eyes. I felt the weight of expectation, like the arm of an old friend, on my shoulders. I stood by the side of my brother and with his sword at his belt, and helmet on, he looked less like a farmer, and had the look of a tough old veteran. When the last few were scrambling to get ready he called out, 'Ready, men of Uppland?'

They shouted in answer.

'I can't hear you!'

They answered once more.

'I can't hear you!' he shouted again, and we bellowed back at him all as one and I lifted the White Boar and let it fly as I led them all to battle.

*

43

It was two hours' walk to the farmstead.

The day brightened about us. Mist shredded off the pine forest. The knotted woods were bright with stabbing sunlight. We could have been strolling to market. Only the rattle of shield cases and the flap of sheaths and axe hoods reminded us our business was war.

Somewhere below, another army was marching up the valley to meet us.

'It'll tire them out,' Guttorm said. 'That will help us.'

He kept up a long, lone conversation, and I smiled and nodded and made brief grunts in answer, but I was too tense to speak. I do not know if it was fear or nerves, but I could not think of anything to say. All I could think was that I was going to fight in battle. It was a little conversation going about in my head.

You are going to kill or be killed. You are going to stand firm. You will not let any man near your brother. You will not shame yourself. No man will ever call you a coward.

My mouth was dry. My stomach empty. I would not shame myself before the battle had even begun, I swore. I would not give men any reason to say, Look, there is Harald, too young for a fight.

Someone behind me started singing. It was one of Budli's sister-sons, a cheerful lad named Vikarr. It was a sad song about a pair of lovers who do not meet for many years. It was not the *Bjarkamál*, but I think it did more to lift their spirits.

All the company joined in. Only I remained silent.

It seemed all my life was building to this moment. I brought back all I had learnt: swordplay, courage, fury, discipline; every poem I had heard; each tale that had filled the winter's nights; each afternoon riding, hunting; each morning I spent chopping lumps out of a wooden post; each day I spent holding my shield out to get strength in my left shoulder.

I was like the new-forged sword that is taken out for the first time, to see if there are hidden faults or cracks that will make it break; or if it was forged true.

*

44

Guttorm and I were the first men on the battlefield. The homestead's owner had fled with his family. A herd of grey goats watched from their wicker pen as we found a broad stretch of level ground with a wood on the left and the homestead on the right. We stood in a broad meadow bright with buttercups. It looked as though it had been grazed until the day before and Guttorm planted his heel and wrinkled his nose, and said, 'Thin soil.'

It was as if the place was not worthy of a battle. I looked about. Behind us, in the east, the mountains reared up like hunched shoulders; north and south the valley slopes steepened to bare crags; and in front of us, where the land fell down towards the setting sun, there was a scattering of pine trees, more fields full of half-grown crops of barley, just coming to ear, and a patch of surprised tufts of turnip.

I breathed it deep. The land was ancient when our people came here. It did not care who lived or died, this day. Whatever happened, the mountains and fjords would remain.

It was a strangely consoling feeling, like forgiveness, or confession.

'Six deep!' Guttorm shouted as our companies filed into the meadow. 'That's it!' he shouted, and whistled to the men at the end as if he were rounding up sheep for winter.

The wind tugged at the boar banner as each man arranged himself behind, according to rank and courage. It was just as I learned from tales as a child. The first comers are not the richest or the most noble, but they are, of men, the bravest and the best.

As the Upplanders took up their positions, one by one the various companies came in behind us, and I saw with a panic that I would be too far away from Olaf.

His retainers stood about his banner with the Swedes, and then the men of Ostford, and Vestfold, Emnet and the stout Dalesmen on the other side.

Panic rose in me like a sickness. I had to be with him, I

thought. I had promised, but I could not walk away from the men of Uppland who I had brought north to battle. It seemed a churlish thing to do to reward their service. So I wavered between cleft futures.

Olaf rode out a little. 'Guttorm, move right!' he shouted through cupped hands. We walked sideways a little, made the end of our line a stand of gorse. The Swedes raised their banner on the left, and Olaf's retainers stood about his banner with the blue cross.

'What's up lad?' Guttorm said.

'Nothing,' I told him, but he saw in my face what I wanted and put his hand to my arm. 'Go,' he told me. 'Help hold the centre. I will lead the Upplanders.'

I opened my mouth to argue, but he smiled. 'Don't worry. Budli can carry my banner.'

I was sheepish as I walked towards Olaf's band of gold-honoured veterans, and I almost lost my nerve, but Rognvald called out to me. 'Come, Harald, stand with the poets! They are to witness Olaf's deeds and memorialise them in words.'

The poets were in the third row of his retainers, fighting men: tough, hard, prickly as old blackthorn. Their names were Thormond Kolbrunarskald, Gissur Gulbraaskald and Thorfinn Mudr. I nodded towards them and they nodded back, but Thormond was the only one who spoke to me. 'How old are you?'

'Fifteen,' I said.

He grunted and nodded towards my sword. 'Can you use that?'

'Some men say so.'

'Sure?'

'I'll strap it to my hand, it you like. To stop it falling.'

Thormond laughed, but Gissur didn't. He was famously tetchy before battle.

'Keep back when I swing my axe,' he said. 'I won't earn any fame killing a boy.'

I was too nervous to respond. I needed to piss, but there was no more time for fear.

'Here the bastards come,' Thorfinn shouted, and I turned and through the heads of other men I saw the glint of steel through the trees below us.

Their banners bore the Black Bear of Thore Hund; the yellow cross of Kalv Arnasson; Harek of Tjota's Red Raven, but there were many more behind that I did not know.

I looked to see the White Boar to my left, carried by another man's hands, but I was glad. I was with Olaf, and he and I and Guttorm were the only men here to share the same womb.

I was ready. I watched what other men did, puffed out my cheeks, rolled my shoulders, checked my sword for the umpteenth time. As the column of our foes began to form up in a line across the turnip field, I began to feel calm. Death is just a long sleep, I thought. It cannot hurt. Only life hurts.

We started pacing forward as one. I ran a finger under my helm strap, checked my belt, hefted my shield, drew my sword.

'*Fram! Fram!*' Olaf called out. 'Forward! Christmen. Crossmen. Kingsmen!'

This is it, I told myself.

Thorfinn was coughing to clear his throat, Gissur traded a joke with one of the others, and Thormond started playing with words, repeating Olaf's own.

'*Fram, fram,*' he muttered, as he reached for the right words to speak that night when the battle was won and the feast-fires lit.

I concentrated on each step forward, felt the turf lie under my feet.

Rognvald was next to me. He caught my eye. Stay with me, his look said. The man in front of me started to jog. I kept pace with him as his stride lengthened to a run, and then we roared as one as we drove like a fist into the guts of the foe.

CHAPTER FIVE

The Battle of Stiklestad

You leave a tooth on every battlefield.

I lost this one, here, at the front. God knows when.

As a boy I spent my days sparring with a wooden sword, chopping the bark off a tree, but trees did not bleed. Nor did they fight back. Men did both. Battle was a blur of shouts and swords and raining axes. The first man I killed, my very first, was a sudden shouting face with yellow teeth and a leather cap. He seemed mad with fear. I wish I remembered him better, but I was mad too and we were jostling and pushing and shoving with our shields, and I rammed my sword point into his mouth, and he died still raging.

The next man I punched with my sword hilt, and felt the crunch of bone. The third and fourth were blurs, I cannot tell you if I killed them or not.

'On, Harald!' a voice urged in my ear. 'Stay with the king!'

It was Rognvald.

The next was black-bearded. He terrified me and I him. We battered at each other like a pair of blacksmiths. His sword splintered my shield and I hacked at his till the rim burst and he slammed the boss into my face. I drove him back with the rim of my shield. He fell forward. I chopped down. His helm burst with the blow. I caved in his skull-dome with all my fear and anger, and jarred my hand and notched my father's sword like a fool.

I just kept moving, forwards, ever forwards. A slash under the shield, driving down over the shield rim, boxing with the boss, following in the red wake of King Olaf. My mother's voice came to me, driving me on, farther Harald, faster Harald, stay with your brother, keep your brother safe.

I will, Mother. I will!

Then night came.

Ask any man who was there. The day darkened, as if a thunder-head had blotted out the sun, and then turned darker yet, so that there were white stars in the sky staring wide-eyed in terror.

As a child I had heard tales of Fenris the Great Wolf, and looked up and saw that a great chunk had been bitten from the sun. The day's candle was devoured.

I understood now what the red sky had been for. It was a warning to us all.

'Ragnarok!' someone shouted, as if Christ himself would arrive on his chariot and drive our foes from the field. Day became night, good became evil. I tried to remember the last time I had sinned, and told God that I was sorry, as I killed another man.

Olaf was the only one who did not stop fighting. He was about ten feet to my right. I knew that this was my moment, to stand with him back to back, and take the blows that were meant for him.

Thormond and Rognvald were nowhere to be seen, and the retainers about him were all dead.

'Harald!' I heard Olaf shout, or it may have been 'Christmen!' or even 'Why Lord?', I could not tell, but the words summoned me, as a hound is whistled from across a field, and I ducked under a sword-swipe, knocked a man aside with my shoulder, used my shield as a ram as my feet slipped on gore. I came within an arm's length of him, a shadow clotted from the darkness and took the shape of a man.

Some say it was Thore Hund, but I saw a stone-troll with a cloak of human pelts – and knew he was the Devil. Yet the sight of Lucifer did not terrify me, but drove me instead to a pitch of fury. I knocked two men out of my way. 'Olaf,' I shouted. 'Olaf!' and drove my shoulder into the Devil's side.

It was heavy and solid as a tree trunk, and with the slap of one hand he threw me back as a child could toss a doll of straw, and I stumbled back and stared in horror as the Devil rose above my brother, as if to embrace him, as a father does to a son.

I shouted and screamed, but there was nothing I could do. I had met a Fate stronger than my own.

That killing was strangely intimate. Olaf was leaning back against a standing stone. The Devil stepped in to lift his mail shirt. I saw the spear go in. I saw my brother's face as the blade was dragged out. I heard it too: a dull wet sound, like slapping a half-full wineskin, and through the puncture gushed my brother's blood.

The groan stunned me. Now Olaf was wounded his foes were like women at the well, shoving and pushing and queuing up to strike the next blow.

Five times they wounded him, in arms and legs and belly, but it was Kalv Arnasson who killed him. I saw the side-swung sword catch Olaf in the neck and my brother slumped and slid and fell and his gold helmet tumbled into the mud.

'Olaf!' I shouted. 'Olaf! Olaf! Olaf!' But my words were lost as thunder rolled and the darkness was abroad and the air was cold and it started to rain.

I had heard much of battle, but the skalds have it right: it is the roar of Odin, storm of Valkyries; weapon-clash; spear-storm, edge-wind; sword-rain; wound-wind; killing of men; wolf-feast; the judgement of warriors.

Berserk strength came upon me. I knew that I would die that day. I cannot say clearly what happened next or even how I survived those moments. The sun came out again and there was spray on my face, and I thought that it was rain. I held another man's shield in my hand, blood stuck my hand to the hilt. My second shield was splintered by an axe blow, I caught up a third, and it lasted long enough to kill two more men.

There was a brief pause and I sucked in breath, wielded the boss like a fist and broke men's noses who came near me. I heard voices, and suddenly there was Guttorm beside me. 'Let us avenge our brother!' he shouted. He trembled with fury. He'd lost his helmet. There was a cut above his eye, and blood down his face, but he did not seem to notice. His voice was hoarse. 'Come Harald, come!'

It was like Pentecost, I think. The Holy Spirit entered us. We were all battle-mad. We fought like starving wolves and all about me men grunted and died, and the rain spray grew fiercer, and then I realised that I was the centre of the storm, and that I was the killer.

Guttorm was struck down. I avenged him in moments. His killer had a surprised look as I sliced his neck in two. I caught another man's sword on the remains of my shield, stabbed at his face and heard him shout out in pain. It was fast and brutal. Men fell like wheat stalks when the scythe is swung. All about they were crashing to the ground.

I did not see the man who cut me down. It was a blow in my thigh. I think I had forgotten that I had no shield left. I do not know. It is not clear. All I remember is that one moment I was fighting, the next I was lying in the sheaves of the slain, my mouth in mud as someone put a boot in my back and speared me through. The blow was hard enough to pin me to the earth. It was quieter down among the dead. Cooler as well. It is just sleep, I thought. It will take away the pain.

Blood splattered, raining from swung sword edges. In front of my face was a buttercup half red with blood. I knew I was dying. A hand grabbed my shoulder. This was to be my end. A murderer's knife across the throat.

I felt for my sword, so that I should die with it in my hand, and felt blind panic when my scrabbling fingers found nothing.

'No,' I groaned. But the knife did not come. Hands held me under the armpits and dragged me backwards.

'No!' I moaned when I understood that these were friends and they did not mean for me to die trampled into the dirt like a common man. 'Let me die by Olaf. I am Harald Sigurdsson. He is my brother. Give me a sword!'

I was almost too weak to speak, and I could not raise my head. There was blood sticking my eyes shut and I could not tell if it was mine or not. The light began to grow, as if it were dawn, even though it was late in the afternoon, a few weeks after midsummer.

I was thrown belly-down over a donkey's back, like a deer that's been gutted where the hounds caught it. I did not know if my captors were friends or foes, who meant me ill, or worse. Someone jumped up behind me. The beast started. I was tall, but not thick, and I do not think I was too much weight. Hands wrapped about me as if I were a child.

The clamour of battle was fading behind me. I did not know why they were not fighting.

'Give me a sword!' I hissed.

The light was failing again, and I could not tell if the darkness that filled my vision was dusk or dawn or curtains of death closing about me.

'He still wants to fight,' one said.

'His fight is almost over,' said another.

'Will he last?' the first voice asked.

There was a long pause before the second spoke. 'I do not think so.'

CHAPTER SIX

The Mountain Hut

'Lie still.'

I did not know the voice. I did not know where I was. A damp cloth smoothed my forehead, cheeks; then around my eyes. It took a moment before my gummed lids peeled open. Sudden light made them water. I blinked and lifted a hand and turned to my side.

A rough man spoke. His words were whispered into my ear, from behind, like a murderer. A goat was bleating. I smelt fresh meat, the regular puff of a fire being stoked.

'Still,' the voice said again. He wanted me to know. 'This will hurt.'

I groaned each time he pressed the iron to my flesh. The smell was that of burnt hair, burnt skin, burnt flesh that was my own. I had been branded like a thrall. Someone poked me with a stick.

'He's still alive,' a child's voice said.

Much later a woman's voice said, 'He'll die.'

Outside came the thud of an axe chopping wood. Suddenly the hut was full of the roar of battle. My own voice rang out. Olaf snarled as the spear was pulled out. His face was white, his blue eyes wide. I lay on the floor. The spear ran me through again, slower this time, as slow as a dream can make it. Fenrir's son, Sköll, was eating the sun. Doomsday was come. I would die fighting. It was raining blood. Will he last? Strange voices say, I do not think so.

I saw Rognvald's hand scratching the back of his spotted lapdog. The black boggle eyes close with pleasure.

'Lie still,' the voice said.

I tried to speak, but did not know what I was saying. A hand was rough on the back of my head. He stroked me as if I was a child. 'Hush. Sleep,' he said. 'Dream. The gods will send healing.'

My breathing slowed. I did not want to dream, but in my head the millstone of guilt wheeled on and on. The battle kept returning to me. I saw Olaf being surrounded and tried to help him but my feet would not move, or Thore Hund was there, knocking me backwards, and my voice was a scream and at some point I opened my eyes again.

Hours have passed. Days perhaps. It is sunset, or sunrise and the door is open. A shaggy old hound stands silhouetted on the threshold. He lifts a leg against the doorpost to piss. That piss is sparkling gold, the sparkling gold of Olaf's helm as it tumbled into the mud.

I've never seen the wound on my back, but men have described it to me. If the blade had gone lower, or if it had been turned true, it would have gone straight between my ribs and I would have bled out on the fields about Stiklestad.

But luck saved me from death that day. Luck, God, and Rognvald. I learnt that much later from the family who took me in. They fed and cared for me, and brought me back to strength and hope, and helped me nurse my grief.

It was they who gave me life.

The father was named Oswi. He was a small man, with little hands and a lopsided face. It gave his thin lips and lined face an odd, bemused look. He had a high voice, and for the first month I think he was the only one who spoke with me.

'Rest,' he said when I was awake to the world, his open hands gently pushing me back down. 'Sleep. I will bring you food.'

I lay as he fetched something. A bowl of greens and beans. Sometimes an egg, stuck with feathers, that he cracked into a bowl and made me drink in one gulp.

They had three sons still living. They all took after their father: both in looks and in manner, with odd eyes that seemed sad. They reminded me of three skulking fox pups, waiting for their dame to bring them food. They sat across the fire and stared at me, flames in their small blue eyes.

The wife was taller than them all: a troll of a woman, large and ungainly, but quiet as well, awkward and clumsy. She had an embarrassed air about her and bore no ornamentation, bar an iron ring woven with wolf-fur about her wrist. She brewed up dark potions from pine resin and roots. 'Take this to him,' she'd whisper to one of her boys, and if my eyes were open they would stalk towards me as cautiously as if I were a bear in sleep.

It was easier to keep my eyes closed. The mother would not speak unless she thought I was asleep. Not that she had much to say about the world. 'Fetch the grindstone,' she'd say. Or, 'Hurry, lad.' Or, 'Where's your father?' Or, 'When the wind changes your face will stay like that.'

It was maybe two months past midsummer, but the family were already putting away stores of firewood, roots and vegetables that they pickled in salt.

One day I heard the father talking to his wife. 'Men came up the valley yesterday,' he said. 'Strange men. They were not gathering their herds.' I tried to hear what she said in reply, but her voice was so softly spoken I could not make it out.

Next day the three boys came towards me in a nervous huddle. They stood before me, a drip of green snot hanging from the middle one's nose. They prodded each other and it was the youngest who spoke. 'What is your name?'

'Harald,' I told him. 'Harald Sigurdsson.'

'Are you the one they are hunting?'

'Come away boys,' the father said. He'd been sharpening a knife with a long whetstone and the wet blade was still in his right hand and droplets hung from the knife blade like silver blood.

For a moment I had the sense that he was going to gut me and cook me, as old wives' tales have it, and knew there was little I could do to stop him.

He looked up as if reading my thoughts, then looked down at the knife and spat on the whetstone. After each rasp he spat on the blade, turned it in the light of the doorway, and rasped again.

I felt like a pig that waits for slaughter.

The boys did not move. The snot hung like green candlewax, but did not fall.

'Out you go,' the father called.

When they were gone, I said, 'There are men?'

He looked at his knife, then me and nodded.

'They're looking for me?'

One eye looked gloomy, the other defiant. I looked into the defiant one. 'Hush,' he said. 'Rest.'

The next day horsemen came to within a mile of the house. I heard the horse hoofs echoing up the stony stream bed and pushed myself up. The scabs itched and I could reach those on my leg, and picked them to reveal raw, red skin, underneath. But my back still tugged at my skin as I limped to the doorway and looked out.

Summers are short in the mountains. It was autumn already. The trees were yellow, the pines still green. The goat was tethered by the rear hoof, the wife had the wood axe in her hand and was striding across the yard, bent forward like a man striding into a heavy gale. She looked up suddenly and said, 'Sit! Stay!'

I was so astonished that she'd spoken to me I ducked back inside and waited inside the doorway, my head pressed against the wattle, said a prayer, felt the distant tremble of horses through the ground. The man came back at a run.

'Under the bed!' he said.

I felt sick at the thought.

He became nervous. 'They can't find you here. Stay inside. Please.'

I could not hide or skulk away from my enemies. I could not have it said that Harald Sigurdsson was found hiding in a pigsty or in a water barrel. I would have to go and tell my mother's ghost. Imagine an eternity of her anger.

'I'll go up the valley.'

'You cannot,' he said, but I was already grabbing a staff and a piece of bread. I could see in his eyes what he was thinking. He looked up at the mountains. Their peaks were like a mighty stockade the giants built in defence again the Swedes. 'Men do not cross those this time of year. Not living men, anyway.'

A horse neighed. Closer this time. I had no choice and my face must have made that plain.

'Take this,' the father said, and pulled an old homespun blanket off his bed. It made a rough cloak that I knotted about my neck and then he gave me a broad-brimmed grey hat to keep the rain and sun off my face.

'Thank you,' I said. 'I shall repay you one day. I promise!'

'Go!' he motioned 'Go!' and I was already hurrying across the yard as the pounding of hoofs came closer.

I cut my fingers on rocks and brambles as I scrambled up the hill. Twigs tried to hold me back. They tore at my skin and clothes, but still I ran till my breaths were heavy and I could taste blood in my lungs, and I drove myself so hard the cut on my thigh opened again and the pain drove me faster.

But all the time I heard the sound of pursuit, and did not pause till I had reached a high black crag, and knew that I could go no further. All I had with me was my eating knife. I found a hand-shaped rock, and got ready to throw. I would not flee any more, I told myself. I would stand and fight. But it was not Thore Hund who burst from the bushes below, or any of his warriors, but Oswi's son.

'I thought I had lost you,' he panted. Our chests heaved and I lowered the knife. 'You will die up here. There are few tracks that lead to the sunrise. But I will show you. Come!

We went slowly at first through a wood of twisted and stunted birch and yew. Then the hardwood gave way to pine, dark and gloomy and thick with old needles, and the land was steeper and crueller, and more wild.

I sucked in breaths, leant heavily on the stick, and felt sweat and blood drip down my back.

'It's opened up,' my guide told me as we paused at a stream. I swallowed back the meltwater stream, cold as ice in the gut, and as we looked down from the high place I saw six horses tethered under the tree by the side of the hut. The riders had dismounted. They were talking to the father. One of them turned and looked up the valley. A troll of a man, with black beard and a hairless cloak.

The Devil stared straight towards me. I jumped up. 'Let's keep going!' I said.

The lad was lean and brown as a mountain goat. We climbed without pause and late that day we reached the head of the valley, where miles of bleak moorland stretched away before us. 'Your friends went that way,' he said, pointing at the low ground between two white-capped peaks. 'The lands of the Swedes are on the other side.'

I looked at the snow-tipped crags and felt as though I was being given an impossible task, like a man in tales asking for a king's daughter in wedlock. 'How many days?' I said, as if I were walking to a market just over the next hill.

He shrugged. 'I've never been that way. Some men say a week. Others less. But that is in summer.' We nodded. 'At least the snows have not yet fallen.'

Yes, I thought, ever hopeful, such good fortune.

We stopped in the shadow of a withered spruce. A black scar ran down the trunk where lightning had struck it. He touched the place where last year's resin had dripped out and hardened almost to black.

'This tree has been marked,' he said. 'It is lucky. This must be a good place for partings.' He put out a hand. It was smaller than mine, but his fingers were hard and tight, and sticky with resin. It stuck our hands together for a moment. I drew in a deep breath and it was only as I was about to say farewell that I realised that I had nothing to give in thanks, so fumbled at my belt and took off both that and my eating knife.

The belt had a silver buckle and the scabbard was made of a matching red, with coiling creatures worked into the leather; the knife was English, with a beautifully knotted red leather handle. 'Here,' I said.

'No,' he said and tried to give them back, but I pressed them into his hands.

He looked at the sky, and saw that the afternoon light was already failing. 'I should go,' he said.

As he picked his way back, I turned and looked at the wilderness of forest and peak before me. The spearheads of pines stood sharp against the twilight. A half-moon was bright in the pale blue sky. As the light failed the mountains' northern faces were dark, the southern crags bright with yellow light.

It gave them a cruel look, cold and hard and defined. The words of the Seeress came back to me.

> Rivers run wild, Wolf-torn men,
> Dark grows the sun, in summer storms.
> Would you know yet more?

I did not want to know more, but Fate controls all, and my Fate had forked off in a way that I had not foreseen. This was the path that I was to tread. I puffed out my cheeks, pulled my cloak about me, and turned to the rising slopes of pine and peak as, far off, the mountain wolves began to howl.

CHAPTER SEVEN

The Keelback Mountains

The Horned God filled the path before me, twice my height, its black nose snorting steam into the chill morning. Its shaggy mane caught flecks of snow that were falling from the sky. I could not defeat this foe. It was taller than I, with horns the height of a man. Defeat, I thought, again. All my childhood fantasies lay in scraps before me.

It turned its head to the side to watch me with hard, sloe eyes.

I stopped and held out my hands. Behind the spread of its antlers I saw the vast spread of the mountains and forests that still lay before me. High up the slopes, another elk grunted. The low snort echoed on the still mountainsides.

I picked up a stone. It scuttled along the track, but the elk did not move. 'Ya!' I shouted, and clapped my hands.

It took a pace forward; head sideways, bowing slightly, tipping its vast horns towards me. It was the king of the forest, and I was on its migration path to the lower pastures.

A hundred yards behind I saw a young doe elk standing under a dead pine. Then another. They were still as stones. Only the flick of a tail, or the snort of a breath in the cold betrayed them. They were all watching him and I knew then that he would not step aside. He was their king, and they his folk; he was leading them to safety, taking them down from the mountains for the winter. He snorted a puff of steam through his wide black nostrils.

'I mean no harm!' I called out. 'I have to cross the mountains!' The sound of my own voice gave me courage. He snorted once more, his fat nostrils flapping. He started forward. He was their master, their lord, their protector. He was the one who would fight and die for them.

I jumped back.

'I will go round you,' I told him. 'I mean no harm.'

His hard black eyes watched me as I moved a little way off the track, and continued on my way. When I came alongside him he turned to stand across the path. He started towards me once again, as if to charge, and then as one the hinds started forward with dainty flicks of their tails, and with a final bow of his head he turned and followed with a low grunt of success.

I was through, and rising before me were the pine-toothed saw edges of slope after slope, silhouetted by drapes of winter mist.

I did not know the names of the mountains, but they were my only companions, and I had not been walking alone for more than a few hours before I named them Blackcrag, Whitespear and Old Grumpy.

They watched my struggles with utter disdain as I trudged slowly forward under an albino sun, like an ant crossing a field, sometimes losing the path, sometimes weeping in despair, singing rowing songs to cheer myself. I needed something to spur me on, and thought, I must find Rognvald and thank him and let him know that I live.

I was a week into the climb when the first heavy snow came. The flakes were large and fat and gentle, but they brought bitter cold, and my feet were soon wet with slush.

The land about was marshy, and I was starting to look for a place to shelter when thick clouds brought the night early and I picked my way through ferns and brambles and nettles into a stand of pines that filled a steep valley. I was on the east side of the dale. There was ice from last year's winter still cupped into the hollows, but at least I was out of the wind, and I could push my way through the low branches, but my fingers were so cold they stung with each touch, and I ended up finding bare shelter under a fallen pine.

In the morning I crunched out of the hole I had made, and stood and looked out. The snow had stopped but the world was white and still. The only sound was my breath, the only movement myself, or the occasional hawk that balanced on outstretched wings, and watched me and wondered how long I would last.

Night came on early with the gloom, and I was just ending a long dispiriting trudge round yet another lake when the wind picked up and I heard it singing in the tops of the pines behind me and the note grew more wild and hostile as the light darkened and the snow was no longer soft and fat, but small and hard. It stung my cheeks. I staggered on, barely following what I hoped was the path till I saw a dark patch in the snow, and slipped towards it and cursed as I landed hard, and the cold stung.

I half-pushed, half-fell, and found myself in a low burrow in the snow, at the foot of a large granite rock. It was large enough for two men to shelter. I felt before me, burrowed deep into the hole, smelt damp earth and roots, and the scent of dry grasses.

I lay in a ball, my forehead pressed into my knees, and if I had had the strength left to me to weep, then I would have.

I do not know how long I lay there, both hands cupped in my crotch, thighs pressed tight on either side, too cold to move or stir, too miserable to sit up, bat-blind in the night darkness listening to my breath and the muffled moans of the storm. But slowly, slowly I warmed and with warmth came the pain.

But not all pain is bad, I learnt, and pain is better than despair. It is, when times are at their lowest, at least a sign of life. So telling myself, I at last sat up and felt about me.

Someone had placed stones against the rock, and covered them outside with turfs. It must be a summer shieling, I thought, or a drover's shelter, built against sudden summer storms that come often so high. I felt about me. There was straw and old hay on the floor, old sweet-smelling sheep droppings and a pile of dry sticks in the far corner that made me laugh out loud till my frozen fingers dropped my flint and I could not find it for the longest time.

I was like a mountain hermit, who talks to himself because there is no other. 'I must thank Rognvald,' I kept saying to myself as though it was a prayer. When at last I found my flint I cupped my hands to warm the kindling against my skin, and when I felt I could hold them both, I bent over them and carefully struck them together. The sparks were like shooting stars in the dark of night, streaking and falling out of sight.

Spark after spark fell this way, but at last one caught on the kindling.

The spark grew. Shy at first, then growing in confidence, and I bent over it and breathed on it, and I felt such joy when a glow of blue flame appeared, rimmed with yellow.

This is how God must have felt, I thought, when he shaped clay and blew on it, and the clay became man, filled with the spark of life.

I added more kindling, cupped the precious fire from the draughts outside, blew warm air onto it, and when it was ready, I added a few broken twigs, and prayed.

At last a tiny, amber flame appeared. And another. I watched each one with the care of the poor shepherd who helps each frail newborn lamb to stand and walk and find its mother's teat.

I thought of Rognvald standing before me and held my hands out to the flames, and started to cry as the flames grew in size and warmth and confidence and they threw both cold and darkness back.

Next morning the light that fell through the entrance tunnel was tinged blue.

The entrance had been blocked with snow. I used a stick to poke a hole through it, and widened it and then crawled out and brushed the snow off me. The white was angelic and clean, as a well-wiped slate.

I will find Rognvald or whoever dragged me from the battle, and thank him, I told myself, and set off once more heading towards the sunrise.

My leg wound had stiffened with the cold and it was difficult keeping to the track with the snow, and a number of times I plunged up to my knee in freezing water, and had to drag myself backwards.

It took a long time before the sun cast any warmth. I reached the top of the valley and saw that a herd of elk had passed by that morning and marked out a route for me meandering across the bleak moors.

I remembered the day Olaf had held me out over the killer whales. I had not felt fear, but I had just been a child, and I was fearful now. It clutched my guts in its cold fist, and held them tight; it hung onto my shoulders like an old man, and never quite left me.

My only hope was to press forward into the wilderness, and trust to my luck that cold or hunger or wolf would not take me.

I marched all that night, and the next, and each step was a misery. I never knew such pain. Every moment was filled with the fear of putting the one foot down, just as relief flooded into the other foot as it was lifted from the ground. So the miles went on. And the miles turned into days, and the days became a dream of torment and the night skies were lit with elf-lights that lure men to their deaths.

But on the third day of that march, the land began to fall, and in the madness that had come over me I laughed and wept in turn, and hated every brief upturn of the path before me. But at last I came down from the high moor, stumbling on feet leaden and blunt with the cold. I trudged down through the scattered pines, thick beds of dry needles, which were a blessing to my sore feet.

In the growing light I saw through the trees a clear wide bowl in the pine forest, that had to be a lake, frozen now with winter.

I stumbled towards it, expecting nothing but a level crossing, and wished I had bone-skates to fit to my shoes, such as the mountain men use.

The reed beds rattled as I pushed through them, using a stick to steady myself as I stalked out onto the ice.

It creaked and cracked as I put my weight full onto it, but it held and so I skidded and pushed myself along, hoping to get to the far edge before the sun was lost behind the low mountains ahead of me.

But as I pushed myself along I thought I saw a thin line of blue smoke rising against the white and dark of the forest. It stood up straight into the still morning air like a finger raised in warning, but I did not care, I was up and running and skidding and stumbling across the ice. 'Steady,' I kept telling myself, and the ice creaked and cracked beneath me, but I did not care. I was a winter ghost: hoary, ice-rimmed, desperate.

'Halt!' a voice called. I was two-thirds of the way across the lake, and as I stopped I saw a fur-clad figure, standing on the shore, fifty yards to my right.

I stopped but I could not answer.

What were words, when all I'd had were mountains for company?

'Who are you?' the voice called.

I paused for a moment, thinking I had imagined the speaker, but he walked towards me and I could see that in one hand he held an axe, and in the other a stiff, frozen trout.

I was fearless, in a way that was beyond caring, and limped towards him, heedless if he was friend or enemy. All I wanted was to be warm, and then I could die happy.

When I was ten feet away I could see his thick beard, his young face, the thongs of his bearskin jacket pulled tight across the hide; the dark dapple on the trout's silver scales.

'Who are you, stranger?'

I paused for a moment, as if I could not remember my name.

I could not speak.

'Are you man?' he said.

I laughed and nodded and closed my eyes to stop the spinning. 'Ganglari,' I croaked. 'I am Ganglari.'

'Welcome "Wayweary",' he said. I had chosen one of the names that Odin took when wandering the world. He took in my beard and old cloak and hat and staff. 'From where do you come?'

I waved a hand towards the mountains.

'You crossed the mountains?' He looked me up and down, as if assessing the truth of my words. I held my hands out to show I was no threat, but they were red and black and scabbed, and trembled like an old man's.

He waved me forward. He had green eyes and a thick beard that hid his top lip, icicles where his nose had dripped. His eyes looked sad, even when he smiled, and his teeth were neat and straight, and he pointed to a hut a little way up from the water.

'You look cold,' he said.

I made a face and we both laughed.

'Come,' he said as we crunched through the snow towards a low shieling, dug half into the ground, and walled and roofed with shaggy turf. When we got close I could smell the warmth inside and stopped as he pushed the wolfskin door open and beckoned me inside.

'This man is called Ganglari,' he said, speaking to a figure inside. 'He says he came over the mountains.'

CHAPTER EIGHT

Sacred to Freya

The figure hunched over the fire turned, and I was surprised to see a young woman, with wide green eyes, like fjord water. She had an upturned nose, a rack of split trout in her hand, fish guts on her apron. She wiped a lock of hair from her face with the back of her arm and wrinkled her nose, and looked at me, bent and hobbling like an old hag.

She said nothing but went back to her work and he pulled up a stool and took the bowl from my hands and held it to my mouth so I could drink. It was a thin stew of fish and grain. I slurped it down, and shook terribly.

'Come here,' he said, as he lifted a rack of trout out of the way so that I could get close to the fire.

'I saw him,' he said. 'Crossing the lake.'

The woman was across the fire from me. She looked up and watched me without expression.

'Is he hungry?' she said.

She picked up another trout, slid the knife into its chest, and with a quick neat slice, opened it out from chest to tail, pulled out the guts and dropped them onto the dirt floor. 'He's shivering,' she said.

He nodded, picked out a small log and carefully nestled it into the embers.

'You're lucky,' he said. 'This time of year we are usually down the valley.' He trailed off and I nodded, but I had no idea what he was talking about. My toes ached. My fingers tingled. I stared at the embers and shook uncontrollably.

The return of real warmth was a delightful pain, but it was an hour at least before I stopped trembling enough that I could take the bowl for myself, and I held it with both hands and closed my eyes and felt the warmth grow slowly inside me.

I ate five trout, bones and all, and licked the warm grease from my fingers. She stood watching me wolfing down the food in great gobbets. She did not speak but the man did.

'I'm Grim,' the man said, and nodded towards his wife. 'She's Fritha.'

I nodded.

'Maybe he has been sent to us,' she said. She turned her back on both of us and picked a brown trout from the basket, and started scraping out the frozen-guts. I held my hands out to the flames. The man paused at the door, and nodded.

'I will go get the fish,' he said.

The first night I looked for a bed, and as they climbed under the sheets, Grim said, 'Come, sleep with us.'

It was odd bunking up with the two of them, but I was dead tired and fell into a deep sleep where I dreamt I was kneeling by the pool again, as I had that morning, but that now it was high summer, and the pines were deep summer green, and the sky was white and blue with clouds, and in the still water I saw fat trout swimming, and over them my own reflection, and on my head was a golden helmet, such as a king might wear.

'Come,' a voice said. It was morning. Fritha had already coaxed the flames to life. The larch gave off a sweet resin scent. It was dry and sappy, which left your fingers sticky, but it burnt quickly and hot if you let it, the resin cracking and splitting.

Grim was already out. I could hear his grunts as he used a pole to smash through the ice that had formed in the night. Sound travels far over snow.

'It is time to work,' she said.

Fritha and Grim were heathen folk, and each day they went out to leave a sprinkling of flour or beer for the elves and dwarves, and once I caught her in the woods, licking out the sacrificial bowl. She started when she heard me.

'I am sorry,' I said and held my hands up, for I had trespassed on something I should not have seen. I backed away, my hands raised, and she watched me as she kept on licking.

That evening I told them everything. The *Bjarkamál*, the charge, my brother's death, the bite that had been taken out of the sun.

'We saw it too,' Fritha told me. 'The day the sun was eaten by the wolf was three days after midsummer. That was what caused night to fall. The wind must have been the Valkyrie coming to collect your brother's spirit. They fly over battlefields and pick the bravest fighters for Odin's Hall. All men are brothers in Valhalla.'

I put the bundle of packed trout onto the pile and handed her the next rack. We sat in silence for a while, then she said, 'Did you run away?'

I shook my head. 'I thought I was dead,' I said. 'Friends dragged me from the battlefield. I was too wounded to make the crossing. They left me at a farmer's hut. To die, I think. But I lived, and when I came back to myself I had nowhere to go, so I'm following them.'

'They did not come this way.'

'No?'

She shook her head, but said no more and that night, as we sat in silence, she said suddenly, 'And you crossed the mountains.'

I nodded.

69

'Those are great mountains,' she said. 'They were carved from the bones of Ymir, in the time of giants, in the days before anyone remembers. They do not let any man pass over them. Which is your family god?'

'Christ,' I said.

She frowned. 'Why follow the Nailed God?'

'He has conquered death.'

Her voice was mocking. 'Yes. I've heard it all. And he has a hall in the sky. But if Olaf was your brother then you must be a king's son.'

I nodded. 'I am Sigurd Sow's son, who was descended from Harald Finehair, Great King of the North, descendant of Odin, whom you call the All-Father.'

She smiled. Her teeth all leant into her mouth. It gave her a strange wolfish look but I saw that her opinion of me had changed. 'Your family must be sacred to Freya of the Falcon-feather cloak. Her powers are life and death and coupling, and whose sacred beast was the boar.'

She looked to Grim, but he was staring into the flames. He did not look up, but nodded slightly. 'He *has* been sent to us.'

Grim's gaze had been caught by the flame-weave, but at last he looked up. His eyes seemed very sad and he nodded, but said nothing.

That night as we three lay in bed I felt hands on my breeches and pushed them away.

'It is the gods' will,' she whispered.

'No,' I said, my voice was thick.

Grim coughed, and I knew that he was awake, and heard and knew all.

'I cannot,' I said.

'It is the gods' will,' she said, but I resisted and after a short while she relented, and I lay awake for a long time and could not sleep.

But the next day I watched her, bending to break the ice on the lake, carrying the buckets on the pole across her shoulders, and I admired the swing of her hips, the softness of her skin, and the firelight on her hair as we sat in the evening and listened to the wolf packs howl.

Grim led me to the back of the shieling. There was a low mound of earth in the shelter of a pine, so the snow had not fallen so thickly there. It was not much bigger than the belly of a pregnant woman. The clods were frozen, but it had been dug fresh in the autumn, for no grass grew there. It had been swept clear of leaves and twigs and pine cones and fallen brown needles.

Grim stood over it.

We both stood for a long time in silence. 'His name was Nokki,' he said at last. 'He was seven.'

'What took him?' I asked.

'Sickness,' Grim said.

'I am sorry,' I said to him. As we stood there, Fritha came out and turned and saw where we were, and what we were doing, and she turned away without speaking. 'She does not like to leave here without him. Even in the winter.'

The next night I climbed into bed, and turned my back to them and slept, but in the night I had a dream where I was washing in the lake, and it was summer, though the water was still icy cold, and Fritha was naked in the water next to me, her hair long over her breasts, her wolfish teeth grinning at me. There were ripples all about her, dark and bright in turn. She spoke, but I did not understand, and she slid forward, and took my hand.

'You are the wanderer,' she said, and sliding the hair aside she took my hand and put it on her breast. They were fine breasts: full, firm, excited to be touched. 'You are the All-Father,' she said.

I woke and found that somewhere my dream had mingled into truth. She was next to me, her breath was hot, and my hand was inside her skirts. I found her breast. I pressed against her and she pressed back, and then I surrendered to lust, and we pulled and tugged till we had shed what needed to be shed.

71

Her hands were insistent. Her legs parted, and I rolled on top of her.

When it came to the moment to spill my seed, I tried to pull out. I did not want to shame my host, but she wrapped her legs about my back and pulled me deep within her.

'Give me your seed,' she said. 'Son of the Sow.'

I only stayed there a moon-turn, but it felt like a year had passed.

During the day Grim and I would rise and go out fishing or trapping, and then come home as the short day failed, with frozen fish over our shoulder, or a white hare, or nothing, depending on God's grace.

At night I climbed into bed with them, and we made no pretence at silence or secrecy. Grim would turn away as I pulled up her skirts, or if it was afternoon and lust overtook me I would put her over the table, and he would look up and walk outside.

There was no tenderness afterwards.

When I had been there a month or more, she said suddenly, 'Aren't you sick of trout yet?'

'Why?'

'It is time you left, Ganglari.'

'Where to?'

'Follow the eagle back over the mountains.'

The peaks were thick with snow now. 'It is death to walk that way.'

'Then follow the streams,' she said, 'go down the mountain. But remember to pay thanks to Freya, mistress of Valkyries, chooser of the slain.'

I nodded, but knew that I could not. I was sworn to Christ. But where could I go? All my childhood I had dreamed of standing by Olaf's side, but now he was dead, and I was lordless and roaming without honour or position.

'You should go to King Onund's hall,' Grim told me. 'He is always looking for warriors.'

I nodded. The Swedish king had helped Olaf before. I would go to him, I thought, and see if he would take me into his band of retainers, even though the notion filled me with dread. Here I had forgotten much of the last few months, but now I would have to come out into the open, like the hedgehog after winter's sleep.

What could I offer King Onund of the Swedes, who could not even help his brother in battle? The retainer who lives when his lord is dead is not respected by other men.

On the morning I left, Fritha stood at the door, a poor mountain woman, standing by a wolfskin door as I fetched my cloak and hat and staff. She did not speak as I took in a deep breath. I feared the cold and the wilds but knew that I had to brave them once more.

'Farewell,' I said.

She leant against the doorpost and said nothing.

'Let's go,' Grim said, and took his own staff, and the axe, and set off, going surely like a mountain goat jumping down from rock to rock, and I followed after.

As we reached the edge of the pinewood I stopped and turned, and looked back at the shieling, and in my mind's eye it seemed as if it was not a house, but an old mound, where ancient kings are buried. Fritha had gone.

All I saw was the mound, a trail of blue smoke, and an eagle circling high in the blue sky.

CHAPTER NINE

The Road South

The land fell away and the great forest of pine trees was replaced by a wide flat land thick with forests of oak and broad sparkling water, and far off, the hammered leaden sparkle of the sea.

I did not see a cross for a month. Only heathen offerings hung in trees, stones smeared with blood, dark valleys knotted by woods.

The sight began to sicken me. I was a stranger to these men: in reality and in spirit. They brought spears when they saw me approach, and I held up my hands to show that I was not armed. I was no threat and hoped that they would let me pass by unmolested. Some nights I slept wild, but I never slept well, and my imagination tormented me with thoughts of being seized and bound and hung from a sacrifice tree, my throat cut ear to ear, my lifeblood dripping onto the ash tree's roots.

At last I came to areas where Christianity had reached, new-cut simple crosses set at crossroads and at meeting places. When men seemed hospitable I approached them, and did odd jobs for a night's food and hall. Chop wood. Thresh grain. I even carried water, like a girl.

One day dawned late and dark, and I could see the southern sky was full of cloud.

I spoke to myself cheerily, saying that it would journey on, but as I watched the clouds they seemed to drift towards me, and then I saw the dark skirts of rain, and the wind whipped up and there was a brief half-rainbow, hanging over the forest slopes, and then the downpour came.

I trudged on, but it was bleak beyond words, and the day only grew colder and grimmer, my clothes were heavy with rain, and I began to shake like an alder leaf. I thought myself done for, when I saw the shape of a fence through the trees, and as I stumbled through the mud I came upon a clearing, with a long, low hall, roofed with turf. It was bedraggled-looking, with old dead grass seeds hanging low over the doorway. There was a well with a wall of timber about it, some wicker pens, a crab-apple with the buds beginning to show, and a store of firewood under a dripping turf roof – but I could smell woodsmoke and warmth, and splashed through brown puddles to the door.

The animals in the pens looked as bedraggled as I. A herd of goats looked at me over the wicker fencing and bleated warning, but I was beyond care and banged on the door, and put my weight upon it and found that it was not bolted, and I fell inside.

I had a brief image of dark shapes huddled about a fire when a hand grabbed me and pushed me face down into the musty reeds. He drove his knee into my back, and I grunted as he hissed into my ear. 'Who are you?'

'Ganglari,' I tried to say, but my mouth was full of dirt and I could barely speak. I tried to throw him off but I was weakened from the wet and the wound and the days of walking, and he was too heavy for me.

'Is he alone?' a woman called out.

'He's alone,' a third voice said.

'Alone,' I agreed, and got a kick in the ribs for my temerity.

'Shut up, you!' the first man hissed, but then he let go and I pushed myself to my feet and saw the room before me, lit by the low, red light of a single small fire.

Most of the hall was taken up with the beds of six oxen, the sweet scent of summer hay filling the room as it filled their trestle manger. The inhabitants had a small end of the room, about a low fire, and pieces of soot-slimed bacon hung above the fire, grease-drips hanging from their ends. They were a family, all of them with the same round eyes and the same look of stupidity and suspicion.

The man who had put his knee into my back was small, with a bad leg, that gave him a rolling gait, his thumb hooked into the V of his staghorn stick. The other had a wide mouth and heavy chin that seemed to take up half his face.

'I come from a royal house where we greet strangers with more honour than this,' I said, and brushed myself down, but my clothes were so wet I felt as though I had a mail shirt on my shoulders.

'Oh yes,' the old woman said. She had no front teeth left, which meant she spoke with a lisp. Her tongue slid out like a snake and licked her lips as she spoke. 'And where is that, young stranger?'

'Uppland,' I said.

My cloak hit the floor with a wet slap, but none of them made way for me so I stood there like a thrall as they discussed me.

'We had Norsemen stay three months ago,' the man with the big jaw said. 'They were King Olaf's men. Heard they fought a battle, and lost.'

'Which hall do you come from, kingling?' one of the children said. He had the same heavy jaw as his father, and took after him in manner and looks.

I'd regretted speaking so freely, but now I had to tell the truth. 'I'm Olaf's brother, of Norway. My father was Sigurd Sow. He was chief of Uppland.'

They laughed. 'Listen to him,' the lame man said, thumb still hooked into his stick. 'King and chief and all that stuff.'

'If I was Olaf's brother I'd watch out,' the old woman said. 'You know what Knut did when he took over England? He had all the princelings hunted down and killed. Edmund's wife came to the King of the Swedes, so I heard. Knut sent them here and gave word

76

that our king was to have her babies murdered. He wanted the blood on Swedish hands, you see, but instead our king sent them on the Eastern Road. That's as good as leaving them in the woods. Eats men, the Eastern Road with jaws of ice.'

She went on at some length and I stood there, shivering and desperate to get warm. 'Knut does not care about me,' I said, but the way she looked at me it was as if she was already thinking how much my head would bring her, if it was sent to the king of England and Denmark.

'How come you survived when so many others didn't?' the old woman said. 'Did you run away, young man? Battle too terrible for you, was it? Not quite up to the terror? We don't want cowards here. You never heard of a woman running away from childbirth, did you! Ha! I give you battle.' She clicked her fingers and licked her lips again, as if tasting her words.

'I fought,' I said and she rocked with pleasure.

'Ah-ha!' the old woman said. 'I knew it. Valhalla only takes the brave, young man. And now you want to take my ale and bread, do you?'

'Yes,' I said. 'If I may.'

I was more afraid that she would send me back out into the rain, and what I really wanted was warmth and shelter. I'd had my fill of cold. 'I can work for my meal.'

'What work? You'd steal my goats, I'd bet. Like the last one.'

'I am not a thief,' I said.

'That's what he said.'

'I cannot speak for the last one.'

'No, but I can!' She licked her lips once more. 'I can. He took the suckling kid with the black spot about the eye. The one we were saving for Easter.'

'I do not steal.'

'Let him chop wood,' her son offered.

'He'd steal my axe.'

'Well, name a job for me,' I said.

77

'You can muck out the horses,' she said, and pointed with her chin to the other end of the hall, where the animals wintered. She waved a thrall forward, a limping, beaten-looking man, with a bruise on his left cheek. 'Bjorn. He can muck the cows out. Don't let him touch the pregnant ones. I don't want their bellies being cursed.'

That night the soup was a poor meal for any guest. I sat with the thralls, farthest from the flames. The old lady ranted about her dead husband, the son she had lost in the lands of the Rus, the feud she had settled with a man named Strut Trofi, who she'd had burnt in his hall, and the cock-eyed slave girl she had buried with her dead husband. I was too proud to ask for another bowl of soup, but I took a crust from one of the hounds and hid it in my sleeve, and all the while I felt the two men watching me.

'Are you really Olaf's brother?' the lame man said. 'I heard Olaf was short and stout, not tall and skinny. You're a beanpole. He the bean!'

The big-mouthed man laughed at the joke.

'We shared mothers,' I said. 'But his father was different to mine.'

'What's that?' the old woman said.

'His mother was a whore,' the lame man shouted for her, and even the children turned to see if I would react.

'No whore,' I said.

'She's a whore if we say so,' the old woman shouted.

I stiffened at that. They were trying to goad me. It would make it so much easier to kill me. Honour or death. I gave up honour, but I knew I had to leave that night, as soon as the family lay down to sleep.

I kept my head down but it was not long before the old lady yawned.

'Get a log,' she called out. 'A nice thick one.' She felt the weight of one the boy handed her, but shook her head. 'No. Not that. That is birch. I don't want birch. I want oak.'

He picked out another.

'That's not oak,' she said.

He picked out another – a rough quarter of a thick trunk, which looked like it was an off-cut from a piece used for a boat rib. She felt it and reached for another.

'This is oak?'

Her son nodded. She screwed up her nose. 'Put it on,' she said.

The oak was duly lifted to the fire, and dropped with a shower of sparks.

As hay and cloaks were piled up to make mattresses, I started for the door.

'Where you going?' the big-mouthed man said.

'To piss,' I said.

He nodded with his chin to where the cattle stood. 'Piss in the straw.'

'It's bad luck to piss inside a house.'

'Not here, it isn't.'

'I piss outside.'

'Then leave your cloak,' the lame man said.

'It's raining.'

'The rain has stopped.'

I put a hand to the door and peered out. It was true. The sky had cleared, the waxing moon had risen, and the forest sounded with dripping branches. I took off my cloak and hung it on the nail by the door and stepped outside, and did not waste a moment.

I sprinted across the clearing, splashing through puddles, and startling the geese who hissed and honked, and a dog began to bark. I was already into the trees when the men shouted after me. 'Thief!' they called out. 'Thief!' and I heard the barking of dogs being let loose behind me, but I did not care.

Cloakless or not, I was free and alive and I just kept running. Terror, I have found, makes a fine goad, and I had escaped from a treacherous death at the hands of these forest folk.

The night sky was clear; the path before me sparkled with puddles of moonlight: white and clear like a trail of stones leading me away from danger.

CHAPTER TEN

Helgulf's Son

I earned my passage south: mucking out stables, cutting wood, fixing fences, sawing birch, splitting oaks in the forests. I worked. I ate. I made my way from the lakes and mountains to the flat forests, and was only a fortnight from King Onund's hall when I stopped at the house of a local chieftain, who saw me passing. He was a tall man with heavy jowls and a slight hunch, dark eyes and sunken cheeks, and a beard that he combed straight as a brush. We traded a few words, and having asked my name and business he invited me into his hall which was across a spring meadow.

'At least until the night-meal. And then you may as well stay overnight, take some bread and be on your way on the morrow.'

His name was Helgulf. His wife was Ljufa. She was short and narrow-faced, with hard brown eyes, and a look in her face that seemed to pity all the world. 'Oh, look at you,' she fussed, and took the shoe I had removed, and wiped it with a handful of straw and stuck a thumb through one of the holes. 'Stay at least till I get this fixed. I doubt there's time to stitch some new ones for you. Where are you bound?'

I gave her a sideways look, not sure that I was staying any longer than the meal, but after so many suspicious men it was good to be welcome.

'King Onund's hall.'

'Dressed like that?' She slapped both knees with her hands and let out an exasperated sigh. 'Well, that is sorted then. You cannot go to see the king with your toes sticking out. I shall fetch the cook. He must have some skins we can use. We'll find some clothes as well. Go as you mean to be received, I always say. Alfrun!'

A young girl entered from what looked like a private chamber.

I guessed she was their daughter from the silver hoops in her ears, and the fact her dress was cut from the same red bolt of cloth as the mother's. She took after her father, with honey-brown hair, brown eyes, and even though she had a mannish look about her, she was not ugly. She nodded and smiled. 'Welcome,' she said. 'Has Mother fed you?'

I smiled. 'Not yet.'

She gazed at me intently. 'I'll fetch you a loaf at least.' But instead of bringing food she brought word that a neighbour had brought a cockerel over for a fight.

My father had never approved of wasting a bird in this way, but Helgulf clapped his hands and jumped up. 'Come!' he said and took me to the yard where the men were standing round sizing up the birds.

'This is mine,' he said and showed me his prize fighter: a black bird with a long yellow feather mane, and a combless head: small, hard, thick-beaked. 'I've seen him take down birds twice as big as him,' he told me. 'He never gives up. Never knows when he's beaten. Do you now?' he said, and stroked the unblinking bird, and let it peck grain from his cupped hand. 'Do you want to put him in to fight?'

'No,' I said, feeling foolish. 'I will stand and watch.'

Helgulf plucked a few tail feathers to anger his bird, then cupped him in two hands and on the signal let him drop.

The birds leapt at each other, pecking and clawing, but I saw that he was right, he knew his birds. The bigger bird gave way in the end to the tougher fighter, and Helgulf grinned as he shook hands with the other man.

'Come,' he said after, 'I smell food.'

They were good, kind people. We sat and ate as the daylight failed. I soon learned their story. Their son had gone to Dublin two years before, and his ship had last been seen in Orkney, and never made it down the sea-lane to the Isle of Man.

'He's lost to the waves,' Ljufa sighed, and allowed herself a little sigh. 'So there's just Helgulf, Alfrun and I, and our servants of course. They keep us company. But it's good to have a man about the house again.' I took from this that she meant a warrior. 'How old are you?' she asked me.

'Seventeen,' I lied, not wanting to admit that I was still fifteen.

She put down her knitting. 'You're not,' she said. 'Well, I thought you were twenty at least. Now tell me your story. You're an Upplander, if I know my accents. What are you doing wandering down from the North? Were you with King Olaf?'

I paused for a moment, remembering the glint in the eyes of the last place I had told the truth to, and how they were sizing me up for slaughter as if I were a fatted calf. But Ljufa had a good look in her face, and I trusted her. They had dressed me in warm clothes and I had done little for them in return. I will tell them the truth, I thought.

'I'm Olaf's brother,' I said, and she put her hand to her mouth and shook her head.

'You're not! He's Olaf's brother, good husband.'

They all stared at me.

'My! You poor lad. We feasted with Olaf, not six months before. He came here, on his way north. He took quite a shine to Alfrun, didn't he, husband?'

'He did,' Helgulf said. 'Well, sit down! I'll see if there is any beer. If not, will warm buttermilk do?'

'And bread!' Ljufa called to him. 'It was baked just yesterday.'

As I took all their generosity they sat across from me and stared at me, as if they had never seen a young man before. 'Olaf's brother,' Ljufa said. 'My my. He's Olaf's brother. Olaf was king, you know. Of the Norse.'

She gave her daughter a nudge and Alfrun blushed charmingly. 'Ask him something!'

'What was it like to be in battle?' Alfrun said.

I wanted to sound brave and fearless, but after I had given her my answer she half-smiled and picked a nail. 'I wish I were a man.'

'Do you?'

'You get to go and fight and then come home again, full of stories. All I get to do is milk goats and weave wool.'

'Listen to her!' her mother laughed, but I could see pain in the father's eyes, as if he too felt the loss, of a son.

Helgulf had wine brought that night. A jug of it that he and I shared, and we piled the fire high and laughed and talked, and after we had eaten a bowl of beans and bread, he stood and said, 'Oh, while I remember. I found this in the chest, and thought that it might fit you.'

He lifted a cloak and a kirtle from the back of his wife's chair. He lifted them up while his wife rubbed the wool lovingly between her finger and thumb. 'The kirtle might be a little short, but the cloak looks fine, and it will be better than those old things.'

There was a belt to match, only a little worn, and my new red shoes were given to me and later that day, when one of the maids came in with a basket of firewood, she dropped it in surprise, and as I looked up, she put her hand over her mouth and laughed at herself. 'Oh my, I thought that was the young master back at last.'

'No,' I said. 'It is me.'

She smiled and bobbed and I understood that I'd been dressed in their lost son's clothes. My immediate response was to give the clothes back, but Ljufa shooed and tutted as if I were a broody hen. 'No,' she said. 'Keep them on. They look better on you than locked in my chest. It's good to see them worn again. I stitched them myself. Each hem. I wove the kirtle-cloth too.' She reached over and inspected her own handiwork. 'He looks very handsome, doesn't he, Alfrun?'

The girl nodded shyly.

Ljufa caught my eye and winked as if to say, go on, the girl likes you, say something kind. I blushed and looked down and scratched my head, but my father had never been one for idle talk, so I said, 'I hope I look as fine as your daughter.'

It was something I'd heard Olaf say, but for him it was practised, and for me, the words came about as easily as ploughing with unmatched oxen. I blushed and Alfrun blushed and the father swallowed and only the mother seemed pleased.

Next day was bath day.

Helgulf took me across a sloping field, where a spring filled a deep pool and then ran down a narrow rocky bed to the stream at the bottom. The water was so clear that you could see the last year's brown leaves lying at the bottom. The water bubbled and rippled as the water flowed up from the earth.

Helgulf started to strip down, trousers first, then pulling his kirtle over his head and dropping it on top.

He stood naked before me. His body was lean and strong, his skin slackening with age, and the hair between his legs was wiry and grey. 'It's a little cold still,' he said, striding down into the water, hands trailing at his sides. He stirred a little grit and dirt up from the bottom as he stood and splashed himself and then ducked his head under. 'Come!' he called, and I left their son's clothes folded and put a toe in.

It was only a little warmer than ice. I splashed in, felt slime between my toes, and the swirl of dead leaves about my legs as I kicked myself back up to the surface.

I came spluttering upwards, but the cold squeezed the breath from my body and my teeth rattled and I could not breathe. Helgulf laughed. 'Keeps you fit!' he said and slapped his own chest. 'Look at me. Fifty-three winters.'

He splashed his head, and shook the droplets from his beard, and ran his hands back over his head. 'I need someone to leave this place to. Someone to look after my daughter.'

'There must be someone nearby,' I said to him.

'You would think so,' he said, and held out a hand to me and hauled me back towards the side. 'Up you come! Now, let's get dry.'

The shock had brought life back into every inch of my body. I was not sure I'd ever felt so vital, so alive, so transformed. My skin burnt red with inner heat as I rubbed my hair and back with my cloak. I dressed and tied my laces about my legs.

'It is good, yes?'

'Very good,' I said.

He seemed pleased. 'Come,' he said, 'the women will be waiting.'

That evening as I gobbled down my second bowl of porridge, Helgulf watched me with satisfaction. 'Nothing like a little chill to put hunger into a young lad.'

All three of them stared at me, and I grinned in answer, and swallowed my food. 'Alfrun, go and sit over there,' Ljufa said, 'your father and I want to talk to Harald.'

She went across the room to where her loom stood, trailing threads. Her dog followed her, and sat down as she rubbed its ears, its tail sweeping back and forth across the hearth stones. The two of them looked at me. There was a leaden silence, then she gave her husband a poke with her elbow and he stood up and said, 'I'll get more ale.'

He pushed himself up stiffly, and took the jug in one hand, and walked to the end of the hall where the barrels stood. As he found the sieve and shook off the old lees, Ljufa leant into me. She lowered her voice. 'Are you betrothed, Harald?'

'No,' I said. 'I'm not.'

'Did you ever think of settling down?'

'Of course,' I said. 'But not till I have done something.'

'Like what?' I had no answer, so she leant into me and said, 'What do you think of our daughter. She's comely, yes?'

'Yes,' I said. 'Very.'

'She has a sweet nature,' Ljufa said to me. 'Kind. Loving. Loyal. She's not afraid of hard work, and she sews so well.'

'She would make any man a fine wife.'

'Not just any man,' Ljufa said. She put a hand on my knee. 'My husband likes you. He needs a lad about the place. What would you say to marrying Alfrun?'

I looked across the room to where the girl was teasing her hound. The loom, the hearth, the hanging threads still unwoven. It was such a domestic scene, and she was pretty enough, with long legs, a plump backside, and high breasts.

Part of me wanted it; part of me felt sick at the thought. 'Thank you. That is very kind, but I do not think that is for me.'

Ljufa looked affronted. 'What's wrong with her?'

'Nothing,' I said. 'But I . . . I have to take revenge on my brother's killers.'

Ljufa tutted and looked disappointed in me. 'Vengeance is not something to live for, Harald. It is a poor guide in life. You should live to love and raise children and feed your family. Those are reasons to live.'

At that moment Helgulf returned. He had a vaguely cheerful look on his face, but Ljufa wasted no time. 'He said "no",' she said.

I started to speak, but it was true, and the old man looked at me. 'No?'

I had to repeat the word for him and he let out a breath and looked across the room to where his daughter sat. 'What's wrong with her?'

'Nothing,' I told him. 'But I. I am too young to settle down. I have not done anything in life yet.'

'What do you mean? You've fought in a battle, and crossed the Keelbacks in winter. A man could settle down for life on those two tales.' The old man had a hurt look in his eyes, but I wanted so much more from life than this.

'I'm sorry,' I said.

I could not flee their house as I had done before. They had done me great honour, and their only fault was generosity. Not many families offer their daughters to their houseguests. Not for free, anyway. But it seemed they had come to the same decision overnight as well.

Next daybreak as I sat and drank a cup of ale, Ljufa greeted me with a tight smile. 'Here,' she said. 'I've fixed your shoes.'

I held them up. They looked like old friends, only her neat stitches had closed the holes in them, and they had a new sole now of stiff rawhide.

I thanked her.

'It's nothing,' she said, a little brusquely.

'I'm going to leave today. Shall I give you back these clothes?'

She pursed her lips and I thought she might cry. 'No,' she said. 'Keep them. A man meeting a king should be well dressed.'

'Thank you,' I said. 'You have all been very kind.'

She sniffed and nodded and found a loaf and a handful of last autumn's crab-apples, and wrapped them all up in a cloth for me.

'Come back, if you can. Send word,' Ljufa said as a parting, and Helgulf stood silently and opened his arms to embrace me as if I was a son, and he held me a long time and I felt him take in a great breath.

'Be safe,' he said. 'Be safe.'

I looked for Alfrun, but did not see her, but just before I left she appeared with her dog. It was clear that she had been crying as she handed me a purse that she had made, heavy with a handful of coins inside. I thanked her and she stood with the rest of them when it was my time to leave; I wanted to say something private to her, but I could not single her out. So I said to them all, 'Thank you all. I shall miss this hall. You gave me a royal welcome.'

It was hard to walk away at first, but with each step away from that house my sadness lessened, and soon I was humming a song to myself, and feeling the gap between me and Onund's hall lessen.

The one who leaves feels little grief, I have found. It is much harder to be left behind.

CHAPTER ELEVEN

King Onund's Hall

From a distance the town of Sigtuna, where King Onund kept his hall, looked like a tapestry, with thatched houses gathered close to the skirts of the king's hall, and white tents strung along the road. The walk took me twice as long as it ought, but I was glad to have arrived at last. The size of the place and the crowds of people shocked me after so long alone and on the road. I stopped and looked at all the wares, which were marvellous and strange, I listened to all the strange accents, stared at strange boots, strange faces. There were traders from as far as Holmgard and Wendland with white Russian fur hats; silks and slaves, pots and wine, amber, jewels, spices, walrus ivory; all discussing kings, prices, raids they had just finished, and the prospects for the next spring's raiding.

I was thrilled as I paced about the stalls.

My footsteps led me to an old oak, with a dead crown – twigless and bare, each branch tipped with a seated black rook. The fingers of the lower branches were thick with swelling buds, and from them all hung offerings of meat and cloth and sacred charms.

I realised that this was a tree sacred to Odin, and I remembered the tales I had heard as a child that it was here, at Sigtuna, that the Old Gods had landed when they sailed from the East in time beyond memory.

I took one of the silver dirhams from the purse, and hammered it into the elephant-hide bark of the oak.

'Thank you, Odin,' I said, my hand pressed against the bark. It was not a prayer, and the Old God understood. It is not wrong to honour your forebears, even if heathen men worship him as a god.

Across the market square a missionary had built a timber church, where beggars sat waiting for alms. A man in a red cloak with a sword at his belt was standing on a bucket, talking about the Lord God, while a few curious Lapps stood and listened for a moment.

I thought I should go there as well, and thank God for his help in bringing me through the wilds. About the church there was a wicker fence to keep out the goats, and a wooden cross was set into the ground before it, freshly carved. You could still smell the pine sap.

The priest was sitting in the sunlight by the door. His hair was unkempt and grey, his eyes were closed, and he was enjoying the last light of the day. When I swung the gate open he sat up and bowed his head.

I stopped in the shadow of the doorway and saw myself then, as he saw me. Travel-stained. Mud-spattered. Lean. Hungry.

'Welcome, stranger,' he said. He was a Northumbrian. From York, I'd guess.

'May I go in?' I said.

He stood up as I spoke, then cocked his head like a sparrow and said, 'You are from Norway?'

I nodded.

'Have you come by boat?'

'No,' I said. 'By land.'

He thought he had misheard me. 'By land?'

'Over the mountains.'

'Ah,' he said and smacked his lips. 'You were with Olaf the Stout?'

I had stopped using other men's names and named myself true. 'Yes,' I said. 'I am his brother.'

He sucked in a breath and then nodded slowly. 'You know men are starting to talk about your brother.'

'What are they saying?'

'You are really his brother?'

'I am. I fought at his side.' I had no tokens to show him, but I lifted my kirtle to show the wounds I had taken in my back. 'Look, this is where a spear hurt me.'

He put his hand onto the place in my back, where the spear went in. 'Like Christ,' he said.

I felt guilty then, for paying my respects to the Old Gods. 'Can I go in?' I asked, fearing that he somehow knew, and would turn me away.

'If you were with Olaf then you are blessed, my child. There was a ship before the storm. From Nidaros. The man on that ship told me that the night your brother's body was brought there for burial, a light shone out in the sky, and a blind man's sight was restored to him. It's the third such story I have heard. Men have started coming here and asking to pray to Olaf the Stout. Saint Olaf, men are calling him. I saw it in a dream. He is sitting on the benches of God's hall, with all the other saints, and when he speaks on behalf of those who pray to him, God listens.'

I had not heard anything, but then the man said, 'There are many Norwegians at King Onund's hall.'

'Do you know their names?'

He shook his head, but the news gave me hope.

'They all came to pray last week.'

'I think I know them,' I said.

'Then you should go and see them.'

I went into the church. It was a simple place. A single room, a wooden altar, two reed lights burning smokily in the gloom.

I wondered at this news, said a prayer to my brother, and closed my eyes and listened, but I did not feel him there. I did not feel God, either. But I prayed to Christ and then to my brother. 'Speak to God for me,' I said. 'Have me treated with honour when I arrive at Onund's hall.'

The reed-lights flickered, but it was not much of a sign. I did not know if he had heard. But as I closed my eyes, I felt my mother and brother in the room behind me.

They said no words, but there was a feeling. If there had been a rift between them, it had been mended. I felt the shadows behind me and almost turned to see their faces, but even though they spoke no words, I had an odd sense that I should not turn back, or I might lose them.

Onund's hall watched over the market like a seated warrior.

There were high earthen ramparts with timber palisades, where his warriors stood guard. Their cloaks flapped in the breeze. They may have had colour, but from below they looked black against the grey sky, like rooks. 'I am Sæbbe, doorward of Onund, King of the Swedes and the Geats. What brings you here, in the dark of winter, like a thief?' a voice called out as I walked up.

'I am Harald Sigurdsson,' I called up, 'brother to Olaf the Stout, king in Norway.'

The cloaks flapped once again, and one of them stepped backwards and shouted down. The gates opened like a mouth, and I strode forward, into its shadow.

Inside the yard was thickly strawed against the winter mud.

To either side were barrack halls, and pale-eyed Swedes stopped and watched me ride through their king's gates. One of them had a helm with gilt cheek-guards, bright with boar emblems, and a face-mask bright with gold. All I could see were his eyes, and his teeth, which were jagged and broken.

'Others came two moons ago. With Rognvald leading them.'

'I was wounded,' I said, and I saw that the men had formed a circle about me. Their faces were pale with winter, they were neither friendly or unfriendly. 'But now I am well.'

Sæbbe nodded. 'Come. My lord will want to see you.'

*

We crossed the yard and turned and faced King Onund's hall. It was a magnificent building, rising before me like a temple to the heathen gods. From the outside it looked more like a church than a mead-hall, with carved gables and pillars of carven wood holding the hall-mouth closed.

We mounted the steps. 'Wait here,' Sæbbe said. 'I will take word of your name and arrival to my king, and he shall judge whether you are worthy of welcome.'

I stood uncertain then, unsure of what kind of name I had made for myself.

I tested my memory, and felt the cold press of earth on my cheek. I had failed Olaf, but we had all failed him, who lived.

Sæbbe emerged a few minutes later. He stood more smartly when he spoke to me now. 'King Onund says he has heard of you, Harald Sigurdsson, and that you are welcome to his hall.'

We mounted the steps, and the wooden boards rang out our arrival. I began to doubt myself. What if Onund did not welcome me, what would I do then? I should go back to Ljufa and Helgulf's hall, I thought, but then the doorward announced me, and I strode into the wide, pillared hall. On either side stood tall warriors, their hard faces all turned to me. I willed myself forward to where King Onund sat on a high chair at the end of the hall, a white bearskin thrown over the seat, and a carpet of brightly woven wool at his feet.

'Greetings, Lord,' I said, though my voice failed me and I felt my cheeks blush.

'You are Olaf's brother, Harald?' he said when I had bowed.

I swallowed. 'Yes, Lord.'

'You don't look like him.'

I didn't know what to say, but he stood and opened his arms as if I were his brother, and embraced me. 'Harald Sigurdsson.' He patted the bench next to him. 'Here, lad! Come sit by my side and tell me your tale!'

I took my seat and started to talk, slowly at first, then as he prodded me with more questions I relaxed. Laughed, even, and the circle of men grew tight about me, and I saw that they were not unfriendly and I was with my own kind at last: like the wolf that finds his pack.

As my horn was refilled and they stood and smiled and listened, my words started to spill out. I told of the elk, the mountains, the cold, and the family who thought to send my head to Knut.

I felt my throat tighten as I recalled that night, and tried to swallow back my grief, but my throat was too tight. It was as if I had poured it into my water-skin and lashed the end tight. Only now could I let the drawstrings go, and as I did I found that my few drops had multiplied and it was like trying to hold back the sea.

I felt a fool, but Onund looked at me for a moment, then put a fatherly hand on my leg.

'Hush, lad,' he said and gave my knee a squeeze. 'It's alright. You are safe in Onund's hall.'

CHAPTER TWELVE

Many Meetings

Onund's men welcomed me. One found an axe. 'Here,' he said. 'It's a little off-straight, but it'll do.'

It was good enough to get the feel of a weapon in hand and to train until my shoulders ached.

Across the yard one of Olaf's men had killed two brace of broody hens. He puffed his hair back from his face as he hacked off a yellow claw and tossed it to the dogs who were fighting over the blood, then sniffed and swallowed and sat to pluck.

'Come, Harald!' a warrior shouted. He was a small, fat man named Bjorn Punch. His nut-hard eyes were intent on my every movement, but the falling hen feathers kept distracting me. 'I could have had you then,' he said, his teeth crooked through his scraggly beard. His wooden sword hit me on the cheek and smarted. 'And then!'

I came for him again, but my blows were weary and slow, and he stepped back and struck so hard that later, when I checked, I could see the weave of my trousers embedded in my skin, but he danced back from my blows, and struck me again, on the back. 'Keep your shield up' he said at the end, when I was striped with welts from his sword.

The last time I came for him he knocked my shield back into my nose and I fell down with a groan. My eyes filled with water, and I turned away, expecting another blow, but he stopped, and I blinked the tears away, and tasted blood in my throat.

'Best break it early,' Bjorn said as he pulled me up. 'And better here than in battle.'

Sæbbe found me sitting alone, smarting from the shame and still blinking away the tears. He lifted my chin and looked straight at me.

To Bjorn Punch he said, 'Been beating up younglings, again.'

Bjorn Punch turned and laughed. There was something of the mule about him: stubborn, stupid, defiant. 'Better now than on a battlefield,' he said. 'I'd have chopped him into kindling by now.' He wiped his beard on the back of his arm. 'No good being Olaf's brother if you're dead.' He reached out and ruffled my hair. 'Is there now?'

I forced a smile. Sæbbe chuckled. 'Well. Fetch a clean cloak, Harald. Someone wants to see you.'

I was so glum I could barely speak. 'Who?'

'Onund's sister.'

I did not know who he meant for a moment, then I understood: Olaf's widow, Astrid, was here. I counted back in my head. It had been three years since I'd seen Astrid. In Norway, I thought, before Olaf had fled. I remembered her as she sat on her horse, waiting for the hunt, a white cloth pulled tight over her head in the French style. When I'd seen her then, she'd seemed the most exotic and beautiful thing. I remembered so many moments: as she brushed her fine fair hair back from her cheek, or absent-mindedly pulled at a lock and turned it about a single spindle finger, then let it all fall free.

Her nose and cheeks were as fragile as blown glass, her hair as thin and silver as a thread of summer silk that hangs in the air, or like a thread the jewel-smith twines into an earring for a chieftain's daughter. Her eyes were large and storm-blue; imperious as a hawk's on a glove.

And of all the people here, we alone were kin.

'I cannot go like this,' I said, and showed my blood-smeared kirtle.

Sæbbe fetched me a cleaner cloak, and I threw it on, and wiped the worst of the mud off my boots on the steps of the hall.

Astrid was sitting with her back to the door. I knew her straight away from the white cloth she wore about her head.

'It is rebellious hair!' Olaf used to say, and put a hand to one of the stray locks, and rest it there as if it were golden thread. 'Look at that hair! See how it catches the light. Mother, have you ever seen anything so fine?'

'Harald!' she said, standing to greet me. Widowhood had aged her, but it had not taken anything from her beauty. She stood and embraced me. I smelt a perfume I could not name. It must have come from England or France. 'Look at you!' she said.

Women made me blush in those days. 'Harald wasn't this tall last time. See!' she said to Onund. 'I have to look up to him now.'

Onund and she laughed, and I stammered something.

'How long has it been?'

'Three years,' I said. 'When Olaf went into exile.'

'Are you sure?'

'Yes,' I said. I had counted each day.

She seemed surprised. 'I think you're right.' She sighed, and her eyes fell on a girl who was sitting with a cloth in her hand, from which hung a red thread and a bone needle.

'This is Wulfhild,' she said. 'My daughter. Olaf's daughter.'

'We've met,' I said. 'But you were little then.'

The girl pushed herself up and tilted her head in the way her mother did. She was Olaf, in girl's form. The same short legs, wide shoulders and thick neck. There was none of her mother's beauty about her. Poor girl, I thought, but then she smiled and spoke, and I saw her eyes were as keen and blue as Olaf's, without the hostility his held, and I liked her at once.

96

I was not the best at making conversation with anyone, never mind royal ladies, and stood for a moment thinking of what to say to the child. 'What are you stitching?'

'It's not stitching,' she said, looking at the crumpled cloth in her hand. 'It's embroidery.' She held it up and showed me the cloth. It was a Christ's head, upside-down.

We looked at each other, unsure and nervous, and Astrid said, 'Come sit. No, here, by the fire.'

Astrid made me tell my tale again. I did so, but it was a different tale with only her. She had freckles that I did not remember. They were faint. You had to sit close to see them. She screwed the top of her nose up when I mentioned some detail that was unpleasant, but seemed to delight in the tale of my wounding, and rescue.

'Thank God,' she sighed at the end. After we had gone through all the pleasantries, she put a hand to my arm. 'Was the sun really eaten?'

I nodded. 'It was as dark as twilight,' I told her. 'There were stars. Then *he* came. Thore Hund. He was dressed in skins and charms. He was like a troll. No weapon would hurt him.'

She watched me as I faltered. 'Go on,' she said gently.

Onund was staring at his hound, whose front paws were twitching in a dream. He looked up. Even Wulfhild looked up. The child's face was silent and intent as I told how her father was killed.

Astrid put her hand to my thigh and squeezed it. 'He was wounded five times? You are sure of that?'

'I would swear an oath. In the thigh, both arms, the stomach and the neck.'

Her bosom rose as she nodded. 'Just like Christ.'

'I tried to help him,' I said.

'There was nothing you could do. It was God's will. Have you heard? There are miracles at his tomb. Even among the people of Lathe men are talking.'

'A priest told me the story in the market.'

'Have you prayed to him?'

'Not yet,' I said, but then I thought of the cave, the snow, the frozen lake, and wondered if it had been Olaf watching over me, not the Old Gods. 'Although maybe he has been helping me.'

I listed the occasions and she kept her hand on my thigh, listening to each example. 'Olaf always thought well of you.' I must have looked surprised, because she said, 'Oh yes. That Harald. He's the best of the lot.'

'A bad lot,' I said.

She tutted and shook her head. 'Olaf has helped me. I feel his ghost about me.' She sat back and looked triumphantly to her brother. 'I shall build a church and dedicate it to his memory.'

Next day I was in the sparring yard. There were a few other early birds. Bjorn was painting the stripes on his shield with a badger-hair brush, another man was fashioning a length of yew for a bow. I was trying to straighten my axe head when Sæbbe entered. 'Harald,' he called. 'Come now. Onund wants you.'

'What is it?' I asked, but he did not answer. I followed him to the king's hall, my mind working through all the things that could have me summoned like this.

Perhaps someone had accused me of theft; maybe someone's sheep had gone missing, and I had attracted the blame. Wandering young men are blamed for half the wrongs of the world. I thought of the family who had wanted my head for Knut. They had followed me south. They would accuse me of theft or worse.

As I turned the corner to the space that lay before the hall I saw strange men standing outside, and a sheaf of spears and swords stacked against the wall. They watched me approach with casual interest. They were Danes, from their voices. Zealand, I thought, though I was not so good at their accents.

Sæbbe led me up the broad stone steps.

The doors stood open. I swept inside and saw the king sitting on his throne, his warriors about him, their hands on their swords. He saw me enter. 'Ah! This is he.' Onund beckoned. 'Harald, come forward.'

There was a band of men standing before him. They turned and

I felt all their eyes on me as I strode forward between the stacked-up benches. I saw with relief that I did not know the men who stood before Onund.

'What have I done to be summoned like a thief?' I demanded.

Onund did not answer, but turned to the man before him. I took him in. He was a large young man, with staring green eyes. 'This is Olaf's brother?' the stranger said.

'Yes, I am Harald Sigurdsson. Tell me your name, stranger.'

He squared up to face me. 'I am Beorn Estridson, nephew of Knut the Great. I come bearing greetings from my uncle.'

'What tidings?' I asked.

'They were for King Onund's ears, not yours,' he replied.

'Did they concern me?'

He laughed. 'No. He mentioned that Olaf's brother had arrived, and I asked to meet you.'

'What chance has brought us both here together, at this time,' I said.

'Chance indeed!'

'Evil for some, perhaps,' I said.

'I hope not.' We stood and took the measure of each other. I was the taller, but he was thicker, and darker, and he had a dangerous air about him, like one who cannot control himself, and goes berserk in battle. But I liked him, and liked him even more when he said, 'I heard you fought well at Stiklestad.'

'It was a hard battle,' I said.

'And Olaf fought well.'

'He did. Though he was surrounded. It was a shame that Knut sent other men to fight his battles. It is not a brave man who pushes others before him.'

I meant to sting him with my words, but instead I saw the flicker of a smile about his lips, as if at heart he thought the same. 'That is how my uncle works,' he said. 'He has deep sight. Only the fool fights when other weapons will win.'

I started to speak but Onund spoke over us all. 'Beorn and

99

Harald, you are both my guests here. Let there be peace between you all, as long as you are welcome in my hall. I will have no fighting between you both. Do you understand?'

There was a long silence.

'Do you understand?'

'Yes, lord,' we both said.

'Shake hands on it,' he told us.

The strength of Beorn's fist astonished me. It was like gripping the bull's halter as he runs amok. 'I shall abide by King Onund's law,' he said.

'And I,' I said, trying to match him in demeanour, but that night at the feast I felt the eyes of these Danes on me, and I could not settle. Astrid caught my eye, and I could see that she felt as uncomfortable as I to sit with Olaf's enemies.

She came to find me when the feast was over and the benches began to break up. 'How can he have him here?' she said. 'And what tidings has Knut sent at this time?'

'They do not concern me,' I said.

She looked at me as if I were a fool. 'How can you know?' her look said.

Next morning one of Beorn's Danes barged into me as I passed him in the yard.

'Sorry,' he said, but his smile put the lie to his words and I saw how this would go. It was an old trope in poetry, how oaths of peace and brotherhood were put to the test by old feuds. I thought, I cannot stay here, wearing out Onund's welcome. At some point, Beorn or I, or one of his ship crew, would take a wrong step, or make a joke about Olaf and his death, and I would be honour bound to challenge him to a fight, or be named a coward – so that in losing I would be dead, and in winning I would have broken my own word, and would be sent out like a thief.

I had no one I could talk to except Astrid, and I found her sitting under the shutter, with a warm posset in her cupped hands.

'Lady,' I said, 'may I sit with you?'

'Of course,' she said.

I pulled up a footstool and sat by her side and breathed into her cup as she waited for me to speak.

'I do not think I can stay,' I said. 'Not now.'

'Has he said anything?'

'No,' I said. 'But his men talk, and if I stay much longer, then it will only get worse.'

'Come and stay at my hall. I will clothe and feed you.'

'Thank you,' I said, 'that is kind.' But the truth was I did not want to sit and listen to Astrid's talk of Olaf and vengeance. I wanted my own life, my own pattern, my own star to follow. And I wanted to be away from Knut's long shadow.

'You are kind,' I said, 'but I do not think so. I should leave.'

'Where would you go?'

'I don't know,' I said. 'I only thought of reaching Onund's hall, but now I see I cannot stay here. Not with Beorn.'

She nodded. 'I will send a man to the harbour to see which way the ships are bound.'

'No need,' I said. 'I will go.'

But she insisted. 'Let me do this for you at least.'

When Astrid's man came back there was little option. There was a ship bound for Iceland, after a stop in Orkney. I could get a boat there, and sail south to York or west to Dublin, but there was no place for me in either hall, and no fighting where I could make my name. And there was a boat heading east.

'East?' I said. 'I've never thought to go east.'

Astrid forced a smile. 'I went that way with Olaf when he was in exile. It's hard. We lost many men. But if you reach Eilief's or Jaroslav's halls, then there will be many who remember us well. Do you have good war-gear?'

'I had my father's sword,' I said, 'but I lost it at Stiklestad.' Now, no doubt, it was gracing the belt of some Lathe chieftain.

She pursed her lips. 'You'll need sword and helm and shield. Fighting is the way a man makes a living in the East.'

I drew in a deep breath. I knew she was right. But the Eastern Road had a hard name. 'You think there is no other way?'

'Yes,' she said. 'Come and live with me. Or go home and raise cattle.'

The captain of the ship was named Sigurd Crow, and he was a fur and salt and steel trader who had been working the western routes for the last few years, but had fallen out with the earl of Orkney and now thought he would try the Eastern Road.

'You're Olaf's brother,' the captain said. 'Why's Onund sending you away? Taken Knut's coin has he?' He laughed at me. 'Don't look so sour, lad. What do you know of furs?'

'Not much,' I said. 'But I can learn.'

'Good. And you can row?'

'Yes.'

'And you've a sword. Can you use it?'

'Yes.'

'Yes, no. Got any other words?' He pointed. 'Get your sea-chest. No one else is going to carry it for you. We don't have ranks upon this boat, except captain, which is me.'

I nodded and looked over the crew. They were a rough-looking bunch, with salt in their grey beards. Some of them were oiling the rigging, others were buried under the loose deck planks, making space for the cargo that was still to be loaded. They were Danes and Icelanders, Norse and Irish and Orkneymen. A typical landless lot of sailors, not warriors; outlaws and misfits, not sea-kings. There was a goat in a wicker cage, and an orange cat that lay on its side, eyes closed, asleep. As I set my chest down the Crow called out, 'Shorty! Look after this lad. He's Olaf's brother.'

The figure had his back to me at first. He turned slowly. He was younger than me, perhaps, with a patchy beard, and dark eyebrows that met in the middle.

'Olaf who?' he said.

'Olaf the Stout,' I said quickly, but he seemed none the wiser.

'I'm from Iceland. I've been exiled. You?'

I made a non-committal response.

'My name is Halldor,' he said. 'And this is Tooth.' He lifted his axe. 'On land I pray to Christ. On sea I pray to Thor. But however much I ask, Tooth is the only one who answers my prayers.'

We shook hands, though I felt low, as if I had fallen into the company of thieves and murderers and halfwits.

If I had had my choice I would have slipped away next morning, in the dark hours before daybreak, but when I got up and walked down to the strand, the captains all shook their heads. No one would sail east that day, not until the gale had passed.

Each day was the same. Bitter easterlies that brought hail and snow and sunshine one after the other.

Word spread that I was taking the Eastern Road, and then it seemed that men treated me with a new respect.

It felt odd still lodging in Onund's hall, but I could not bring myself to camp out in the ship with the others. It would be my last taste of a retainer's life: sitting on the king's benches as the fire fell in on itself, and the harpist warmed up his strings.

Bjorn Punch made me train with him every morning. He taught me all his tricks and feints, and each time I seemed to end up cursing and on my backside in the mud, with him putting a hand out to pull me up. But I never fell for the same trick twice, and near the end I was ready for him. 'When nothing else works, use your size and weight,' he told me.

Sæbbe took me to see a stone near his father's hall that had been carved with runes. *Here Torfi set out he died on the eastern road Sæbbe, his son, carved me*

'I was seven when he left,' Sæbbe said. 'Each year we thought he might return. I watched for his sail. Still now, I find myself looking into the April seas, and wondering if one of those sails might be his ship.

'I went to find him, when I was your age. I got as far as Holmgard and turned back. It had been nearly ten years, and no one could tell me if they'd seen him. There are many bones on the Eastern Road. Few men know their names. Don't add yours to them.'

'I shall not,' I said, as if my words had power. 'Shall I say a prayer for him?' I offered.

Sæbbe smiled. 'Yes. And if you find the place where he lies, tell his ghost we raised this stone in his honour. Tell him that the fields here have not forgotten him. Even the stones bear his name.'

I had avoided Beorn and his Danes at every opportunity, knowing how easily trouble breaks out, but one day he came and found me.

'You're leaving,' he said.

'I am.'

'Me too.' I feared for a moment that he too was sailing east. 'No,' he said. 'West. To England. My mother's sister is married to an earl there by the name of Godwin. He thinks there might be a place for me there.'

'I've heard England is a fine place.'

'Yes, and there is always fighting against the Welsh.'

We shook hands again, and this time I tried to match his grip. 'Good luck,' we said to one another, and then parted.

Next morning the gales had subsided, and I packed my few belongings into a sea-chest that Onund had given me, and said farewell to the few men I knew well.

Onund was not there. He had gone hunting, and so I walked alone through the market tents and down to the place where the ships were drawn up.

I was glad my mother was not there to see it. She had often told me how she handpicked a sea-captain for Olaf when he was a lad, how she had picked the crew, and feasted them all to ensure that they cared for her son, and how splendid the longship was: lean and low and long.

The ship that I was to sail in was a shoddy little tub, more trader than Viking. I took it hard, as if I was being shipped off like an outlaw. No family, or friends to see me off, no feast, no glory, nothing. Maybe I should not have been so rash, I thought, but I was too proud to turn back now.

I made a vow to myself that I would make it back alive, and when I did I would come back with all that my mother had promised me, all that the poems had spoken of: fine longships, gold, a host of fine warriors, and a name to rival Knut's own. Or I would not return at all.

I helped push the craft out into the water, swung myself up and took my last look at the North: the snow-capped mountains, the blue sky, the tumbling arms of fjords, the hammered-lead waters.

Then we raised the yardarm and let the winds fill the sail, and I wrapped myself in my sea-cloak, and tried to see what lay ahead of us, through the chill Baltic mists.

CHAPTER TWELVE

The Crossing

The Eastern Road is all water.

You cross the sea for three days and then enter a wide river mouth, and then another sea, with winter-bound shores. From there it took us two weeks to find the river that led south, and I understood why Sæbbe had insisted on me taking a thick shearling coat to wear, and boots of the same. In Norway in April the snows are melting, but here the land was still locked in ice.

I never knew such cold. Mist and spray froze on the rigging and the land was a wall of white, silent, watchful, unchanging. At night I lay along my planks, head on my empty sea-chest, heard the grindle-slap of water along the side of the boat, and wished I was not here. If I never see snow again, I thought, I shall be happy.

Along the wide river banks were small Swedish stockades with log cabins, firewood stacks topped with snow, and the lazy blue columns of smoke. I let my eyes linger on them, the only point of civilisation in this wilderness, and saw the smoke from their fires, or a man – thick with furs – come out to piss or clap his hands together, and silently wished I was with them.

When we stopped at one, I went with Sigurd to learn the craft of trading, but it all seemed so much effort over things of such little worth. We could spend an hour arguing over the cost of a goat, or a hen, or how much salt pork for a measure of grain. I learnt it all.

But mostly we saw nothing but pinched and mournful trees; bent and scrawny, their branches clinging to a few dry leaves, and under the snow, long beards of lichen hung. There were hosts of them crowded together; sickly and ragged as a crowd of starving thralls.

'So this is Mirkwood,' Halldor said. 'It is an evil-looking place.'

I nodded. It was wolf country, wild and bleak and empty; treacherous as a rabid dog.

Most I knew of the East I had learnt from fireside tales: how Attila had broken the Burgundians, and taken their sister to marriage in the Tale of the Volsungs. They were all full of gold and treachery and women and murder. And all I saw of this land seemed to reinforce this image.

Every so often we would see runes carved in a trunk or split timber.

Otli's crew died here, one said.

Another, *Thorbjorn killed many Serkis. Valete. I am Grey-Gunnar and made these runes.*

'Who are the Serkis?' I asked.

'All the people here who ride horses and shoot bows,' Sigurd told me.

I wanted to laugh, thinking that I never saw a horse that could run through such snows, but instead I shivered.

I did not want to see one, or fight them.

I did not want my end to be a name carved on a stick by an empty river, a thousand leagues from home. The only upside was that there was little work to do. The river meandered south and we let it carry us on its back. But it left me with a drifting feeling, as if I were being moved by others' will, and not my own. And each day grew colder and colder, till Sigurd warned us all not to touch iron with our fingers, or they would stick to it.

'Just wait till we get to Holmgard!' he laughed. 'There is food and warmth and Eilief keeps a great hall. And the marketplace. You will like it, Harald. There'll be Arabs there. They love nothing more than to argue all day long!'

He rubbed his hands, just thinking of it. I closed my eyes and dreamt of sunrise, of fire and warmth, of ashes, and of new beginnings.

At Muddy Bank we had to beach the ship, and unload her, and then drag her up onto the ice and drag her across to another river that would take us further south.

The next portage was at Beaver Lake. The land about was forest, and local tribesmen had cut a way through and sat guard on their crossing. They were an evil-looking band, with dark skins and narrow eyes. Their leader was named Svan. He claimed to be chieftain, though his land seemed to be nothing more than the path between one river and the next.

Svan was short and lean, and his head jutted out from his neck, so that it seemed to lead him along the way a horse is led. He said simply, 'You need ten hands and ten shields.'

It was how men were counted in Rus. Hands or shields. Hands for pushing and carrying, shields for protecting us from the Serkis.

Shields cost three times as much as hands.

'I do not need shields,' Sigurd Crow said.

'No shields, no hands.'

'Six shields,' Sigurd said and at last the price was agreed.

At Shingle Point, three days later, the spokesman was a short, dark fellow, with a bloodshot eye. The crossing was short, but it went over a low hill that was thick with trees. His people had cut and smoothed a passage over the hill, but they wanted twice as much money for each hand.

'Pay them,' Arnbjorn, one of the Swedish crewmen, said. 'And let us be done with this.'

'It'll come out of your share then,' Sigurd Crow said.

Arnbjorn laughed. 'Reduce my share and I'll shorten you by the same amount.'

The last crossing was at Battle River.

The guide here was named Wolf. He said it was too dangerous to cross alone.

'The Pechenegs are far north this year,' Wolf said. 'Hunting for fat ships like yours. My mother Khazar. Pechenegs are my enemies. Their horses fill the wide grasslands. They war with the people of the walls and boats. Their king drinks his wine from the skull of Jaroslav's father. But the grasslands are their ocean, and they ride wherever they choose, and leave death and sorrow, and widows in their wake.'

I took little notice. All I wanted was a roof and a hall but at that moment one of the squatting tribesmen started to speak in their own language. Wolf nodded, and at the end he turned to us and said, 'He says wait for more longbeard ships. When there are more we can all cross together.'

We kicked our frozen heels, and waited. It took six days for three more boats to gather. They had spent a month at a trading post named White Dog Post, on a different river, trying to buy mink pelts. 'The Pechenegs had caught three ships before us,' their captain, Ake said. 'They piled the hands and feet and heads by the side of the river.'

He shook as he spoke. We sat and listened. I felt a dull dread go through the company. This country sapped men of their courage. Our spirits were low. No one spoke.

'All men must die of something,' I said, trying to be cheerful. 'I would rather meet the Pecheneg than freeze.'

I got a laugh at least, and so it was agreed that we would start in the morning.

That night we all prayed, I to the White Christ, the Swedes to their old gods, and Halldor had his axe in one hand, whetstone in the other. He held it up, to reveal a rim of freshly whetted steel.

'Now that's a fine smile,' he said.

109

CHAPTER THIRTEEN

Battle River

We set off early, as the sun rose, and made good time.

But the feeling grew on me as the day went on: that we were being watched. I turned – suddenly at times – but saw nothing. But others felt it too. They would turn and glance over their shoulder and one of the mounted guards rode up to us and spoke to us in a tongue I did not understand. But I knew the word Pecheneg.

We drove through noon, laying down the timbers and heaving the ship across them, but we hit a soft patch and it was slow, slow going. We were stopping and looking at the problem when a band of horsemen rode into view along the top of the river bank. They were the ugliest men I had ever seen, with beaked noses, cruel hunt-ing spears, horn-tipped bows, and quivers of black-fletched arrows. Everything about them – the way they moved, the way they sat on their horses – even their horses – seemed strange.

'Pecheneg!' someone shouted, and then the horsemen wheeled towards us and let out a war-cry that was so unearthly and horrible that the memory of it still makes my skin tighten about me. It was half gabble, half wolf-howl, and with it came the thunder of their approaching hoofs. Brass horns blew as we tore off our fur mittens and scrambled for weapon and shield. It was as sudden as a summer storm that rides on chilling winds.

I can feel it now, even after these years. Look, my hand is still trembling, just thinking about it.

'With me, Harald! With me, Eric!' Sigurd Crow called but he did not know what to do. Any more than any one of us there, but we ran out with him as he threw his spear. As he drew his sword, one of the horseman – at a gallop – pulled an arrow from the quiver at his saddle, fitted it, drew, and loosed. I did not see it, but I heard it hit Sigurd's shield with a low thud, like striking a full barrel.

I turned and saw Sigurd. The arrow had gone straight through his shield, and straight through Sigurd. The end jutted out of his back, and he was dead.

I thought of all I had learnt from Bjorn Punch and the other king-garth brawlers, and saw in a moment that we were strung out, leaderless, helpless. I saw terror in Eric's face and knew it was a reflection of my own. I was damned if I was going to let wild horsemen kill me where Knut had failed.

'Together men! Stand fast,' someone shouted, and men said it was me. 'Stand together! Stand firm!'

I had no brothers left in the world, so it was good to feel Eric's shoulders against mine. Then there were more of us, all facing outwards, shields raised high in a desperate defence.

'With you!' Halldor hissed as the Irish lad, Bjarke, took an arrow in his chest. It buried itself to the feathers, the end coming out, right between his shoulder blades. The man at my side – one of the Icelanders – was hit in the head. Valdi groaned as he took an arrow in the chest. Blood ran from his nose and mouth. He tried to speak.

'We will get out of this,' I said to him as he fell against my legs, but he shook his head at me, and reached up for help and squeezed my hand so hard it hurt.

All the time the Pechenegs howled as they wheeled about us, penning us in. We had no choice but to stand our ground and fight them off. I knew what would happen if we were scattered, or fled. I had seen it at Stiklestad. But here we were dying regardless. Their darts could kill from afar. In the time it takes a man to take a shit, we would all be lying on our backs, breathing our last.

'Into the boat!' I shouted. 'Into the boat!' I dragged a few of the most foolhardy backwards, and we ended up ducking down behind the bulwark.

'Come!' I shouted to the others.

Arnbjorn was right beside me, helping me up. A black-fletched arrow thudded into the timbers between my arms as we hauled the men up, one on each hand. It hummed as it quivered, and I kicked out at it in hatred.

Arnbjorn winked at me. 'The boat will shield us for a little time,' he said, and slapped my back. He and Halldor dragged out the oilskins that had kept us dry on the Baltic crossing.

He and Arnbjorn gave me hope.

One of the Pecheneg tried to seize hold of the oilskin. I leapt out and stabbed at him, and missed. Three came in next time and stabbed at us. I threw my spear and hit one in the throat, and they wheeled off, still howling.

I cannot tell you truly what happened. I was mad with fear. We threw everything we had. Nails, bundles of ropes, spare wooden rigging blocks.

Someone found bows under the loose planks. I loosed a shot that missed, ducked behind Halldor's shield and loosed again. It wobbled as it left the bow, and just as it started to fall it hit one of them low in the chest and he fell back over his saddle and toppled from the horse.

Halldor clapped me on the back as if I had killed a giant.

'That is one, and there are many more.'

Half of us were already dead, but at least we were dying more slowly now. We were there an hour or more before our Khazar guard returned, howling and blasting long brass horns. They came at a thunderous gallop and the Pechenegs wheeled about to face them off, and then the rest of the day was them circling one another, and wheeling away again. It was like watching flocks of birds mobbing one another. Our captains lay dead and we stood, stunned, exhausted, still trembling.

The third boat crew came at a run, loping through the snow with slow exaggerated steps. The captain of the third boat was a man named Armundr. He saw that his brother was not among the living, and wanted to see the body. 'Here,' I said, standing over the body.

Armundr pressed a hand to his brother's cheek, and then looked up to me. 'Did he die well?'

'He did,' I said. They had all died terrified, but they had not let their terror show. Even their faces looked calm, when we had wiped away the blood.

The land was too hard so we could not bury our dead, so we piled then up on the boat, and cut off beech branches and set the boat aflame. Many of the corpses had already frozen. They made an awkward pile. The Pechenegs had not left many dead, but we stripped them of what they had and added that to the pile.

Armundr put the torch to the brushwood. It was too cold for tears. Too cold, almost, for the kindling to catch, but at last small blue flames began to appear, crackling and splitting like dogs chewing on bones.

'You should choose one of your number to be captain,' Armundr said.

I looked at them, and thought, Eric? But then a voice called out my name. It was Arnbjorn. It felt strange looking into his Olaf-pale eyes. At first I thought he was asking my opinion, but then the next man said, 'Aye. Harald.'

Armundr looked at me. 'But he is so young.'

Halldor rose. 'The captain is the one who leads. It's already been decided. It is Harald.'

And one by one they all agreed. 'Without him we would all be dead. This is a hard land. We need a tough fighter. Let Harald lead us to Holmgard.'

And so, nearly seventeen years old, I sailed into Holmgard with eighteen men and a ship, and a cargo of goods, and made my way straight to Jarl Eilief's hall to offer him service.

I was with Jarl Eilief two years. He ran the fur trade in the whole of the North. As soon as I got there I thought to myself, 'I shall be his best warrior', and when it was time to shake out the mattresses on the floor, I lay with my eyes closed and imagined leading a band of brave warriors north and raising all Norway to my cause, and defeating Knut in combat.

Killing him, as he had killed my childhood dreams.

Each summer we dug forts and palisades from the wilderness, each winter we took empty dog-sleds out over the white and frozen land, and took tribute from all the tribes in that wild land: the Chuds Beyond-the-Portages, and the Chuds Within-the-Portages, the Ves, the Perm, the Pechera, the Yams, the Ugra, the Livs and the Wends. I knew them all by headdress, manner, customs and meeting place: by the bent yew, Oli's Stone, the fork in the black stream, the Clearing-above-Dead-Man's-Mound, White Dog Post, the giant's tooth two days after the full moon.

The meetings would all start the same way. We would pick a way through the snow and cold, unhitch the dogs, and light a fire and wait.

Halldor would have his axe with him. The rest of us spears and swords. We did not wear armour. We were already bundled in bearskin trousers and coats. That sound was all we could hear as the forest stretched silent about us, then a figure would appear, first one, then three, and then when they were satisfied they would all come out in their shaggy furs and unkempt hair.

'Come!' I would say to them, beckoning them closer to our fire. 'Cold is the foe of us all!'

I never turned my back on them, never went without a sword, and when I went to shit away from the others, I took my spear with me.

Other captains were not so lucky. The first winter we served with Eilief, Rolf the Fat was hung naked from a yew tree, a red gash where his privates had been. Poor Armundr came out of the forest without his hands or nose or tongue. Gustav the White came back down the river in his boat, his head in his lap. The Livs were the most treacherous. In my second year they set upon me after getting me drunk and tried to take my scalp. I left their bodies in the swamp and took their heads to the camp.

'Here!' I said. 'I found these at the end of a knife that was trying to cut my hair.'

The chief was a lean and wiry man with teeth filed to sharp points. I have no idea what his name was, but I will never forget the look of murder in his eyes, and I knew he would try, so I walked to the edge of the clearing and pissed against a tree and waited. He came at me with a spear, but I laughed as I shattered his spear shaft with my sword, and split his skull to the bottom teeth.

'If Knut could not, then a hairy savage shall not have my soul!' I told his ghost.

There was one chieftain I took a liking to. His name was Nurmi, Chief Beyond the Portages. Each winter I saved his people for last. If we had done well in the other places, I would not drive such a hard bargain with him. It was usual for his scouts to come days out of their winter camp to lead us to him. When we came he would use his spear to unhook a piece of meat from around the smoke hole, and his girls would cut slices off, and we would chew them slowly, and wash away the salty taste with ale.

'Your jarl wants too much,' Nurmi always said, but once a deal was done he at least had the sense to smile and laugh.

The previous year I had said, 'It is his lord who wants more.'

And he had scowled and coughed in the smoky inside of his tent, whole sides of salmon hanging above our heads. 'Who is this lord?'

'Jaroslav. In the south.'

'And who is his lord?'

'The Great Caesar,' I said. 'In Micklegard, the city of stone.'

'And who is his lord?'

'God,' I said. 'None other.'

Nurmi smiled. 'Then you should serve the Great Caesar. He keeps all his own furs.'

'Maybe I shall,' I said.

He had laughed and we toasted that thought, and I was looking forward to seeing him, and telling him that I was thinking of taking his advice.

But in my third winter with Eilief there were no scouts, and when we came to his camp, at the end of the fur-gathering season, it was not Nurmi who welcomed me, but another man with a thick black beard that reached almost up to his eyes, which were very blue, as blue as winter skies, with dark rims. They were wolf's eyes. Or the eyes of a hawk.

'I am Meri,' he declared. 'I am chief of the Chud Beyond-the-Portages.'

'Where is Chief Nurmi?'

'Dead.'

'How?'

'I killed him,' Meri declared.

As I went to the hut, Halldor touched my arm and I nodded, and tested my sword was loose, before stepping inside the dark tent, still hanging with smoked trout and salmon and strings of elk as tense as a hunted deer.

Meri stepped to the wall opposite the door, where his chief objects were displayed. He took one, no bigger than my fist, and turned it towards me.

There was a tiny head, all lips and nose, sitting in his hand, with sandy coloured hair bound into a top-knot. I took it for a child's toy at first, but then I saw the texture, and realised it was not stone or clay, but made of skin.

The realisation hit me like a blow. It was Nurmi's head that sat there, lips sewn shut with gut-thread. Meri explained to me how it had been smoked and salted, but I felt sick with it in the room, and at the end I said, 'How much for that head?'

Chief Muri seemed amused. 'You like my trophy?'

'I liked the man more. Here,' I took my dagger from my belt. The scabbard was of finely knotted red leather, but it was the steel he was interested in. The blade swirled with light and dark. It was the finest Damascus steel. So I took Nurmi's head and buried it by an old oak, and said a prayer for us all, to get out of this hell alive.

So it was in a foul mood that I returned to Eilief that season, and when I heard that a new boat had just arrived from the North, I was eager to get back. There is nothing that an exile thirsts for more than news from home.

I had hoped for Norsemen, who might bring news from home, and was disappointed to hear that they were Danes. But it only got worse when it turned out that they were sent by Knut to bring his good wishes to Eilief.

'The Great King would like to be friends with you,' their spokesman said. He went on to list all the deeds that Knut claimed for his name.

We listened to the tales of how he had subdued the kings of the Irish Isles; accepted the fealty of the kings of Dublin; how he had marched north and taken oaths from the Scottish kings Malcolm and Macbeth. We sat through the tale of how he had gone on pilgrimage to Rome and had been called 'brother' by the Bishop of Christ. How he was now king of the Danes, the English, the Norse and the Swedes of Helgea.

I listened to it all and I felt sick. Here was I, scrounging furs from wild Chuds and Livs, and my enemy was heaping titles and honours upon himself like a harbour-side whore. But what hurt most was the welcome that Eilief gave these men. He sat them on the benches above me, brought out his best wine, had a calf slaughtered, feasted them as though Knut himself had come here, and accepted both gifts and friendship from the great king.

I scowled throughout the feast and thought that Eilief was like an old man on his wedding night to a comely young girl. Even here, it seemed, I was in Knut's shadow.

I did not sleep that night, but rolled about on my mattress like a ship on stormy waters.

By morning I had made my choice and went straight to him as he sat before the embers of the night's feast with a bearskin thrown over his shoulders.

'Lord,' I said. 'I think you have shown me little honour by showing my enemies such a welcome.'

He tried to dissuade me, but the words and the hurt came out altogether. I was done. I would go and find a better lord.

I'd come to my decision alone, and did not know if any of my men would come with me. But that night, when we gathered together and they could see my hurt, Halldor said, 'You have led us well, Harald. I for one will stay with you.'

And one by one the others agreed. They stayed with me as we travelled down the Land of Rus, doing whatever we had to do to get money and food and shelter. We took service as bodyguard, escorts, dabbled in the fur trade – everyone in the East deals in furs. Furs, slaves and iron weapons. That is all men are interested in. And silver, of course.

But I did not have the nose for prices, the patience for haggling, the interest in inspecting each skin for blemishes, and I gave up too easily, and made bad deals more than once. 'They've made a fool of you,' Halldor told me more times than I can remember.

'Fuck you,' I'd say, and we would not talk for days. Or, 'You do it next time.'

'I will.'

We suffered much, but the shared hardships brought us as close as brothers. It made us stronger, as the hammer brings out steel from the iron.

Only once did we make money. It was autumn, and the leaves were changing and winter was sharpening its cold knives.

We made a fortune on a load of white mink pelts, but I remember sifting through the coins. Silver dinars from Babylon and Micklegard; the tiny bronze coins no bigger than a fingernail, and all the clipped and worn faces of emperors and kings who did nothing of note, and whose names no one remembered, and I thought, there are places in the South, where all these coins have come from, where men have more coin than sense.

So at last we came to Kiev, where Olaf had once stayed, and where I met up with Rognvald once more. And for a while there I was happy, but then again Knut's emissaries came bearing gifts and sweet words, and even though Jaroslav and Rognvald both insisted that I stay, I decided to push my men southwards.

I was overly proud, perhaps, as far as Knut the Great was concerned, but wanted to be somewhere where I did not have to hear his name.

Jaroslav wanted to honour me. 'I see I cannot persuade you to stay, but I need a good captain to take my tribute south to Micklegard. Will you do this for me?'

I felt ungrateful and foolish, but was glad to accept. It seemed a job worthy of me.

'I will,' I said. 'And I will carry whatever kind words of friendship you would like to the King of the Greeks.'

And so next summer, the fur tribute for Micklegard was finally loaded onto a row of five barges. We were ready to depart and Prince Jaroslav gave us gifts of fine red silk clothing.

'When you meet the Great King in Micklegard, stand proud. Do not let him think the Lands of Rus are filled with savages. And send him greetings from his brother Jaroslav, Prince of the Rus.'

He was intent on the wording. Brother Jaroslav. I committed it all to memory, and bowed. 'I shall, Lord.'

We had a Byzantine merchant with us, a small, dark man named Probus, who had his own trade in furs, but whose ship had been burnt by Pechenegs.

He was grateful for the ride back south, and promised to lead us the safest way over the rapids and across the seas to Micklegard.

So we poled the barges out into the middle of the wide river, and let the water do the rest. We were lean and young and tanned, and we stood, naked to the waist, and watched all that world fall behind us: the steppes, the Rus, the fur trade, the constant threat of Pechenegs, even the boastful talk of Knut's emissaries retreated behind us, like snow in spring, and all we heard was the laughter of unlocked streams, and the promise of warmth and bounty and beauty before us.

The church of St Olaf, in York, is a beautiful little building, near the river bank. It was founded by Earl Siward, whose son was killed by Macbeth, and the first church in England to be dedicated to his brother's memory. There is a marvellous rood screen and coloured glass in the windows.

I took your father there to swear oaths with Earls Edwin and Morcar. Tostig insisted on using the earl's quay, but your father did not care. His longship grounded on the river bank, and he vaulted over the front of the boat, and landed in the mud.

'So this is my brother's church,' he said.

It was as if he was on a sightseeing trip, such as pilgrims in Rome make, once they have stabled their horses in the Saxon Quarter. 'In Norway they build our churches out of wood. You stand inside and smell the resin, and feel you are within a forest. It has the same light, filtering down through high windows.'

He turned to his men. They were old, lean warriors, who had been in the south with him. He slapped the stonework. 'Feel the width of these walls. They are solid as the hills.' He seemed impressed, and when all were gathered he gestured to us all. 'Come, let us go inside!'

Your father paraded me through the whole ceremony as if I were his new wife. 'My little English bishop,' he called me.

Brother Edwinus, a helpful man, brought out St Olaf's relics.

Their most prized one was a slashed cloak that was said to have been worn by the saint when he was killed. It was made of a fine blue wool, with many slashes in the cloth, and dark stains of saint's blood. 'Look, Lord King,' he said. 'This is the cloak that your brother was wearing when he died.'

Your father went very quiet. His face darkened ominously. 'Are you mocking me?'

'No!' Edwinus managed to gasp.

Your father ripped it from his hand and balled the cloak up in his fist and shook it in his face.

I stepped forward. 'Is something wrong, My Lord?'

Your father ripped the cloak into two, and threw both parts onto the floor. His nostrils flared with fury. 'My brother was not wearing a cloak. What fool would wear a cloak to battle?'

PART II

The Middle Sea

CHAPTER ONE

Micklegard

I had imagined Micklegard many times. In my mind's eye I saw something built of wood and ditches and thatch, like Kiev, but grander – like Odin's Hall in Valhalla. So when we saw the first Greek city, on the shores of what they call the Black Sea, the sight of stone buildings piled one upon the other, wide colonnades, streets paved with slabs of white marble, dredged harbours with walls of dressed stone – then wonder winded me.

Picture, if you can, all the stone churches you have seen all piled one upon the other in one place, and roof them with red clay tiles, not thatch, and set a stone wall all about it – so high that you could see only the tops of the cypress trees over their battlements. That would be nothing compared with these cities. They had domes of gold, terrace after terrace of olive groves, where goats waited in the small puddles of shade; wall-paintings, their colours bright as a bed of summer flowers.

When we rowed round the first mole that protected a deepwater harbour I was like a mountain goatherd who stepped inside his lord's hall for the first time and saw gold and carvings alive with firelight. My mouth fell open. 'Is this Micklegard?' I said, and we all thought it had to be until Probus, the local who we had hired to navigate our way, set us straight. 'That is Constanta,' he said dismissively, wrinkling his nose at the thought. 'No. That is just a little town.'

As we sailed south with our cargo of furs the cities grew larger and more splendid, and I thought we had seen the finest masonry and palaces and cathedrals. But when at last Probus led us into the narrow sea which is called the Bosphorus, and told us that we were only two days from Micklegard, we picked up on his excitement and were like children at midsummer, who cannot wait for the bone-fires to be lit.

The Bosphorus is as narrow and long as a fjord. You passed silver olive groves, herds of sheep, fertile slopes where wheat grew, stone-built farmsteads with terracotta roofs, and tumbling in marble terraces down the hillsides were the rich palaces of the greatest families: each one with a stone jetty of its own, each one with stone walls and guard towers, and paddocks full of the finest black stallions I ever saw.

It was wonder upon wonder. But as we saw the glimmer of golden domes over the next headland, I had to order the men back from the same side, lest they tip the boat over. The winds could not blow us there fast enough. It was like a beautiful woman, slowly disrobing – veil, headscarf, cloak, girdle, gown, linen undershirt all puddling at her feet. So Micklegard appeared to us as she was struck with noonday sunlight, the glare of white marble, the crenellated battlements of vast city walls, tiers of columned colonnades, each one a little smaller than the rest, cypress trees and dark laurels set in geometric shapes, palaces built with the lines of black and white marble, which the Byzantines love, and her shadows dark as the night, and just as unknowable.

Sharp against the clear deep blue of the Mediterranean sky the Queen of Cities rose from the black waters of the Bosphorus – ageless, golden, brilliant with the morning sunlight shining on her golden domes – and I fell to my knees and Halldor shook my hand

126

and he tried to get words from me – but I could not do anything
but laugh. He laughed with me at first, then grew concerned.

'Harald!' he said. 'Are you ill?'

I tried to answer but I could not. If this was a city then no other
was worthy of the name, I thought, and the crew looked at me as if
I was a fool and at last Halldor stood up and said, 'He's still drunk.'

But I had seen with sudden clarity that the worries that had
driven me south were gone. It was as if the shadow of Knut had
been purged by the bright Mediterranean sun.

It was how Adam and Eve felt when they ate of the apple, and
were given wisdom and understanding. I felt like a boy who brings
his wooden sword to the hall of warriors. This was civilisation. This
was power. This was the hub about which the world turned. Who
cared what Knut called himself? Nothing was great that was not here.

Probus enjoyed our astonishment. As we approached the city,
we could make out the serried walls, the golden domes of churches,
the stone shoulders of Hagia Sophia – and we were all dumbstruck.

'That's the palace,' he told us. 'There the Empress Zoe rules.'

'A woman?' I said.

He nodded, and I imagined having to greet a woman and give
her Jaroslav's greeting. I imagined a dark, Greek beauty, such as
we had met by the docks at Varna or Burgas or Constanta. 'Is she
married?'

He laughed. 'Yes, barbarian. She is an old woman now. Old and
bitter. She has worn out two husbands already.'

'And she has no sons.'

'None. Only a sister, whom she has locked away in a monastery.'

He kept talking, but I did not listen. I was staring at the stones
of the palace. Each stone was the size of a horse. Only giants could
have raised such a place. Or angels. Or God himself, in a holy
miracle.

War galleys, that the Greeks call biremes, were berthed on the
northern side of the city. They were long and sleek and I would like

to have had a closer look at them and their crews but Probus led us to the harbours on the southern side. 'There!' he said, and pointed to a narrow beach between two rocky headlands.

We did not know it then but we knew it well in the years that followed. It was the harbour of Eleustherios, where the city walls – pale yellow in the bright sunlight – came right down to the water, and rose up like a cliff face, and behind were the towers that were houses, each four or five floors high.

That first time a young boy was standing on the battlements, pissing over the side, before his mother's hand appeared and dragged him back.

'There!' I shouted to Halldor, who was my steersman. I called to the rowers to make a good show. 'Remember we are the equal of any Greek!'

The drummer gave them a smart beat and they drove our boat high up the beach. Our keel crunched ashore with a hiss of foam and shingle, and the steep beach brought us to a sudden halt. I could not wait, but leapt down into the water, and it was hot, like a woman's body, and I strode ashore and smelt the city all about me – spice and gold and power.

There was no dignitary to greet us, only the gang of dockers, who sat on the narrow beach, naked from the chest up, dark as Moors, dirty and sweaty, black beards down to thier chests. They waved me on to the dock-master, a sour looking fellow, with heavy, bullish brows.

I had picked up a little Greek, and had rehearsed the words I was to say to the Great King, and practised them now. 'I am Harald Sigurdsson,' I said to the harbour master. 'I'm from your brother Prince Jaroslav, of Kiev. We bring gifts for the Great King.'

He made a face. 'Whose brother?'

'Your brother, Prince Jaroslav,' I told him.

'Who?'

'Kiev,' I said, and waved to the north.

'Where?'

'Rus,' I tried, and he shook his head. I gave up and thumped my chest. 'Varangoi!'

'Ah! Varangoi,' he said and shouted to the harbour master, who came out from under an awning. Everyone knew the Varangoi, it seemed.

The harbour master was short and fat and sweating, and had a horse-hair swat, which he absent-mindedly swiped about his face as if the beads of sweat were flies. He yawned, open-mouthed, and took his stylus from behind his ear, and frowned as he tapped the end against his teeth. He spoke to me so quickly that I had no idea what the words meant, and Probus had to come down to help me.

I had thought Probus as civilised as any man, but here he seemed not much better than the labourers, and the harbour master flicked his hand at him as if he were a goat-boy from the mountains. 'He says unload the ship. They have a custom here that gift bringers should carry the gifts ashore, and so the deed is done.'

We formed a chain, and within an hour the oilskins of precious furs were piled high on the sands, above the high-water line. Nine of the boats brought tribute from Jaroslav. The last one brought a gift from me to the Empress herself. It was those I was most concerned with. I knew the forests from which these furs had come. I had followed them on sleds, on horse, on barge, past Pechenegs, rapids, Chuds, the lot. Now, I thought, they will grace the shoulders of some Byzantine prince, or maybe even those of the Empress herself.

As we stood the harbour master counted and scratched, and counted some more. 'You are short,' he said at last.

'Impossible,' I told him. 'That is Jaroslav's, and these are mine for the Empress.'

'I say you are short,' the harbour master said, and tapped the wooden rim of his wax tablet.

'Count it again,' I told him.

'We have just counted it.'

'It is all there,' I told him. 'And more.'

I was getting exasperated. We were all hungry and we could smell fires being lit on the other side of the walls, sticks of spiced meat being grilled over racks of charcoal. My men just wanted to go inside. 'Have done,' Halldor said. 'Set a guard and let the rest of us go up into the city.'

'No,' I said. I counted it before him. Load by load. The harbour master got bored and squatted down on his heels, and looked up at me as if I were a fool. The third time I was done he pushed himself up and rubbed his forefinger and thumb together.

'*Asimi!*' he said.

'*Asimi?*' I said.

'Yes,' his laughter said. '*Asimi!*'

The dockers had risen to their feet. They had clubs and sticks in their hands. I got his drift now and my anger rose quickly.

'I promised my lord I would bring his tribute here safely, and that is what I have done. That is his and that is mine, and I am going to give it to the Empress personally.'

He laughed at me when my words were translated. I did not have to turn to look. I knew my men were behind me. I stepped to the side to go round him but he stepped in front of me. I leant into him. I was a good head taller. We were so close our beards touched. 'No,' I said and shoved him back.

Someone swung a punch. It hit me on the side of the head. I punched back. My knuckles caught a chin and I heard the thump of a body being thrown backwards and I knew that Halldor was at my shoulder.

I thought that would be it. But then one of the dockers drew his knife: a short nasty blade of freshly whetted steel.

The man was small but moved lightly on his bare feet. He came in low and fast. I leapt back, but too slow. The slash opened up a cut across my right palm. I smelt blood, felt it dripping down my palm, between my fingers, dripping from the tips.

He grinned at me and came in again, thinking to do the same.

He was a street fighter, and that is a different way of fighting to a stand-up brawl, but I had learnt a few things in the five years in Rus. From the Chuds, mostly. They liked to feel a man's breath on their cheek as they cut his throat. On the third attack I stepped in close and I could see the shock in his eyes. I had caught his arm with my bloody palm. He was held fast, like the shark that bites upon the fisherman's hook and knows it is caught. I grinned down on him. Let him wriggle on the line for a moment, like a silver herring. Then with a roar of anger I twisted his arm and brought it down. There was a sharp snap as I broke it over my knee.

The man howled as he dropped his knife.

Someone swung a club. I knocked him back and he shouted 'Barbaroi!' and spat. Halldor threw himself at the man, and the two of them rolled over like angry dogs. It seemed the whole beach would be engulfed. But at that moment I could see the red horse-hair helmet plumes of armed guards coming at a trot. They were a fine-looking band, with dark skin and magnificent black beards, their seven-foot spears held straight up, like real warriors. I grabbed Halldor and dragged him back as the guards came to a stop, held up my hands in a gesture that meant peace. My fingers were sticky with blood. Now it dripped down to my wrist.

'We shall be hanged like thieves,' Halldor said.

But I expected better of the Emperor. I had a naïve faith in our common honour and status. And we had come a long way to make the Emperor here our lord, I had faith that even in a city this large, he would hear and would protect us.

The captain pulled off his red-plumed helmet, tucked it under his arm and strode towards me. He had the rolling gait of a man who has spent most of his time on a horse, and an oiled black beard that covered his cheeks, and stopped just below his eyes.

He shouted to the harbour master. The harbour master shouted back, and pointed to the knifeman. His face was white and sweating. He held out his arm, which hung at a sickening angle.

131

The captain spoke again and the Greek's response was more timid this time.

The captain turned to me. I had no idea what he was saying. He took my bleeding hand, turned it over so he could see the cut, and then he tutted and shook his head.

'This is Katalokon Cecaumenus,' Probus said. 'He is one of the Emperor's captains.'

I explained I was a king's brother, from far to the north, and that I was bringing tribute to the Great Emperor from his brother Jaroslav, in Kiev.

The harbour master said something and Katalokon kicked him and shouted. I caught the translator's eye, but Probus was listening intently. 'He says, "We will count the tax now. And see who is lying."'

A tax collector was dragged down to the harbour by his gown. His unhappiness was evident, but he clearly knew what was in his best interest. The furs were unloaded and Katalokon had the man witness the tribute. 'All correct. Put your print here,' he said.

I used my bloody hand, and pressed it into the tablet.

'I will make sure it reaches the palace,' Katalokon said. 'I promise.'

At last I relented, and he put his helmet on his head. All I could see was steel and beard and two small points of eyes. 'But now,' he said, 'you must come with me.'

CHAPTER TWO

The Varangian Guard

Even if you took all the other cities you have ever seen and put them in one place they will not compare to Micklegard.

The city is built on a wide promontory. To the north is the Golden Horn, a narrow harbour where the warships were berthed in the shelter of watchtowers and sealed each night by a mighty chain they row across the opening. That is where the war galleys lie, painted with stripes of deep red and Turkish blue, which the people of the city love.

That clear morning, we threaded through narrow streets, cobbled with flat stones and flanked by houses so tall the sky was just a stripe of blue above your head.

Everyone, it seemed, lived in houses of stone. Most of them were as high as a tree and within them ten families might live, each one piled one atop the other like stones in a wall. We had stayed in one of those, on the fifth floor, which made all of us feel queasy. None of us slept well, and we were glad next morning to step on the cobbles, and feel the ground beneath our feet.

The street led us to a broad white marble thoroughfare, that we later learnt was called the Mese. It was flanked by columned porticos where tradesmen were taking their wooden shutters down from their shop-fronts, and journeying traders were setting up their fruit and vegetable stalls between the pillars.

Bakers were carrying trays of fresh bread upon their heads, and old women leant out of the high balconies and lowered baskets on ropes for the salesmen to fill. A pair of old men were playing some game on a step that had a chequer-pattern board scratched into it.

Songbirds, bright as paintings, trilled from delicate black wooden cages; by a doorway, an old man leant back against the wall, a wriggling baby in his lap. Every so often the road opened up to left or right, and there would be a wide square, that the people call a forum, where they meet and gather in the shade of the stone arches, each one marking some victory over their enemies, or great columns, or life-size marble statues of men and women, naked and beautiful. We looked at them with amazement, but they watched us pass without interest.

We strode past the Forum of Theodosius and Constantine. As we came about the end of the promontory we passed the Praetorium, which is the vast building from which the whole empire is run, and then colonnades fell away and we turned the corner and saw a towering building loom before us, lit brilliantly by the rising sun . It was like a giant's hall, three times as high as the greatest oak, built of white marble, three stories high, each one held up by huge pillars of stone. There were hundreds of them. A forest of stone trees holding up the curving arches, the pictured walls bright as meadow flowers.

My mouth was dry. 'Is that where the Empress lives?'

Our guide laughed. 'No, that is the Hippodrome. It is where the chariot races happen.' He liked my wonder. 'Come, the Boukelon is this way.'

We crossed the white-flagged square towards the gate with the morning sun bright in our faces, and passed under the Million, the milestone from which all distances were measured.

Sweat trickled down my side. The palace walls had seemed small from the sea, but now that we stood in their shadow I saw how high they were: tall as a mountain pine, at the least, with stern guards looking down, their steel helms stars in the bright glare. Each one carried a round shield and spear, and they had long plumes on their helmets that hung down their backs. They were giants, and as we came closer we saw that they were made of metal. But you could see the lines of their muscles, their veins, each hair on their head. 'What sorcery is this?' Halldor said, then turned to me. 'How big do you think the Empress will be?'

The Bronze Gates stood open, and once we had passed through them we were led through courtyard after courtyard, some lined with neat low bushes, some echoing with fountains of tumbling water or laughing girls, others ringing to the sound of warriors training, and once we passed a guard post where tall dark warriors stood, each one wearing silvered mail and gilded helms, silent and still as the statues in the Hippodrome.

When we reached the palace itself we had given up on pointing things out to each other. We walked in awed silence through the gates of black and white marble, through reception rooms, empty dining chambers, small candlelit shrines and chapels, walls hung with silk and laurel wreathes, our booted feet moving across mosaics of bear and lion hunts, past walls of gold, through curtains of embroidered silk, under paintings of Christ that were so real I stopped and thought he was looking at me, and reached out to touch and my fingers flinched at the stone-cold.

At last we were led to a pair of great timber doors, carved with the figures of saints, one of which was ajar. There were ten warriors posted there. They wore long shirts of finely knitted steel, gold-worked helmets with silver face-masks, clothes of white and blue silk, and great baggy leggings tucked into calfskin boots.

One of them spoke to us. 'Wait!' he said. The man spoke with a thick Orkney accent and I felt a sudden thrill of relief. It was true! Varangians were at the very heart of this kingdom. They were bodyguards to the Emperor and Empress themselves. I knew then I wanted to be one of them. I imagined myself serving here clad in silks and mail as fine as trout scales – protecting the body of the Emperor with my own, like this Orkneyman before me. The boy inside me bristled – how is he better than I? The man was respectful.

'I will tell you when you may enter.' When some of the men started talking, he put up a hand. 'Silence!'

I stood for an age. Men came in and out. Some looked glad, some broken, all of them looked weary.

'What does the Emperor do to them?' Halldor said.

I shook my head, thinking of the metal statues outside. I could feel my heartbeat in my fingertips. I sucked in deep breaths, tried to appear calm. At last the Orkneyman nodded. 'You may go in.'

He used the singular you, '*þú*' not the plural, '*þér*'.

I panicked. 'Alone?'

He nodded. I turned and looked into the faces of my men. I had been through fire and battle and hunger with these men. I felt naked without them, but they nodded and motioned for me to go. 'Do as he says,' Halldor said, and pushed me forward.

The Great Hall of Micklegard is domed like the sky, but the sky was golden, and painted with figures of Christ and his angels. The walls were golden too, and the eight-sided room was faceted like a gemstone, and each wall shone back candlelight. All about me was the light and the gleam of gold and power and beauty. A dragon's den could not contain more riches.

About the walls stood the great and the worthy. Some were beardless, but most had broad black beards, curled and combed and hanging to their waists. All wore cloth of silk and golden thread, buttons of garnet and turquoise, and the richest furs about their collars and their shoulders.

In the middle of the room, on a high dais, stood two ceremonial chairs of gold and minutely carved ivory. Six Varangians stood to either side, faces hidden by mail and helm, and on the steps before them counsellors on stools.

On the floor before the dais were the skins that we had brought. Katalokon had been true to his word. They were divided into two piles. Those from Jaroslav, and those that I had brought. They seemed crude and wild in that place. I felt a little ashamed of them as I turned towards the throne.

A hand pushed me forward. I bowed so low I think my nose touched my toes. I've never bowed so low before, or since.

'Varangoi, rise,' a voice said, and I stood and found myself looking into a woman's face.

The shock ran through me, though I'd heard that the last emperor had died without a male heir, and so his daughter Zoe ruled, with her consort, Michael. She was old, perhaps forty or more, and little. No bigger than my mother's maid, Thorhild, and she seemed weighed down into her seat with clothes and jewels and a great crown of gold. But there was a light in her eyes that disturbed me, and as I stood there all the words I had learnt to say left me, and I stood dumb and mute as an ass.

'Announce yourself,' said the chamberlain, who sat on the step just below the Empress. He had no beard and was dressed in a white tunic, with a red doublet, and boots of red as well. But his voice was shrill as a girl's, and from his smooth, plump cheeks I guessed he was a gelding.

I had planned to announce myself as a royal prince, but now I was here something held me back, an old shadow that bore the shape of Knut the Great. Who knew how far his powers ran? a warning voice sounded. The Bishop of Rome had called him brother. Was he also a brother to the Empress and her consort?

I started to speak but my voice failed me. 'Harald,' I said, clearing my throat, and left off all my proud titles.

The man did not pause. His high voice rang out. 'Do you bring the tribute from Kiev?'

'Yes,' I said, and beckoned towards the furs that I had brought.

There was a royal ransom there, but the Empress barely gave it a nod.

'I brought my own gifts ...' I began, but the man behind me tapped me on the shoulder and I fell silent.

'You seek service with the Emperor?' the chamberlain said at last.

I cleared my voice to speak. 'Yes, Lord.'

'How many men?'

'Two hundred,' I told him.

How are they armoured? What battles have they fought? Are you their leader? How old are you?

I answered all his questions.

'You know the cost?'

'Yes, Lord,' I said. Micklegard ran opposite to all I knew. Here a warrior had to pay the Emperor to take him on. 'I have also given one whole load of the white marten from me. A gift for the Great Empress.'

He consulted a roll of vellum, sniffed and nodded. At the end he said, 'The Empress Zoe accepts your service. Tomorrow you shall swear service, and you and your company shall join the Varangoi Outside-the-Palace.'

And then I was shown out, like a bull from the market ring, when its price has been fixed. The Empress never spoke, I realised. What kind of ruler was this, who let others talk for her?

My men were amazed to see me return. They were like children at midsummer as they leap the bonfire. 'Did she take your gift?'

'What did she say to you?'

'What was she like?'

'Will they give us silk to wear?'

I puffed out my cheeks and tried to describe what I had seen, and they listened like amazed children. 'We are to be made Varangoi Outside-the-Walls.'

'What does that mean?' Halldor said.

'I don't know,' I said.

'Did you send them Jaroslav's greetings?'

My face showed my horror. All the things I had learnt and

rehearsed had gone unsaid. I had done nothing that Jaroslav had charged me with.

Next morning we strode about the Hippodrome's eastern end and approached the Bronze Gates, but the guards stood as we approached, and barred our way.

'The Empress told us to come back tomorrow,' I said.

'Did she now?' The man who spoke was a Dane. He wore a silk cloak of blue and yellow stripes.

'Yes,' I said.

He looked at me. 'Varangoi Outside-the-Walls report there.' He pointed and I saw the next gatehouse, a long bowshot away. 'Are you the Norwegian, Olaf's brother?' I nodded. My men had talked, I thought, and readied myself for danger, but his tone softened.

'Have you heard about Knut?'

'What?' I said, trying not to tense up.

'A boat came last week from Frankia, and the captain said that Knut has died.'

'Dead?' I said.

He nodded.

'But he was still a young man . . . How?'

'Not battle,' the man laughed.

I puffed out my cheeks. That was what I had felt, I thought, when I sailed south. It was Knut's shadow not just leaving me, but the whole of Middle Earth. I laughed and then apologised, thinking the man was a Dane and might be related in some way, but he smiled and shook his head. 'Don't worry. It doesn't matter here whether you are Dane or Swede or Norse. We are all barbarians here. If you're quick there's a new expedition setting out this month. See if you can't join it. Tell them that Halvdan sent you.'

I was as light as a swan as I entered the barrack master's hall. It was just inside the lower gate, in a hall of brick and stone. The barrack master was a fat man, with a grey-shot beard, and broad, fleshy hands. He was picking his nose when we entered, and rolled it round for a moment before letting it drop onto the floor and then picked up a wax slab that he used for writing.

'You will serve in the Varangian Outside-the-Walls,' he said, scratching runes with a metal pick. 'We have four companies that are short. We will assign your men.'

'These men are bound to me.' He looked up. 'I am Harald Sigurdsson, son of King Sigurd, brother to Olaf. I am the son of a king. My men will not accept being broken up, going here and there, like a flock of sold sheep.'

I had lost all my fear now, but he gave me a look that said that there was nothing he could do, and I felt like a bride, who thinks that the day is about her, and begins to understand that her bedding and her maidenhead are in the hands of other men.

'Halvdan the Dane sent me,' I said. 'He thought my men could serve together. In the new expedition.'

The barrack master whisked at a fly with a horse-hair whisk. He clearly knew the name. He looked through his lists and sucked his teeth and shook his head, and sighed. 'How many men again?'

'Two hundred.'

He sighed again and tapped the stylus against his teeth. 'Then you will have to serve on Swein Blackbrow's dromons.'

'What is a dromon?'

'It is a ship of war. You'll see them. They have two banks of oars. Your squadron is led by the *Sanctus Nicolaus*. It's a good name. Saint Nicolaus came from my home town. He is a friend to sailors.'

I repeated the name. It felt strange to name a ship after a man, but it was the way of the Greeks, and it was good to have a friend in Heaven. 'But first,' the barrack master said, 'you must be trained.'

'Trained in what?'

'Signals. Orders. The way the army works.' He tapped his stylus against his teeth. 'I will send word to your ship. Now, swear your oath.'

'I thought I made it to the Emperor,' I said.

'You do. But you make one to me, with your hand over this cross, so that God is your witness.'

In the North when you swore service to a lord you stood before him and looked him in the eye, and he gave you a gift in return. I had played it out in my mind, and how, as I knelt there, I would repeat the greeting that Jaroslav had charged me with. Standing in a barrack master's hall was not the same. I was disappointed, and it showed.

Afterwards the barrack master gave me a brass token with Zoe's head on one side, and her husband Michael's head on the other. I looked at it. 'This is it?' It was bad enough to swear an oath to a clerk, but then to be given this paltry token in return. 'I have brought two hundred men, and they are warriors.' I clenched my fist and the cut stung, but I did not care. 'Warriors,' I said. 'Not serving men.'

'That is a token,' he said. 'You take that to the paymaster of your division. He will pay you.'

'Pay me what?'

'Your wages,' the barrack master said. 'Forty aureii a month.'

'What is an aurei?'

He handed me one. It was a golden coin. Astrid had a necklace of them, and other noblewomen had them as earrings or hanging from their brooches. It seemed good, I thought, though I did not show that I was satisfied. Greeks would take the milk from a baby's lips if they thought they could get away with it. They had no honour where gold was concerned. He held out a hand and took the coin back.

'So,' I said. 'Where do I find this Swein Blackbrow?'

The paymaster looked at me. 'In a wine house, I should think.'

'Which one?'

He shrugged. 'The Three Magi? The Flag and Lamb?' He pointed past the Hippodrome, over the tile-thatched roofs, to the south-west. 'Or maybe the Cross Keys. Ask for the Varangoi. You'll find it.' He looked at the sun, as if gauging the time. It was about two hours after noon. 'But I'd wait till tomorrow, if I were you. You don't want to meet him when he's drunk.'

*

That night, as the moon rose, Halldor and I and the best of my men strode along the Mese, and found it more busy at night than it was during the day.

Lamps were lit along its length, and where there had been bread and bean sellers, there were now men sieving wine from large pots, grilling meat over red coals, women with painted eyes and unbound hair stroking your arms as you passed. Figs had fallen and were rotting in the street; languid cats stretched out on the cobbles as if before a fire; we passed a chapel which rang with the deep sound of monks singing; a man with a child in his arms, stood with his back to us, looking into the chapel through a grilled window. Grapes hung about us from the vines which shaded the street, but it was still early summer so they were still green and small and sour.

I breathed it all in and felt joyous. In Greece a northern heart cannot walk long in the heat and the sunlight, and not feel lifted. Even at night it is so warm a man does not need a fire, and so we did what others have done, and found a little shop and learnt the word for 'wine', and then the words for 'more wine', and then it did not matter. We could speak any tongue that we needed.

The Greeks fed us platters of meat and olives and hot bread, freshly baked in the domed ovens at the back, and they knew how to celebrate.

I felt as though my cares had been lifted from me. I was here, in the heart of the world. Knut was dead, and the shadows of the past had curled up like fallen leaves under the Greek sun. This is civilisation, I thought. I wanted it all: the learning, the wealth, the wine, the stone-built cities. I was like Thor, whose horn held all the seas, who tries to drink it down. One life, I thought, is not enough to learn all that I could learn. And to crown it all, Knut was dead.

We clapped and cheered, the old lady of the bar came out and danced, and her husband joined her, and soon we were all up and clapping as we learnt the new steps.

CHAPTER THREE

Swein Blackbrow's Company

My mouth still tasted of wine next morning. I found Swein in his barrack-yard, sitting under a cypress tree on a low stool, his knees up to his chest, and beside him a wooden bucket with a rope handle and a dented beaten-brass pitcher. He was stripped down to his trousers, and his hair was gold and his skin bronzed and weathered. He looked at me with his one eye, reached for the pitcher and emptied it over his head. The water dripped down his scarred torso and the parched soil sucked it down like a dying man. 'You're Olaf's brother,' he said. It was not a question.

I nodded.

'Have you heard?'

'About Knut? Yes, I have.'

'Elfshot,' he said, which was what we called a sudden death. 'What do you think?'

'I wish I'd known he was about to die,' I said. 'Maybe I would have sailed north this spring, not south.'

He looked at me as if I were a fool, and looked about the yard. 'You would have missed this?'

I laughed. Maybe that was the point of Knut, I thought, to bring me here, to the centre of the world. 'No,' I said.

'That's what your brother did. He went back to Norway and look where that got him.'

'Maybe God sent him,' I said.

Swein laughed. 'Pah! A fig for God. Why would God have him go die in Norway? I bet he would rather be alive. I bet he'd rather be here, swimming in warm water, drinking warm wine, and holding a warm woman close to his side.' Swein reached for the pitcher again, and repeated the drenching. 'Your brother could have been a great leader here.' He waved his hand, and that gesture seemed to say everything he could not be bothered to express: slavewomen, silks, war, battle. 'Instead he went back to those farmers and fishermen, and they killed him for his trouble.'

'Perhaps it was his fate.'

Swein nodded. 'It is all our fate eventually. Serve with Jaroslav?'

I nodded. 'And three winters with Eilief.'

'Eilief's a bastard. I served him once and that was more than enough.'

'He kept me for three winters. I took twice as much tribute from the Chuds.'

'The Chuds,' Swein laughed, and leant against the table where his breakfast of bread and white cheese and black olives remained half-eaten. 'Hunters and cut-throats. You saw the Empress?'

I nodded.

'What do you think?'

He didn't bother waiting for an answer. 'She's an idiot. Frivolous. Nasty. Evil.' His gesture took in the whole city. 'Don't fall for the glitter. It's rotten. The whole place. They send us out because they can't get their own people to fight. They're so craven they pay money *not* to fight.' He paused. 'So, why should I accept you and your men?'

I was not expecting this. 'We are good fighters.'

He laughed. 'What did you think of Jaroslav?'

'He's a great man.'

'I never liked Jaroslav,' he said. 'Too much of a builder. The

Pecheneg king drinks his wine from Jaroslav's grandfather's skull. If I was Jaroslav I would tear the guts out of him, and throttle him with them.' He grinned, took the bucket and upended it over his head in a great shower and let out a roar of shock and pleasure. He set his hands on his knees, reached for the pitcher, and this time he offered it to me. I took it. He filled it with wine. We tapped our cups together and drank. He emptied his in one gulp.

The wine was strong, and so sour it made me shiver.

'Can't take your drink, huh?' he said, but I felt as though I had passed some test, and when he put out his hand I gave him my sword, hilt-first. He took it, paused for a moment to read the runes on the hilt, and nodded. 'Now, make your oath properly. Like a Northman!'

I put my hand on the sword and swore that I would take no other as my lord but the Empress and Emperor of Micklegard. That I would serve them and protect them, as long as they rewarded me with food and roof and honour.

'Good,' he said at the end, and we tapped our cups together. 'Welcome to Swein's Company.' He refilled our wine. 'How did your brother die?'

I told the tale as we finished the wine. I did not feel it so keenly now, I realised. I was free of its shadow here, where the sun shone so bright and so hot. He called his girl from outside. She was the kind of girl you would see hanging about the Hippodrome on an evening, looking for work. Dark-haired, dark-skinned, with kohl about her eyes, a simple white robe girdled at the waist.

She was pinning her tar-black hair up from her neck, and I could not help but notice that free within her robe was the swell of wonderful breasts: heavy, full, firm.

'Bring us more wine,' he said. 'Not from Demetrius, though. This stuff is shit. Go to Alexander of Ephesus. Get him to fill it from the pot on the top shelf.'

She took the pitcher from his hands and nodded and left. She had fine hips and bare feet, and I was a little sad to see her go. But I enjoyed her re-entry even more than her first, because she had seen that she had an audience now, and moved with the casual elegance of a black swan, carrying a wine jug and two silver-rimmed horns, such as we use in the North.

'Do you know what the Greeks call us?' Swein said as he filled our horns. 'The Emperor's Wineskins!'

We toasted each other and drank. Ten minutes later she was sitting on his knee.

'Look at these tits!' he said, and pulled down the top of her gown. 'Aren't they something?'

Her eyes were hot and lazy as she looked at me. She wanted to see how I would react. My cheeks coloured, and I was thankful for a beard. It seemed churlish to look away, so I paused to look.

'They are,' I said.

The girl kissed his cheek but her eyes were on me. She did not pull her robe back up.

I had not seen such a thing before, and he saw it in my face. 'This is Micklegard,' he said. 'You are cheap. She is cheap. We are all cheap. We are cheap and we all get rich. But none of us ever make it home again.'

I had fallen for Greece and felt wounded by his words, but I hid my feelings and made a promise to myself. 'I will make it home,' I thought. He took a handful of her flesh and I saw her frown.

'She does not care,' Swein said. 'I will die before her.'

She kissed his head again.

'I took her as a slave. But I treat her well. You should see how the Greeks treat their slaves. And the Arabs. They treat them like swine. With me, she is well looked after. If I die, and she falls to you, look after her well.'

I took his words seriously. 'I shall,' I said.

He took a swig of wine, and turned back to me. 'Where are your men?'

'I have them refitting the ships.'

146

He nodded. 'Enjoy the city while you can,' he said. 'I had my orders through from the palace this morning. We leave in five days.'

'Where to?' I said.

He poured us both more wine. 'Fuck knows,' he said. 'We just man the ships while the Greeks sail us to battle. You'll know the enemy when you see them. They'll be the dark-skinned bastards trying to put a spear in your gut.'

We emptied the jug and his girl got more. As we drank our way through that I twice caught her dark eyes watching me. Each time, she looked quickly away, and her cheeks darkened beneath her tan, and I thought she was lovely.

Her name was Helen.

CHAPTER FOUR

Pirates

Swein's Company was a mean-looking bunch: tough, cheerful, fierce as mountain bears in spring. But they welcomed us and my men mixed with them and found that some had relatives or friends or neighbours in common.

Dromons turned out to be small galleys with single masts, a high fighting deck, and underneath two rows of benches for the oarsmen. They were not particularly seaworthy, but the seas never were that rough, and we spent most nights beached somewhere, letting the tide ebb and flow. Next day we would push them into the blue water.

We could not sit and watch other men lifting the sails, so we helped them pull the sail up.

'Don't do that again,' Swein told me later that day, but I was a king's son, and he was not. 'We're warriors, not sailors.'

'Where I grew up we were both.'

'Well. You left there for a reason.'

'I did. But a different reason to you.'

I made a point of hauling ropes after that. It kept the men strong, and they could get bored sitting around waiting for battle. They turned to dice, and drink and bragging. It was better to keep them busy.

*

Sometimes the sea was blue and sometimes green, and it was always warm, and so clear that we could count the black spikes of the sea urchins on the seabed. And the water was warm as fresh milk. One night we found the ruins of an ancient temple. A few pillars were still standing, and the dark cedar beams had been roofed with canes and turf. It had been left in a foul condition by the previous cohort of Bulgars, but we cleaned it out, patched the roof and lit a fire. The wind was off the sea. I lay and smelt the sea, listened to the water slap the shore, the stream note changing slowly as rain fell in the hills, and I closed my eyes and thought of home, of my mother, standing in the doorway, and I slept better than I had ever slept in the lands of the Rus.

I had arrived, I felt, where I was meant to be.

They were joyous days. There were no Pechenegs to chase us. We were the sleek sailors, we were the masters of the seas, and yet there were always pirates to hunt down, like the rabid dogs they were, and kill. They came through the islands, burning, looting, raping, enslaving. Singly, for the most part, but I remember one day when I shaded my eyes and saw a black sail and turned our prow towards it, but then spied a second sail, and a third, and I knew that we had a real fight upon our hands.

My squadron had the best rowers, who were Armenians, and I promised them a share of the treasure if they got me there first. So Swein's dromons soon fell behind. 'This is our first real battle,' I told my men, and gave them a few lines of poetry to bolster their courage. 'You must make a fine display to show the others what mettle you are made of.'

Swein shouted at me to wait, but I waved back to him, as though I had misunderstood.

Halldor stood at my shoulder. He clearly approved. 'Why should we share the glory?' he said.

'Keep it up!' I called to the oarsmen, and they bent their backs and with each swing of the oar-wings we skimmed over the clear blue water. We were blessed that day. Dolphins rose up, as if carrying us on their backs, weaving beneath our boats and snorting gouts of steam into the air. That scent of dolphin breath took me back to the day I'd stood with Olaf, watching killer whales in the cold fjord water.

Never flee, I thought. Never fear.

I did not fear as a child, but I feared now. Only a fool feels no fear, though I would not show it. That is the mark of an experienced man. He knows fear and makes friends with it. It can drive you better than any other goad.

Our ships were better than the Saracens'. My squadron gained on them slowly through that morning as their captain lashed his rowers with a long whip. They were slaves, and slaves do not row as well as free men, but the Saracens were too foolish to understand this, like those masters who think they can beat a dog into loving them.

The first arrows hissed into the water about the ship. One slammed into the deck at my feet. It was only then that I called for my mail shirt. As it was taken out of the oilskin wrapping, I stood at the mast, tied my hair back from my face, lowered my mail shirt over my head, hitched it up and tightened my belt. It had been a long time since I had felt such battle joy. It blew through me like a storm, a shiver that ran from my groin to my shoulders. It was as if the world was mine now, to shape as I wanted. All I had to do was to reach out and grasp my future. The only limits were those I placed upon myself.

Foot by foot we gained ground. Now our sail stole the wind from theirs. For a moment they wallowed and I threw the first grappling hook. It caught on the second throw. I braced my legs against the strakes, and foot by foot I dragged the Saracen ship into our deadly embrace. It was the way that Olaf had taught me, hauling in a net.

I was the first to leap onto their boat and felt my men leap after me. The ships pulled apart again, but the grappling ropes groaned and twanged, and held, and battle was joined.

The first man was dark and hairy, with fierce blue eyes and bright white teeth. I killed him with one blow to his neck. The next two were short and skinny, but surprisingly strong. I batted away their scimitars and smashed the nose of one with my shield-boss, dealt the other a blow that shattered his skull-dome in one strike.

I strode ahead of my men with the wrath and noise of a thunderstorm that turned the air cold and whipped it into chilling gusts. The Saracens rose up like serpents all about me, a palisade of faces, furious, hemming me in. I gritted my teeth and hacked and slashed as their swords clawed at my mail. I felt a blade in my calf, a slash on my forearm. Something hit my shoulder – maybe an arrow, I could not tell. I was not dead, that was all I knew, and I roared with fury. I was Olaf. I was Harald. I was a thunderbolt from the North, I raged about me, cleared the ship the old-fashioned way, sought out their captain. He pushed men before him like an old lady, and when he leapt into the waters rather than face me his white robes billowed out and he floated like a jellyfish, even after my crew shot him with arrows and turned the waters about him red.

Each man chooses the manner of his death, I thought, and turned as Swein's ships caught up. His face was red with fury. 'You should have waited,' he shouted to me, but behind him on his boat I saw Helen – like a shadow, though not like Knut's, but a Greek shade, that offers shelter from the heat and the sun, a place where a man can sleep.

CHAPTER FIVE

The Inland Sea

Deck by deck, ship by ship, land fort by castle, we cleared the Sporades and the Cyclades of pirates, left nothing in our wake but smoke and squabbling flocks of black carrion birds. It was off an island named Ikaria, as we chased down three black-sailed Saracen galleys, that Swein took an arrow in the thigh.

When I saw him later that day, on a blood-splattered Saracen deck, he laughed at the wound, which had been washed with wine and bound with dried herbs and cloth. But the dart was poisoned, and he sickened, and a week later, as a nail-clipping moon rose above the dark sea, we buried him in holy ground next to a small white chapel, by a pale pebble beach.

His captain, Rolf Ironhand, took command, as was the custom. Rolf was not a daily drunk like Swein. He was a good man, and I liked him. 'I'll get you all home, lads,' he always said when he was with wine, as if that was what we all wanted from this world. He claimed Helen as his prize, and I envied him, but sometimes she would sit on his lap and look brazenly at me, and I would look away for shame.

Rolf never kept his vow to bring us home. He died that Yuletide at Lefki. It was sickness that took him, not an enemy blade. Helen sat with him as the flux wasted him away. I had thought she was a woman of little character, but when I saw how she cared for him I understood her a little better. She had her own kind of gentle, resolute spirit. She would have made a fine warrior, if she had been born a man. In the North she could have made a chief, like Hervor, or Aud the Deep-minded. But she thought like a Greek, and there were things that she could not do.

When Rolf died the women tended to his body as they did to their own, tying up his mouth to stop his soul returning, and washing him with oils and then swathing his body in a clean linen winding sheet. They prepared a meal of boiled meat with dried fruit and nuts, and then once his body was consigned to the earth, the wine was sieved from the great amphora, and carried in jugs throughout the company.

We had to select a new leader before we got too drunk, and I had only been with the company for a few months, but I put myself forward, not thinking to win. I have royal blood, I told myself. It would be shameful not to stand.

Swein's other two captains, Freystein and Grey-Gunnar, stood against me.

Grey-Gunnar spoke well, but he was an unlucky man, and everyone knew it. Freystein was a fearsome warrior, but he kept his purse strings tight.

'I am Harald Sigurdsson, brother to Olaf, who was king in Norway. I am of the line of Odin, who saved me from the mountains. I took command on the field when the Pechenegs attacked us. I led my men away from the clutches of those enemies. Each year my following has increased. Each year I bring more victory.'

'But what of Stiklestad?' one man shouted. 'Olaf lost that battle, or so I heard.'

I braced my feet, rooted them to the earth, and lifted my voice so that they could all hear. 'My brother lost the battle and his life,' I said. 'But he won a place in Heaven, where he sits on God's benches, and intercedes on my behalf.'

'And how old are you now, youngling?' one of Grey-Gunnar's men shouted.

'Do not ask a man's age. Ask him how many battles he has won and how many he will yet win. Here – ask Arnbjorn and Halldor! They have been with me since we took the Eastern Road. They are my brothers. Whoever stands with me in battle is my brother.'

I have seen the Greeks at their elections. A vote, for them, is a secret, hidden thing. They have a special pot with two chambers inside. Each man takes a stone and drops it into one side or the other, his hand unseen. But we kept to our northern traditions. Each man who wanted to be leader stood up and made a short speech, and when all were done, each stood behind his choice so that each might see who he had voted for, and that all had been done fair and right and in the open.

When all was done, Freystein had fifteen men. Grey-Gunnar had thirty. I had the rest. They were a great crowd. I didn't know what to say. I felt the weight of their expectation like a heavy sack that's dropped across your shoulders.

Arnbjorn slapped my arm. Halldor laughed. Freystein came over to embrace me. 'It seems to me likely that you will keep your promises to us, Harald.'

I gripped his hand in mine. Both grips battled against the other. 'I shall,' I said. 'And remind me if I fail.'

Grey-Gunnar shook my hand, but he was not happy. His cheeks were pink, and he could not look me the eye. But after one night's sleep, he let go of his hurt, and served me well. 'Maybe your luck will make mine better.'

I respected him because of that. He never challenged my authority.

My first action was to let the men divide up Rolf's treasures amongst them.

At the end, as they were already at dice, losing what they had won so easily, I thought of Helen. I had not gone to Rolf's tent to take her, so she came to me. She had thrown her cloak about her shoulders and head, and clutched it with one hand at her throat, the other tucked under the armpit, in a gesture of fear. 'I was Swein's,' she said. 'And then Rolf's. What now, am I to be given to the men, like a whore?'

'No,' I said.

There was the slightest change in her eyes when I said this. She lifted her chin as she spoke. 'Then what?'

'Where would you go?' I said.

She laughed. 'Where would I go. I would find another lord who would protect me.'

'Do you know of one?'

'Yes.'

'Where is he?'

She had drawn close to me by now. She put out a hand. It found mine. Her fingers were soft, and they wrapped themselves up with my own, till our two hands were a single knot. 'Here,' she said. Her voice was husky as she lifted the cloak just a little to pull my hand inside, and placed it on her breast.

I pulled away, not wanting to offend her. 'Let us first put Rolf's ghost to rest,' I said.

'He did not wait.'

I stood, and pushed her back gently. 'And he died soon after,' I said. 'If anything is worth having then it is worth waiting for. Sleep in my bed, if you like, so that none of the men trouble you. But I shall sleep on the floor until Rolf's spirit is rested.'

CHAPTER SIX

Harald's Company

In the autumn of 1035 we joined up with the rest of the fleet at Skyros, and drove the pirates back to the African shores. I had seven ships with four hundred Varangians, and whenever we came to a large port I found many more captains who asked to join me.

Many companies kept to the northern tradition of swearing a year's service to their captains. 'Are your vows up?' I'd ask them, and if the answer was yes, I would take them in, if not I would refuse to accept them and they would turn away, crestfallen; but I would try to cheer them up. 'Do not come to me as an oath breaker. Wait until your year's service is done. Then I will welcome you, and you will be able to hold your head high. There is no shame in keeping your word. Men trust others who hold their oaths dearly.'

I felt like a sea king as I led my own company to war, and it was during those years that I thought well enough of myself to say, why, if I can make myself king of these warriors who have all made it to the ends of Middle Earth, why not make myself chief of Uppland?

Or even the king of Norway?

It was a quiet thought at first, and I took little notice of it, like a child at court, that men pay little heed to.

There was wine, and Helen, and so many other wonders to

distract me, but the child did not go away. He was always there, just off to the side, playing with a kitten, watching, listening, biding his time, and slowly growing.

The Saracens kept to their ports over winter, so there was little fighting in that season, but as retainers of the Emperor we were expected to collect taxes and be the representatives of the throne.

In our third year we wintered in a place named Corinth, where I shared the season's plunder according to law. I gave the men their third, and sent the other two shares north: one for the Emperor and one to Jaroslav, who wanted books and crosses and other fine things for his new city. Or so I told myself. But already I was thinking that if I was to go home I would need a great treasure to win men to my cause.

The port of Corinth is half a day's ride from the city. We left our ships in the port, with a warrior guard, and looked along the dusty tracks that led to the great rock that dominates the land.

We spent the morning crossing a fertile plain that climbed through orchards and ancient olives, before switch-backing steeply up in the shadow of the ancient yellow stone walls. The cliffs stood almost sheer, and there was a bustling new city at the foot of the crag.

Helen told me that Corinth was famous for its silk. She was eager to see what was for sale, but as soon as we marched through the dark gates you could feel that the city was tense, like a place under siege.

The streets were narrow and winding, no wider than was needed for two donkeys to pass each other. Some streets were flagged with rough white marble, others a black stone that was common about the place, and here and there was an old pillar or pedestal, set into the wall or used as a flagstone.

As we tramped through the streets, our war-gear in bundles on poles on our backs and in the donkey panniers, the people's eyes clung to our backs like leeches. The chief citizens welcomed us formally, and showed us to our quarters high on the summit. I was glad when we reached the top of the crag, and shut the gates on them, and were alone. The summit was bare and rocky, with patches of dried grass that the goats had nibbled short. The well was clean, the slopes about us sheer.

A low wall ran about the circuit, and there were simple stone-built barrack halls and kitchens. Halldor scuffed through the dead leaves and the caked bird muck, and looked out through the shutterless windows and curled his lip.

'I thought this was supposed to be a good place to winter. It's a bit bleak,' he said, then turned about. 'And where's the bedding?'

I did not know, but the water tasted good, so I sent the men to the market to buy all that we needed: fresh straw, firewood, wine, grain, olives, cheese and pigs. 'And pay the market price,' I told them. 'We have to spend all winter with these folk.'

We cleaned out the quarters, burnt the rubbish, stuffed bags with the fresh straw, hung old sailcloth over the empty windows, and burnt all that was not needed in a great fire that could be seen across the plain.

When we were settled in, I sent a young Danish lad named Svarni, one of Grey-Gunnar's company, to buy a dozen goats, and to bring them back to be slaughtered. Our mood was low, and I thought that I would feast the men in style.

While he was out, I took my chief men down to the local church to pay our respects. Sailors and soldiers are superstitious folk, and we were both. It is always sensible to honour local saints. The people watched us come down from the rock with the same hollow eyes. I managed to get the priest to talk to us. He was a tall man, with an outsize mouth and ugly donkey teeth, but he was softened a little by my curiosity. All men like to talk of their home town, and he started to talk quite freely: how the church there was founded by St Paul himself, who spent many years teaching in the city, and went on to die in a lion pit in Rome.

We stepped inside the whitewashed church. The air was cool and dark and damp. The only illumination came from high, small windows, and brass oil lamps hanging from the rafters. Gold icons hung around the walls. They were the faces of Christ, of saints, of Mary. They held crosses, books, scales, shoes, ointment, a sheath of arrows, or branches of dates. Only one of them held a sword. It was the image of the winged warrior, dressed in gilded scale armour, with a red tunic and curling brown locks that hung, like ours, to his shoulders. His cheeks were shaven clean, but he did not look boyish, but hard and handsome. In one hand he held a sword, in the other a white banner, He looked like a man you would want to follow. But it was what he had just fought that caught my attention, for under his feet curled a subdued dragon, mouth open in despair.

The priest was at my shoulder. 'That is Archistrageos, the Archangel Michael. He leads the armies of Christ.'

'He fights a dragon?' I said.

'Yes. The dragon is the Devil.'

'I want to be there with him when he meets it.'

I took a gold arm-ring from my forearm and placed it before the icon, as a man does who takes service with a lord.

Afterwards, I said, 'My brother is a saint.'

He thought I had misspoken, so I told him the tale – how Olaf's enemies hid the sun as they worked their devil-magic.

'So you have faced the Devil?'

I nodded. 'He was in bear-shape when he killed my brother,' I said. 'He swatted me away as if I was a child. But next time, I think I could handle a bear. Next time I want to face him as a dragon! That would be a fight worth watching!'

He smiled indulgently. 'Well, you took your chance,' he said. 'Not many of us can say that. Be resolute and bold,' he said, lifting his voice so that all could hear. 'Take the battle to the enemies of Christ!' he said, and sprinkled holy water over us all, and as we were making our way back up the hill I heard the bells of the goats as they were driven to the slaughter. I could hear my belly rumble. As the day darkened the cauldrons were simmering and the amphoras of wine were brought up loaded onto the back of a cart drawn by two unhappy oxen.

The men rubbed their hands as they unloaded each jar and laid them in the wooden racks. I was keen to taste it, and had a jug brought to my room before it had settled. It had been sieved already, and was dark and purple in the horn. In the green glass goblets I had taken from the pirates, it looked black. I took a gulp and smiled. It was good stuff. Not the usual vinegar some men tried to sell to us, thinking we were barbarians.

'Give the wine merchant meat and bones,' I told the men, and they gave him a foreleg and a pair of goat heads to boil. Experience had taught me that it was not just the local saints you wanted to keep sweet.

The sun was girdled with purple as it set, and a chill wind blew across the bay, and made the stones about us moan.

We had our cloaks drawn tight about us and the fires stacked high, and the side-blown flames were just starting to catch as the first jug of lightly watered wine was passed about my captains. From the stable yard came the mounting noise of a cock-fight. Grey-Gunnar's men had a fine cream bird named Thorin. I heard that Halldor's men were to put their best bird up against it.

It was then that young Svarni dashed into the chamber. He was breathless, and I thought at first that Thorin had been killed, but he said, 'Sir! There's a crowd of townsfolk coming up the street. Hundreds of them!'

As I stood I could hear the hum as they approached, like a swarm of hornets. The noise grew steadily louder. Halldor already had his axe in hand.

'What if they come in peace?' Grey-Gunnar said.

I dragged my mail shirt from its woollen bag, and pulled it over my head.

It fell onto my shoulders and I belted it in place and took

Arnbjorn and Freystein with me. Halldor didn't need telling. He came anyway, with Tooth.

The crowd had stopped before the fort's ancient stone gates. My immediate thought was that one of my men had stolen something, or taken a girl by force, or that they had forced the straw-sellers to sell at too hard a price – these were the usual things that excited a mob – so when I put a foot onto the battlements, Freystein beat his sword pommel on the inside of his shield and I held out my hands for silence.

At last they stilled, like choppy water. 'What is wrong?' I called out. 'Have we dishonoured you?'

They started talking all at once until I motioned them to silence, and as they did not seem hostile to me I had the gates opened and went out to talk to them. Six or seven of their chief men surrounded me – well-bred men, well-dressed, fine sandals of calfskin – but all of them had the same look, their cheeks dark with emotion. Anger, fear, indignation – I could not yet tell.

As soon as they had come up, three or four of them burst into speech.

'Hush! Pick one man, and let him speak for you all, and I shall listen.'

They debated this for some time, and at last one of their number stepped forward, a lean grey-haired man with a close-cropped beard. 'My name is Gregoras. I am a quaestor here in Corinth.' He went on at some length with the compliments, and how since the death of someone I had never heard of, the law had been eroded, as the sea waves break down the great cliffs of the shore. At last he got to the point.

'There is a nobleman named Pardus who lives not far from the city. He has six sons and they are lawless as wild dogs. They do whatever they choose, and they beat men who resist them. He robs and makes us pay his taxes for him and no one stops him.'

I thought of Olaf, who had always upheld the rights of small farmers against more powerful men. 'Who is this Pardus?'

'His grandfather was cup-bearer to the Emperor. His family have a villa outside the city.'

'I will send word to this Pardus, and tell him that I want to see him. And then I shall hear both sides.'

My words were greeted with a stony silence.

'He will punish us if you do this,' the old man said.

I never found hunger bettered my thought, and I could smell the boiled pork, so my stomach grumbled as loudly as the people.

'No one will punish anyone until I have spoken to both sides.'

They clung to me, and my belly was a hollow pot, and I grew tired of it all and agreed to send one of my men. 'Svarni, go with these men. Take horses. Tell this Pardus to come to speak with me.'

Our bowls were filled with meat, and as we dipped in the spiced bread, Helen insisted on serving us all the wine. To the Greeks' horror we usually drank the stuff unwatered, and she had the sense to always add a cup or two of spring water. When she came to fill my horn I caught her with my hand, and she leant into me for a moment, before slipping away. I watched her move about the room, watched as she leant to tilt the jug, her arms dark and smooth, bare to the shoulder.

'More, my prince?' she said, and gave the hint of a smile.

It was a joke she had used since hearing my brother was a king.

I held my horn out to her and she filled it almost to the brim.

It was a strong brew they had in Corinth, I thought as I took a sip. We should take a load of amphoras with us in the ballast decks.

Night had fallen, a cold wind was blowing through the marble halls, and we were an hour into a second round of meat and broth when I heard a shout from the training yard and felt a cold finger of premonition touch the back of my neck. It was just a momentary thing, but I shivered for a moment, and remembered the great horned elk, blocking the mountain path, and my own voice steaming in the air about me.

I have to cross the mountains! I mean no harm.

Helen caught my eye and smiled. She could see that my mind had wandered. 'More wine, my prince?'

I held my horn out but did not settle. The noises were unusual. When they came into the room they brought Svarni to me in silence. His footsteps faltered. His hands held those of other men who stood about him, and they led him forward, like the horse that is to be sacrificed.

Helen put her hand to her mouth. I stood. There were gasps all about.

There were streaks of bloody tears down both of Svarni's cheeks. His sockets were hollow, the eyelids trembling like an unfeathered chick that has fallen from the nest. Both his eyes had been put out.

'You are standing before him,' one of Grey-Gunnar's men said to Svarni, and pushed the lad forward. Svarni held out his hands and stopped. He did not know where to turn, so I stepped forward, and took his hand, his own blood still wet on his fingers. I swallowed as his face found my direction. His eyelids were sunken. His face was scratched and bloody.

I felt sick. I had to clear my voice. 'Speak to me, Svarni. Tell me what happened? Who did this?'

His lips trembled, but my hands encouraged him. 'Pardus,' he said at last. 'I spoke your words to him, and he beat me. I told him that my commander would kill him for it. He flew into a rage. He told his men to rip out my tongue, but I bit their fingers so they said they would take out my eyes. I did not let them do it. I fought them, Harald.'

I put an arm about his shoulders. Halldor, Arnbjorn, Freystein, Grey-Gunnar all stood before me, and Helen, with the jug in her hand, clutching it as if it were her child.

It was my words he had spoken to this Pardus, my orders that had led him to this.

'I fought,' Svarni said again. 'But I could not stop them.'

I took the lad into my arms and held him, eyes closed so that the darkness could sink into me, let the sounds of breathing, of shock, of slow-mounting fury rise.

I was hot with wine as Helen helped me slide my mail over my head and handed me my sword belt, then gave me my helm.

'How could they do such a thing?' she said. 'He's only a child still.'

I said nothing, but Helen saw in the set of my jaw that I understood. Svarni was me, he was Helen, he was all of us who had been driven out – far from home and kin and country. He was a boy still, and we had failed to protect him.

Halldor entered the room, his feet scraping on the grit and reeds. 'The men are ready,' he said.

Helen reached up to kiss me. 'Be safe, my prince,' she whispered, and I nodded.

Svarni was sitting in the yard, shivering still with shock.

I touched his shoulder. 'Svarni,' I said. 'Will you ride with us?'

'I can't,' he said.

'Ride with us,' I said to him. 'Grey-Gunnar. Bring his mail and helm. I will lead you.'

I took his hands, and lifted him, and led him forward.

The townsfolk said that Pardus lived like a pirate in the hills, with a watchtower and slaves enough to till all his fields, and that they were as surly and violent as their lord.

I took two of my three companies: nearly two hundred and fifty men in all. There were torches on the city gateways, the flames flickering off into the darkness, illuminating a myriad of faces, some young, some old, all stern and nervous, and willing us to succeed. The townsfolk had given us horses to carry us, and we rode out in full armour, under the black-star sky, cold and clear and watchful.

The Corinthians crowded at the narrow east gate of the city, winter cloaks wrapped close about their bodies, fur hats pulled down to their brows. Their eyes looked different now. They no longer sucked at us, but gleamed bright with reflected fire.

Only one man walked, and that was me. I gave Svarni my horse, and I led it, going on foot, like a penitent.

Pardus's fort lay a few miles distant, on a rocky crag in the foothills of the mountains there. Someone had clearly ridden from the town to warn him, and as we crossed the plain we saw lanterns lit along the battlements, and his slaves welcomed us with clubs and the whirr and crack of slingshots that bounced about us, and caused more pain and cursing than harm.

My men dismounted, the horses were tethered in long chains, and we took our shields from our backs, found a bough of fallen tree, formed up in a hollow square about the men who carried it, and using our shields to protect the whole, we stove in his gates.

The bravest of the slaves put up a brief fight, but we cut through them as a man through children, and they fled into the night.

In the stable yard a line of fine brown Saracen coursers were saddled and ready with saddlebags stuffed with food and gold and wineskins.

'They expected us to wait till morning, like Greeks, as if our vengeance could wait,' I thought, 'or as if we could sleep with the image of Svarni's face in our dreams.'

I led my men to the base of the tower. A few large stones rained down on us, but we fetched the ram from where it had been dropped by the front gates.

'Peace,' a voice shouted down. From the light of the lantern he held he looked as though he had to be one of the sons – a handsome fellow with fair hair, a warm, curly brown beard, and pleasant words.

'I have punished the one who hurt your messenger,' a voice called down. 'We have gold we can give you. Let us speak.'

I was trembling with fury and lifted the length of timber myself, and called the others to shield us as we swung.

The door was small and stout, and firmly barred, and as we pounded on it we could hear it being barricaded from within with barrels and chairs. Lumps of carved masonry started to crash down about us, and one of the shieldbearers' arm was broken as he deflected a rock as large as a hogshead.

'Back,' I told them, and we retreated ten paces.

I had let my fury get the better of me.

'Peace,' the handsome fellow called down again, and this time he threw a handful of coins. They fell like hail, bouncing and shining in the torch light. There was gold there, and silver. 'There is more if you depart now in peace. Let us talk.'

No one touched the coins. I called my captains to me to discuss what to do. It was Halldor who said, 'Burn the door down.'

We got a fire going, then carried faggots, piled them around the doorway, and threw pots of olive oil against the wall. The oil caught and spat and dripped into flame, like the fat of a suckling pig roasted too close to the embers. They did not have enough water in the tower to put out our fire, and when they tried to drop an amphora on it from one of the windows, the long pot caught the tower's flanks and spun off course and crashed to the side, and the dark wine drained away as the flames licked higher.

By the time the half-moon had cleared the eastern peaks, the flames had done their work, and we smashed through the charred timbers, dragged the barricades away, and I led the men inside.

The first man to resist was a middle-aged slave with rolls of fat above his belt. I killed him with a single sword blow, and he rolled down the steps as I stepped over him.

The stairs wound up the tower. Each level was a single chamber, and as I appeared women screamed and shrieked and tore at their hair and rubbed ashes on their faces and covered their half-naked bodies with tapestries and cloaks.

I kept going up, killing two of Pardus's sons till I reached the top, where the handsome lad had a spear in his hand. He was no slouch, and cut my thigh with a spear thrust before I knocked him backwards over the battlements, and leant over to see him land head first on the rocks below.

Grey-Gunnar found Pardus and his remaining sons. They looked ridiculous as they were led to me, dressed as women, kohl smeared about their eyes and their beards shaved off in their haste.

It was plain which one was Pardus. He had a long head, small, low mouth, and eyes set one a little higher than the other. He would have been a handsome man, I thought, if it were not for the look in his eyes, which was hatred and fear.

I had Svarni led toward him. 'Did you do this to my man?'

He acted as bullies act, when they have found someone larger than they, and denied it all at first, then blamed one of his sons, and then begged for mercy.

Svarni gave me all the confirmation I needed. 'I know that voice. It was he who gave the order.'

Pardus squealed as I gave the order to have him brought forward. 'An eye for an eye,' I said, and called to Grey-Gunnar's men to hold him down.

Pardus would not lie down, so they kicked his legs from under him and pinned him to the earth with their knees. I led Svarni forward, helped him kneel and led his hands to Pardus's shoulders. After that they needed no more guidance. They felt their way, blind, to his neck, his cheeks, and then his brow. They felt for the corners of his eyes, the place from which all tears flow.

'Should I?' he said.

'It is what the Lord commanded,' I told him, and he pressed inwards.

We arrived back in Corinth as the next day was dawning, the smoke of Pardus's estate rising into the sky behind us.

Pardus and his sons came with us. We cut off their hands, and turned them over to the monastery, and let them try to heal their wrongs with the salve of prayer.

I visited Svarni every day after that, had physicians come and apply salves to his eyes, gave the monks of the local church gifts of silver so that they would pray for him, and I gave Grey-Gunnar an arm-ring.

Svarni was one of his warriors, and he had been dishonoured by the whole affair.

'What will you do with him?' Helen said to me that morning, when all the captains had gone to rest.

'I shall keep him,' I said. 'He is one of us. He is of the North. I will bring him safe home. I shall deliver him to his family.'

She smiled, but there was a sadness in her eyes.

'You have a home,' she said.

I nodded. That I did, I thought, and pulled her to me.

I have a home and a hall and a country, I told myself, and tried to picture them, but in my mind I did not see fjords and snow and mountains, but a blue sea twinkling in the heat of a Greek sunset. I smelt spices, I smelt grilling goat meat on the warm evening air, and I saw the *Sanctus Nicolaus,* silhouetted against the swift Greek sunset, waiting for tomorrow and a good wind.

Helen's head was against my chest. 'Would I like it?'

I laughed. 'Do you like the cold?'

'No,' she said.

I laughed. 'Nor I.'

I thought we were to winter in Corinth, but a fortnight later an urgent summons reached us from the command at Athens. The Moors were moving ships north to Crete. It seemed that they were chancing their luck on a battle. All Byzantine ships were to report to an island named Delos. I had never heard of it, but the Corinthians said it was a place of great omen. The old gods lived there, the gods of wine and sunrise and pleasure. They were glad to guide us, and so we hopped through the Aegean, from Kea to Kythnos to rocky Naxos.

The harbour was a rocky bay, with low stone houses stepping down to the shore. We arrived at an island named Delphos before the rest of the army and we had the place largely to ourselves. We walked among the ruins in wonder. There were stone lions, goddesses, warriors, a marble hand as high as a man is tall. I took Svarni with me, mounted on a mule, and described the places that we saw.

The spring sunlight was warm and gentle; the skies above us deep noonday blue.

Each evening, as we sat to a dinner of olives and bread and grilled goat I sent a pot of wine to each of my companies. Battle and death would come soon enough for many of us, and with each passing day the bay beneath us filled with many ships and men and accents; Greeks, Latins, Syrians, Varangians, Armenians, Romanians, Bulgars: all of those many peoples who paid homage to Micklegard with fighting men.

When the Grand Domestikos arrived from Micklegard he brought with him a state in miniature: scribes, paymasters, eunuchs, cupbearers, keepers of the inkstand, governors, minor commanders, stable masters, the keeper of the table.

They took over the houses along the harbour front, while the Grand Domestikos took over the church, and lived in the halls that the monks had built. We were all to report for duty, and when I reached the front the clerk was a tired-looking man, with heavy lids and a befuddled air.

He tapped his stylus against his teeth as he thought. 'So, you are the Varangian captain, Araltes Sigurdsson?'

'Yes,' I said.

'You shall join Strategos Cibirriotes' division.'

'Who is he?'

'He is the strategos,' he said. 'The general who leads.'

I was happy enough. Our worth had been recognised. We would protect the body of the strategos as if he were the Emperor. It seemed the reputation of Harald's Company had reached even to the ears of distant Micklegard.

As I walked back to our camp, in the ruins of some ancient Greek temple, Svarni was waiting with one of his guides.

His guide left him as I approached, and Svarni called out to me. 'Harald, may I speak with you?'

The fallen stones made walking awkward there, so I stepped over them and sat next to him on a half-buried round column.

'What is it, Svarni?'

'I have a favour to ask,' he said.

'Name it.'

'I want to fight in the coming battle. I want to be in the front line. I want to strike a blow against our foes.'

I sat for a long time, watching a squadron of triremes row into the harbour.

'I do not want to die an old blind man,' Svarni said. 'I want to die in battle. With my brothers. I want them to remember me fondly.'

I was glad that he could not see the tears in my eyes.

'If that is what you wish,' I replied.

'It is.'

We sat in silence for a while, and the wind blew from the north, and brought a chill to our backs.

'So be it,' I said, and led him back to Grey-Gunnar's camp, and after that I sent an extra pot of wine to Svarni's fire. He was only sixteen, but bravery does not grow with age, I've found. The young can be as courageous as the old.

CHAPTER SEVEN

The Battle of Milos

The Saracen fleet sheltered off Crete, a great island which lies a day's sail south of the isle of Santorini, then they threaded their way north, up through the Cyclades, burning as they came. The beacons were still burning on Naxos and Mykonos as the sun set into the burnished waters at our stern, and we cast anchor into the blue shallows off the lone rock of Antimilos, and waited. We could see the smoke on the far horizon, as the fastest skiffs sailed back and forth with tidings.

Half of all you hear in the marketplace and hearth-side is rumour, and more so in times of strife, so I held my own counsel and waited as the rest of our ships anchored along the same bar. Wherever the Saracens were bound, they would have to come up this channel. Clearly the Greek admiral thought the same, and so, on the third day, when the Saracen black-sailed boats rounded the stark white cliffs of Milos, our whole fleet lay in wait.

The Byzantines saved their dress sails for harbour and battle. Ours was red, with a white bar across the top, with three black crosses. We hoisted it up, hauled up the anchors with eager hands, put on our mail shirts, fresh from their oilskins.

Dawn came grey over the water, but the air warmed as the sun rose, and soon all was sun and sea and sparkle. The following breeze was light, but we let the rowers rest as we lined the deck with shields, cleared and scrubbed the castle and the foredeck, strung our bows, then brought up barrels of arrows and pitch and set the braziers to light.

The Greeks clustered about the general's flagship, many of them two-masted boats with sails emblazoned with the figures of saints. About them the Varangians and Armenians and Italians rode with their quartered sails, with red crosses.

I caught a sight of Svarni on Grey-Gunnar's ship.

It was a good day to die, as well, I thought, but said a prayer for him.

'Give him the death he wants, Lord.'

I did not look for a signal that he had heard. It was not a prayer for me, and prayers for other men fly straightest to Heaven.

I had left Helen behind, on Delphos, but I missed her now as a headwind blew into my face, and below us the rowers heaved against the swell, the wings of oars rising and falling with each beat of the drum.

The sea was dark blue, almost black. By the time the wind came round and the sails were raised, the rowers lay stretched out among their benches like spent hounds after a long day's hunt.

With Grey-Gunnar's and Arnbjorn's ship to my left, Freystein to my right, Vestein and Otkell right behind me, I waved to each captain, and they waved back. Their men gleamed with mail and helms, their spear-tips silver in the bright sunlight.

I sent a boy running to fetch wine. It came twice-mixed with water. I took the jug and gulped and then handed it to Halldor, at my side.

As we approached the oarsmen took up their positions again, and fitted their long oars into the locks. The drummer stood in the stern, before the captain's awning. He set up a steady rhythm.

It happened slowly at first, a few ships about us joining in, and then all of our ships were beating the hollow drums, like the heart-beats of the fleet gathering power and speed.

I paced up and down like a chained wolf. I wanted it raging, already, I wanted it to start, and shielded my eyes as the Saracens came towards us.

As the Greeks lit the dragon-fires on their ships, the stink of the black smoke filled our nostrils. The lead ships of the enemy were drumming as well, their voices rising, over and over, but I did not know what they were saying. I heard the wail of whipped slaves, the shouts of command. I smelt Greek Fire.

As we came within half a bow's length, the lead Greek ship, a great high-sided galley with three banks of oars, breathed fire like a dragon.

It was a narrow spray, a hundred feet long, that splashed on the water like a bucket of flaming oil, and kept burning. It brought screams of pain and fury as the living flames licked up the first ship, then the next. Flames crawled like rats up the rigging, chewed at sails till they hung in burning tatters, and rained embers onto man and deck. The Saracen ships wallowed and careered into one another, and the flames, like panic, spread. Nothing would put the fire out. It was a terrible thing to behold. Even men who dived underwater still burned. I saw them sink like stars into the blue water, their eyes and mouths open in horror and despair.

Still the beetle-black fleet came on, drums booming and men screaming and shouting their many war-cries – the Saracen general driving his men before him.

As the wind broke up their formations I signalled to my ships. Our heartbeats quickened, the waters broke white before our prow, and through the black ships I saw a giant's boat with golden swirls on the sail, a hundred oars each side, decks thick with black-bearded warriors, chanting together and waving their curved swords, and I knew it was the chief ship of the enemy.

I was awed by the sight of her decks, thick with dark warriors, and all thoughts of protecting our general were lost to me. I could not resist the chance to reap fame for us all. 'Their chieftain!' the Greeks shouted to me. They were in terror of his coming.

'Forward!' I shouted, waving to Grey-Gunnar and Freystein through the smoke, and took the drumsticks myself and beat out a rhythm that the rowers could only keep up for a short time. The black ships could not bring themselves about in time. We were surrounded but we ploughed forward and the enemy flagship rose like a cliff face before us and some of the crew men wailed as if we were to be dashed onto rocks.

Smaller black craft tried to halt our approach. They showered our decks with hailstorms of arrows. They slammed like fists into the ship timbers, snapping oars and making the boat lurch. I felt each blow reverberate through my shoes and up my legs as we slung wet cloths along the side of the ship, but still the *Sanctus Nicolaus* swept forward, wounded, defiant, fearless.

I started up the *Bjarkamál*, and the men all joined in, chanting with me.

Arise, awake! Not to wine or women, but to the game of war. Look now for Odin, the one-eyed wanderer. Where is the foe-chief, find and fix upon him your furious blows.

At the last moment the enemy's flagship turned and rammed *Sanctus Nicolaus.* I was almost thrown over the bulwarks, but held desperately on as the timbers beneath us groaned like a wounded beast and our ship started to list.

Grappling hooks flew and caught as fast as eagles' claws. I shouted to my men as they tried to row off us. It was like harpooning whales. 'Haul her in my lads!' I shouted, and we dragged the beast towards our embrace. The ropes strained with tension. One of them broke. 'We cannot hold her!' a man shouted.

I raged at him.

But he was right.

Sanctus Nicolaus was holed. Water was pouring into the lower decks.

This is a good day to die. My own words mocked me. I felt a sudden fury as our ship shook and breaking ropes whipped about like maddened serpents. All about me was smoke and black and the screams of dying men. For a moment I was back at Stiklestad, the storm of steel raging about me. Heathens leapt aboard my ship and I cursed their mothers, cursed myself for driving us into danger, cursed the luck that had snared me here.

'Olaf! Save us so that we may revenge your death!' I shouted, but all about me was smoke and black and the screams of dying men.

CHAPTER EIGHT

The Last Stand

There was no one left alive. I stood on the hull and said farewell to *Sanctus Nicolaus* as she wallowed in the waters.

My skiff was waiting. 'Quick!' the captain shouted up to me. 'The strategos said to come at once.'

I was parched, burnt, and bloody as I slid down the tarred hull, still wearing my armour. I was weary too, and do not think that I could have swum if I had slipped. I would have sunk like a rock, but hands reached up for me and pulled me in.

The boat was lean and light, and the twenty rowers were fresh, and heaved us through the debris of battle. All about me was a vision of Hell. There must have been ten thousand men drowned, their spirits lost in the waves, looking for land. Dead men were thick on those waters. They were mingled with barrels, chests, bits of charred sail, arrows, spear shafts, shields, boys. One man stood at the front of the boat with a pole to shove them aside, and they drifted past, face up, face down, facing their sins before the one who shall judge us all.

As the curtains of smoke parted, the Greek flagship reared suddenly up. Her timbers were charred, but she was hale and whole, and the dragon spout at the front of the ship was stained black with soot.

Somewhere I heard the sound of a woman laughing, and I thought of Helen and wanted her. I clambered up the rope and swung myself onto the deck of the Greek dromon. Strategos Cibirriotes turned as I was announced. I knew him from Delos. He was a fat man, who padded about the deck as if he had been born to sailing. The tight black curls of his beard had been freshly oiled that morning. It gleamed as he came towards me, slipping a paring knife back into his belt-sash.

He had to look up at me as I dripped a puddle of water at my feet. 'You are he?' he said.

I nodded.

'What is your name?' he said.

'In my country I am known as Harald Sigurdsson,' I said. 'My father was king over my people. My brother was king as well.'

'Come. Eat. Tell me all!' Cibirriotes sat me down on cushions. He tossed glossy dark dates into his mouth and let me tell the tale.

I told him how, as soon as we had been holed, and the flagship was pulling away from us, I knew my ship was doomed and swung myself up, caught a leg over their strakes and dragged myself over as they stabbed at me with spears. But the mail shirt protected me as I batted them away and stood my ground.

'We're coming, Harald!' my men shouted from behind and below. I heard the shouts as some of them were knocked back overboard, and set about me to clear a space for them.

My mail shirt saved me, just once of many times, snagging their sharpened tips from wounding my flesh. It seemed as if I stood alone for hours, but then I felt a man behind me, and knew it was Halldor long before I hear the axe thud of Tooth.

We were like giants to the foes, beating them back with great swings of sword and axe, while more of my men came clambering up behind me. I was Death that day, dressed in bright mail, my sword smoking red with blood, but the fighting was furious and relentless and soon my muscles burned. I did not think it was possible to lift my sword arm for one more strike, but I kept hacking down because it was death to stop, even though their numbers seemed endless, and behind them I could see their captains, lashing more bands forward with whips, and killing any who would not fight.

Grey-Gunnar's ship hit the foe amidships and snapped her oars like kindling. The boat tilted, like a ship in a storm and we all staggered sideways. Somewhere above the tumult, I heard Svarni shouting, 'For Harald! For Harald!' and his voice was like the gale from the north that fills the longship's sail and drives its oak keel through the dark waters.

At last their general appeared. We had piles of dead to climb to meet one another, walking on decks slick with blood. He was a tall man with big eyes and a hooked nose, like an eagle. His gold-worked helm and white horse-hair plume were bright in the sunlight, but in his shadowed eyes I could see fear.

Yet he was fresh while I was weary. He slashed at me, and I at him. My mail protected me, his scale mail him, but despite my fatigue my blows begin to tell, and when I landed a heavy blow on his shoulder I heard bone crack and saw his face turn pale and his shield arm fall useless. That was brutal work. I landed another blow on the same shoulder and his white teeth ground out curses, but I kept hitting the same arm, till he could barely defend himself. He cursed me as I stepped in close, and caught his head by the helm-strap and swung down.

In a moment it was done. I staggered as I held up his head, white horse plume and all, and knew that we had won this day, and as I faced the cheering ring of faces I looked hopefully for Svarni's face among my men.

But he was gone ahead, on the road that all men travel in the end. He was not among the living any more.

'If only you had taken him alive,' Cibirriotes said at the end of the tale. 'I could have paraded him through the Hippodrome. Just imagine how the plebs would have roared my name.'

He gave me a Saracen sword with a golden hilt, but I was too weary to speak, and the thought of parading an enemy through the streets like a slave seemed foreign to me then. My mood must have shown this, so in the end he feasted me, gave me well-watered wine, and sent food to those men of my company who still lived.

I gave away his other gifts, a third for my men, a third for the Emperor and a third for me.

Arnbjorn of the Olaf-eyes had been killed I learnt. So had Grey-Gunnar's banner-bearer, and poor Svarni. Men said that the blind boy led the charge off Grey-Gunnar's boat, and killed three of the foes before he was struck down.

I found Helen in the women's camp on Delphos, a week later.

It was for her that I fought. She was Greece for me and I felt my pulse quicken as she put her hand to her mouth when she saw me, and then ran to greet me and flung her hands about my neck.

'I heard you were dead,' she said, and I realised that she was crying and held her out and laughed at her as she wiped the tears away with the heel of her palm.

She hit me with her fists, and we both laughed, and later that night, when the men had found their girls, and the dead had been remembered, and the food and wine were done, I took her to bed, and afterwards we lay as one, her head on my chest, my hands on her back, as the sweat of our bodies cooled.

'They swore you were dead,' she said again. 'I did not want to believe it. But men were sure, the *Sanctus Nicolaus* was sunk.'

'Hush my dark dove,' I said and pulled her tight to my side. 'The battle is done.'

Next day I rose late, and found an imperial messenger sitting outside, drinking a cup of wine with Freystein. He stood as I came out and held out his hand.

'My master has good news,' he said. 'You are to sail to Cyprus tomorrow.'

'Is there war there?'

'No,' he said. 'But the wine is very good. Cibirriotes has recommended you for this. You must be there within the week.'

My men were not happy. Nor was I, to speak true. I had lost many of my warriors, and hoped I might pick up some new captains as the fleet disbanded.

The winds were not helpful for the sail north, but we made the crossing in three days and rowed into the rocky harbour. A ship was there, with blue- and red-striped sail, embroidered with the face of Holy Mary. Everyone stood in awe. Helen came to stand next to me. She wanted to warn me. 'Harald,' she told me, 'only the imperial family travel in such ships.'

I looked. There were Varangians on board, with the unmistakable red cloaks of the Palace Guard.

'Oh Harald,' Helen said, holding my hand with her own. 'You have been summoned by the Emperor himself!'

I was giddy with excitement as we moored alongside the imperial craft. The nearest Varangian was a short, good-looking man, with small, shining eyes. He said his name was Ake. He was Hoplitarkes of the Varangians Inside-the-Walls.

'Whose ship is this?' I hailed him.

'Theodora's!' he shouted back. It was good to ask a simple question and get a simple answer in return.

I was disappointed. 'Who is she?'

'Sister to Zoe.'

Ah well, I thought, so the Emperor had not summoned us, but his wife's sister instead. This would at least be interesting.

His men took our ropes and lashed us to the shore. When I stepped onto the harbour side, he was waiting. 'So, are you Harald Sigurdsson?'

'I am!'

'Greetings. I am Killer Ake!' He spoke as if I should know him. I did not, but he seemed friendly, so I waved back and he cupped his hands and called out, 'We have heard of you.'

180

I laughed. 'What have you heard?'

He laughed in turn. 'We heard you killed a Saracen chief.'

I nodded.

'Are you a religious man?' I nodded once more. 'Good. Have you not heard?' Killer Ake laughed and clapped his hands together. 'So, you have not heard. We're going to Jerusalem. The Holy City. Where Christ was crucified. Where he rose into Heaven.'

I cannot remember how I reacted. It was like learning that a place you have always thought of as a myth, or a high crag on the mountains, impossible to climb to, is just around the bend in the road.

He kept talking, and I realised I had missed half of what he'd said. 'What stonemasons?'

He repeated himself. 'At Acre. They're going to rebuild the church where Christ lay dead. You escort them.' Killer Ake winked. 'We get the princess.'

I remembered all that I had heard of Zoe in the drinking-houses and brothels and barrack yards. That she had rotten black teeth from the sweetmeats she loved, that she dyed her hair black, but that it was grey as the sea. That she was barren, and jealous, and unfaithful as a bitch-hound. So I imagined the sister would be like her – old, fat, withered – and I laughed. 'Lucky you.'

He caught my meaning and smiled. 'Oh,' he said. 'You've not seen Theodora then.'

'No,' I said. I had not yet taken the measure of him, and did not know if he was one of those little men who talk big. We stood in silence for a moment, then I said, 'So. Is the land between here and Jerusalem safe?'

Killer Ake slapped my arm. 'If it was safe the Emperor would not be sending three hundred Varangians to make the journey!'

CHAPTER NINE

The Holy Land

We barely saw Theodora. She went in a sedan chair that was slung between four horses, and remained curtained all day, attended to by her chamberlain and maids.

As we marched down the coast Theodora let it be known that she wanted us to clear out the bandits, so that poor pilgrims might follow behind without violence.

I heard her say the words through the closed curtains of her sedan. Her voice was deep for a woman, and from the bare glimpse of a sandalled ankle, a long and shapely foot, the skin pale for a Greek, I began to assemble a picture of the whole.

In my mind she was shapely as a gazelle, and as spirited as well, too good to lock up in a nunnery.

The Holy Land. How we laughed at that name. I cannot think of a more benighted place. The writ of the caliph did not extend here. The locals were a law unto themselves. The land itself was treacherous. It bred men with the tongues of snakes and the hearts of jackals.

Men still tell the tale of how we scoured the coastal roads of bandits and towers and hideouts and caves, and by the time Killer Ake and I reached Jerusalem, we began to see a trickle of holy Christian men and women – footsore, wondering, weather-stained – whose way we had opened up once more.

We found lodging in a caravanserai on a narrow street that smelt of thyme and freshly baked bread. On one side worked a row of silver-beaters. They sat on the floor, bent-backed and tap-tap-tapping on little anvils that they held between their legs. On the other side lay a Jewish temple and a monastery for a people who are named Ethiopians and whom I celebrated a few hearty feasts with. They live just above the fires of the South, have skin as dark as a cow's, and laugh and sing and drink mead like Saxons. We told each other many a long tale and let our faces and the tone of our voices do the telling. It's easy when you're drunk. Wine is a common language.

The caravanserai was a massive square building, four storeys high and set about a central courtyard. The best rooms were at ground level. They had high windows, mosaic floors and walls of plaster with bold scenes of birds and plants. That was where Theodora stayed with her monks and priests and palace guards. We did not see her much. Ake had all the imperial duties to perform. He was the Varangian Inside-the-Wall. We were just the warriors.

I had brought Helen with me. She had been with the company longer than half of us, and she knew us all by name and habit and humour. It would have felt strange to leave her behind.

That first night she had set up a curtain to screen off our bed. She had found a boy – a pretty young lad with cow lashes, long and dark – who rode a donkey slung with water-skins. He brought it fresh from the spring, he promised.

'It had better be,' I told him, and he pointed and smiled.

'It is cold. Straight from the spring. Clean! Good, you try it!'

I took a sip. It was. He grinned at me. 'Tomorrow I bring more?'

'More,' I said. 'Samesame. No river water!'

He went out rattling the coins I had given him in his closed fist.

I used a jug of water to clean the dust from my body. The water was refreshing after the long heat. I tipped jug after jug over my head, just to feel its cool fingers run down my shoulders and sides and thighs. I was all muscle then. Lean as a wild lion that spends its time hunting gazelle among the rocks.

As I washed, Helen threw the shutters open and looked out. The day was funnelling westwards into night. All the colours were slipping down, leaving a pale blue sky, and the silhouette of domes and towers and temples.

Sunset was on her. It made her skin dark, warm, youthful. She turned to me in that gloaming half-light. 'Did you ever think you would come here, to the Holy City?'

I set the jug down and laughed. 'I never thought I'd come to Greece!'

She turned her face back to the sunset and breathed in deeply. I joined her at the open shutter.

'Can we go,' she said, turning to me. 'To where Christ died. Please?'

'Now?'

She nodded quickly. 'I would like to pray.'

Half the men were out already, drinking, seeing, whoring. The other half were bent over a game of dice.

'Who wants to come to the church?' I called out to them.

My men looked up. Halldor had a hard, tight-lipped look on his face, while a young Orkney lad named Eirik was clearly winning.

'No?' I said.

None of them were interested so I went with Helen. Neither of us knew the way. We stopped an Ethiopian monk and he pointed along the street, but each street was bent and confused as an old man's rope-work, and we soon gave up and just wandered the streets and alleys.

The night air was warm. The stalls were lit with oil lamps, and the scent of grilling meat rose on the air. I thought of my parents, my brother. All those who had taken the faith of the Nailed God to their hearts, and here I was, walking the very stones that he had once trodden.

It made the skin of my back tighten for a moment as the thrill ran through me. It was like a baptism of cold spring water. The feeling never left me. You could not walk through those streets without sensing God. Not a god of mountains and streams or snowstorms, such as I had felt on the Keelbacks, but a God of cities and books and learning, a God who had conquered Death. That was a fight worth winning, I thought.

When we found the place where Christ had been crucified, I had expected to see ruins, but there was nothing but an empty courtyard, strewn with odd heaps of old stones, ferns growing from the cracks in the bare rock, and a few tiny clay oil lamps set in recesses, their flames guttering in the wind.

'This is it?' I asked the man who had brought us. We paced about the cracked rocks, where small weeds grew among the goat droppings.

Helen translated. 'He says that this is it. He says that there was a church here when his mother was a girl. It was pulled down by the Caliph's father. He says they dug out the foundations, right down to the bedrock.'

'Where exactly was Christ crucified?' I asked him.

He led us to the spot. He stood and pointed to the hole in the ground which held the cross.

'He says it was here,' Helen said. 'This is the place.'

I knew it. I felt it within me, and I found myself kneeling and turned and saw Helen beside me, her dress pulled up so that her knees were bare on the ground where Jesus bled.

As we stood, a file of dark-robed Latin monks came up a side street, singing words I did not understand. My throat tightened. I smelt frankincense and found my eyes pressed shut, and words tumbling clumsily out in prayer.

'God, my Father,' I said. 'Make a place in your hall for Olaf. My father Sigurd, and my brother Guttorm. My mother also. She is a tall lady. You will know her when you see her. She looks like me, men used to say.' I stopped then. It is customary for a man to ask God for a gift or blessing for themselves, but I did not know what to ask.

I backed away from that place of death and victory and the rending of temple curtains and a voice said, 'What did you ask for?'

I knew the voice, though I could not place it. It was deep and assured, and I looked up in a moment of confusion and saw a tall woman standing before me. She was swaddled with fine silks, gold hoops stretched her ear-lobes, and her large dark eyes had been painted to look larger.

I was dumbfounded for a moment as I put the Theodora of my imagination against the evidence before me. They were similar, to be sure, though my imagination had added an extra curve here and there, and the real woman was older, leaner, and as her dark eyes glittered I thought she was laughing at me, and was suddenly conscious of my barrack Greek.

When I told her what I had asked for she nodded. 'It is what my father always said, "By their petitions shall you know them."' She paused. 'He always asked for a son to be his heir.'

She turned away and I saw that her priest was hurrying up to intercept us, and realising I only had a few more moments to talk with her, I said, 'Did he enjoy ruling so great a kingdom?'

She turned her dark eyes back on me. 'No,' she said. 'I do not think he did.'

I wanted to ask more, but her priest touched her arm as if to tell her to come. She took his hand and squeezed it and then laid it aside, as she might do to a naughty child, but he would not leave and I could see that she did not want to argue in front of me, and bowed and left.

'Did you feel God there?' Helen said to me that night as we lay in our room, and the sound of snoring rose and fell from the men of my company.

'I felt something,' I said.

There was a long pause. 'I felt him. I felt his pain.'

Her fingers were on my chest. I could feel that she wanted me to say more, but I did not know the words to describe how I felt. 'I prayed for the souls of my family,' I said at last.

'I prayed for all of us. I prayed for you. Did you pray for me?'

'Yes,' I said.

The air was still warm, even though the sickle moon had risen. Its light fell in a square of white upon the reed floor. Neither of us could sleep.

After a while Helen sat up on one elbow. She pulled herself up to my head, and kissed me.

'Thank you,' she said.

'For what?'

'For bringing me here.'

She kissed me and put her head on my chest.

'Do you feel it?' she said.

'What?'

'Lighter. He has taken the weight of some of my sins.'

I laughed. 'What sins do you have?'

She sat up again, her hair falling dark over one bare shoulder. 'We all sin. Lust,' she said, meaning us, in bed.

'This is not lust.'

'Pride then.'

'It is not wrong to be proud.'

It was her turn to laugh. Her God was different to mine. Hers spoke of humility, forgiveness, faith. Mine was a warrior, proud, resolute, defiant in the face of darkness.

Greek rulers locked themselves away from their people. It was not our northern way to build walls of stone and custom and ceremony between us and our folk, and Helen was always in awe of Theodora, and kept silent when she was around.

I had no such qualms, and after I had spoken to Theodora, Helen treated me as if I had just spoken to Christ, or the Archangel Michael.

'What did she say to you?' she asked me.

'Not much,' I said.

She gave me a look as if to say 'How can you be so calm?'

I reminded her that my brother was a king, and she nodded and snuggled into my shoulder. 'Zoe is barren. All the empire knows it. She's been through three husbands already, and keeps Theodora locked up for fear she will marry and have children.'

It seemed a shame. Not for the first time, God had sent the children out into the world in the wrong order.

Helen kissed me as the scent of spices rose to our window. She lifted me onto her as a drunk man sang in the street below us, his voice rising as he came towards our window, and then receding as his footsteps led him away.

Afterwards, as Helen slept, her head on my chest, her fingers twitching in her dream, I smelt the oil in her hair, the dust on her skin, watched the moon's light cross the floor of our room.

You are the Varangian captain, Araltes, her words had been. And as dawn came to summon me back from dreams, I lay for a long time, entwined with Helen's naked form, thinking of Theodora.

CHAPTER TEN

Theodora

My men and I did all the things that visitors to the city must do. We went to the place where the good Samaritan had helped the wounded man. At Gethsemane, the place where Jesus and his retainers fought off the warriors of the priests, we sat under the olive trees and chanted the tale of Hrolf Kraki and Hrothgar. We were baptised in the River Jordan. At the place Christ was brought back to life, we walked into the cave and touched the walls, the rolling stone. I even lay in the place where Jesus had lain, and closed my eyes as if in death.

Only about ten of us made our way to the place where Christ had fought Death and beaten him. 'You do not want to see?' I said to Halldor, but he and the others were bored.

Killer Ake had bought a puppet on strings, and the men were clapping out a dancing tune as he made it leap about. 'I'm sick of ruins and places where Jesus did this or that,' he said. 'What did we come south for? To carve our names on old stones?'

Each morning Theodora's servants were up two hours before any of us. They fed and brushed the horses. Readied her clothes. Donned their armour.

The noise of their feet, shuffling with sleep; the tall groom with the hacking cough – his hawk and spit and cough again; the low voices of the women as they used the hems of their skirts to waft the embers back to life; the smell of sweet resin kindling smoke. It was to these that I woke each morning, and lay, eyes closed, and waited for the sound of her priest coming from his own prayers to join in hers.

He had a high, almost girlish voice. 'Slept well?' he said each morning to the guards who slept across her threshold. He never failed to laugh at his own joke. The guards laughed too. Eventually I found myself lying awake and smiling with them.

Once or twice I went with Ake and his guards to the place where Christ had died. The local caliph had given us permission to bear weapons within the city, and Killer Ake and I would rest a hand on our long axe shafts. 'Here they come,' he would say, and as crows descend on a freshly mown field, the boys and young men of the city would come and stare at us.

They had never seen our like. I was taller by a head at least. The thing that amazed them most was our trousers. The bravest of them would walk up and tug at the cloth, to see how it was sewn together.

'Off!' Killer Ake said, and slapped their hands. He couldn't stand being pawed. I did not care. We were wholly strange to them, and they to me. They marvelled at our beards, our laughter, the sound of our words. Sometimes they would mimic us – *riff raff ruff,* the brown-eyed children would say, and pull fierce looks, knitting their brows together, and look stern.

Sometimes we would frown at them to scare them off. Other times, after breaking fast, and much more so in the last weeks, when we knew we were soon to leave, we would laugh with the children.

We had brought fifty masons with us from Cyprus, and they had already set up their tents and lodges. They had their own smithy for their chisels, and were examining the cliff face for stone to quarry.

One day Theodora finished her prayers, and came and spoke to

Ake and me. 'The masons have already started work. Christ will be pleased, I am sure. Now, it is hot. Let us go back.' She always spoke like that, as if it had just crossed her mind, as if we had a choice in the matter. Let us go back, she would say, and we would retrace our steps.

It was like a great wedding procession each day. When we got back the horses were unsaddled, and brushed and fed. We walked back to our fellows, stripped off our mail, and joined or watched them dicing, snoozing, telling each other tales.

All this theatre is for her, I thought, and understood how the empire took so long for anything to be done. If I were a king, I thought. My childish dream had grown and lost his chubby looks.

'Halldor,' I said, one day. 'What if we went home to make ourselves kings?'

'"We"?' he said.

'Me.'

He snorted. 'You're not rich enough yet.'

'No?'

He shook his head. 'You might have enough to make yourself king, but how long do you want to stay king for? A year, two? Your brother lasted twelve, and how much did he bring back? And chiefs want more now. And their wives. They will not take hack-silver any more. They want well-worked gold.'

Helen was sewing a hole in my trousers. She ran the thread between her pursed lips as Halldor talked. Our talk was strange to her. The Greeks did not choose their kings like this. They were granted to them by God.

As we spoke a shadow from the doorway fell into the room. It was Killer Ake. He leant against the post and nodded to Helen. 'Harald. What are you doing tonight? I'm a guard short.'

'I could send one of my men.'

'I think she wants you,' he said. 'She asked especially. At least, I think it's you. She couldn't remember your name. "The tall one," she said.'

'Fine,' I said and yawned, as if I did not care, but the rest of the day Helen and I were giddy. 'She might talk to you again,' Helen said. 'You could ask to join the Varangians-Inside-the-Walls. Oh Harald! We could live inside the palace.'

She insisted I did what the other men did when they were summoned to Theodora's company. I went to the baths and was rubbed and scrubbed, my hair was oiled, I dressed in clothes that Helen washed that morning, rubbing and slapping them on the stones by the well, and hanging them over the warm rocks to dry.

Theodora's chambers were on the bottom floor. They took up a whole side of the caravanserai. When I stepped inside I understood now why we had over a hundred mules to carry the iron-bound chests. Brass lamps cast faceted light and shadow about the room. The walls were hung with fine rugs and embroidered clothes. There were red rugs on the floor, and there were stands of fine carved wood and ivory, and a prayer station with an icon of Mary and the God-Child.

I stood at the back with six other Varangians, and watched and listened and took it all in.

Theodora had a couch of her own. Her guests were local Christians, Greeks who professed loyalty to the Byzantine state. They were here to discuss how best to finance the church that she was going to build. They lay on carpets and cushions on the floor and she encouraged the men to eat and drink. As I stood there, keeping my own council, I day-dreamed what I would do if I were king. I would bring stonemasons from Frankia and Cologne to build stone churches for me. I would bring all the wonders of the South to my people. Learning, books, churches, stone walls. I would make the poor land rich, the cold seas warm . . .

At the end of the evening her priest saw me out and she did not even turn around. She was born to this life, I thought, she does not even notice us, and I thought that would be that, but I stood guard twice more. By the third time she caught my eye as I watched her, and I blushed and looked away. But a few days later one of her ladies came to me and asked me to go up to her.

'The mother wants you,' she said. The maid was older than Theodora, but it was a term of respect they used for her.

'Tonight?' I said.

'Now,' she whispered.

I made a face and passed my bowl to Helen. 'Like this?'

She waved a cloth at me, and I understood she meant yes.

I gave Helen a look and she raised her hands in a gesture that said, 'Go, you fool!'

It was an hour after noon. The sound of the Saracens, calling from their holy buildings, began to rise into the air, first one, then another, like strands of goldwork, one serpent twining with another.

I suddenly thought that I should bring a gift as well. I cursed myself for not thinking of this earlier, but there was a market nearby that I had seen, where they sold bright birds that sang the sweetest tunes, and so I grabbed what coin I had, and dashed through the crowds that were heading to their churches.

The stalls were quiet this time of day. Some of the salesmen were already packing up. I looked along the stalls where the blue and yellow and orange birds sat and trilled from their carved cages, and could not buy one. Not even a bird of blue and yellow and red, which turned and looked at me with a single black eye, and said, 'Sallam', which is the word the Moors use to greet each other.

Theodora's own life seemed too close to that of the caged birds. I walked along to where the cages ran out, and stopped and sighed. I needed something special. How often did a man meet the heir to an empire as vast as hers?

There was a man with a yellow and green snake curling about his arm; another with a pair of sulky peacocks who would not display; a man with yellow-eyed cats, and at the end a spotted cat with a plaited leather collar, long whiskers and milky blue eyes. I saw its tail first – it was very long, and lay along its side, the end flicking in displeasure.

I bent down to ruffle it behind the ear and it stood on its hind

193

feet and hissed at me, a soft sound, almost like the hiss of a snake. When I reached out a hand it hissed again, and batted it off with a forepaw.

'How much is this one?'

The salesman was talking with another man about something, and I had to ask twice for him to hear. He answered me, and I presumed I had misheard. No cat could cost so much.

'I will take it,' I told him, and the man made a face as if to say, 'Are you sure?'

I nodded. I wanted it. Alone among all the other animals here, this one had a royal, fighting spirit.

The salesman kept talking to me, and held out his hands as if to say, this cat will grow as big as a dog, but I was done and felt sick as I handed over two months' worth of coin, and thought to myself, I shall not tell Helen how much I paid for this.

I cradled the cat in the crook of my arm as it kept hissing at me. It had teeth, but it was too young to hurt, and somewhere along the way back it did not bite me but licked me instead, and I knew that I had found a beast with a noble heart.

The maid was scowling at having to wait, but as soon as she saw the beast in my arms her wrinkles puckered and she put out a hand and let it hiss at her, as it had to me, and stroked its head, and I felt the vibrations as it began to purr.

'Does it have a name?'

'The man called it "Fad",' I said. She nodded and gave it another rub before a voice from inside called her.

'Yes, Ma'am,' she called. 'He is here.'

I waited outside as the maid went in and the curtains fell together. I knew the two Varangians on the door. They were both older than me. One of them winked. I smiled. I felt a little silly, to be honest. They both wanted to touch the Fad.

'Is it a lion?' one asked, but the other shook his head.

'Lions do not have spots.'

The maid returned and beckoned to me to follow her, and as

I stepped through the doorway she announced me. 'Mother. The Varangoi named Araltes is here.'

Theodora was lying on her couch. Her priest was standing at an open book, humming absent-mindedly to himself. He stopped as I entered, darkening the door for a moment. Theodora did not look up. 'You may leave me,' she said to him.

'Lady,' the priest said, and bowed.

Only then did she look up. 'What is this?' she said.

'The man called it a "Fad". I think it is like a lion. It is a gift, for you.'

She looked at me and laughed. 'We call it a leopard,' she said, and held out her hands to take it. 'Is it for me?'

The leopard cub hissed at her as she turned it onto its back and stroked the fur of its belly. 'It is so young,' she said. 'We should find some milk.'

A little meal of sweet pastries, dates and wine had been laid out for me, but it lay untouched for an hour or more as we bent over the little cat and she fed it drops of milk from a brass pick the Byzantines use to clean the ear.

Only after the thing was asleep in her lap, belly stretched wide with milk and meat, did she shake herself and say, 'I have not thanked you.'

'It is nothing,' I said.

She sat over it, like a mother over a sleeping babe that is full from the breast, running a hand gently along its head and body.

'Well. Jerusalem is full of surprises,' she said when her next guests arrived. 'And I have asked you nothing.'

'Next time,' I said, and stood and bowed and left. A milking goat was bought and the cub's coat became thick and glossy.

Next time came the next day, when a similar spread was laid out for me. The leopard cub lay on its back and clawed its own tail as we sat cross-legged on the floor, and I answered her questions.

'So your brother, Olaf, was not a king's son.'

'No,' I said.

'How then did he make himself king over the whole country?'

I had to explain how kings were made in the North. It was not the same as Byzantium, where the eldest son of one king is then made king after he dies. In Norway a chieftain had to win the others over, by friendship or force, and by exchanging gifts and oaths of loyalty and protection.

'So, anyone can be king?' she said.

'Not anyone,' I told her. 'Only the best of men can make it. Those who have a good name.'

She laughed, and shook her head. 'How strange. Here, we pick the eldest child of the last king. That is why Zoe rules. My father only had girls and he would look sadly at us, and you could see he wished for one of us to be a boy. But as he grew sick, he would lecture us. Both of us. Stay together, he always said. Help each other. The court is a cruel place for young women. When she was young all the men in court wanted to marry her. My father picked the man to wed her, a solid type, diligent and studious at the matters of state.

'But as the years went on and she did not bear a child, men began to whisper that she was barren and the young men began to court me. I never felt so flattered. But Zoe struck me across the face, and accused me of trying to unseat her, and had me sent to a nunnery. And so I sit, while she goes through husbands, and the empire that our father cared for crumbles at the edges.'

'Do you ever wonder what would happen if she died?'

She raised an eyebrow at the question, and I almost expected her to bare her teeth and hiss at me, like her cub. 'Yes,' she said, with a deep sigh. 'Many times. But she was my big sister, and I loved her. How can I wish her harm?'

CHAPTER ELEVEN

Jerusalem

Looking back now, that time of my life feels like a dream. The world was sun, fine food, and wine. But even on the brightest days I had a sense that a cat's shadow was following me, sly, languid, its tail flicking in taut displeasure.

I sat each month with the chests beside me, and handed out the pay to each company captain, for them to distribute. What next? I thought. Is this how you want to end your life, counting coin?

I spent my coin on a splinter of the True Cross between two slivers of crystal.

'Is this real?' I asked the seller.

'Real!' he said and put his hand to his heart. 'Kill me if I lie!'

I gave him a look, but bought it anyway. 'I'll need it when I meet the dragon,' I said, and he did not understand me and I laughed and did not bother to explain. I hired guides to the holy places, I feasted the Ethiopians, I bought the best drink and food and fine weapons and armour, and I bought silks for Helen, a pair of twined silver earrings that she held in her palm when I gave them to her.

She scowled and said, 'They are too much!'

But she put them on and asked me how they looked.

'Beautiful,' I said and my words brought a little colour to her cheeks.

She took them off and hid them and later, when I had done my rounds I found her feeding a stray dog that had come into our camp. It was a handsome pup, with long ears and gangly legs. It nibbled at her hand as she looked up at me. It was always hungry, that hound, drooling till you tipped out the wine-lees, or tossed the crust onto the floor.

I sat down next to Helen. 'Would you come north with me?'

'To Constantinople?'

'No,' I said. 'The true North.'

She did not look at me, but laughed. 'What would I do there?'

I did not have an answer for her, but I wanted it, nonetheless. I saw her dressed in rich furs, sitting in my father's hall, holding her hands to the flames, her dark skin and beauty amazing all my pale, freckled kinsfolk.

'You could wear your earrings,' I said. 'And more. I will give you more.'

She laughed but said nothing, and I could not tell what she was thinking, but a few days later she brought the matter up again. 'Do you think you will go back home?'

'Of course,' I said, as most Varangians said, though fewer did it.

'When?'

'I don't know.' The truth was I could not yet see how I could go home. If I go home, I thought, it must be to be the king of Norway. I would not settle for anything less – and yet it seemed such a distant possibility. A king needed warriors and gifts to win men's loyalty. I had warriors, I thought, but how much money did a man need to win over Norway?

'How much did your brother have?' Helen asked.

'Three chests,' I said. 'Of coin mostly. But treasures also.'

'Then start to gather,' she said. 'Build a treasure of your own.'

I had already sent many treasures to Kiev for Jaroslav. Things he needed and could not get easily, like books, paintings, silks, spices. But I knew what I had sent to Jaroslav would not be enough.

On our last night in Jerusalem, I was drunk and I went out alone to get grilled meat, but in my drunkenness I missed my way, and wandering decided to go for one last time to the place where Jesus died.

All the streets looked the same at night, and I gave up and found my way to the Ethiopian church. There were three steps up, the doors were unshuttered, the air inside cool and empty.

My footsteps echoed as I strode inside and saw images in the gloom that came to me like visions. A ladder reaching up into Heaven, with Christ greeting the worthy, while sinners were pulled down by black demons. I saw Christ suffering on the cross, while angels put their hands over their faces and wept. I saw Christ Victorious, but standing against a wall of gold, being raised up from the earth, being made King of Heaven.

I knelt then, and prayed, and came out into the street and saw Helen standing in the doorway of the caravanserai with Grey-Gunnar.

'There he is!' Grey-Gunnar said. They hurried across the street.

'We could not find you,' Helen said. 'I was worried.'

'Do not worry,' I told her. 'I just wanted to pray.'

They were drunk, I was drunk, and that night we fell into our beds and slept and did not need to dream.

Next morning the water-lad brought our last load of water from his spring.

I finished a skin on my own before we had finished loading the pack animals, and then we set off though the narrow winding streets.

The heat of summer had passed, and everyone had heard that Theodora was the sister to the Empress Zoe, and it seemed the whole city turned out to watch us leave. Theodora had the curtains of her chair drawn back, and sat on display in all her gold and silks, her cat on her lap, baring its fangs at the crowd. The dark faces of the people looked up with wonder and admiration, and then the crowds and the noise and the city all fell behind us, and the curtains were closed once more. We trudged up through the hills, and as the details began to blur with distance, I turned back for a last look at the Holy City.

The sun was setting, and it seemed to fall so quickly, blazing off the burning domes of the city, and then it was gone, and all the colour seemed to drain from the world – and distant stars began to appear, like peepholes from the past.

I have changed, I thought. I was all barbarian before, but I had seen and learnt in the service of the Varangians. I had seen the world, and no man can see his home in the same way, once he has travelled to Jerusalem. But I had learnt as well. I knew how to govern armies, manage wages, oversee the government of Imperial districts.

The steel of my hard upbringing was folded now with southern learning: and iron and steel make the strongest swords.

What I could do, I thought, if I went home and as we retraced our steps through olive groves and dry farmland, past ruins and the lairs of bandits that we had burnt, then the wording in my mind had changed and I wondered what would I do if I went home. By the time we saw the sea again I had an idea: I would bring home some of the things that I had seen. I would change my home as I too had been changed.

By the time the serving men were tapping in the tent pegs in the grassy dunes the sun had already set. The tide was coming in with long, low waves fretting up the sand, and once we had eaten I stripped naked, strode waist deep into the surf, stretched my limbs out into the warm, clear water. As I swam through the black water the water sparkled with green light. I hung in the dark water, with green fairie lights swirling about me. It was a miraculous thing, and I took that as a sign from God himself.

As I swam back to shore I was full of myself, thinking that God had a mission for me, as he had for Olaf before, but by the time I came to my tent, and Helen was waiting for me, then my mood had changed. I did not speak of it. This was a secret thing between God and myself.

We marched back up the coast and when we got back to Acre, our ships were waiting in harbour, and our new orders had arrived. There were good winds and I was eager to be off before they changed.

While the boats were stacked with figs and cheese and fresh water I went to pay my respects to Theodora. Her priest led me in. Her cat was asleep, and she was standing over it. She wore only a nightshirt with a cloak thrown lightly about her.

'He is asleep,' she said.

I nodded. 'We're leaving. We're joining a force that is going to Sicily.'

'Sicily?' She looked at me with her painted eyes. 'There should be good pickings there.'

'I hope so. Good luck to you.'

She put a hand to the leopard's side, which rose and fell with each breath. She was going back to her nunnery. 'Pray for me,' I said. She nodded, and I bowed and left, and thought of the caged songbirds in the Jerusalem market, and how they sang of their captivity.

Last was Killer Ake. We chatted for a while and then we stood and nodded at one another, and neither of us wanted to say more, so I shook his hand and made my way along the wharf to my ship, and swung aboard.

Halldor was standing next to me. 'Where now?'

We were to set sail as soon as we had enough fresh water for the journey. 'Back west,' I said. 'We are to conquer an island called Sicily.'

'Is it rich?'

'The richest in the Mediterranean.'

Halldor smiled. 'Maybe we'll make you king after all.'

'Maybe,' I said. He tried to read my face, but I gave nothing away, and I thought that God was giving me this chance to make myself rich and that I must not squander it.

PART III

Constantinople

CHAPTER ONE

Sicily

Have you heard the one about the warrior who was dying as he besieged a town and wanted a Christian burial, and so the townsfolk, being good Christians, let his men in, carrying a coffin, on the promise that they would leave peacefully after; but the leader was not dead, and as his men carried his coffin into the city, their leader leapt up and under him, in the casket, were swords and spears for his men to use, and so they took the gates and held them open while the rest ran up?

Or have you heard the one about the men who tied burning faggots to the tails of rats and let them loose, and they ran through the town, putting all to flame? Or the one where men dug a tunnel under the walls, and came up like rabbits on the other side? What about the men who built a wooden horse and rode it over the walls of the town and killed all inside?

We told each other all these ludicrous tales as we sat and waited and stared at the city walls, and waited for something to happen. I grew tired of starving towns out, and I lost as many men through sickness as battle, and it hurt to see great warriors die shitting their guts out. Better to die with a sword in hand. It is quick that way.

'Fuck it,' I'd say, and pull my mail shirt over my shoulders, feel it fall in place with its own weight. 'Let's storm the fucking walls.'

Sicily was a slog of a campaign. The place is all mountains and villages hard-baked to the colour of clay. The houses were tiled, and packed tight as lice-eggs in the seam of a jacket, and set high on rocky crags with curtain-walls all about them. We camped, we marched, we dug in, we stared up at the walls and started working out how to break them down.

They made Pardus's tower-house look like a fort made of sand on the beach by a child. And there were dozens of them. Each a tough walnut that had to be cracked.

A year and a half into the campaign, we were stuck outside one town with walls set with square towers of rough stones, and I flicked a pair of mating flies off my bread. They lay on their backs and buzzed round in circles as I saw a shape on the wall-top and saw a veiled woman tip her chamber pot over the battlements onto the shit pile at the base of the wall, deep enough to bury a man standing up. She shouted and gesticulated and I raised my middle finger in response. It was a tired ritual. I took the leaf off the top of my horn, and sipped. The ale had been sour when we'd bought it. Now it tasted foul. I drank it regardless.

A horse clattered up the road, trailing a slow-settling cloak of white dust. The rider was as white as a miller as he came towards me. I sat in the cool shelter of the olive groves and called for wine.

It was purple as it poured into my horn, but dark as the Baltic Sea when I looked down into the depths. I drank three cups before I would see him.

When I was done I motioned him forward.

'Katalokon has reached an agreement with his town,' he said to me.

'He's got them to surrender?' I said.

He nodded. 'After their festival. Some heathen thing.'

'Fuck,' I said. I had bet Katalokon that I could take my town before he could take his, and now after four months of watching the townsfolk tip their night pots over the walls the bastard was about to beat me. 'How many days off is their festival?'

'Five.'

I walked out from under the olive, waving flies from my face. They buzzed in my ear. I swatted at them. I had the shits, my men had the shits, and worst of all, Katalokon was going to win our bet.

I called all my captains to me. 'Right. We've got five days to take this fucking town.'

There is no siege where you cannot let a soul in or out. Each morning the south gate opened and a few boys hurried out with their few remaining goats. They tugged the last grasses out by their dry roots.

We counted the goats for want of anything else to do. They started with a hundred. A month later they were down to sixty. On and on, till there were fifteen. Now they were down to ten.

'They're starving,' Halldor said.

'They're still shitting,' I said, as the woman waved her chamber pot at us. 'So they must be eating something.'

That night the ale had turned my guts, and I felt the shits start to rumble, and knew I would have to go, and lay there, waiting.

I slept little and was up before the flies as grey and purple light crept up from the east. The walls were too high. They were too strong. I stood and stared at it, and cursed myself for coming to this place. The sky paled. About me my men slept on the ground, their shields and swords and spears lying between them. When dawn came I had horns blown and I summoned my men. They shook the night from their clothes and came towards me. 'Today let all men compete for prizes that I shall give. There will be rich rewards for those who perform well!'

They were uninspired, but when I passed about the last pot of wine they cheered up and I offered a fine Moorish helmet with a gilt rim, set with red-veined agates, as first prize.

On the first day there was racing, horse-racing, bear-baiting, wrestling and cock-fighting. I gave out prizes, and let it be known that tomorrow there would be more of the same. The townsmen crowded on the walls to watch as Grey-Gunnar's prize cockerel was matched with another. Feathers flew. Bets were won and lost, and when it lost its third bout, there was a groan from the battlements.

The townsfolk were more bored than us. They took sides on the wrestling, and had taken a shine to a small lithe lad named Orun, who was good at flinging fatter men over his knee. They cheered him on whenever he stepped up, and he turned and waved at them and some of them waved back, and some of them swore at us.

As the day went on the side gate creaked open. Nine goats. A few lads came out with them, and whistled at them to stay close. The goats did not know Varangians from Sicilian. We were all their enemies. They did not care who ate them.

On the second day we held the same games. Orun was matched in the final of the wrestling against a great ugly beast of a Swede with filed teeth, named Abbe. Abbe had his fair hair bound up into plaits and coiled up on his head.

Orun had tied his hair back.

Halldor was with the men who were standing guard.

We started the games. The gates opened. Seven goats led the way. The boys sat on rocks, chewed dry grass, waited for the wrestling to start.

Abbe had once broken a man's back over his knee. Orun came forward warily. I was fearful for the little lad, but he was brave and fast on his toes, and soon the people on the walls were cheering for him.

At that moment Halldor jumped up and ran up the slopes. The boys thought they were meaning to steal the goats and ran back and forth, gathering them back up. As this happened the wrestling seemed to mesmerise the townsfolk. By the time the last goats were being herded through the open gateway Halldor and his men had reached the gates and killed two of the boys.

They pushed the gates wide open, and now all of us grabbed weapons that we had hidden and sprinted.

It was a close-run thing. By the time we got there Halldor had lost three men, and he had taken a cut to his face. He was an ugly, sour-faced fellow before then. 'You were late arriving,' he said to me after.

I put up with a lot from him. Bloody Icelander, I thought. Never bloody happy.

The next day I rode to Katalokon's camp. He came out, grinning through his black beard.

'Araltes!' he boomed. 'You bastard!' He laughed as he clapped me on the shoulders. 'You crafty northern bastard! Tell me, how did you do it?'

I shrugged. I drew in a deep breath. 'I pretended I was dead and my men asked the locals for a Christian burial . . . ' I told him.

CHAPTER TWO

The Battle of Syracuse

In Sicily I led a thousand men. They were Norse and Danes and Swedes and Flemings and English, and I don't think I ever loved a company of men as much as them. I loved every single one of them. We shared our lives and deaths. We could have conquered the world together. We all shared the same boots, as we liked to say.

It was my chief task to keep us all alive; and get rich.

We fought our first full battle on a day so hot the white sun cast a glare that made us all squint. My Varangians had broken the Saracens with our great axes, cutting through man and horse in one sweep. I was parched, my undershirt soaked through, as I pulled off my mail and threw it over my shoulder and led my men to the baggage train, eager for loot, only to find that the Lombards and Greek auxiliaries had got there before us, and were still picking through the carts and pack-mules, like dogs.

They looked as though they had come straight from the parade ground. Not one of them had drawn a blade in anger – unless it was to bicker over a girl or a silver spoon.

I cursed them all. 'We'll have to be quicker next time,' Halldor said.

'Sod that,' I said. 'Who did the fighting here. Us or them?'

I led my men, still in their mail, to the Greek tent where their commander, Maniakes, stood before a great pile of plunder. His men were still bringing up armloads of armour and weapons, silver, gold, clothes, food and a few silver trinkets.

'Araltes,' he said. He could see the anger in my face, and motioned to his men to step forward.

I wiped the blood from my face. 'I have come to admire the booty your men have brought back to you. It is a mighty pile. Your men are thorough.'

'They are,' he said.

He was watching me with dark, suspicious eyes. I was all smiles and made note of each piece that was brought in. 'That is a fine saddle,' I said, or, 'That goblet must weigh as much as a stone, let me feel. See the gems on this. Such beautiful work.'

When the Greeks had thrown all their treasure onto the pile I said, 'Right, let us divide the treasure now, before the sun sets, so that we can all see that it is divided fairly.'

'This is our plunder,' Maniakes said. 'Not yours.'

I slapped my head. 'You are right. Men – forward.'

They added what little we had taken: silver rings, buckles, sword hilts. Then I had a bag of swords brought forward, and tossed them onto the pile.

'This is what we faced on the battlefield. Swords and spear-points. I could give you blood as well, but it would spoil the beautiful things here.'

His face darkened, but he could not deny the right of my words, and with everyone's eyes upon him, he started to pick out a few choice treasures that he wanted, but each time he did so it made him look miserly, even before his own, and in the end he cursed, and had the pile divided into two parts, with the rings scattered by the handful back and forth onto the piles. 'There,' he snorted, as if I was the one who had been miserly. 'Satisfied?'

'Yes,' I said. 'Though I think you have been a little generous to yourself and your men. Clearly you value those who can rob a baggage train more highly than those who win your battles for you.'

I held out a hand for him to shake, but he looked at it and would not put out his own. 'I think you consider your own value a little too highly,' he said.

'I'll remember that next time you ask me to take the centre.'

He snorted and stormed off, and I had a cart brought up quickly to fetch our heap before he changed his mind.

'You have an enemy there,' Halldor told me, as the last pieces were thrown onto the ox-cart. But I knew it already. Saracens, Greeks, locals. Everyone was an enemy on Sicily.

I always took ten men and my sword to council with Maniakes, but he did not repeat the mistake of trying to rob my men of their plunder. And each battle won, or city stormed, brought me more treasure, and each ounce of gold and silver brought our home-coming closer.

'Got what you need to make yourself king?' some of my captains would tease me.

I'd reckon it in my head. 'Another twelve-pound of gold,' I'd say, and when a year passed and I had half that, then I'd say, 'Half a twelve-pound.'

And the closer I came to saying I had enough, the more they were drawn in. It was like a young girl who starts to see visions, and make prophecies about the future. The more I believed, the more they did too, and soon they were throwing some of their treasure in with mine, which was all sent by trusted captains to Jaroslav's care.

Soon it was not just my dream but theirs as well. 'How long till you go home to make yourself king?' changed to 'How long till we all go home and make you king?'

We started to count the fighting seasons till we would be done, and when I had enough gold we held a great feast and drank so much wine we could hardly stand on our own two feet without the world shifting from under us.

Next morning I lay with my head feeling as though Thor's hammer had been tapping on it through the night.

Helen tutted and shook her head, but she made me a drink that she said would cure my hangover.

'It's foul,' I said.

'It should be.'

I tipped the black dregs away when she was not watching and poured myself more wine. That helped, a bit.

That evening some of my men talked of leaving as soon as the fighting season was done. 'We are not going to leave the Varangians like a thief,' I told them. 'Besides, there is a month's travel before we even leave the lands of the Greeks. First we have to conquer Sicily, then I will ask the Emperor to let us leave with honour.'

If I could I would have kept all my men alive, but it is the fate of fighting men to die young, and I lost too many of my friends in Sicily, when it seemed our departure was so close. Orun and Orkney Eirik died of the bloody flux, and fifteen other men within a single month. The last had been a young man named Brand, a tough little warrior, always the first to step forward to the front. I had marked him out as a possible captain and I came back from the latest funeral heavy with loss.

Helen cheered me. She was fat with child, and this was her first and she was full of joy. 'He will have your golden hair,' she said as she squatted over the dough, scraping her hands clean and rubbing them with flour.

'What if she is a girl?' I said.

She shaped the cakes and pressed each flat, then fussed over them for a moment so that they would not burn. 'He is a boy!' she said.

'How can you know?'

'I know,' she said as she flipped the hot buns into her skirts. I squatted down next to her and took a hot cake, and broke it into pieces, blew on them till they were cool enough to eat and imagined a plump girl just like her mother: dark and kind and beautiful.

Next morning orders came for another march. Helen came out to see me off. She was too big for travel, and I left her with the men who were too sick to fight, with half a company to keep guard.

'When will you be back?' she asked as she stood with a hand under her belly, the other behind her back, her breasts hanging fuller than ever before.

'A fortnight,' I said. I could not tell. War is uncertain.

'Be safe,' she told me. I smiled and winked and heeled my horse up the slope.

There was a band of thieves who were raiding one of the villages. They ran back to their high fastness, thinking themselves safe; but I led my men up the rocks at night, and we caught them in their beds, and slaughtered them.

I hanged those who survived the fight, pushed their walls down the cliffs, and pulled down their stronghold so that others could not take it over.

All in all I was gone only a week, and I was in a good mood, having lost only six of my own men and taken a good deal of plunder which I split three ways between the men, myself and the Emperor.

We came down the same path we had taken, my horse skidding on the loose scree as we started down the slope. It was nearly noon and the heat of the day was on us. The cypress shadows clung close to the tree skirts, cicadas sang from tree to tree, the leaves of the lemon tree hung limp in the air, my throat was dry with dust and I was looking forward to a long draught of wine.

My men stood as soon as they saw me approaching. I was glad to see many of those that I had left behind had healed, and that there were only five new humps of soil in the field we used for burial.

I was looking forward to washing the road dust from my skin, a bed of soft straw, so it seemed strange that the men's movements should look so slow and glum. Hrothi led them. His face was grave. 'Harald,' he said when I was ten feet off from him. 'There is news.' I could tell it was grave, but I was not ready for the keenness of the blow. It was aimed too low.

'Helen,' he said, 'died.'

Two words. That was all. But I looked from face to face for confirmation and saw the truth of it. 'Impossible,' I said, my voice hoarse with dust. I swung my foot over the horse's head and slid down. They led me to the pregnant swell of earth in the field, second from the end.

'She fought it,' Hrothi said. 'She was very brave. But the child would not come out. She grew exhausted. We fetched a woman and prayed for her, and the little one.'

'Was it a boy?' I said.

He shook his head. 'I couldn't look.'

That hurt me afresh. I nodded and he put his hand to my shoulder and squeezed it and then I wanted to be left alone.

That night I cursed Sicily. I cursed the town and the people. I cursed the skies and the land. I cursed the robbers who had taken me away. I cursed the gold that had kept me here. We should have left, a voice in my head told me, and escaped back north. If I had been there, I thought, I could have done something. I scourged myself with thoughts of her asking for me, hoping to hear the sound of my horses, waiting to hear the first-breath cry of a child.

I stood for a long time away from my camp. I had charge of a thousand of the best warriors in Christendom, towns fell at my command, and yet I felt powerless, he who had such power upon the world, then I felt guilty. It was my babe that had killed her as it lay within her belly, curled and cruel and innocent as a cat.

I can feel the emotion still. It chokes me. What a brew grief can be.

The sun set. There was no moon that night – only the twisting flames of our camp fires – but I could not go to them. I could not face the light and the men sent Halldor to me.

I heard him call to me from about fifty yards distant. I refused to turn to him.

'Harald,' he said, coming close.

'Leave me,' I said.

He walked closer.

'I heard,' he said, and put a hand to my shoulder. 'I'm sorry.'

I had no words.

'The men are worried,' he said at last.

I nodded.

'Come in,' he said. 'It will feel better by the fire. A man should not be alone with his sadness.'

I let him lead me, stumbling, towards the fire. The flames licked over the knotted black branches, blue and purple and yellow and red.

The men lined up to embrace me. I held each one for a moment, as if he was my son, and we laughed, because sometimes, when the Fates have been their cruellest, there is nothing else you can do.

It was three months later that we finally brought the Caliph to battle.

I was numb to the world, and angry. I tried to dress myself for battle, but my mail shirt snagged on my shoulder, and I cursed and summoned someone to help me. This had always been Helen's job. The lack of her left me stricken.

We took our place in the battle line eager as hounds for the day's hunt. I looked at my men, dressed for battle, and I felt my throat tighten.

'One more battle, men,' I shouted, 'and then we go home!'

They let out a great roar at that. Tears of pride welled up in my eyes, and my throat was too tight to speak and they saw the emotion within me, and they felt for me. 'Varangians!' I managed to shout at last, and my men made a bristling line, all spears and shields and bearded battle axes. 'Forward!' I called, but my throat failed me, and I led by example, and my men followed.

We met the enemy on the plain outside their capital city. They were the door through which we had to pass, or never see the North again, and as they streamed out to meet us their numbers were uncountable, their black banners filled the sky like carrion birds.

The Caliph had warriors from ten tribes; he had three elephants with great horns reaching from their mouths, each with twenty men on its back, with bows and arrows and spears; Italian infantry.

We were in the centre, as always, and one of the three elephants was driven towards us. 'Hold,' I called and my voice was steadier now, even though I felt terror at the sight.

Its horns were tipped with brass, a wooden fort was strapped onto its back, and heavy cloth fell down over its sides, so that arrows snagged into the fabric, and gave it a look like a vast hedgehog. It was a ship on legs, a charging barn. You never saw such a thing, and nor had we, but we had to fight it.

'Spears!' I called, and the best among us lobbed their javelins towards it.

A few of them struck. One of them caught in its trunk. Another hit the rider, and he tumbled backwards and he slipped under its massive feet, and all I saw was a man being crushed like a rag doll.

Rudderless now, it ran towards us, all ears and trunk and legs, swinging its great grey head from side to side. 'Christ!' I thought as I felt the earth shake beneath me. My men felt the same terror, I am sure. The spears became a storm, and then it was within the range of throwing axes, and I grabbed one from the hand of the man next to me, and threw, and the thrum of thrown axes was like the sound of a flock of geese rising suddenly from a field.

The elephant bellowed its fury, and then it hit the shieldwall as a wave hits a wall of straw, and men and bodies were flung about like kindling.

I found myself lying on the ground with a dead man on top

of me, my helm askew. There was a line of dead and dying where the beast had rampaged down the hill, and now we could see its tail as it ran, riderless, towards the river.

I looked about. My banner still stood, and I heard Helen's voice in my ear, her last words to me, *Be safe;* and I thought I understood, that she had given herself for this, to turn the beast away at the last moment.

'Up!' I shouted. 'Up!' and the men had panic in their eyes, but seeing I lived and was fearless settled them and they re-formed quickly.

'Shieldwall!' I shouted and the men formed up, with me in the centre, and I led them forward, axe in hand, my shield bearers about me. We routed a company of spearmen and the Italian conscripts behind, and were into the Emir's household guard with their black flags and curved swords. They charged straight for us and we held them off on the rock of our shieldwall, and as the battle raged I formed my best warriors up in a boar's snout about me. My voice came back then, louder than ever before. 'Ready men?' I raged, and they roared back in answer, and at my command the shieldwall before us opened up, and we charged through and hit the enemy like a hammer blow on a stallion's skull that makes the legs wobble at first, before it crashes chin-first to the ground.

My weapon that day was a great two-handed axe. The Saracens had nothing that could defend against such a blow. Even men in mail died beneath the crushing weight of it. I could not tell you how many men I killed, though men said they had never seen me fight so fiercely. I carried no shield, but trusted to my men and my mail shirt and swung and swung until I could barely walk another step, and could not lift my arms above my head for a week after.

But we had broken them. The Emir fled from the island.

They had not thought to meet such hard warriors that morning. Sicily was conquered, our oaths fulfilled, and I had all the gold I needed to make a throw at claiming the kingship of Norway.

*

A month later boats laboured with the weight of the treasure and armour we had taken, but the weight I felt most keenly was of all the men I had loved and left behind. And especially the absence of Helen. And all I could think of was the image I had seen in the Ethiopian church in Jerusalem, of men climbing a long ladder into Heaven, and how the next time I saw her she would be radiant with light, a child in her arms, cured of pain and loss – and through Christ's mercy, she would be healed of death itself.

Your father broke off to show me his banner. I had seen it in battle, of course, and it was a marvel, as it flew without wind. Landwaster, he named it, and it had always brought him victory. 'I cannot unfurl it all the way,' he said, 'or I should have to kill you. But I will show you a little of it.'

'Is the black raven not a heathen symbol?' I asked him.

'It is not a raven,' he said to me. 'It is a black dove.'

You must have seen the banner many times. It was made of fine white silk, and your father said it was a saint's gown, and that he had been given it by an Archbishop of Rhodes.

'Which saint?' I asked your father.

'I don't remember.'

'Why did he give you such a relic?'

'Why should you ask?'

'Because it seems a kingly gift.'

'I am a king.'

'Yes,' I ventured, 'but you weren't then.'

'Do you question me?' he said.

I bowed. 'No King,' I said. 'I do not.'

'If I had stolen this do you think it would have brought me victory? Do not be a fool. This was given to me, and there is magic within it, that has always brought me success.'

'May it always do so,' I said, and when no one was watching I went up and touched the staff of the banner. I had heard much of Landwaster, but when I touched it I felt nothing. It was just a staff of wood, and a wrapped length of embroidered white silk.

CHAPTER THREE

Michael the Caulker

I asked to be sent to Micklegard so that I might petition the Emperor to let us go, but we were in port in Italy when word came that the Norman, Guillaume, who had been our ally in Sicily, had grown so enraged by Maniakes' division of the booty that he had decided to set himself up in Italy as a warlord. He'd started with his three hundred cavalry. Within six months he had an army of twenty thousand similarly disaffected fighting men.

The local commander begged us to help put their rebellion down. I spelt it out to my captains. 'What do you think?'

Halldor said, 'I say leave. We have what we came south for. Gold. Honour. Tales to tell our grandchildren, that will make their mouths drop in wonder. Let us leave, before we lose any more friends.'

I let the other men have their say. 'We could leave, but men will say we fled, and left the others to fight without us,' one said.

Another said, 'Let us fight. We'll leave with our honour intact. And we'll get more gold.'

This seemed to be the majority opinion, and I weighed all their views, and decided to stay. I was proud, and would not have Guillaume say that I had refused to meet him in battle.

*

We did not have long to wait. The two armies met on a wide plain, traversed by a river, where the locals told me that a Moor named Hannibal had defeated the Romans in battle. Cannae, they called it, but now the place was named Montemaggiore. It took three days for our army to file in. We outnumbered the Normans and their allies three to one, and it should have been an hour's business, but our commander was a nobleman who barely knew one end of a sword from the other, and the local recruits were either drunk or unhappy to be compelled to fight.

We lined up, my men in the centre, and the Normans' three hundred heavy cavalry formed up opposite. I'd seen them fight many times, and knew what to expect, but the Normans had more sense than to charge us. They hit the Lydians on our left, and the Lydians crumpled like a sackcloth. One by one the allies gave way, our general fled, and then the panic turned into a rout, and only my Varangians held firm.

It is the hardest thing to keep a unit together in defeat. The Normans came at us again and again, and we held the shieldwall firm despite all they could throw at us. We saved the Byzantine army that day, stopped defeat from turning into rout. But it cost my brothers dearly and I strode from that ghost-haunted battlefield with my mail coat hanging in shreds. There was blood on my face, blood on my hands, and blood in my shoes, much of it mine.

That night I went through my men, embracing each one. I had a boat full of coin that I was about to send to Jaroslav, and I had the chests unloaded, and shared out what little booty I had won to all the survivors.

When I found the Byzantine general I wanted to throttle him.

'It was not my fault,' he said.

I bared my arms: they were covered in cuts and bruises, where the mail had been driven into my skin. 'These are the arms of a man who fought this day. Instead of using arms to fight, you used your feet.'

I caught Halldor's eye. They were as angry as mine, but angry with me. I told you so, they said. You overreached yourself for pride, and now our friends are dead.

We holed up in Bari while the Normans set about laying siege to the town. It was a miserable time, everyone blaming each other for the defeat, and I did not want to be boxed up in a city under siege. I had seen sieges enough in Sicily. They are long, tortuous, unhealthy affairs, and I began to doubt that I would ever leave the Varangian Guard alive.

It is in the time of greatest darkness that the most unlooked-for light comes. And so it was for me. Whether Ake or Theodora had put in a good word for me, or whether Maniakes had grudgingly given us some credit for Sicily, I do not know, but the year after Helen's death we were summoned to Bulgaria to fight in a new campaign alongside the Emperor Michael himself.

My thousand men were loaded onto eight two-masted biremes, and we took over the whole ship from aft to stern, and loaded all our war-gear and treasure in the bilge deck. It was summer, and the light winds winnowed our minds as they cleaned away bad airs. I lay on the deck and watched the sights drift past. Time and days seemed to merge into one long dream. I would wake to see thunderheads over Olympus or lookout towers over the burnt ruins of a pirate camp, and a few times dolphins raced the boat, weaving through the waves, blowing great breaths from their foreheads. Smelling their breath, once again I recalled the cold killer whales massacre a shoal of silver herring.

Thinking of that moment was like reaching through water to pick up a fallen coin, and finding your fingers close on nothing. I felt like a different person, I felt numb, I looked forward to nothing except the moment when the anchors splashed into the water, the oarloops were closed, and I could dive from the boat and swim by myself, and climb out after to drink unwatered wine. I was carried in God's palm, cradled like a child on the aft-deck of the bireme, feeling the rowers' drumbeat through the deck timbers and enjoying a time of stillness that I had not known since we had sailed south from Kiev.

That trip to join the Bulgar campaign was good for us all. We had gathered a legion of ghosts about us, and the two-week sail northward helped clear them away, like cobwebs when all the doors and windows are thrown open to the winds of springtime.

The weather was clear and hot and pleasant as our ships rowed past the harbour bar at Thessaloniki and found a river mouth, a strong stone jetty, and a stone city rising behind.

The city had been besieged that summer by the rebels, but the rebels lacked ships, and never cut the sea lanes, and I never saw a city that shrugged off its war footing anywhere near as fast as this one. The markets bustled, the streets were thronged with elite Byzantine units, and whenever they saw Varangians, the local traders cheered.

That first evening I supped with the Emperor Michael himself. I had told my men that I would petition the Emperor to let us go, and when I did he heard me out, which was kind of him, and promised that when our year-oaths were done, in March, then he would release us.

He could tell from my face that my men wanted to leave earlier, and so he said, 'To signal your courage, I will raise you all to Varangians Inside-the-Walls.' He gave me the white cloak of office, a belt of gold, and he sat me at his right hand each night, and asked me what I thought; and when I spoke he listened.

My men were delighted at the news. Varangians-Inside-the-Walls were the elite bodyguard of the Emperor. They were paid three times what other Varangians were.

'So we're doing the same thing for three times as much pay?' Halldor said.

'Yes,' I told him, and even he seemed impressed.

'Well, as long as he lets us go at year-end.'

The Bulgars were a tough, warlike lot, but they fell to infighting, and so won half the battle for us. You will have heard all the poems.

In each battle I was the conqueror of the Bulgars, and at the end the Emperor rewarded me handsomely.

I was twenty-six years old and I had gold; I had men, I had the grip of a warrior, I had the confidence of a king. One night as we marched back to Thessaloniki, I was summoned to his tent to share a dinner of figs and cheese and grilled meat, and he poured unwatered wine, and he seemed in a fine mood, though tired.

'Sir,' I said. 'You have been the best of lords, but I would like your permission to return home. My men wish to leave before the winter closes the ways north.'

I had more to say, but he put up a hand. 'Not yet, Araltes. There is yet the Triumph. You should be there with me. Speak to me after that. Then I will listen.'

'Yes, Lord,' I said, and promised my men that we would all be going home soon.

Peace settled at last through the empire, our homecoming could not be long.

I had been to the Hippodrome for the chariot races. It is the first thing newcomers to the city do, once they have said a prayer of thanks at the Shrine of St Nicolaus, Protector of Sailors, that is set into the wall at the harbour of Theodosius. But I had never seen it so full, never heard such a noise, never known awe to run through me like lightning from a clear sky.

We could hear the crowd as we stood in the Great Palace, checking the last details. Emperor Michael had fallen more sick the whole way home, and in the ten days that we had been back, and once I had escorted his sedan chair up the steps from the Emperor's private jetty, I had barely seen him. All my time had been taken up with my duties now that I was a Varangian Inside-the-Walls.

When he did appear that morning, carried in a chair by a team of plump eunuchs, I was shocked to see how much he had declined. I did not know him at first, did not think this bloated shape was a living man, until he lifted a hand and gestured to where he wanted to be put down.

I came towards him and bowed, and said some words, but I felt sick at the sight of him. His fingers looked like sausages. All his rings had been cut off, but there were still purple bruises about his fingers, and he had refused to take off his signet ring. It was buried in his flesh, like a tick that gets its whole head under the skin. His eyes turned to me, and I tried not to show what I was thinking.

'Araltes,' he said, and smiled, and in that look I saw the man, the Emperor, the victor, who had led us through Bulgaria and back again without rancour or regret.

The eunuchs spoke in their high shrill voices and I stepped back for them to do their work.

They lifted him up, rubbed his limbs with oils, helped him walk across to where his white gelding, Delphos, waited, head buried in hay, swishing his tail.

It took an age to get him up the steps of the mounting block, and so to guide his foot into the stirrup, and then to swing his leg over. Delphos started at the smell of him, and only settled when he spoke in reassurance.

Someone had found a cavalry saddle, with a brace he could lean against.

I stepped forward to cover it up with his cloak. It would not be right for everyone to see his shame, at this, his Triumph.

'Thank you, Araltes,' he croaked, and forced a smile. 'Who can win a campaign if he can't sit upon a horse?'

He tried to heel the horse forward, but his legs were so swollen and painful that it was beyond his power. No one dared step forward. They will leave him like that, I thought, for fear of action.

I leapt down and bowed before him. 'Let me lead you, Lord,' I said.

I could see in his eyes the pain and the fear.

'Please,' I said. 'I have been in your personal service for a short time, but you have always treated me well.'

He gave a short nod, and so I led Delphos forward, down into the wide flagged tunnel that leads into the Hippodrome, and as I did I heard a sound like angry bees that grew louder and louder as the bright end of the tunnel approached, and I looked about, and realised it was the crowd that awaited us.

The tunnel ran level for a while, and then began to rise upwards. Each step the noise increased, while I led Delphos further up the slope, and spoke soothing words to him when he tossed his head and snorted. As we stepped out into the light, I was blinded for a moment, then saw about me the massed ranks of thirty thousand faces, all shouting and cheering. I had stood in battle, and never known such noise. It assailed and almost stunned me. I had to concentrate hard to take each step, hold tight to Delphos's bridle, yet not appear to do so, and always I thought of the Emperor, and that I must not let him be shamed.

Behind us came all the chief men of the army who had won in Bulgaria, but the Varangians got the biggest cheer. 'Emperor's Wineskins' we may be, but they loved us also.

When we came to a halt to watch the captives pass before us, Delphos had calmed, and I looked up and the Emperor nodded.

'I think I can hold him now,' he said.

'Did you remind him?' Halldor said to me that night.

'I could not,' I said.

'I said you wouldn't. He'll be dead soon, and then who will take over? Whoever Zoe takes to her bed, that's who.'

'I will,' I promised, and went to see him one last time, in the autumn of that year. His fingers were the width of a man's arms and his face as bloated and misshapen as a child's clay doll, and I did ask, but I said, 'Lord, about our returning home . . .'

He winced and nodded and waved a hand to silence me, and it would be brutish to press one who looked to be lying on his death-bed, but I was like a man caught between wife and mother. I had promised my men that we would leave, and yet I had promised the Emperor that I would be his man.

And so, instead of pressing him I put my energies into helping him recover. I found herb-women to come to mutter charms over him as they rubbed his swollen limbs with fragrant oils. I prayed twice a day, and told my men to pray too. I went to the church of Hagia Sophia and gave gold to the monks there, and prayed for over an hour to Olaf, knowing that he would intercede with Christ – and hurried back to pick up my duty that evening.

I set the guards on the palace gates and harbour, and felt a tingle of expectation that when I found the Emperor he would be feeling better. 'Yes,' he would tell me, and sit up and rub at an arm or foot. 'The swelling has gone down.'

And I would thank Olaf and hold my tongue, for it does not serve a man well to brag about his benefactors. That is for the children who claim their fathers are giants.

But when I came to the Emperor's chambers, the chaplain signalled for me to tread quietly.

'Any change?' I asked, but he shook his head, and again in the morning, when our shift was over, and my men were relieved from their posts, I went back once more, and could hear groaning from behind the carved screen, and a serving girl carrying a chamber pot, with a perfumed cloth pressed close to her nose, and I felt that Olaf had abandoned me.

When Emperor Michael spoke at last, I could barely make out what his struggling mouth was saying.

'The Empress will need you when I'm gone. She will need strong men about her. Promise me you will stay and help her.'

I started to say that I'd vowed to take my men home, but he closed his eyes and repeated himself.

'Promise me you will stay and help her.'

I felt sick, but took in a deep breath and nodded. 'Yes, Lord,' I said.

Halldor was furious. I felt sick and wearied by it all. Sometimes your swan turns out to be a goose.

I grieved. My men were downcast. The whole Varangian Guard was in mourning. But the Byzantines did not seem to notice. The eunuchs all slipped the prettiest of their relatives into the palace in the hopes that one of them would hook the old trout, and Zoe had already taken up with the nephew of John the Chamberlain – another gelding that men called John Thousand-Eyes, because he saw all that was happening.

This lad was also named Michael, and everyone despised him. Especially the local nobles who thought one of their number should be Emperor, not some eunuch's blow-in. 'He's the son of a ship-builder,' I heard them curse, and they named him the Caulker, on account of his poor upbringing.

The Caulker was an ill-bred fellow: pretty, in a girlish way, with just a wisp of beard, vain, and jealous. He did not care that the Emperor Michael was dying slowly in the yard opposite, but would sing and squeal and carry on like a lovesick boy.

I received him icily whenever he emerged from her chambers, often drunk, half-dressed, his cheeks smeared red with the Empress's kisses. But our loyalty to the Emperor did not serve us well when he finally died, and it seemed that Zoe had decided to marry her low-class sop.

The whole court was scandalised. The city, even. Half of them could not believe that a handsome young man found anything in that rotten-toothed old hag. The other half were scandalised that she had taken such a limp-wit to the marriage bed.

'Why not just fuck him?' some of them said. 'But to make him Emperor as well? She cannot,' I heard more times than I could count – in the barracks, the courtyards, the stables, the fish-market, the armourer's smithy, the steps of Hagia Sophia, in the shade of the Hippodrome, by the Shrine to St Nicolaus. Even in the brothels the madams sucked their teeth, the half-dressed girls stood about to hear the latest rumours, and their frowns said it all. 'Make the Caulker Emperor?'

'It's not much a man has to do,' I said to Halldor, 'if his only challenge on the way to the crown is to persuade Zoe to open her legs for him. Why, half of Ake's men claimed the honour.'

'I told you so,' Halldor said about three times an hour.

I was sick of it. 'Next time you say that to me you must give me a denarius,' I told him.

He reached into his purse and gave me a handful of coin.

'There,' he said.

I had promised the dead Emperor to help his widow, but it was the hardest oath I ever swore to serve the Caulker, and I regretted it before it was done.

We glared at him and he at us, and none of us had forgotten what had previously passed between us. He had already started castrating anyone who objected to his bedding Zoe before her husband was dead. He picked on the weak at first, punishing noisy and unpopular citizens, but he found he liked the taste of power, and each time he finished his cup, he poured himself a larger one.

The job of gelding fell to Varangians, of course. He did not ask me, he knew what kind of response he'd get, but he found a man from Ake's old company, a giant named Bjorn the Troll, and made him his champion.

'Bjorn the Balls,' I said, and that name stuck.

Bjorn laughed at first, but as the days wore on and the whole joke grew nastily real, none of us found much laughter, least of all Bjorn the Balls. He was a brute and a bully, and there was something about his manner that raised the hackles on my neck. One day he pushed into one of my feasts, got drunk on my wine, and sat there, large and smug, and ate my grapes. 'Is this it?' he said, when he had finished picking the plates clean.

'What else can I feed you?' I picked up a dark brown fig. 'Catch!' I told him and tossed it to him. 'Have one of my balls.'

Bjorn caught it, and held it up. 'I thought you'd lost these at Montemaggiore.'

I slapped the horn from his hand. It skittered across the room, and the wine was dark and spreading on the floor like blood. He was up in a moment and we butted up against each other like rams. He was one of the few men taller than me, but I did not fear him.

'Enough,' our men said, and pulled us apart. 'Enough, we are brothers together.'

'Clearly not,' I said, and Bjorn laughed and shoved me once more, and I was thrown backwards.

Halldor was waiting for me that night, when I had finished checking the guards. I had lost half my gold buttons in the brief altercation, and someone had gathered them up and given them to him and he put them into my hand.

'No coins then,' I said.

'No.'

I sat down and rubbed my forehead. I was sobering up slowly and my head hurt and I reached for more wine. I knew what he wanted, and it did not take long. 'We have to leave, Harald,' he said to me. 'Otherwise we will never get out of here.'

I closed my eyes and nodded, and rubbed my temples.

'I know,' I said. 'You're right. I will go tomorrow to the Caulker. I will beseech his better nature.'

'Why bother? Let us just leave.'

'A thousand men? On what ships? How will we manage that?'

'Then leave the rest.'

'So who do I take?'

'The men who have been with you all along. Since Battle River.'

'So we leave those like Skall, who fought with us throughout Sicily. Or Hedin?' I could have listed thirty men who were beyond deserving. 'Who then?' I said at the end, but he could not answer me. How could I leave any of them behind, having made my vow to them?

'We have to leave somehow,' he told me, and after he'd gone I knew that he was right.

I would go tomorrow, I thought, and buy our release, if need be, with the gold I had taken in Bulgaria.

CHAPTER FOUR

Inside the Walls

Zoe and the Caulker spent their afternoons drinking and fucking, but they started the day with good intentions, and after Mass they held a brief council, where the palace eunuchs reported to them.

That day I was up with the dawn, washed with water from the rain-butts, dressed in ceremonial armour, white cloak of office, strapped on my sword, and dagger, took off some of my rings, and hid them under my straw mattress.

I tipped out half the coins in my purse, took off three of the five golden armbands. I did not want to show how successful the years of Byzantine service had been for me.

My sandals creaked along the mosaicked colonnade that led to the throne room. I knew the mosaics beneath my feet. I barely noticed them now.

At the end of the colonnade, before the throne room, I expected to see Bjorn the Balls's men on duty. I ran through the captains' names in my head. Most of them were good men, as unhappy with their new captain as the rest of us were. But as I came forward I saw men in a uniform I did not recognise. They wore scale armour and gilded helms set with white horse-hair plumes. I looked over my shoulder, and saw more of them following behind me.

'Since when did Scythians guard the Emperor?' I said when the guards stopped me. The Scythians were slave troops, captured children raised to serve the Emperor.

'No more room in the honeypot?' the leader said. He was tall for a Scythian, with hook nose and buck teeth. His men laughed and I did not have a retort in me that morning, did not have to give him my name.

I stepped into the throne room. The chief counsellor, John the Thousand-Eyes, sat on a stool before the Empress and her new husband, his hands gathered about his belly, his hairless cheeks plump and pink.

'What do you want, Varangian?' the Caulker demanded.

'My Lord, my name is Araltes. Sword-Bearer to Michael IV, of the Varangians Inside-the-Walls.'

'I did not ask for your rank, barbarian. I asked what you wanted.' The Caulker edged towards the front of his seat. If the lad was drunk on power, then Zoe was like a fellow drinking partner who delights in some new game. Six months earlier I had been marching through Bulgaria with the Caulker's predecessor. Now I was answering to a nineteen-year-old milksop.

I saw a shadow pass across John's eyes, and thought, he is not happy with his nephew, and I took this as a good sign. 'I did not mean to correct you, sir,' I said.

'Call me by my title, barbarian.'

'Which one?' I said. I did not think he would like being called 'the Caulker'. There was a titter from someone at the back of the room. The Caulker's cheeks coloured.

'Emperor,' he said, but he was a fool for even deigning to answer my question.

'Yes, Emperor. There is a favour I would like to ask of you both.'

He came right to the front of his chair. 'Indeed? That is interesting, for there are matters that we would like to question you about!'

'Question me?'

He did not like that I was the one giving the instructions, but he was eager as the hound when it wants to taste the hare's blood. 'Is it true that in your own country, you are a king?'

'No.'

'Tell me then, what are you?'

'My brother was king,' I said. 'My father was his vassal, and the last to bear the name of king except my brother.'

He waved his hand as if my answer was a trifle in his way, like a child or an old hag that stumbles in front of your horse. 'You know the ban that there is on men of royal rank entering the Varangian Guard?'

I had heard, but it was an old law that no one bothered with any more.

'I have had the scribes check the records. You did not declare your lineage when you arrived.'

'I apologise for that,' I said. 'I was young, and I had a feud with a king in the far North, who wanted me dead.'

'Why, were you treacherous towards him?'

'No,' I said. 'He paid the nobles of my homeland to rise up in rebellion and kill my brother.'

The talk went increasingly badly, so I brought up the idea of buying us out.

'How much do you have?' Zoe said. She leant forward to listen to the answer.

'A thousand marks of silver.'

She sat back, smug. 'Where did you come by such riches?'

'You must surely know how you pay your soldiers,' I said.

She had a way of jutting out her chin and narrowing her eyes. I had seen it before when she wanted to look intelligent. 'You tell me,' she said.

I explained to her how we were paid. For each captured ship I gave a hundred marks to the Emperor, and the rest was mine to keep. When we took booty from an enemy then we divided it three ways: one part for the Emperor, one for me, and one for the men. I had been in the Emperor's service for so many years, so many campaigns, battles, by land and by sea. 'Battles can be generous to a brave warrior who stands his ground and does not flee,' I said.

It was at that moment that they brought out the man who had led the Sicilian campaign, Maniakes. He smiled at me as he walked to my side, and bowed. 'A thousand honours, Lord Emperor of the Latins and the Greeks.'

You can guess how it went. 'Our beloved servant, General Maniakes, commanded you in the Sicilian campaign.'

I had many quibbles with this sentence, but decided to let them go for the sake of clarity. 'Yes,' I said.

'Did you serve him well?'

'Yes.'

'Did you obey his orders?'

'Yes.'

'Did you disobey him?'

'Yes. When his orders were foolish or dangerous I did not obey him. I remained ever loyal to my oaths, which were made to the Emperor Michael, who came before you in the Empress's bed. *He* did not doubt my loyalty.'

'Silence,' the Caulker told me, and turned to Maniakes. From the way the black-bearded general answered their questions, I could see that this had been arranged in secret between them.

'Yes,' Maniakes said. 'This is the man who fought under me on Sicily. No, he was never content with his own plunder, but would march into camp and take what I had put aside for the Emperor.'

They went on and on, stacking the accusations and slurs on me like stones upon a cairn. My temper grew. 'Lies!' I shouted, and the room went silent as I put my hand to my sword hilt to defend my honour there and then.

In an instant there were four Scythians on either arm. I snarled as I tried to throw them off, but more of them ran up, punching and kicking, and I was lost in a flurry of body blows as I twisted and turned and tried to protect myself.

At last they threw me grunting onto the floor, where I lay, with a bloody lip, and my cheek lying flat against the smooth stone flags.

'Araltes, you have done nothing but enrich yourself at our expense. You have rebelled against the Empress and the oaths you swore to God. You have spurned even the honours we have given you. Tear off the sword that he wears. Tear off his red boots. Tear off his cloak! Lock him up, until he deigns to tell us the truth.'

CHAPTER FIVE

The Night of Dreams

I did not miss my boots or white cloak – white is the wrong colour for prison – but I could have done with its warmth.

Two days after my imprisonment, Halldor was thrown into prison with me. I was glad at first. 'Did they harm you?'

He opened his mouth and I saw that he'd lost two more teeth. He spat out blood and glared at me. 'I said we should have left,' he said. 'You should have listened to me. And don't ask me for a coin to say that.'

'Yes,' I said. 'You're right.' We soon ran out of conversation.

We were locked in the cellar of the Numeri Tower, that stood in the same street as the Church of St Mary, which was the Varangian church. I have heard that it still stands, and that Northmen in Constantinople still call it 'Harald's Tower'. It is odd that it should bear my name. I hated the place, and saw little of it beyond the cellars: which were damp and dingy and stank of stagnant water.

Rats infested the place. They were especially bad when the rains were heavy and they were driven out of the flooded drains, but at least they were an enemy we could fight. Halldor and I waged war on them. With little but our hands and heels and eating knives, we cleared the cellar as we cleared Sicily: efficient, relentless, unmerciful.

The guards refused to take the bodies away at first. The stink of rotting flesh filled the room and made Halldor even more miserable. I had to pay for each rat to be removed, but in the end I thought it wiser to bribe the commander, who made them do it for fear of his whip.

The only air we got came from an iron grate too high for us to reach, even when we stood upon each other's shoulders. A unit of the Palace Horsemen were stationed there. All day and night all we heard were the clop-clop of hoofs on the cobbles, the sweet stink of dung, and the neighing of the horses.

Hopeless situations bring out the steel in a man, but steel rusts in the sea air, and I saw little chance of escape.

My gloom deepened when I heard that the Varangians had indeed been replaced by the Scythian eunuchs as the palace guards, and I thought that my chances were slipping away.

Had Bjorn the Balls fallen from favour, I wondered. Or did he know all along?

'They'll put out your eyes,' Halldor said. 'Or slit your nose. Or cut off your ears. Then they will parade you on a donkey on race day, through the Hippodrome, seated backwards, for everyone to mock.'

'Well, you'll be there with me.'

'I will not.'

'You will.'

'Why should I be punished?'

'They'll cut out your tongue,' I said. 'Once Bjorn cuts off your balls.'

I scratched a mark on the wall each sunset. We counted out the days. We had been imprisoned in February. Now it was April, the cold was beginning to relent and our guards had grown quite fond of us. They would come into the cellar and play chess with us, or bring us wine at a price that Halldor could have bought half of Iceland for. I used to sit and watch him, and wonder if I liked him better drunk or sober.

When he was drunk he would stand up and talk through

battles we had fought. We gloried then in the great deeds we had accomplished. Every battle a man fights in and survives is a victory against Death. But one day he was morose and touched the scar on his cheek and said, 'Remember that town in Sicily, when you left me to hold the gate all alone.'

I rolled my eyes.

'You were slow in coming, Harald. Without me you would have failed!'

'All I have to do is look at your ugly face and be reminded.'

I had a moment's warning. He punched the wind out of me as he drove me against the cell wall. We fought there, hand and fist, till we had exhausted ourselves, then I started laughing. Out of despair, I think. Or madness. Too much time alone with his thoughts can send a man insane.

He stopped suddenly and said 'Why are we fighting?'

I laughed so hard I fell over. He scowled at me. I sat up and eventually I could rub my lip. There was no blood.

'I do not know,' I managed to say, then even he could smile.

The days grew longer. We slept on the floor, on rough straw mattresses. There were some old rags from the stables as bedding, but these had fleas, and I had paid the guards to burn them and bring us something more suitable. We became strange to each other and to ourselves. 'I'm the brother of a saint,' I told the guard as he took five silver coins from me.

'Oh,' he said. He kept his palm out. I paid him the last three pennies agreed, and he smiled. 'Bless you.'

'I am Harald Sigurdsson,' I told another.

'I am Thor the Thunderer!'

They nodded politely, and took the money.

Bastards, I thought.

'Listen,' I said. 'I need you to take word to one of my men.'

They laughed at me.

'No really. You must send them word. They will help me.'

'I will ask.' He came back each day with news, but it was no more than you could pick up in gossip from the palace gates.

I don't believe he ever found any of my men. He was content to spin me a tale in return for coin.

Each night we lay and listened to the night watchmen walking the streets, and then Halldor would start snoring, slow and loud and interminable, and I waited for the bed bugs, which were as big as beetles, and fought my own war against them, but it was futile.

'It's your blood,' Halldor said. 'Or mine.'

One morning, when the bed bugs had fled to their corners, I saw a rat snuffling through the rotten sacking against the far wall. I was eager and excited. Killing was a joy and a release. I found my rock, and turned as slowly as a hunting bird. But then the rat's head appeared. That was when I realised that this was too big to be a rat.

I did not move.

Halldor snored.

The head lifted up from the ground, and licked the air and then began to slide towards me. Its tongue flicked out. It had diamond patterns along its smooth-skinned back. It undulated forward.

It was hairless, it was slithering, it was as long as I was tall. I edged towards the wall and looked for a weapon. Halldor kept snoring. It veered towards him and I swung a filthy rag around my arm as a shield.

'Ya!' I shouted to divert it. Bjarki himself could not have been more challenged by his fire-breathing worm. At least he had an ancestral sword and an iron-bound shield. I had a snoring fellow, an old cloak, and a fist-shaped rock.

'Come here you bastard,' I whispered.

Halldor sat up as if I was talking to him. 'What?' he said, and I shoved him aside. 'Ya!' The snake wavered between us.

'Christ's nails!' Halldor swore.

'Keep still!'

'Kill it!'

'I'm trying to!' I hissed.

'Try harder.'

'Will you ever talk about that town again?' I said. 'Will you ever say, "I told you so"?'

'No,' he hissed, 'and no!' He pulled his knees up to his chin. 'Quick!'

It speared out fast from under the dirty straw, and I felt its weight on my arm when its fangs sank in and were caught in the woven fabric. I wrestled for a moment, wrapping it around in my cloak as it lashed like a rope in a storm, until at last I caught hold of it and put my foot on its neck. I do not know if I knelt or bent, but I clubbed its head till it was bloody and flat as bread, and Halldor kissed me and we linked our arms together and danced about our cell like drunken monks.

CHAPTER SIX

Saint Olaf the Stout

For some days Halldor would re-enact my fight. It was so ludicrous, like serving men who squabble in the kitchen, waving an eating knife and thinking themselves mighty warriors. We laughed so hard our sides ached, and the guards came to see what was the matter. I showed them the snake.

They shrank away just to see the thing. We hung it from the rafters, and Halldor said one day. 'It's really not so big is it?'

I was reluctant to let the snake corpse go, but it started to attract flies, and as spring warmed the foul air would make us sick.

'Big news,' the guard told us that night, the bastard who claimed to have contact with my men. 'Emperor Michael the Caulker has deposed the Empress and seized the throne! The whole city is abuzz. The patriarch is furious!'

I had given up believing him and thought he wanted another coin, but he was as excited as if he had seen a snake. I suppose the Caulker was a snake – treacherous, poison-tongued, slithering his way into power. Now he would lock Zoe away and gather all the power and wealth to himself, like any serpent. Everything, cup and throne and all.

The guard closed the door, and I picked up the piece of

hard-baked bread that he had left. I turned it in my hand. Halldor took the piece I proffered, without comment. The bread was still warm. He cupped it in his hands and I picked off morsels and chewed them slowly, feeling the gaps in my teeth, and trying to remember the battles where each was lost.

In the cold, dark isolation of the cellar, that warmth brought memories of a hot bread oven, warmth, comrades, the freedom to walk out of a door and slap a slavegirl's backside, to feel the sun on your face or to smell the scent of griddling lamb.

'So Zoe's gone,' Halldor said.

I nodded. I had no speech in me.

'Wonder how long she'll survive.'

I half smiled. Not long, I thought, but longer than us. The Caulker would not wait long. Men who seized power usually needed another man to blame, and why not pin responsibility on one of the Varangian Guard?

The guard's footsteps retreated slowly up the steps.

Abuzz, I thought. That's a word I haven't heard for a long time.

That night I had a dream. A vision. My brother came to me, like Christ. He was clearer than you are sitting before me with the firelight on your face. 'Harald!' he said to me. 'Harald!'

'Is that you?'

He laughed when he saw my astonishment.

'It is I,' he said. 'Look.'

He pulled back his cloak to show me the wound in his neck.

'Give me your hand,' he said, and the eagle claws of terror clutched me as he pulled his kirtle aside, and I put my hand into my brother's insides.

'Do you believe now?'

I believed. I was frozen with belief. It stunned me, like the ox who is struck by the axe. 'Do not be scared,' he said. 'Have hope. Have faith. Christ will not forget that.'

243

I had no idea what he was talking about, but he clutched my hands very tight and kept telling me, 'Have hope, Harald. Christ will not forsake you. Never flee. Never fear. Understand?'

Yes, I thought with all the strange clarity of a dream. *I understand.*

Dreams are often indistinct. Misty. Mysterious. Hazy. But it was not this way with me. That dream was vivid, bold, more real than life itself, and once the message had been given to me, it dropped me like a stone and I woke at once in the darkness and sat up. The world was less real than my dream. I could feel Olaf with me still, as if he sat in the room just out of reach. He was like a cloak I could wrap myself in.

Then Halldor snored, and the feeling left me.

I still do not know what my brother meant, but he gave me hope, and it was hope that had kept me alive in the crossing of the Keelbacks. I sat up. I could smell smoke, even though morning was still far off. I listened, and heard the rustle of rats in the gutters above us. Then I heard voices.

I thought at first they were coming from the street above and I thought little of them. But then I heard – what? It was footsteps on the stairs and the clink of armour. I felt for my sword, and cursed myself for my madness. 'Halldor!' I had to shake him. 'They're coming for us. Quick!'

But before I could tell him to be silent, I heard the jangle of keys, and in the touch of his hand I knew he was as wide awake as I.

'Araltes,' a voice summoned me. 'Come forward!'

But it was not a Scythian voice. It was a woman's, though I could not see who. The light of the lantern blinded me. It was only an oil lamp, cupped in a hand, a single yellow flame, but the flame shone in darkness, and I was blind. For a moment I thought that Zoe had come to torment me, but then the woman spoke again, and it was a voice I felt I knew. 'Is that you, Araltes?' the voice said again. 'I need you. The city needs you. Come!'

As my eyes grew accustomed to the dark, the speaker was revealed. Dark-painted eyes, the scent of purple, and at her side a full-grown leopard.

'Theodora!'

Looking back now, I cannot tell if we were the movers of the chess pieces, or just the pieces themselves, directed by the mobs and the anger of the people of Micklegard.

Theodora rushed me to the Varangian barracks, and my men saw me and put down their weapons and let me come to them. They had the same downcast look that they'd worn when a Sicilian siege dragged on, or after our defeat at Montemaggiore, but when they saw me and recognised me despite my unkempt beard, they hailed me with joy, and all the months of worry and concern fell from my shoulders.

We were like a ship driven by a great storm, and I was at the helm and must steer her well. There was no time for answers or discussion. 'The throne has been seized. Remember your oaths. We must find the Caulker. The people demand it!'

They cheered and Halldor brought out my banner, Landwaster, and others brought mail and my axe, and helm and shield. They seemed heavy to me at first, but you don't forget the weight of a mail shirt, and I was overjoyed to be free of those four cellar walls.

'Theodora, your leopard will scare people. Perhaps it should stay hidden.'

'All men know that this cat is mine,' she said. 'We will fight and die together, if need be. For if we fail here I will be killed. The Caulker has gone mad with power. He will leave none of us alive.'

I looked into her eyes.

I felt God with me again.

There was a flurry as a procession came down the road.

'Is this the Caulker's men?' someone said.

I drew my sword and strode out to meet them.

'Halt!' I shouted. 'I speak in the name of Theodora Autokrator and Empress of Constantinople. Who do you serve? The Caulker or the rightful Empress?'

There was a moment's panic, then an old man came forward, looking sinister and fierce. He was dressed all in black and he carried a staff bound with silver.

'Who speaks?' he called out.

'I, Araltes, Commander of the Emperor's Bodyguard. Varangian Inside-the-Walls.'

There were muffled voices, then the man – who must have been a monk – stepped aside and the crowd brought a stooped old priest from within itself. I knew his grey-streaked beard and bald head well. I had seen him leading processions through the streets, and had led him personally to the throne room. It was the Bishop of Micklegard, whom men called simply 'the Patriarch'.

I knelt before him. He came forward and put his hand upon my head. His skin was warm and soft and leathery. It was clear he had no idea who I was, though I had met him half a hundred times.

Barbarians all look alike to Greeks.

'Does he speak Greek?' the old man said to the man next to him.

'I do,' I said, but he did not seem to understand, or did not think that such a thing was possible.

'Tell him we need his aid,' the old man said. 'We have to stop the Caulker. He must find his men. He must protect the Empress.' And I played the part of the dumb barbarian as his words were translated, and squeezed his hand to show him that I understood.

CHAPTER SEVEN

The Wolf Runs Free

It was the depth of night, but the city was bright with burning and looting. We marched out of the barracks in four great squares, shields raised to cover each side, and the mob fell back. They were like wild dogs, starving and desperate, nipping at our heels.

They did not care who they were fighting for. They were out to loot and burn and rampage.

It was a short walk to the palace. As we came closer, I said to Halldor, 'Unfurl my banner!' He loosed the bindings, and Landwaster flapped angrily in the wind of our passing. It was red with reflected firelight. The colour of blood, which is the marker of brotherhood, anger, birth and death. It was fierce with foretelling: portents, omens, and men called out, 'The Raven!', as if they had seen some image on its surface.

My men cheered when they saw it. A fell mood had come upon us all. The city was burning and we were the disciplined centre of the conflagration.

A great mob had answered the Patriarch's call and had gathered at the palace gates. They were hurling stones up at the walls and calling for Zoe's return.

My job under Michael IV had been to protect the palace. Now, facing Michael the Caulker, it was to storm it.

'This is a strange reversal,' Halldor said.

'It is,' I said. 'Come. Let us get to work.'

The mob was a living thing of women, men, boys, children, priests, soldiers, aristocrats with their servants in their livery. It seethed like a wounded animal, back and forth, but like the beast that protects its young, something greater than fear drove them forward: it was a kind of madness, a fury at what had been done to their Empress.

I held my own men back and assessed the troops still loyal. There were Scythian Guards in their garish colours. There were other Varangians on the walls. Halldor pointed at their chief, but I knew him. It was Bjorn the Balls. He was marching back and forth, keeping his men in place.

Good, I thought as I led my men forward then, a man worth killing.

The mob parted like the Red Sea for the Israelites, and we passed through, mail gleaming forge-red with flames, shields high, swords and spears gripped. There were overturned carts set against the wall ready for burning, but the mob was losing momentum, and I knew that if they were beaten here then we would all be dead.

The tide of opportunity would ebb away. I have never seen anything so clearly in my life, and I made my choice. I would win victory, or die in the attempt.

I ran at the nearest cart and jumped onto it, scrambled up the sacks and leapt for the walls. On the second jump I caught a hold on the battlements and swung myself up – mail, helm and all.

'Up!' my men were encouraging each other, as a eunuch reached through the battlements to stab me. I grabbed his arm and yanked him over the wall, then hauled myself up and rolled onto the battlements.

I felt spears stab towards me as I leapt to my feet and my sword struck left and right. Blood sprayed down like rain. A bearded man drove a spear at me. It grazed my side. I kicked him in the midriff, knocked the teeth from the next with a punch of my sword hilt. His head came free a moment later, as I jumped down, gathered his shield where he had dropped it – a single-handed brass thing, not much bigger than a bucket top – and punched it into another's nose so hard my knuckles bled.

Six came at me. I broke the first man's arm through his shield. The next lost his head, I kicked the third off the wall, backhanded the next, and heard the crack as my hilt shattered his skull. An arrow hissed past my ear. I heard a man scream and did not know what had killed him. Someone jumped on to my back, his breath hot on my ear. I flung him over my shoulder and heard his heavy gasp as he landed. Someone grabbed my leg. I swung the shield side-on. The first blow had no effect, the second loosened his grip, the third was my axe, and he died with an angry sigh.

One threw his spear. I caught it and returned it with interest. It hit his cheek and his teeth sprayed out as it drove through his mouth. I shivered his helm, the blow so fierce that blood started from his eyes and he fell groaning from the wall. The next two paused, and that was their death. I slammed them back with the shield. My sword-point silenced one, and then I kicked the other so hard he knocked the men behind him onto their backsides.

Two archers crouched on the ground below. I saw them notching arrows to their bow strings, and swung wildly again as more men closed in. Two eunuchs came together, for courage. I ducked back as the bows twanged. One hit the eunuch low in the groin. He squealed like a pig. Two more pushed past him. They were scared and soft and fleshy. They clawed at my eyes. I cursed as one hand raked nails down my cheek. I shoved him back. They came at me again.

I hacked them down. One hand flew up, then another. I kept hacking and kicked my legs free. Shreds of flesh splattered up onto my face.

This all happened in the time it takes to draw three breaths. The next was a Varangian, who hovered, his spear held ready. I came at him and broke his spear-shaft and he died with a low moan as I ducked a Turk's wild sword swing, and barged that man off the wall with his own momentum. He clung to me as he fell, and I swayed and saw a long drop before me. I found my hand in someone's mouth for a moment and tugged down before he bit my fingers off. The bone cracked as it met my knee. I took the head from another man with a backward swing. Blood splattered into my face.

A hand grabbed me.

It was Halldor. 'Careful,' he said. Just one word. Landwaster flapped above us. It was like having a lover in battle. I was already moving on. My brother was with me. I was possessed with the Holy Spirit. I was fearless. I was murder. I was Death.

If any were with me I could not tell you.

I cleared the walls. I killed three Turks as the fourth fumbled with his arrow. He let the arrow fly, but it was a rushed shot, and I caught it on my shield. 'He's mine!' Halldor shouted, and led my Varangians past me. I looked about me, assessed the fighting. The defenders were in flight. Only about the gatehouse was any resistance gathering. And there stood a giant with a white horse-hair plume. 'Bjorn Balls!' I shouted.

The troll stopped and looked for me through the fighting. I bellowed his name again, and this time he found me and grinned. He had blood on his sword, splatters of gore across his face, and he was boiling with the thrill of killing. 'Take him!' he shouted to his men and they ran at me to slow me down. I killed the first two, Halldor knocked the third to the ground, and the last one fell to his knees, as if he thought that cowardice would save him.

'Bjorn!' I raged, and came at him like the Archangel Gabriel at Doomsday, when he leads the armies of God in battle against the Devil. Bjorn picked a fresh shield from the ground, and paused for a moment to catch his breath.

I had seen him sparring in the barrack-yards, slow and monstrous and unstoppable. He was a heathen in all but name, and had the trick of summoning the spirit of the bear and going berserk. His fury was a terrible thing, and I saw the madness come over him as he gnashed his teeth and sucked in the breaths as fast and deep as a running man. 'Stop howling, dog!' I shouted, and he came at me with a roar like a spring bear, woken hungry from its slumber.

His overhead swing rang through the shield and jarred my arm. The next came fast and hard to the side, the third a low sweep, and I only just jumped back in time; it whistled past me, and I felt the breath of death as he barged past me.

He saw that I was holding my shield arm back, and came at me again, raining blows down on the brass shield as if ringing a gong or beating the metal like a smith, till it was bent and folded onto my hand.

That hand was numb. My fingers had no strength in them. He saw my pain and his eyes grew wide, but he took an old foot-feint that Bjorn Punch had taught me, and as he watched the sword in my right hand, my left drove the sharp buckled edges of the brass shield into his face with such power that I heard the crunch of his nose as it flattened against his cheek, and he flew backwards in a spray of spittle, teeth and gore.

Halldor said I lifted Bjorn the Troll from the ground with the force of my strike. I have seen it re-enacted many times in the hall when men gather to tell tales of epic battles they have witnessed. When I see the fight in my mind's eye, I see no watchers, only Bjorn's panting face as he lifts his sword to strike again, the white horse-hair plume swinging with the build-up to the blow, his unhurt features, and within me I feel the terror and horror and fear as I realise that he might best me, Harald Sigurdsson, in combat, and I feel my feet brace against the earth, my shield arm straight before me, my body one line, a brass arrow that strikes at his head and hurls him back.

Each man tells only half a tale, but I tell you how I saw it. The next thing I remember my hand was in agony and I was looking down and Bjorn lay groaning on the floor, and Halldor stepped forward. He was laughing so hard he could barely stand up straight.

'What?' I asked him.

He put a hand to my shoulder, and pointed to where Bjorn groaned on the floor. The berserk spirit had fled. It was as if I had exorcised a demon. I believe that was what I had done.

The great clod was stupid, both legs outstretched, shaking his head like a drunk who has just had a bucket of water tipped over his head. He shook himself and pushed himself up, spat out his teeth, and came at me again. But the berserk frenzy had gone from him. He was punch-drunk and it felt like cutting down the village halfwit.

My first blow sheared off his white plume. The second hit true and burst the rivets of his nose-guard, the third rang out like a minster bell. It stunned him and he fell back against the wall, and at once I saw my brother at Stiklestad, held up by the rock, and I stepped in close, lifted his mail shirt and drove my sword through his guts.

'Go to Hell, heathen bastard!' I told him, and then dealt the death blow to the neck; his head flew over the wall, and my sword hit the battlement bricks and showered sparks. You can still see the notch it made, men who have arrived from Micklegard tell me.

I wiped my sword on his white silk cloak, and tutted to see the dent the wall had made on the edge. It is true what men say, I thought. No man lives beyond his allotted hour.

We took the gatehouse a little after midnight, opened the gates and the mob streamed in. The remaining Varangians loyal to the Caulker died to a man. A shame, I thought, but they kept to their oaths, and you cannot fault a man for that. Better to die on a battlefield than in a bed.

I was standing there when Theodora arrived, pushing through the crowd on a fine black palfrey. She looked older, taller and more gaunt, but this also gave her a stern and serious aspect, like a warrior. 'Empress!' I called out, and the crowd began to chant her name. By the time she crossed the fifty feet to the palace gates, she had to shout over them. 'Araltes,' she said, 'I need more. The Caulker has fled. You must find him. He cannot be allowed to rule again. Understand?'

I nodded. I knew what that meant. All our lives were at stake this night.

CHAPTER EIGHT

Doomsday

The Caulker had sought sanctuary in the Monastery of St John of Studios, which stood in the southern quarter, near the Golden Gate, overlooking the Propontis. The abbot was at his gates when I arrived, desperately trying to hold the mob back. The noise was overwhelming. It was fury, excitement, hatred and joy. I could see the abbot and a few dark shapes pushing at the jaws of the mob, one, two, three times, but on the third time he and the monks were shoved back and then the mob was inside, and the old man disappeared in the crush.

Fighting my way through, I shoved past the abbot, burst through the doors and marched into the church. A great crowd had gathered, but no one dared lay a hand on the Caulker. He had taken holy vows and had his hands upon the altar and was loudly proclaiming that any who touched him would be cursed. His voice was commanding and he held them back with the force of his will. He saw I did not fear him and his voice became shrill as I strode towards him.

'I have taken Holy Orders,' he called out. 'I am in Sanctuary. You cannot seize me here.'

'My brother will speak to Christ for me,' I said, and grasped his arm and dragged him from the altar. He caught a candlestick and swiped at me. I backslapped it from his hand, and he hung from me like a dead hare, as if that would slow me down. 'I have taken Holy Orders,' he kept saying, as I shoved my way through the angry, milling crowd. As soon as he was outside the church the mob set upon him and they pulled him from me. There were hundreds of them. It was like trying to hold a beast down.

I saw him briefly, warding off their blows, and then he broke free for a moment, before the mob caught him once more.

It was like watching a cat prey upon a wounded shrew. Again he got away and again the mob was on him. 'Stop!' I shouted, but nobody heard me. 'Back!' I shouted again, wading through the bodies. At last I shoved the final bunch aside and caught him up.

The Caulker lay bloodied and groaning. He clung to my legs as stones flew and one man tried to pull him away from me. 'Back!' I shouted. Halldor and the rest of my men drew their swords in a ring about me.

'Kill him!' the crowd shouted.

'Give him to us!'

'He is ours!'

'Back!' I told them, and they cringed away. 'I shall judge him. The Empress Theodora has given me the right.'

The name of Theodora stilled them. The fact I had called her Empress gave them something to think about, and when a mob thinks, then they are a mob no longer.

I knew that I could not kill a monk, despite the damage he had done to us all, but I had to do something. The answer came in a moment. I took him to a high place so that all could see the judgement. The steps of the monastery seemed the best place. 'Stay close,' I told my men, and the crowd stepped back.

On the steps of the monastery the abbot lay in the care of his monks. I lifted him to his feet. 'Give him back to us,' the abbot begged, and as he spoke there were shouts and insults and I held up my hands for silence. 'He is one of us now.'

'I will give him back to the care of the abbot and his brothers, I promise,' I said. 'But first I must punish him for his crimes.'

The crowd hushed as I turned to them and spoke. 'Michael the Caulker,' I said, without using his titles, and used the words he had spoken when he threw me into prison. 'You have rebelled against your people, your wife, your Empress, your God and the oaths you swore.'

'Who are you to judge me?' he shouted as I held him up by the scruff of his woollen habit.

'I am Harald Sigurdsson, Commander of the Varangians Inside-the-Wall, bodyguard and strategos, general.'

He thrashed back and forth like a naughty child about to be branded. My men held him down.

I put my knee on his head to hold it still and the crowd pressed close. They were so quiet I could hear a child speaking at the back, and someone else saying, 'Hush! The traitor is being punished.'

'Hold still,' I told him, but he, who had punished so many, could not take chastisement himself. He squirmed like a worm. 'It will hurt,' I told him, but he did not listen.

I got one eye out and then turned his head and that last eye was wide with terror. He was writhing like a serpent, still cursing us all to damnation.

I put my knee on his head again. 'Just be grateful I'm not gelding you too,' I said.

It was him or me, I thought, as I pushed my thumbs in.

Putting a man's eyes out is not pleasant, but I thought of home and wiped my hands afterwards, as he screamed at me.

'Here,' I said to the monks. 'Take him and care for him if he is one of your own, before the mob get him.'

They nodded and helped the Caulker to his feet.

His cheeks were red with tears of blood, his eyes were gory hollows. That is the face of failure, I thought.

*

It took me over an hour to return to the palace. Everyone wanted to shake my hand, and in the end a joyous nobleman gave me his horse, so that I could make my way through.

I rode through the palace gates. Fires were still being dampened down, a scrawny bitch-hound was lapping at a pool of blood, and all about were my men in full armour, on guard. Theodora was in the throne room, pacing up and down. She had a golden cloak thrown over her shoulders and on the throne was Zoe.

It took me a moment to recognise her. Her head had been roughly shorn, and she looked like a hag about to be tarred and feathered as a witch. Whose clothes they had found for her, I do not know, but if I had passed her in the street then I would not have recognised her. There was nothing royal about her now that her baubles were gone.

I turned to Theodora. 'It is done,' I said.

Zoe let out a low moan. Theodora sucked in a breath and nodded. 'Oh thank God!' she said, and crossed herself, then turned to me.

'Araltes. Send out word that the usurpers have been destroyed, and the daughters of Emperor Constantine, the Eighth to bear that name, Zoe and Theodora Porphyrogenita, shall rule together. Until order can be restored.'

I bowed, and repeated the words to the assembled eunuchs, and soon they were being repeated through the city and beyond, wherever the rule of Micklegard held sway.

When I reached my chambers I took off my clothes and poured a bucket of water over my head. I felt the bruises on my body, and massaged my left wrist, which has never been the same since that battle with Bjorn. I set a guard all about the palace and then I slept, almost as well as the dead.

Next evening the bells were ringing prayers. A gibbous moon rose over the Bosphorus. It was the hour of business and food and eating, and a joyful air reigned in the city. Men were singing, people were cheering, crowds were singing hymns – and I thought, this morning they were baying for blood.

I sent a servant out to buy meat for me and my men to eat. The streets were full of men grilling lamb and goat over their coals. We had just finished eating when a eunuch came to my room. He stood nervously, and I wiped my mouth on the back of my hand and said, 'Speak man.'

'The Empress Theodora has asked for you. She is in the Caulker's room.'

I nodded. 'Tell her I will come.'

Theodora was standing at her window, looking out through the open shutters at the palace yard. Below, unaware in the palace yard, three of my men were sitting in the freckled light of a brass lantern, laughing as they passed a wineskin between them. The sound was distant. I could not make the words out.

'It is hard to believe that a battle raged here just last night,' she said.

I nodded. The eunuchs had been rushing about all day. The dead had been buried. The guilty hanged. I walked to her table, where a ewer of wine lay with a weighted cloth over the top to keep flies out.

'May I?'

She nodded. I was a Varangian, her look seemed to say. Why ask?

'Thank you,' I said. 'I thought I was done for.'

'You were,' she said. 'But there was nothing I could do to help you. Not until the Caulker made his move. Then it was not just your life at stake, it was mine and my sister's as well. I needed someone, and you were the only person.'

'Well,' I said, feeling a little less flattered than before. 'I thank you. But what now?'

She looked at me. 'For the sake of the empire, we rule.'

I ate my dinner of spiced meat with the men and then made the rounds of the palace gates. I had posted double guards, and when I stepped back into my room, a shadow gave me just a moment's warning. I cursed and turned, and caught the assailant by the throat and rammed him back so hard I could hear his skull-bone thud against the wall.

It was a young eunuch. Just the kind to take a mission like this.

'Who are you?' I hissed. 'What are you doing here?'

He gargled back at me, and I loosened his throat enough to let him speak.

'The Empress has asked for you.'

'Why didn't you tell one of my men?'

'The Empress was firm on the matter. I carry the message to you and you alone.'

I let him go. 'What does Theodora want at this time?'

The boy blushed as he brushed himself down. 'Oh no,' he said. 'I apologise. My message comes from Empress Zoe.'

'How can I trust her?'

'She wants to apologise. For the way that you were treated. She knows that she was wrong.'

It was a little after sunset. I knew the way to Zoe's private chambers. A pale blue light silhouetted the carved shutters, as a maid went about lighting the oil lamps. Last time I'd been there, the Caulker had been laughing from within. Now all was silent. I knocked on the door and was admitted at once.

The room was dimly lit, but I could see her, lying sideways on a couch, like an old and toothless she-lion.

'Araltes,' she said, and gave me a thin-lipped smile.

I took my place and saw that a glass of wine had already been poured for me.

I did not touch it, even when she motioned for me to drink.

'It is good,' she said, and leant across, her robe hanging open and showing her large breasts. I looked away. I did not find them attractive or alluring. She revolted me.

Her roots had been freshly dyed blue-black, her veil thrown back, with what looked like someone else's hair falling down over her shoulders. Her lobes were heavy with gold, she stank of rosewater, and her eyes were painted dark and large. She could not speak without lisping or showing the black stumps of her teeth.

'I have to thank you,' she said, and sipped my wine to show it was not poisoned, and played with one of the laces to her robe.

I felt sick at the thought that she should loosen it.

'It is nothing,' I told her. 'I just kept to the oath I swore to your late husband, Michael. He asked me to stay to ensure a smooth transition.'

'Thank you,' she said, and tugged at the lace, and the knot unravelled, and I swallowed and sat up, as prim as a young maid.

'The patriarch has pronounced my wedding with the Caulker void,' she said.

I nodded, but I did not care. She began to play with a second lace, and I felt sweat drip down my sides. I who had faced elephants in battle was terrified of this old slug.

'Who will you marry?' I squeaked.

She tugged at the next lace, and as one heavy breast threatened to fall free, I stood straight up.

'That is the guard bell,' I said.

She frowned. 'I do not hear anything.'

'No?' I said. 'I do. It is a soldier's training.'

She gave me a sideways glance. 'Are you stupid?' she said.

'No,' I told her. 'Why?'

She patted the couch beside her. 'Come and sit with me.'

As she spoke her top fell open and a sagging breast broke free, like a shapeless water-skin slipping onto the floor. I did not know where to look. 'I am sorry, Madam,' I said. 'But your gown ...'

I gestured, but she lifted a hand to her collar and opened her top wide.

'Yes,' she said. 'What do you think?'

'Beautiful,' I said.

She patted the couch again, and I could have jumped for terror. 'But I have sworn a vow.'

She let her breasts dangle. 'What vow?'

'I am betrothed,' I said. 'To one of Jaroslav's daughters.' The lie came quickly, and I elaborated it with a few facts, and she licked her lower lip seductively.

'If a better offer were to make itself to you?'

'I swore a vow. Varangians never break our oaths. All men know that.'

She patted the couch again. 'She would never know.'

'Yes, but I would,' I said, and this time the guard bell did ring, and I seized my chance. 'Forgive me, lady, I am summoned,' I said, and bowed and was gone from the room.

CHAPTER NINE

Kingmaker

Theodora was standing at her window, looking out through the open shutters at the palace yard. Her leopard was sprawled before the fire, eyes half-closed, the claws of one paw flexing in upon themselves.

'Araltes,' she said. She looked surprised to see me. I stepped inside, and made a face that showed that I could not speak until the maid had gone.

I stood stiffly for a moment, and then said, 'I have to tell you something.'

Her dark eyes looked up and a faint smile played about her mouth. 'What?'

'I was just summoned to your sister's room.'

'Oh,' Theodora said. 'My. And did you accept her offer?'

'No,' I said. 'Of course not. But I have to warn you. I think she wants to marry. She offered to make me Emperor.'

Theodora lifted her green-glass goblet to her mouth. 'A barbarian Emperor? Well. It has happened before, I suppose.'

'I said no,' I told her.

She lifted an eyebrow. 'Why? Don't you want to be Emperor?'

'I did not want her,' I replied quickly.

She patted the couch where she lay. 'Come. I am not my sister.'

I took a seat. She slid closer. 'Yesterday, when I said to you, "We rule" – what did you think I meant?'

I told her and she looked down and took in a breath. 'No. Not exactly.' She took my hand and ran a finger along the lines in my palm. 'So strong, this line,' she said. 'No wonder Zoe wanted you for her own.'

I was suddenly conscious of her painted eyes on me, her perfume, the low candlelight falling across her, and pulled my hand away. She walked two fingers towards me, and ran them up my forearm. 'Was this the game that Zoe played with you?' She untied the clasp of her gown and slid it off her shoulders. Underneath she was dressed only in a white linen shift. She slid next to me and put on a girlish voice. 'My! What bold hands you have, barbarian. You should not presume. Was that the game she played?'

I had to clear my throat. 'That was it,' I said.

'Did she undress herself? Show a breast, perhaps?'

I could not go through this again, and stood. 'Lady,' I said. 'The late Emperor Michael promised me that when the end of the year had come, then he would let me and my men return home. That is what I want.'

If she had thought to seduce me, my manner stopped her.

'You have the choice of Zoe or Theodora this night, Varangian. Most men would be flattered.'

'I am flattered,' I told her. 'And doubly so, that you would want me as your consort. But these are not my people. This is not my land. Your Greek mountains are strange to me. I want to see the land of my forebears. The peaks where the old gods still send thunder and lightning. I want to see the fjords again. I want to bring my people a little of what you have here.'

Behaviour that came so easily to Zoe was hard for her, and I could see that it had taken all her courage to make a proposition to me, and that in spurning her so quickly, I risked her fury.

At that moment her leopard stretched and yawned, fangs exposed in the open mouth, and turned over onto the other side.

It broke the tension of the moment.

'I understand,' she said, and looked down to hide her shame, and then she was no longer the sister to the Empress, but a handsome unwanted woman.

I felt her grief. I wanted to put out a hand to console her but one of her women knocked on her door, to check if she needed anything before bed.

'No,' she called.

'The Patriarch wants to know if you will be needing Mass before bed?'

'No,' she called again.

I made to get up but she reached out and held my hand.

'My men will be wondering.'

'Let them wonder.' She pressed herself against me and I lay there, stroking the back of her head and wondering just exactly how much trouble I had got myself into.

She pushed herself up onto her elbow and cupped her chin. My eyes had grown accustomed to the dark and her eyes gleamed with the moonlight that filtered down from the high window.

'I wish you were not a barbarian.'

I closed my eyes and tried to imagine myself sitting on the throne of Micklegard, ruling half the world, leading her armies to victories over all her foes.

It was tempting, for a moment, but I wanted my own land, my own people. They needed me, I thought. They needed all the things that the Byzantines had: learning, cities, food, faith, strong defences. Who else could bring these things to them? If I stayed they would continue, as . . . barbarians.

'I am who I am,' I said. 'We cannot change it.'

'No,' she said and pulled me towards her.

Afterwards, when our bodies cooled, I felt as guilty as a sinner.

The silence between us grew. At last she gave me a shove.

'Your men will be waiting.'

*

Zoe announced her marriage the next day. The bells rang through the city, and there was a crowd cheering outside the palace gates by the time I woke.

Halldor found me. 'So,' he said. 'Looks like we're not going to rule the empire after all.'

'What are you talking about?' I said, thinking loose tongues would get us all killed.

He winked at me. 'I heard you went to Zoe's room last night.'

'I did,' I said.

'And did she . . . ?'

'She did,' I said, 'but before you ask, no, I did not.'

He pulled a face. 'Shame. It would have made a good tale.'

I smiled. 'Yes, it would,' I said, but I had become much too embroiled, not just in palace affairs, but in the beds of two sisters. There was no hotter blaze a man could sit in. 'But now, we *really* have to find out a way to leave.'

Zoe's new husband was named Constantine – the ninth Emperor to bear that name. He was standing at the foot of the steps when I came in, with a great crowd of Greek noblemen about him. Clearly they approved of this match. He had the air of a man elected to take up a position. We are taking care of our own business, their expressions seemed to say.

Constantine was a short man, broad and lean, with a close-cropped beard and wide, intelligent eyes. I shook his hand. 'I have been warned against meeting you,' he said when we met. 'After all, it was you who blinded the Caulker.'

I bowed. 'He did not deserve the love of your wife, Zoe, or the people or the Church. I was their servant in punishing him.'

'Good,' he said. 'I would not want to cross paths with Araltes.' He smiled as he spoke, and the men about him laughed, but I sensed a warning there.

'I only serve,' I told him.

The chamberlain, John Thousand-Eyes, had been reinstated. I

felt just two of those many eyes on me. As soon as I came out, I summoned Halldor and explained to him what needed to be done.

'You cannot involve me at all,' I said. 'There are too many little birds that might see me and suspect. I am leaving this to you. It's all our lives.'

He nodded. A man could be killed just on suspicion of plotting.

So I went about my last days in Micklegard as if everything was normal. I set the guards, I sat in council, I drank with important men, attended feasts, and I knew nothing of what was being done in my name.

On the fourth night I was getting ready for a feast at the Numeri Tower, where I had been imprisoned. The captain of the cataphracts there thought it fitting to feast me. We had fought in Bulgaria together, and he was a cousin of Constantine, so it seemed a safe thing to do. But as I dressed in my full ceremonial armour Halldor strolled past my chambers, on the way to the latrine, and said, 'Tonight. Second hour of the second watch.'

'Where?'

'I will come for you,' he said.

'I am dining in the Numeri Tower.' But he had already left.

CHAPTER TEN

The Golden Horn

I had resolved not to drink that evening at Numeri, but nothing would be more likely to rouse suspicions, so I ended up toasting the Emperor Constantine, his family and their rising fortunes, and putting down half a jug at least.

When the bell rang the second watch, one of my men appeared and asked to be admitted.

My drinking fellow was rather the worse for wear.

'Don't go,' he slurred, but my man looked nervous.

'There is a summons for you,' he said. 'From the palace.'

'Nothing wrong I hope?' said my companion.

'No,' I told him. 'Probably just a whore who's not been paid making a clamour at the barrack gates.'

'Another cup!' he said and sloshed wine half over my wrist and half into my goblet.

We drank three more cups, in fact, and then he slobbered all over me and I stumbled as I threw my cloak over my shoulders and stood on the doorstep making a great fuss of having to leave such a convivial occasion.

'I will see you in court,' he called, thinking he had made himself an excellent ally in the palace.

I waved and smiled. 'Ask for me and I will bring you in through the Emperor's Gate,' I assured him. 'No need to queue with the others.'

I did not know if the lad knew what instructions I had given to Halldor, so we chatted about idle things as we passed through the main thoroughfare along the west side of the Hippodrome, but instead of turning right towards the palace gates we continued down to the harbours of the Golden Horn.

The moon had set not long after the sun, and the clear sky turned blue and then black, while the stars gathered brightness. As our horses' hoofs clip-clopped along the flagstones it struck me that I would never see this place again. There was no sadness. The idea thrilled me, and as we made our way over the spine of the city, and turned down to the Prosphorion Harbour, I saw ships waiting.

The Lydian guards waved us through as I came down to the harbour, but rather than a small group of the most trusted retainers, as I had ordered, I saw nearly two hundred men huddled there.

'What is this?' I hissed. 'We're supposed to be leaving in secret.'

Halldor took my elbow and steered me away. 'No one wanted to leave without you. We had to draw lots.'

'The whole world will know,' I said. I felt sick.

'No one else knows,' he promised me. 'All these men would die for you.'

I turned. The men could not have heard our words, but they understood the nature of our conversation. They nodded at me, and I felt humbled.

'Let us go. Now, while our luck still holds.'

My men shoved three boats out into the water and swung themselves up over the sheer strakes. The air was soft and quiet. There was a rattle as the oars were fitted into place. Then we were skimming across the dark water, and on either side the towers of Micklegard reared over us: huge and black, like overhanging mountains in the night – guardians of that narrow way.

There were shouts from one tower as they understood our intention. An alarm bell rang out and a voice shouted, 'Halt!' across the water.

I seized the drumstick.

'Strike!' I told the oarsmen. 'Strike!' I beat out the rhythm, the oars struck and struck again, and I felt the prow lift with each thrust. Ahead of us the boom chain would have been rowed across the harbour at sunset. We had to get over it somehow. Halldor was shielding his eyes as he scanned the dark water for the floats that showed where it blocked the middle of the harbour entrance.

'There!' he shouted and held up his arm, and every man who was not rowing ran to the stern of the ship. The prow rose a good foot more from the water. Alarm bells rang out and the keel ground on the chain links. The impact threw us to our knees.

'Forward!' I shouted, and as one we ran to the prow of the boat, each man carrying his chest with him. The boat teetered for a moment as the weight shifted and the keel righted, and then it tipped forward. Slowly at first, but with gathering momentum, the ship tilted like a merchant's scales, and we slid safely down the other side. Arrows hummed out across the water, but they were wild shots and fell short.

'Row, men, row!' I bellowed, and with every beat of the oars we flew forward, and I thought of northern geese, whose wingbeat quickens as they take off from the water.

We retraced our route north through the Black Sea and up the wide Rus rivers and finally back to Kiev. From the reaction of men we met along the way it was clear to me how much I had changed. When we reached Kiev the place seemed small and rustic, even though Jaroslav's stone gate and church were almost finished.

The old prince came down to welcome me personally. His beard had turned white in the eight years I had been away, but his eyes were still sharp, his grip firm. 'I'm too old to go and fight now,' he said, 'but I can still ride a horse and hold a shield.'

He took me on a tour of his city. 'Look, the gates are finished,' he told me, and I was impressed at how he had brought civilisation to this land.

One night in his private chamber, painted to resemble the Micklegard throne room, we sat and drank spiced wine without water, and he said to me, 'So, then, you killed the Emperor of Micklegard.'

'Blinded him,' I said.

'Well! Is that all? What next, Harald Sigurdsson?'

'I have travelled enough,' I said. 'It is time I went home.'

'You know that Olaf's son Magnus is king there now?'

'So I have heard.'

'He is a fine king, by all accounts.'

'He learnt from you,' I said.

'I would not want any harm to come to him.'

'Nor I,' I said. 'I am his uncle. I love my nephew.'

Jaroslav smiled, but did not seem convinced. 'You have not married, I am told.'

'No,' I said. 'Nor betrothed. I've seen no woman worthy of it yet.'

'Oh really?' he said. 'I heard a tale that you were betrothed by solemn oaths to one of my daughters.'

I blushed. 'It was a tale I told,' I said. 'To get me out of a tight spot.'

'Oh, and my daughters were so excited. "Is he handsome?" they asked me, and I said I could not tell, but he was from good stock.' He acted as if the thought had just occurred to him. 'As we have made no betrothal, maybe you should see them and see which one you would have chosen.'

'I'd be honoured. All men know how beautiful Jaroslav's daughters are. And you're right. I'm twenty-eight winters now. It's time I married.'

Jaroslav's wife was famous across the north for her beauty. I'd taken a fancy to his youngest, Anne, and she, I flattered myself, had taken a shine to me in my seventeenth year, so I was eager to see how the girls had turned out.

The maids came first, tittering and putting their hands over their mouths as the two young ladies were brought forward.

'These are my daughters.'

The two young women bowed. I looked to Anne first of all. She was as I had remembered, tall and shy, like a forest doe that strays into your path, and halts, not sure which way to run. 'Welcome to Kiev,' she said. Her voice was soft and gentle and I thought she was lovely. I almost stood up and clapped my arms about the old fox and kissed him. She was fair and comely, in manner much like the Greek girls I had seen in the South. 'Thank you,' I said, and her cheeks coloured and I wanted to inhale her in a breath. 'I am glad to return.'

As Anne opened her mouth the other girl stepped forward. She was not as fair as her sister, but she looked me in the eye and spoke in a voice that was strong and confident. 'Greetings, Harald,' she said. 'I am Elizaveta. Many years have passed since you were last in my father's halls. Each year men have brought us news of your great deeds. Can they all be true?'

'No,' I said, and she laughed too, without covering her mouth. She had a saucy look about her, breezy and keen and strong-minded, and I realised that there was some air here, some spirit, some personality that I wanted, indeed that I needed. I made my mind up there and then, but did not tell anyone for days, waiting and hoping to see if Anne had any of her sister's qualities, and finding, to my sorrow, that she did not. She was a wallflower, better suited to a Byzantine nobleman's bed than my own. I had a country to run, and if I was to be king I needed a strong woman, who could rule beside me, and help me to govern both household and kingdom.

When at last I asked Jaroslav's permission, he had a look in his eyes, and leaned across and said, 'I love all my children, but with Elizaveta I say you have chosen well!'

I gave Elizaveta a good part of my treasure as dowry. It made her richer than most kings, and was generous with the wealth I'd given her, giving out alms, and commissioning new churches in Kiev and beyond.

I spent two years in Kiev with Jaroslav, watching and learning king-craft. Each year more of my men followed me north from Micklegard. I welcomed each one back, and this time they swore their oaths to me, personally, and my retinue grew, till some talked of me staying on here and founding a principality of my own.

I put paid to that straight away, but Halldor told it true. 'Jaroslav's sons already look askance at the honours you receive. I would too if I were they. You've married their sister. How long till you decide to take their throne? And who would stop you? Men have been singing your name for near ten years now. You're the richest man in Christendom, bar the Emperor.'

Much of what he said was not true, but he was right: it was time to leave. Yet every time I went to Jaroslav he kept putting off my departure, and I was flattered at first, but then began to grow restless. 'My father fears what will happen if you go north,' Elizaveta said, and the force of what she said struck me like a blow.

'He thinks I will hurt Magnus?'

'The strong cannot help but hurt the weak.'

'Well I can't stay here just because a boy sits on my throne.'

She smiled. 'I did not say you should. Let Magnus watch his own back. Your home is not here. I think it is time you went back. Make yourself king.' She took my hand and put it to her belly. 'Can you feel it?'

She was convinced she was with child, and I slid my hand about, but shook my head.

'I know I am with child, but I have not told anyone except my maid. My father would never let you take me north if he knew.'

I left Kiev in the autumn of 1045. I was thirty winters old. I had ten ships, a wife, five hundred battle-hardened warriors, and enough gold to make the ships wallow in rough water.

We passed through Lagoda, and back into the Eastern Seas. Elizaveta was as brave as any man, but it was nearing midwinter and she had never sailed out of sight of land before. Even though she would not admit it, she looked green and pale, so rather than risk the stormy crossing, I had my ships take us to the quieter waters of Sweden, and so on to the hall of King Onund. It seemed fitting, I thought, that my journey should return there, as it had started half a lifetime before.

Elizaveta protested – she had wanted the child born in Norway – but I soothed her. 'It is no matter. I have waited all these years. A few weeks will not kill me.'

King Onund had been in the prime of his strength when last I was here, but now he had grey in his beard, a slight stoop, and the pale December afternoon light showed lines of care about his blue eyes. 'Harald Sigurdsson!' he laughed as our handshake went on and on. 'Look at you! How many winters have we sat and listened to saltbeards' tales of your adventures? My, it is true what they say: either the lone wolf dies, or it returns to the pack bigger and fiercer and stronger than before.'

'I am no wolf,' I said. 'But I have returned.'

'What brought you out from the summer lands of the Greeks?' he asked me.

'Your face,' I told him. 'And the warm welcome at your hall!'

He laughed even louder then.

'Good!' he said. 'Then welcome! And this, this must be Cousin Elizaveta. Such a beautiful bride.'

I helped Elizaveta over the threshold, and all could see how heavy with child she was, and made a place for her by the glowing coals.

'Wine?' Onund said, but I remembered the poor sort that made its way this far north.

'It's been a long time since I tried good ale,' I said.

Onund laughed and clapped his hands and called for the steward. 'Ale it is.'

That night Elizaveta's labours began, and I found myself pacing up and down, taut with nerves. Astrid and the herb-women were in the room with her, and occasionally I could hear a low groan or brief, forced laughter, but all the while my thoughts were of Helen and how she had done this alone, and in pain, and died because of it. I did not want the same to happen to Elizaveta, but for all my powers and feats I could do nothing to help her.

'Sit, man!' Onund called out, and held out the ale-jug, but I kept pacing like a leopard caged.

'It is hard to hear her suffer,' I said at last, thinking that I should make some excuse for not joining him.

He smiled. 'First?'

I nodded. There was a low, bestial groan, like a cow. I swallowed and nodded.

'Sit,' he said. 'It will be over within a day or so. Quicker, if God is merciful and the baby small.'

I nodded. My hands were sweaty. I needed a drink, I thought, and sat down with him.

'Do you hawk?' he asked, brightly.

I thought he would have remembered, but it had been a long time, and much had happened. 'No,' I said.

'Ah well. Hounds?'

'Sounds good.'

'We'll take them out at first light, if the child's not here by then.'

'No,' I said. 'I'd rather be here.' He looked surprised, but I spoke so earnestly that he did not think to argue.

'Well, I'll hunt, if you don't mind. The dogs have been cooped up with rain. They start to fret.'

Before the child had been born we had lain and Elizaveta had taken my hand and put it low on her swollen belly. 'Can you feel him kicking?' Then when he was born, he was a she, but I did not care.

Elizaveta seemed more disappointed than I. 'Next time,' she said.

'Yes,' I said, and forced a smile, and nodded. I could not think about the marriage bed at this moment.

'What shall we call her?'

I knew all the boys' names I would have given him, but daughters I was less sure of.

We settled eventually on Ingegerd, my grandmother's name.

We waited till the babe was six weeks old, and then, as the first buds began to appear, and snow streams ran down the mountains, we took ship again.

The constellation of kings had changed much since Stiklestad. King Knut was eight years dead. His son Harthaknut ruled England, and Olaf's son Magnus was king of the Norse. But a new star had appeared, blazing in the sky: brighter and fiercer than all the others. Men came to offer me their service, and I picked the best of them and turned away any who had fought against my brother at Stiklestad.

So it was with nearly thirty ships we set out from Onund's hall, and this time I took the steer board and turned the prow west, the setting sun golden on our faces.

For three days we sailed, and then I began to see the headlands and mountains of my home, and looking at it then, it seemed so small and narrow a place from which to have sprung.

I was like the autumn bear who returns to the place where it was born, thinking to find shelter, and cannot fit back through the hole.

Elizaveta had Ingegerd swaddled in her arms. The babe had a milky foam on her lips, and was sleeping as deeply as a mountain. 'What is wrong?' Elizaveta asked.

'Nothing,' I grinned. 'There she is, men! Uppland!'

My heart was unsettled to see my home and not feel familiar, but I could not show it. Not to anyone.

PART IV

The North

CHAPTER ONE

Return to Uppland

My brother Halfdan had died in the fifteen years I had been gone. It was typical of him, I thought, who disappointed endlessly. Last time I'd seen his sons, Ottar and Sigurd, they'd been pink-faced, snotty-nosed bairns, now they were bum-fluffed men. They saw me stride up the shingle towards them, and you could see their eyes open in wonder.

I understood their shock. I too had grown up in this narrow northern dale. We shared that at least.

'Uncle Harald,' they stammered. 'You have come here?'

'Of course I have come here. This is my home. Now, you must be Ottar. You Sigurd.'

They trembled before me. 'Of course. We just . . . We are so honoured to see you. You are here for good?'

I had wanted to be wise and kind and generous, but their manner riled me from the start. 'Of course. This is my father's hall,' I said, and held out my arms. 'And this is my wife. She is Elizaveta, Prince Jaroslav's daughter!'

Elizaveta spoke to them, but they stared at her in wonder.

'Welcome, Princess,' one of them squeaked.

'Come,' the other whispered, and hit the fool.

I let them lead me forward as if I were a guest. My father's seat looked small. It looked plain. It looked tired.

'Sit,' Ottar said. He was stout and jowly, like a miller. 'Please!'

He gave me a horn of ale while the others rushed back and forth and stoked the hall fire to a blaze, then they stared at me as if I were a tusk of elephant ivory left in the middle of the hall.

At that moment an old woman came in. I do not think I had ever thought of her in my fifteen years away, but I knew her at once.

'Thorgred.'

My mother's old nursemaid was the last person I expected to see. She was even shorter than before, her forearms were thick with knitted sleeves, and she was hairy about the face now, as old women are. 'I heard that you had come back, Harald. But is that you?'

'It is I. I used to eat your oat cakes sitting by the kitchen fire. How is your husband, Grettir?'

She stumped forward for a better look. 'He is well, Lord. But my! Look at you. Men said you were dead, but I would tell them they were wrong.'

'They are,' I laughed, and took the old woman's hand. 'This is Thorgred,' I said to Elizaveta, 'my mother's nurse, and a second mother to me, after she was gone.'

The old lady shooed my comments away as if they were chickens come to see if the lid of the grain store had been left ajar, but I took her hand and pulled her into my father's chair. She made it look large once more, and it was her place of honour for as long as she lived.

'You look quite the warrior,' she said. 'I don't remember seeing such a man. No wonder they have lit the beacons.'

There was nervous laughter. Ottar tried to shoo the old lady off, which annoyed me all the more.

'Leave her,' I told him. 'She earned honour in this household before you were even born. Now speak. What is this of beacons?'

'Please do not be angry. It is just that . . . ' the eldest trailed off. 'It is just that King Magnus. He said . . . ' they started. 'He said that we should not allow you to land.' He quivered all over like a hound summoned by its master for a beating. 'He said no one should let you land, but you are our uncle and we have heard so much about your travels.'

I fell silent and gave them a cold look that said all.

'Harald,' said a voice. It was Elizaveta. 'Do not be too hard on them. They are foolish men who have seen and understand little.'

The two fools nodded to support her words. I weighed them up and found them little men, just like their father. It was a shame to have kin like these. But as I turned I saw that already a crowd had gathered at the door. Ingegerd started to fuss in Elizaveta's arms. She looked for the wet-nurse and handed her over. 'Harald, look! Your people have come to welcome you home.'

The crowd was timid at first as I turned towards them. I strode out into the daylight, and for a moment, as I bent under the lintel and stepped over the threshold, my hand on the doorpost and the light briefly blinding me, I was fifteen again.

But then I heard the noise of the crowd before me. They clapped and cheered as I brought myself up to my full height. I had fifteen years' worth of speeches in my head, fifteen years of imagining this return, but now I was here I was speechless.

They cheered and waved and I nodded towards them, overcome for an instant with emotion, and then someone shouted 'King Harald!' and soon the cry went round till it was a chant, and then the sun came out, and the light was hot on my face. It made the fjord sparkle with silver, and I felt my throat tighten and wiped my eyes.

Uppland had not forgotten me.

I had planned to ride from valley to valley, farmstead to farmstead, and rally support for my cause, as Olaf had done. But gold has a way of speaking for you, and as soon as word spread that I had returned from the South with a dragon's hoard of treasure, men came from Uppland and beyond and promised to support my claim to kingship.

One chest was made of lead, one of gilt, one had ivory panels carved with flowers, and the largest was so full of gold it took ten men to lift it. Men came just to look at them. I would catch them, wondering what was inside, and trying to lift them just to check that they were not empty. But gold has a weight to it no other metal has. They soon gave up. They could not even rock them from side to side, and they stood and looked at me with new awe and respect.

I was magnanimous. I held feasts, gave out armbands, and made them all my men.

'I am Harald Sigurdsson,' I said to them. 'I am a sea-king no longer, but king of you all. As my forefathers ruled here before me, so I shall uphold the law as my father did, and his fathers before him, and I shall be a good lord to you all.'

Each place I came to the freemen gathered. Those who had helms and mail brought them. They repainted their shields, had their hair combed, their beards plaited, and the lice picked from their best kirtles and brushed clean.

Their chief men would take my hand and hold it high.

'Here is your king, Harald Sigurdsson!' they would shout, and then the whole valley would ring with the sound of weapons drummed on the back of shields. I rewarded each chief. Soon my fame had spread so that they were cheering before I even dismounted from my horse.

Gold speaks loudly, but it calls evil men to it as surely as the good.

Budli's son came to me to warn me that one of the chiefs to the south, along the Elf River, was gathering a war host.

'He has sworn to bring Magnus your head,' he said. 'And take all of your treasure for his own.'

I set sail the next day, with ten ships – half my own men, and half the men of Uppland – against the men of the Elf River. We were men against boys. They stood bravely enough, but my Varangians were mail-shirted, steel-helmed, iron-gripped veterans. We went through them like a hot needle through wax, killed their chief, raided his lands, and when the people came to ask for their sons and fathers back, I said to them, 'Your chief swore he would take my head and give it to Magnus, but where is your king now? He is no king who cannot defend you.'

'We had not seen you,' they said to me. 'We did not know how mighty you had become. It was no crime to abide by our oaths.'

'It was not,' I said, and set the prisoners free, and they all acclaimed me their king and promised to support me against my nephew.

When we returned, Elizaveta had made my forebears' hall royal once more. The carvings I had remembered as a child had been repainted, the floor reeds refreshed, the walls hung with silks and tapestries and costly carpets.

Elizaveta greeted me and my warriors as a queen, with a silver-rimmed bowl of mead, and courteous words. The victorious sat in hall, and as I looked out on their feasting faces I felt as if I'd conquered the world.

I was king of the Upplands, and here were my people, victorious from battle, and there was my daughter, and there was my wife: beautiful, learned, courteous, queenly.

CHAPTER TWO

King Magnus Olafson

It is three days' sail north from Uppland to Sognefjord if the winds are good.

Sognefjord is the most impressive and beautiful of the fjords. No man can see it and not be moved. Great peaks rear straight up from the water, as if giants had sat up and been turned to stone. Their hair is snow, their stubble pine forest, their feet plunge down into the deep water, and between them runs a narrow cleft.

Your ship turns its back on the wild black seas, and as you pass under the mountains the whole view opens up before you of a narrow green fjord, half shadowed by mountains, with the Keelbacks far in the distance.

One of my Varangians hailed from these parts. His name was Gorm, he had lost a finger on Sicily, but he still remembered all the places of his home. He pointed them out to me as our longships nosed into the deep-cut fjord. 'That is Brekke's farm. There is where Ikjefj raised his hall! That is Vadheim, where my mother's brother lives. I pray he is not dead. We were close as children. And look!' he shouted as we rounded the out-thrust hip of the mountain above us, 'that is Magnus's palace of Vik.'

I looked.

All along the fjord there had been barely a scrap of level land wide enough to support a farmstead, but as we rounded the head-land a wide valley flowed towards the fjord, with a curving beach where many longships were moored.

'He has more than ten ships,' Halldor warned.

It could be a trap, I thought, but spoke confidently: 'Each of my warriors is worth two of his. And you forget, he is my brother's son.'

As we came closer we could see a great crowd coming down to meet us, their banners flapping in the wind. Magnus stood on the shoreline. It was the first time I'd seen him since Kiev, when he was eight and I barely twenty. I was impressed. He had a straight back, broad shoulders. He had matured well.

'He looks like a fine man,' I said to Elizaveta. 'Look! He is quite grown. He has much of my brother about him. Magnus!'

Elizaveta put a hand to my shoulder. 'Remember he's just nine-teen. Show him you are the bigger man. Be magnanimous. When you leave his hall, you will have taken from him all that you want.'

The feast went well. There was much laughing and jollity, slapping of backs and arms and embracing lost kinsmen. Magnus presented each of my sixty retainers with a gift according to his station – a sword, a cloak, a shield, a tunic of fine cloth, a gold ring, an iron helm with gilt nose-guard – and I did the same.

'Let us each share what we have,' Magnus said. 'I will share my kingdom and my treasure, and you share what is yours.'

It hurt to give away half the gold I had earned in Micklegard, but Elizaveta's eyes were on me and I assented.

I held out my hand, and we shook, wrist to wrist, and embraced. He gave me half the kingdom, and all the taxes, dues and posses-sions that went with it, and I promised to share my treasure with him, if he would share his.

'You first,' he said.

I could feel the thrill in the room, as I called for an oxhide to be brought out. 'The largest you can find!'

Chest by chest, my treasure was brought in, gold and gems and silver, and tipped out onto it. It took half an hour for them all to be brought in. The men were sweating by the time the contents had been tipped onto the floor. I saw the last fifteen years tumble before me: the silver cup from Lesbos, with the missing piece of turquoise; the golden book bindings I had taken from a Moor's book in Africa; a silver and bronze cross, with Christ hanging nailed to his timbers; the scabbard end from a Bulgar prince; the crosspiece of an Italian banner that we had taken in battle; the hilt of a sword, I could not tell you whose; a jewelled dagger, silver combs, a golden cup, a golden belt buckle, the red leather still attached from where I had cut it free of the man I had just killed, a signet ring with a pair of saints on the seal, a small gold cross, with Christ in the middle, Joseph on one side, Mary on the other, Emperor Michael's signet ring, a golden bowl, now bent and misshapen, and about and in and under them all a heap of gems and rings and sword hilts, and golden coins beyond measure.

That treasure cast a spell upon the room, deeper and stronger than any tale sung after dinner. You could hear each coin drop – the sorry debased *clang* of Michael Comnenus's coins, the brilliant *twing* of the old coins: large, bombastic, regal, pure!

I picked up a great lump of melted gold I had taken from a church in Italy that my men had burnt down. It must have been the altar cross, but now it was fire-formed, with a few embers still embedded in it, as big as a child's head. I was one of the few people strong enough to lift it with one hand. My muscles strained as I held it up like the head of dead king, and let all see it.

'This is my treasure all told. Have you any to match this piece?'

'I have not,' Magnus said, and laughed. It was as if the dragon-sickness was already upon him.

He walked towards the heap, that shone ember-red even in the broad daylight. The sky was flat and grey, the mountains hunched and dark, but here in the middle of the dark room my hoard gleamed like the sun, and cast a yellow light upon his cheeks as he gazed down. He held up one hand and pulled the arm-ring from it and held it up. 'Here,' he said, 'is all the gold that I possess.'

Magnus grinned as he dropped it onto the pile and set off a landslide of golden coins. My mood darkened as the mountains when the storm clouds hit. My stomach hurt. Some of his men began to snigger. I made a note of their faces, and forced a smile.

Be magnanimous. He is young. Youth is something we are all guilty of. I held my tongue for what seemed an age, but I could not resist answering back, despite myself. 'And that is hardly yours to give,' I said. 'That arm-ring was my father's, who was Sigurd Syr, king of the Upplanders. He gave it to your father, even though he was no true-born son, but adopted into his household.'

'He gave it to my father, and so it is mine,' Magnus said.

I forced a smile. Who is this barbarian boy? I thought. What kind of ruler will he be? Nothing better than the chieftains that went before him, without learning or education, caring for nothing but their own power.

'Each man has his own way of earning fame, Magnus,' I said to him. 'You have just chosen yours.'

CHAPTER THREE

The Year of Two Kings

Almost at once, Magnus started to claw back little honours, like a man who feels he has not driven a hard enough bargain. He sent messengers to bring me demands, as if I were bondsman bound to do his bidding.

'When we are together I should take precedence, being the king for longer.'

'When a king comes to visit us, then I should sit in the middle.'

'When our boats are both in harbour, mine shall take the royal berth.'

'When we are together I shall take precedence in greetings, seating, service and salutation.'

'When war comes you shall support me.'

I indulged him at first, but my temper began to fray. Elizaveta had grown up with him in Kiev. She spoke honeyed words in my ear, but it did not take long for her, even, to see what a fool he was making of himself.

'The men with him fear you,' she said.

'What do they fear?'

'They fear a strong king. And look at you. They should!'

I tried avoiding Magnus and his retainers, but Norway is only so large, and men delighted in bearing tales from one king's court to the other, and few of them were good.

It was with a heavy heart that I looked forward to the next feast we would host together. It was at midsummer, the first midsummer I had spent in Norway since the summer I turned fifteen and fought at Stiklestad.

The marigolds had filled the meadows and the village women were making wreaths of green when we set sail. The snow had retreated to the highest peaks, but it had not gone, and the blue fjord water rippled white with its cold reflections.

'Do not quarrel with him,' Elizaveta told me, and held my arm to make sure I understood she was in earnest.

'I shall not,' I said, and I was as good as my word. I let his boat have the royal berth, and I let him sit down before me, as we had agreed.

But when he came to the feast he looked like a Micklegard whore, bedecked in the gold that I had given him. Our seats were next to each other, but his had a fat cushion on it, so that he would not appear so small beside me.

I knocked it onto the floor. 'A king does not need a cushion.'

'Do not tell me what a king does or does not need,' Magnus said. 'I have been king here for many years. You may know about wandering the world, but when it comes to kingship, I have more wisdom than you.'

One of his men replaced the cushion on his chair, and Elizaveta came to my side, and took my hand in hers, and pinched it.

I held my tongue. We sat in silence. I was angry with myself for trusting this lad, and that evening, when we had each retired to our respective halls, my men were angry too. They felt his barbs more keenly than I. He was no nephew of theirs.

'We could burn him in his hall,' they said to me, but I had to still them all.

'Hush!' I said. 'There will be no hall-burning or kin-killing. I did not come home to kill my brother's son.'

But when I was alone with Elizaveta she stroked my arm. 'Be glad! You have achieved all this through generosity, not cruelty. Through faith, not faithlessness. Through a handshake, not the sword hand.'

She was right, but I could not meet him without feeling my anger shake me.

Elizaveta gave birth again that spring. I was a little calmer this time, and the labour passed smoothly, so the women told me. Magnus made a point of coming to see her. 'Another girl,' he said with evident pleasure. 'What will you call her?'

'I thought of calling her Asta, after my mother and your grandmother,' I told him. He never liked it when I pulled age or rank on him. 'But Elizaveta wishes to call her Maria.'

'Are you the master of your house or is she?'

'She,' I said to him, and he did not know if I was telling the truth or not.

Even when we raised our warbands the next year, and invaded Denmark together, we could barely stand the sight of each other. Our enemy was Swein Estridson, who had taken the kingdom after Knut's sons had died. Swein was a coward and a braggart, the worst of men, and had thrown off his pledge to pay fealty to Magnus.

Fifteen years seemed a long time to spend in exile, and I looked forward to turning some of the hardships I had faced upon the guilty: not just the men like Kalv and Thore Hund, who killed my brother, but also the men of Lathe, who filled the shieldwalls. And as time had passed and I saw the events about my brother's death more truly, then I spread the net of guilt wider.

To Knut and Denmark, who had incited the rebels. And England too, who had provided the silver that had paid for it.

We waited for a good wind, and let it fill our sails under a bright spring moon, and rested upon the sea as the mountains rose up on one side, and the water fell away on the other.

We crossed to Zealand, and then to flat Jutland, with its bogs and heaths and poisonous mists, and Swein did not dare meet us in battle, so we burnt and raided where we liked. Without a foe to bring us together, our two forces had drawn half a day's sailing apart from one another. I moored my ships in a wide bay, sheltered by low dunes. Men had been cutting peat. They fled at the sight of us, and so we had the wind for company as I held a feast with my warriors.

Having carried war across Middle Earth, it felt good to be taking war to the Danes, but without Swein's army there seemed little point in prolonging the campaign.

'Let us show the Danes that their king is a coward,' I told my captains as we lit driftwood fires, and watched the flames spiral up into the blue of night.

We were a day's sail north when a fast boat found us, as it scudded over the waves. Its captain cupped his hands to his mouth and shouted, but it took a long time till our boats were close enough for us to hear his words over the winds.

'King Magnus is asking for you!'

'So?'

'He is sick.'

'Send him my good wishes!'

By now the boat was so close that I could throw a line to it, and haul it in like a dead whale. I did not know the messenger, but he did not speak with a Lathe accent, and he seemed a trustworthy man.

'The priest said Magnus would like to speak to you, before the end.'

'Whose end?'

'His,' the man said. 'Men think he is dying.'

I did not take it seriously at first. 'What of?'

'I don't know. His priest told me.'

I took three ships of my best warriors, and we turned back south, and found his army camped in a bay on the east coast of Jutland, not far from Roskilde. I knew his longship, *Bison*, because it had been Olaf's. It was moored in the middle of the bay. The mast had been stepped, and a tent raised along the middle. That was an odd thing to do, and I half-sensed a trap as I had my boat brought alongside and strode aboard and felt the familiar timbers move.

One of Magnus's poets, Thjordolf Arnorsson, greeted me. He had always seemed an honest man. I held his gaze and nodded to him. 'Is he sick?' I said.

'He is,' Thjordolf said. 'It is grave.'

Edward, the English priest, came out of the tent. 'Ah, King Harald, you are here,' he said. His priest is already calling me lord, I thought. Magnus cannot be long for this world.

The tent was dark. I paused for a moment, waiting for my men to join me, and then lifted the flap and stepped inside. Magnus lay on a bed of furs, his hound at his feet, in the middle of the boat. His hands lay at his side, his fists were clenched, his face pale and sweaty.

I walked forward and knelt before him, conscious of the symbolism that this would hold, and took his hand in mine. It was hot. His gaze sought mine, and found me, and he swallowed and closed his eyes. I touched his brow. He was burning up. He moaned and said something but I could not hear the words.

My throat felt tight, despite all that had gone on between us. He was Olaf's son, after all, and no man wants to die abed, like an old maid.

'Have you confessed?' I said.

He made no reaction, but Edward said, 'Yes, King Harald. He has been shriven.'

I stood and looked down at him.

'Care for him,' I said, 'if there is anything else he needs.'

'Thank you,' Edward said.

I knelt by Magnus's side again, and took both his hands. 'Be brave,' I told him. 'Each man's hour is appointed by God. Face yours with courage. You have been a good king. You have led your warriors with great honour. All men will remember you well.'

I left him then, and when I came out there were already ships nosing out of the harbour.

'Whose ships are those?' I asked.

'Those are the men of Lathe. They say that now their king is dead, they are going home.'

I felt ill-served. I had given Magnus half my treasure for a share of the kingship, but it seemed the men of Lathe thought they could pick which one was their king.

Their fathers had betrayed Olaf to Knut, and I was not about to let them break my kingship. I had learnt much in the South: the Byzantines knew much about bringing people to heel. I remembered the Bulgar campaign, where we had burnt and killed and ravaged. Such would be their fate unless they showed me due respect. When Norway was fragmented it was weak.

Magnus died that night. His women washed and dressed him, and shaved his cheeks, and dressed him in my gold. From across the room he looked soft, angelic even, until I came close, when the pallor of death was clear. I said a prayer, and spoke to Olaf directly.

'Your son has come to Christ's Hall. Hear him knocking, let him in and serve him mead.'

That evening there was a great meeting of my men and Magnus's. I walked up the hill before the two groups of retainers, mine and those who had given loyalty to Magnus. They stood a little apart from each other, like an estranged couple. I held out my hands for silence. My men had been my captains in the Varangian Guard. They lived by military discipline. The others were a rabble of voices and opinions.

'Silence!' I called at last.

That stilled them, but I had lost my temper, and I regretted that.

'Magnus, king, is with his father, Olaf, and the Father of all of us. He was king over Norway and Denmark. Now I am king of both Norway and Denmark.'

I paused. There was no answer except the whistle of the wind that was coming from the east, and bringing a chill with it. 'I call all of you to come with me to the Law-Moot, where I summon the Danes to come and acclaim me their king.'

When I came home to Uppland the fields were cut, the ricks filled, the piles of firewood stacked as high as a man's head.

Elizaveta had heard the news already.

If she had cried the tears were done. Serving women brought out food and linen, and she presented my favourite horn to me, and filled it with ale and set Maria on my knee.

The babe was asleep, and stayed so, but in her dreams she reached out a tiny fist and took my little finger in her grip, and held it.

'Some men said you poisoned him,' she said.

'I was not even there,' I said. 'Why would I poison him?'

Now he was dead, I felt little, except the tug of Maria's hand upon my own.

'Perhaps it is better this way,' I said at last. 'It would have come to blows. He will be with Olaf now.'

CHAPTER FOUR

King of the Norse

Onund had warned me that the first year of kingship is a trial few rulers ever forget. But I did not find it so. I was like the horseman who expects trouble and takes the reins firmly, but finds the horse sitting quietly. I think I had learnt all there was of leadership in Rus and Kiev, and then with the Varangian Guard. How to bolster a man who has lost his courage, how to terrify a man who thinks to betray you, how to punish a traitor, and make it both clean and quick. I had so much I wanted to achieve, and I felt I had wasted a year of my reign with Magnus. He was the old kind of king, like his father and like Olaf Tryggvason before him. They were war chiefs who spent their time in boats, cowing their enemies with each visit. I had seen something finer, stronger, more lasting. A king needed scribes and churchmen, he needed tax and coin, he needed a country that could respond in times of war, and he needed to uphold the laws on great and small alike.

I marked the autumn of 1047 as the beginning of my reign proper, and set about my work now with a vigour and relentlessness that reminded some of the way we had cleared the Cyclades of pirates. That winter I went from hall to hall, cowing the chieftains who were most likely to rebel, and rewarding those who did as I demanded. I only killed those that I could not trust. I was not needlessly cruel to their families.

In the chief towns I brought English minters over from the Danelaw, and set them up to strike Norwegian coin, with my face upon one side, and Christ's cross upon the other. I brought in priests and monks and sent off to York and Paris and London for books that might be brought here, and teachers who would teach my people Latin.

And all that winter there was talk of battle, and the vengeance I would take upon the Danes.

As the rivers filled with icy meltwater, longships were brought out of their wintering sheds and their sails were fixed, the sealskin rigging renewed, the seams sealed with dark pine pitch.

I'd seen a longship once as a child sees them: full of wonder and awe, imagining the day he will splash on to an English shore and run up the beach to the nearest monastery, and plunder and kill and make himself rich. But those days were long over. I saw each longship now as a king sees them. Four thousand nails, one hammered out each minute by a handy smith; so many cartloads of bog iron, so much wood to be cut for charcoal and timber, so many masts to be cut and left to season, so many yards of sailcloth, and so on.

I set the whole country to task. Drew up lists of levy from each fjord and district. Each weapontake in Uppland to provide four ships of twenty-four men; Västmanland two ships; Roslagen one, but each crewman must carry axe or sword as well as a spear and shield, and for every row bench there must be a bow and two dozen goose-fletched arrows.

To support all this, I had each district responsible for baking bread and providing salted fish and sewing the new year's sails. Those who rebelled I killed or exiled, and did the country a great service by getting rid of traitors and loudmouths.

Now our talk was all of sailing and plunder and battle, and each night we dreamt of the campaign to come. The sight of the longships filled me with joy. About them the fishing boats and skerries lay on their sides, and the longships rose over them like killer whales on a beach of seals.

One of the first things I did was to let Kalv Arnasson, the man who had dealt Olaf his death-blow at Stiklestad, return home to Norway. I did not want to, but his brothers, who had fought in Olaf's company, begged me to, and I was too full of good cheer one night, and allowed it. 'And you must swear that you will not harm him,' they said to me, and again I promised.

'I shall not harm him,' I declared, but sometimes we swear an oath to keep us to a difficult path. Perhaps it was so with this, but I found that I was not so good a man as I had hoped to be, and remembered the vow I had made a long time before, to Astrid, Olaf's widow, to take revenge.

I was in a cleft stick. One oath or the other would prove me false, and I sat for a long time wondering how to resolve it. I could neither kill him nor allow him to live.

So in that first year of battle I devised a plan that would let me keep both oaths. When the Danes were on the shore to prevent our landing, I gave Kalv orders to lead the attack, and held my own men back until I saw his banner fall. Only then, knowing that he was dead, did I lead my own household troops into battle, and we drove the Danes back in confusion.

His brothers were furious with me, but I slept better that night. Olaf was avenged, my oaths were kept, and when next I found a good man sailing east to Onund's hall, I gave him words to say to Astrid alone, so that she might know her husband's killer was with God.

In the second year of my sole reign, Swein of Denmark sent messengers offering to meet me in battle, and to let the contest decide once and for all who would take Knut's place as king of the north. This was in 1044. We arranged to meet at the Gaut Elf River. I was there with three hundred ships, but Swein did not turn up. Some men said that I had been tricked, and that he would be raiding Norway as we sat here waiting.

I sent the bondsmen and farmers home, and kept a hundred and fifty ships with the best of my war troops. It was good to be rid of the moaners and stay-at-home farmers, and to be a general again, ravaging a foreign land, but the next day Swein's three hundred ships arrived and brought us to battle.

I had my men lash their boats together, and we fought them toe to toe, as Varangians did, and we broke the cream of Denmark and routed them.

Another year we set ourselves the aim of Hedeby, the chief town of the Danes. None could withstand us. We burnt as we made our way across their lands. The chief men of the town closed their gates against me, thinking to keep me out. I laughed at their action. I was Harald Sigurdsson, champion of the Varangian Guard, scourge of eighty cities.

It took me a day.

I burnt the place to the ground. Even now, men who were not in the Varangian Guard talk of that night. They had never seen a city fall so easily. My men had been warriors in the service of the Emperor. They knew how to storm a wall.

Our longships were heavy with booty: men, women and girls for the slave markets, barrels of food, pots of silver and handfuls of gold.

I had sixty ships when at last Swein dared to show his face with at least a hundred. I lost count of his ships, but there was little chance we could defeat them. And why, I thought, should we give battle to cowards who skulk on their boats?

One of his boats came up.

'Harald – maybe you should fight a battle before you make off with those stolen goods!'

'I will fight you!' I shouted. 'On water. Bring your ships alongside. We shall make it easy for you. My axe is eager to meet you, even now she longs for a Danish lover she can kiss!'

The Danes floundered about, debating, and by the time Swein had worked up the guts for a fight it was getting late in the day and the wind changed and we found ourselves approaching what must be Læso Island, when a thick sea fog rolled in.

When dawn came it burnt the fog off, and bearing straight towards us, with the wind puffing out their sails, was the whole damned Danish fleet.

'Haul the yards!' I shouted, and there was a flurry of activity as we pressed round the long sand flats of Læso with the open sea before us.

It was a close-run thing.

'Row you Northmen! Row!' I roared at them, as if I could puff the sails with my breath. It was exhilarating. I would not end my days like an old thief limping through the fields with a lamb under his arm.

'They're still gaining,' Halldor said.

I could have punched the man. But he was right. They were gaining.

'Lighten the boats!' I shouted.

I tossed the barrels of fish over the side of the longship, as my men bent their backs.

The cheap stuff went first: sacks of wheat, smoked hams saved from Hedeby, wool sacks, bolts of silk that men thought to give to their wives. The command was passed along my ships, from captain to captain. But the flotsam did not bring us much speed.

'They're still gaining,' Halldor said.

The captives we had taken were sitting by the mast, heads bent, pretending not to care that we were about to be overwhelmed. I grabbed the nearest. 'What is your name?'

'Eric Olafson,' the Dane said.

'Can you swim?'

He nodded. 'Good,' I said, and pitched him overboard. The command was passed along my ships. One by one we tossed the captives out into the water. It was a trick I had seen the Byzantines use when in dire straits, to scatter gold on the ground to delay the pursuers. I went through all the men we had taken, and any that could swim I threw into the waters. It seemed pointless to waste the ones who would drown, but the world has no shortage of fools, and there were some who lied to me, and sank like stones.

Some of my men were furious to lose their treasure, but soon the sight of the Danish ships stepping their sails to reclaim their kinsfolk made us all laugh. They could not hear the cries of their fellows and pass them by. Only Halldor put effort into remaining woeful. 'That has lost us all a tidy sum.'

'It has,' I said. But the wise man listens and learns as he travels, and worse things happen in the world.

I punished the Danes each year for fifteen winters, one for each of the years I had spent in exile. Peace came at last in 1064, after I had defeated them in a sea battle at Nisa.

Swein and I held a feast together and promised each other peace. I was forty-nine years old, my moustaches were shot with white, and I was master of the North and felt revenged on Knut at last.

If you ask my men, they will tell you that I filled my longships each year, and brought battle to the Danes. And that is true of course, but I did much more than that.

I broke the power of the earls of Lathe, so that Norway would never again be under the thrall of foreign coin. I brought Greek monks all the way up from Kiev. I founded monasteries and cathedrals, gave them land and fine goods with which to decorate their churches. I remembered what had happened to Olaf and turned my country from a string of scattered fjords and inlets to a kingdom. And a kingdom needed a central place where traders could gather and meet and discuss, where taxes could be collected, and churches could thrive. Something more than an annual marketplace where sea-folk gathered. It needed a church, it needed monks who knew letters, a place to trade and gather and grow. It needed a city.

I picked a spot just up from Budli's land, on the other side of our fjord. There was good harbour, even in winter. The ground was firm, and there was stone nearby to quarry, and a summer market had been held there for years.

There was a scattering of islands to shelter the harbour, eight rivers to bring fresh water, forests, elk, flat farming land, and a church, where men could pray, and hope, and at last be buried.

I laid out streets, and plots for workshops and houses, each one six yards wide.

I laid out the marketplace, the place of curing leather, the place of dyers, the butchers' shambles, the dykes that would protect the city from raiders. I delved ditches, built ramparts, I even oversaw the building of the church, and while I wanted a building of stone, I knew how long this would take, and could not wait, so had my finest shipbuilders construct a building with two naves, set side by side, just a central row of pillars in the middle, and set windows along either side, so that the space was filled with light and air and the scent of incense.

And then I brought in Greek priests to fill the building with song and prayer and learning.

Elizaveta had spent her life watching and helping Jaroslav build a state out of the wilderness and she helped me in all these things, and I grew very fond of her in a way I would not have thought a man would feel towards a woman. She was the best of queens. She was like a brother to me. Steadfast, loyal, fierce if any challenged me.

'What should we call this city?' she said to me one night, as we sat over a sketch of the city I had drawn with charcoal on the table. 'Something grand?'

I thought for a while. My father had always envied Budli this bit of land. Its name was Onslo, which meant the 'meadow beneath the ridge', but he had always called it 'Oslo' – the 'meadow of the Gods'.

'Let us call it that,' I said, and so my city was named.

CHAPTER FIVE

Foundations

Oslo grew so fast along the river banks, that in the second year I had to organise a new section of the waterfront, filling the whole promontory. The cathedral was already a frame of wooden timbers and the air was scented with wood-resin as the teams of wood-carvers were busy, shaping, planing, splitting.

The stewards led me to the place where the mill was to be built. The millstones lay side by side, grass growing through the holes in the middle. A team of men were laying planks along a new street where workshops were rising. Each street had a craft: cobblers, coopers, shield-rimmers, Frankish armourers, goldsmiths, minters. As the steward talked, a hopeful trader and his wife caught my eye. They looked newlywed, and worked with diligent care as he gave one end of a cord to her then strode backwards, marking with his heel the end of his six-yard plot. I watched them stand on the side of the plank-covered street and look at the space their home and workshop would contain.

Olaf brought faith to the country, and this is what I have given my people, I thought. They'll never make a saint out of me, but I have given them both peace and hope; the expectation of a life better than that our forebears lived. Knowledge over ignorance, profit over raiding. Trade over warfare. I have given them new prospects.

'Good. Good,' I said at the end. 'Now, show me my hall.'

Halldor stayed with me for many winters, but Norway was not his home, and I was not surprised when he told me that he wanted to return to Iceland.

I gave him treasures to remember our time together, and in typical Halldor fashion, he was not pleased, but took offence where none was meant.

'Good winds,' I said to him, at the end.

'They cannot blow me fast enough from this hall,' he said.

And I was not sorry to see him leave. I was sorrier, I think, that he took part of me with him, the memories we shared, and as more and more of my companions from the Varangian Guard departed – some to sickness, or age, or battle, or because homesickness or love for a women tugged them away from me – I felt myself grow restless and lonely.

'Do you remember that town in Sicily?' I said, and turned to face my companions, and saw them look at me in confusion and wonder. 'That one where Halldor held the gate?' I said and then I saw how time changes us all. Friends and companions were now old men. Even I was old according to some men's reckoning. Forty-nine winters take their toll on a man who has earned his keep with his blood and his hands.

The benches were full of youthful faces. Of the thousand men I had led across Sicily, there could not be more than fifty remaining in my household. The rest were dead or dispersed to farms, where they were raising sons of their own. It made me world-weary to think of the men I had loved as brothers, and left behind.

Elizaveta knew my mood and tried to lighten it.

She looked more and more like her mother as she grew older, and that was no bad thing, for her mother had been an acclaimed beauty in her time, and when I met her she had still been a strong and powerful lady. One September evening, when the sky was clear and cold, she brought me an ale-posset, and I warmed my hands with it.

'Why don't you go riding?' she said.

I sipped the drink. She had flavoured it with a little spice. I closed my eyes for a moment, and remembered the languid heat of the Middle Sea, the warm blue water, the unwatered wine.

'It is not good to sit and brood,' she told me. 'Why don't you take the boats, go north, do something? Go fishing.'

I said nothing, but her words echoed about in my head.

'Ragni,' I called. The steward was brought from his hall. He came, stamping the snow from his feet as he came into the hall.

'Yes, Lord.'

'I want to go fishing,' I said.

'Now, Lord?'

'No. Tomorrow,' I said.

He stammered for a moment as he collected his thoughts. 'I will send word to the men,' he said. 'They were out last week, and caught little.'

'Well. We eat herrings,' I told him, pushing myself up. 'Let us go out and catch some.'

No one else knew why I wanted to go herring-fishing that day, but I did, and was conscious all along that I was taking the same walk out of the hall, down the grassy slopes to the shingle beach. The ships were different of course, and Olaf and my family were not there, but otherwise the journey was the same.

It was a clear, still September day. The snow had come halfway down the mountains and the blades of grass and the crust of the wet ground were frozen stiff.

'May I come, Father?' Maria called out, and despite Elizaveta's concerns, she joined us in the fishing skiff as the men pushed her out and we rippled through the reflections of sky and mountain – and for a moment we seemed poised between Heaven and plunging water. We were, as the ancients said, sitting in the Middle Earth, looking up and down and wondering what was hidden there.

The men dropped the nets, and they rowed us out into the deep water, and came round again, full circle, into our wake, like a dog chasing its tail.

A gull swooped low to see what we had caught. I looked up along the fjord, and willed the killer whales to come as they had done that long-distant day. But the end of the fjord remained still and empty, and all we saw was a seal's snout appear near the shore, and then slip under the water as the men hauled in the nets.

The herring were silver as they slipped into the boat. There was barely enough for half a barrel. Maria caught one that was still flapping. It slapped about her cupped hands, and she laughed then tossed it back into the water, and it landed flat on its side, and lay stunned for a moment, before slipping back through the reflected mountains, into the darkness.

'It'll remember you as a kindly woman,' I told her. 'It's always good to spare a few.'

When we got back to the house, Elizaveta was leaning against the doorpost.

'You should not taken her out,' she said. 'She cannot swim.'

'Of course she can swim,' I laughed.

'Not without taking off her clothes.'

I laughed at that, and slapped Elizaveta's backside, and made her jump. 'If that is what she has to do, then . . .'

That night the frost came again, and as I walked out to see the stars, they were bright as silver in the sky. By the time I got to bed, Elizaveta was already asleep. I slept less now, and I lay listening to the familiar creaks of my family's hall, the sound of snoring, the distant call of a sheep or cow, a tawny owl calling from the trees above the spring.

The old folk still talked of the Norns, the three Fates who wove the thread of men's lives into shapes and patterns. Their names were *Urðr* – Happened, *Verðandi* – Happening, and the strangest of the three, *Skuld* – Should.

Young men always look to *Skuld* and old men to *Urðr*, but too few of us look to *Verðandi*, the mistress of what is happening now, before our eyes. I was just as guilty, I knew. I'm getting old, I thought. I should find husbands for my daughters for when they were full grown. A well-picked betrothal does five times the work of an army.

Next morning Elizaveta had a pain in her side.

'It's nothing,' she said. 'I'll just lie down for a while.'

Maria and Ingegerd went to care for her, and I rode across the bay to see how the plans for a new ward of Oslo were coming along.

I came back a little after dusk. The wind was blowing hard enough to stir the manes of the waves to white. The stars were beginning to show, and the sky was a midnight-blue bowl above our heads, rimmed with mountain peaks. Each day the snows were creeping down.

I threw off my cloak and swapped it for a dry one.

'I'm glad to see you up,' I said to Elizaveta.

She was sitting by the fire on a chair strewn with furs, and an old brown bearskin thrown over her knees.

'I could not stay in bed all day,' she said.

We could feel the chill press in through the hall timbers, and I had finished the evening stew when someone came in through the hall door, brushed the flecks from his hair and said, 'It's snowing.'

There was a time I could have leapt up to see, but I left it to the younger ones, who still delighted in such things. 'Look for the fire lady!' I called out, and the children ran out to see.

'Who is the fire lady?' asked Elizaveta.

I laughed. There was a tale when I was young, of an old lady who carried a bucket of glowing coals to warm the earth in springtime. We called her the fire lady, and all winter the adults would tell us to keep a watch for her, a dark-clad old lady, bent at the back, carrying her glowing pot of yellow coals.

So we sat, staring into the fire, neither of us speaking.

'So,' said Elizaveta at last, with a sigh. 'I wonder what next year will bring.'

I nodded. I wondered as well. With each sunset the days got shorter and colder, till the snows covered us all, and all there was to do was gather about the fire and tell tales.

'Please, Father!' the girls would call, and I took the horn of mulled wine that the traders brought for me, and they would beg to have a sip.

'This is from Cyprus,' I told them. I knew the places where these vines had grown. I had slept in their sacred groves. I had fought under their walls. I had buried friends there.

Like the Norns, I fashioned patterns out of my life. Tales of a fearless young man. A brave warrior. A victorious hero, who brought the princess home, and became king in his own land, and brought peace.

But at night I lay awake in the long dark, and wondered if the places and people I had once talked about remembered me, as I did them. When the moon rose over Syracuse, did it cast the shadow of a tall Norse warrior over the battlements? Did the sea wind still echo with the verses of the *Bjarkamál*? Did the council chamber of Micklegard still feel the weight of my footsteps and tremble? Did the walls there remember the touch of my shadow? Did the wind ever learn to whisper my name?

'What is it, Father?' asked Maria, and I looked at her and smiled.

'Tell me of your morning.'

She spoke to me of autumn leaves and water and trees and frosted spider nets, and how she had found a snail that morning, trapped in ice, and set it on a leaf to thaw.

'You are blessed,' I told her, and gathered her in and kissed the top of her head.

'You look sad,' she said.

'What, me? No,' I told her. 'I was only thinking.'

'What about?'

'Well,' I said, not sure where to begin. 'Do you remember Halldor?'

She frowned, and shook her head.

'He left when you were five or six,' I said. 'Well, he was my oldest companion.'

'In Micklegard?'

'Before that even. We travelled the length of Rus together.'

I saw a brief shadow pass over her eyes. How many of the stories in my hall, told by me or others, began with 'When I was in Micklegard . . . ' It was a joke now among the short-beards.

'Is he dead?'

'I don't know.'

'All your friends are dead.' She spoke with the simple innocence of a child.

'Well, not all,' I said, and laughed.

'What is this?' Elizaveta asked as she brought her embroidery over to the light of the candles.

Nothing, our silence said.

She sat and turned so that the candlelight fell into her lap and she pulled the needle from where she had left it, ran the silken thread through her lips, and went back to her work, but she did not work long before she frowned and said, 'I'm tired.'

Her women helped her to bed, and Maria came and sat on my knee.

'Mother is always tired,' she said.

'She is getting old,' I said.

'Will she die?' she said.

I nodded. 'We all die.'

'Even you?'

I laughed. 'Yes,' I said. 'Even I.'

She hung her arms about my head and pressed her cheek against mine. 'Your beard is so soft,' she said, and looked at me, and I pulled a face.

'What face is that?'

'Angry,' I told her.

She tried to copy it, and asked me to do it again, and I looked angry for her.

*

The next morning, as she sat and combed her hair, I asked Elizaveta, 'Are you well?'

'Yes,' she said, but that morning she only picked at her barley bread, and at night, when the bean and carrot stew was ladled into bowls, she picked out a few lumps of meat and beans and left the rest.

It was Ingegerd who came to see me.

She was two years older than Maria, and serious. 'Father,' she said. 'I think Mother is ill.'

'She is,' I said.

'I think we should fetch the priest.'

'She's not that ill,' I said, but as the spring came on, Elizaveta's strength seemed to wane, and the spans she was up and busy grew shorter and shorter, and at length it was clear that she was not going to get up again.

I could not bear to be around her sickbed. I could not bear to see her in pain. I could not bear to sit and watch her die, as I had with my mother. I found jobs to do across the bay. Chieftains who needed to be visited. A bear that had stolen lambs must be found and killed. There was always something, and at last they sent Maria to me.

She rode bareback up the slopes, one of her mother's fur cloaks thrown about her shoulders.

'Father,' she said. 'The priest says that Mother is dying.'

'Now?' I said. I cursed. I had a chieftain I must visit.

'He said come quick,' she told me.

I cursed again. 'I'm coming.'

I stopped at the threshold to her room. I could smell Death, I could feel it in the manner of the people, and how they pursed their lips and bowed their heads and crossed themselves as they left the room, as if one person's death was catching.

'Good wife,' I said. I meant so much more than that, but pulled up a stool and could not speak.

She did not look in pain. She just looked weary, and swallowed, and closed her eyes, and patted my hand as I found hers.

309

'Be good to my girls,' she said. 'Have faith in Christ. Do not blaspheme so much.'

I agreed to all that she told me, and I held her hand with both of my own. I wanted to leave but Maria and Ingegerd came and sat with me, and I felt as though I lost a limb when she died, and even after her soul had gone, I warmed her hands until they gently pulled me away.

I have buried many people that I loved, but Elizaveta was the hardest. She had been with me through the middle years of life, and those were all good years. Not without hardship or struggle, but years of success and growth and plenty. Years I had struggled hard to earn.

I felt my own winter in her death, I feared the passing of a good and generous stage of life, but more than that, it was the sight of Ingegerd and Maria sitting by her bedside, bringing her a cup to drink, praying for her soul, kneeling by her bed, that undid me.

So passes my princess, I told myself, but saw my younger self kneeling by the same deathbed. I saw my mother. I felt the vast blue depths of the fjord water, and the long-dammed memories rushed through the gap.

I took a few men to hunt elk that winter. I was a good king, I told myself, a good husband, a good father. I had achieved more than I had expected from this life, and there were no rumbles of discontent in my kingdom. I was not continually fighting my subjects, as Olaf had done. I was undisputed, feared and loved in equal measure.

Elizaveta had made me promise to marry again, for the girls' sake and my own, and after a year, when I could face such a thought, I married a noblewoman from Lathe named Tora, who I'd kept as a mistress.

Tora was a good woman. A good match, and I liked her brothers. They had shown themselves brave warriors in the fights against the Danes. They held the North for me when my mind was turned elsewhere, and Tora had given me sons, then I felt as though Heaven had given me all that a man could wish for.

And yet, in the years after Elizaveta's death I was restless.

I felt like the man who sets off at dawn to climb the mountain, and at some points stops and looks back and takes stock of where he is. There were the distant blue foothills, the rocky slopes that I had struggled over, the long grassy slopes where the going had been easier. And ahead of me the slope still rose, the peak was still lost in the mists of the future. I was not yet done, I knew, and though old, there were hours of daylight left, and after a moment's pause I was keen to press on.

Though what summit lay there I could not tell. I took my staff and strode forward and I was impatient to meet it.

CHAPTER SIX

The Year of Our Lord 1066

The horses had already been saddled. They were snuffling in the snow for the last of the morning's hay as I rubbed my hands against the morning chill. We had been cooped up all winter. The hounds licked my hand and jumped up. The months of dark and boredom had made us giddy with the thought of spring.

The hulks of the mountains across the fjord were already lit with a pale yellow rim. It was nearly Lent. Men had told me that the snows had receded enough to open up the paths into the next valley. I wanted to hunt in Hergil's Dale, but most of all, I wanted to take Tora's brother, Eystein Orre, for a ride. I had a mind to betroth him to my beloved Maria, and wanted to sound him out first.

'Eystein!' I shouted. 'Come! The horses are ready!'

He was a handsome young man, his hair falling gold upon his shoulders, his beard already long enough to plait. He wore his moustaches long like mine. I'd set a fashion among the young men in Norway. Travellers said the same of young Swedes and Geats and Danes and Northumbrians. Everyone wanted to look like Harald Sigurdsson.

'Have you ever hawked?' I asked him as I swung myself up. The horse steadied under my weight. He was a young, feisty stallion, always pulling and pushing. It took a strong hand to keep him in check.

'No,' he said.

'Nor I. Never could bear the fuss about them. How full they are, how hungry, are they due for moulting. Give me a pack of hounds. They do the same job, in the end.' Less stylish, perhaps, but thorough.

We set off at a brisk trot and took a winding path up the hillside, and let our conversation ramble with it.

Eystein was shy at first, but I drew him out, and as he spoke freely I began to plumb his depths, as sailors drop weights into the water, and check the fathoms.

'Have you ever been betrothed?'

'Many have asked,' he said. 'But no. My father left it to me. It was his way. Even with the girls.'

'What do you think of Maria?'

I surprised him. It's always good to catch the other man unawares, with his gates open. You have a brief glimpse through the hall doors into his soul.

'She is beautiful,' he said.

'She is. And she is my daughter.'

'She is not betrothed?'

'Not yet.' I rested my hands upon my pommel as the wind stirred the manes of our horses. 'If I was your father, I'd let you choose as well, but I am king. And she is my daughter, and there is a weight attached to who they marry. So she is not as free as others, but I want to find my girl a good husband. A man I can rely on.'

I wanted a Peter, a rock who would help hold up the sons I had with Tora, my country, all that I had built. He opened his mouth to make some protestation, but I spoke over him. I already had a measure of his depths, otherwise I would not have asked. Another marriage between our families would bind the North and South of the country together. This was good.

When he told me he was not the match of me, I laughed.

313

'Nor was I at your age. No man is. Fate forms us. But I do not think Norway needs another Harald. What is it men call me behind my back? Hardrada – "Hard Ruler"?'

'Yes,' he said.

'Well. Better to start harsh. You can always be more lenient. But a man who treats his thralls too well finds it much harder to make them work.'

As we reached the top, the day was at its brightest. I had decided, and I shook his hand. 'I will speak to Maria when we get back. If she is willing we'll hold the betrothal feast at Easter.'

As I spoke, emotion caught my throat. I willed it away, but it is not easy for a man to give his daughter to another. Especially one he loves the best, above all others.

'Have you heard of the tailed star?' Eystein said as we made our way home that eventide.

'No.'

'I've not seen it. But the shepherds were talking. It was in the constellation of the Bear. It hung there for the whole night.'

I thought on this and wondered if it was an omen for Maria and his marriage. I will ask the priests, I told myself. It is their job to know the will of Heaven. My realm is the world of men.

Maria was willing.

She and Tora sat together, hands clasped, speaking of womanly things, and I summoned all my chief men for the Easter Feast. I spent the day picking through the remains of my treasure, for something suitable to give the lad. I have become more grudging with gold. I learned my lesson. I gave too much to Magnus, and he wasted it on his treacherous followers, and now my gold was diminishing and in some of the chests I could see the bottom through the coin, and that felt like an ending of sorts. And that put me in an ill humour, and at last I picked out a golden belt-clasp, a jewelled Byzantine sword, and a fine helm damasked with silver.

This came from – I paused. I could not remember. The ones I cannot place probably came from the palace in the days of confusion when the Caulker seized the throne. Even the names Caulker and Zoe felt foreign to me now.

Tora was in a fine mood all that day. Her family were filling my court. She had given me two sons who lived, Magnus and Olaf, and they were old enough now to have a seat of their own, though they still looked scared when I turned my face on them, and spoke too quickly and apologised too readily for my liking.

It is a challenge for any man who has risen through adversity to give his sons the difficulties he faced. And without testing, how can a boy know the mettle of his heart?

But how to toughen them and love them also? These things were weighing on me, but most of all, the giving away of Maria – my favourite child. She was the one who looked the most like Elizaveta. There were times when she laughed, or reached down to pick up the kitten, or when her cheeks flushed with anger, or when she sang, or danced, or clapped her hands to see my dwarf, that I saw her mother in her, and it made me world-weary.

Not that I meant any disrespect to Tora, but a second wife is loved less keenly than the first – unless the man is an old winter fool, made stupid by a young girl's breasts.

It is the way of things.

At Easter I took Maria's hand and put it in Eystein's and betrothed them both, and managed to croak out the words: 'I wish you both long life, fine children, and years of joy.'

I could barely get the last of the sentence out. I meant to say more, but the crowd cheered, and I took my chance to sit down in silence. Sometimes words are not necessary.

It was after the feast, when I was filled with sadness, that I let some of the young lads, each sporting my beard, take me out to show me the tailed star. The midnight-blue sky was clear and crusted with stars, and the heavens were reflected in the fjord water, and we hung in the middle, oblivious to what was past and what was to come.

'There!' they pointed, and I humoured them, but the truth was I could not see it.

'Fifty winters,' I told them. 'A man's sight is not as clear as it once was. Nor his ears. Even his hand's grip fades.'

I took the fist of this biggest lad in mine, and we tussled for a moment, before I tightened my fingers and I saw his face strain with the effort, and I smiled. I was not yet done, and then they all lined up for the same treatment, and I left them all rubbing their hands and remembering how tight a king's grip must be. They'll tell their grandchildren one day.

This is how it will be, I thought, and looked forward to my last years of peace. Watching my sons grow, my daughters bring forth life from their wombs, feeling the grip of my hand slowly lessen. It was not a death I would have wished for in youth, but it was not a bad death. Better than to have a spear plunged into your guts on a battlefield, while the sky turns dark above your head.

CHAPTER SEVEN

Godwinson

Next morning Maria was in a fine mood, and sadness lay a little less heavily. Treasures of any kind must be guarded and protected, and there is a sense of relief when at last you give them away and let others worry about their care.

Tora was humming in her chamber, and I stumped out and saw my eldest son, Magnus, and sat down with him, and he hung his head and I could see him trying to think of something to say.

I gave him a moment, but he didn't take it, so I did. 'What do you think of Eystein?'

'Maria likes him.'

'She does. What about you?'

'He is always kind to me.'

'He'll help you, when you're king,' I said. 'A king needs men older than he is, when he is young, for strength and force and wisdom. Depend on him until you are a man yourself. When you're old, you should have sons and retainers who can come to your aid.'

He nodded, and put my words away in his heart for safe-keeping, and I worried if he was too soft to be king in a land like Norway.

*

All that spring, men were trading news. I was always interested in the news from the East, and men were talking of a new tribe of Turks, who had taken two cities – one of them Caesarea – from Byzantine rule. They sounded like Pechenegs to me. Wild, ruthless, head-hunting horsemen. I was glad not to be fighting them. They would never come close enough for a man's combat.

I'd kept up with Byzantine news over the years. Zoe had passed away not long after I'd left, and Theodora in the same year that Elizaveta died, after a brief year as sole Empress. She had appointed a nobleman named Michael to be Emperor. I'd known him briefly. He was the same rank as I, a strategos.

I wish I'd kept my white cloak, I thought, but it had been lost on the trip from Kiev. It was white, of all things.

Pilgrims told me that the Church of the Holy Sepulchre in Jerusalem had finally been finished by the sons of the masons I had escorted there. The Chuds had taken a marketplace from the Rus. A Norman by the name of Roger de Hauteville had just conquered Sicily. And here, in the north of Christendom, King Edward of England had died, and a man named Harold Godwin's son had been made king.

'Who is this Harold?' I asked, putting on the English accent.

'He is a Danish prince,' I was told. 'The cousin of Swein, king of Denmark.'

The man I had fought for so long.

'So he's Knut's kinsman,' I thought. I owe him.

It was the time of the midsummer bonfires when the ship appeared, riding the waves straight up from the south like a well-aimed arrow. The sea-captains and fishermen brought me news of it. A Danish ship, with a striped English sail. It was an odd combination, odd enough to bring a man to notice.

It could not be raiders, but it did not look like a trading ship.

'Keep an eye on it,' I said to them, and it sailed up my fjord, as fearless as a conqueror.

Maria stood at the door of the hall and narrated its approach.

'It's beached,' she said. 'The captain has jumped ashore. I see gold on his arm. His men . . . they must be Saxons.'

It was only then that I rose. What did Saxons have to do with me? Were they priests, I wondered, seeking to replace my Greek monks? Every few years some Northumbrian crack-skull would come and argue with me about the use of yeast in my bread. I argued with them at first, explaining how the yeast symbolised the spirit of Christ, but when they tried to tell me that the Bishop of Rome had precedence over all the world, I laughed at them. 'Have you seen Rome?' I said. 'It is a city of ruins and beggars and whores. The church there is smaller than my cathedral across the bay. It has but one nave, and Saracens plundered all their relics years before. It is clear to me who Christ favours. Go to Micklegard and stand in the church of Hagia Sophia, and tell me that the Bishop of Rome is the favoured of God. No one has plundered there!'

That shut them up. The man who knows little but professes to know much is a laughing stock across Middle Earth.

'Well, he doesn't look like a priest,' I said as the company were shown up towards my hall. They looked like warriors and retainers, which meant they wanted to see me. I put a hand to the lintel and bent under it, drew myself up to my full height, and waited, thumbs tucked into my golden belt.

Their leader was a tall, handsome man. I let him walk up to me. My retainers followed me out, and stood to either side of me, like an honour guard. My son Magnus on one side, Eystein on the other.

He stopped ten paces before me, and gave a low bow. He singled me out. There was no mistaking me for another man.

'I have waited many years to see you, Great King, Harald Sigurdsson.' He spoke Danish with a slight accent. Not foreign, but old-fashioned, such as the old women used.

I said nothing. Silence sucks the words out of uncertain men, and I wanted to know his purpose.

'My name is Tostig, son of Godwin. I am earl in England. Of Northumbria, which is a great part of the country . . . ' He smelt of desperation, as a dog who has stolen from the kitchen table cannot stop itself from cringing.

'I know about Northumbria,' I said. 'There was a time, not so long past, when the men of the chief city, York, would send to Norway for their kings.'

'You are right in that. Which is part of the reason why I am here. May I come inside?'

'Will I regret it?'

'I do not think so, Lord.'

I smiled for the first time. It was one of my fearsome smiles. I took his hand and gripped it and I saw him swallow back his pain as I pulled him into my hall.

Tostig took a towel to wash his hands, and sat down on the stool at my feet, and rubbed his hands before the fire. He had the same mannerism as Swein, his cousin.

He's got a nerve to come here, I thought, and I began to make a picture of the man, as a potter will take clay and shape it. The form I made was of a man who was cocksure; arrogant; desperate.

'I must be the last place you have come to,' I said.

He tried to give me some tale, but I saw through it.

'Don't lie. You have come from Denmark. You'd be a fool not to go there first. Swein won't help you?'

Tostig smiled. 'Well. He is Harold's cousin too, unfortunately.'

'So you come to me . . . '

He was still rubbing the hand I had taken, and then put it behind his back. 'As you may know, I was driven out of my land by treacherous nobles.'

'All this is known to me,' I said. 'I thought you said you had news.'

'I do.' He grew a little hot, and looked for the beginning of his thread. 'I intend to go back and take back what is mine.'

'That is not news,' I said. 'Tell me something I don't know.'

He held up his hands. 'Well. Have you heard how I ravaged England this spring?'

'Seafarers told me you burnt some place or other, and that your brother Harold drove you off, and that then you fought a battle, and the Earls Morcar and Edwin defeated you there as well.'

He shrank before me as I set the skew of his tale to right.

'How many ships did you have at the beginning of the year?'

'Sixty.'

'And now?'

'Thirteen.'

'This does not sound like success to me. If I were you I would go home and sue for peace with your brother. Family feuds never end well.'

I had knocked him off his course, and now he struggled to find bearing again. He had learnt Danish from his mother, but he sprinkled his speech with English words. It was charming, I thought, to hear this mix. There were many compliments and much flattery, and at the end I summed it all up in a sentence.

'You want me to lead my army over the seas, to seize back your earldom?'

He nodded.

'And why should I do that? I'm an old man. Fifty-one winters. I am old, I am grey, I have sons who are almost grown enough to take my place. Why should I put my life at risk?'

He tried a number of nets to snare me. He went on at length about how my deeds had been done far away, and no one was here to see them or sing of them, or to understand them.

'If you conquered England,' he said, 'what fame that would bring you! Saxon and Dane and Irish would all know of your prowess!'

'They know it already,' I said, and he tacked again to find some breath of wind.

None of his reasons held me. 'No,' I said. 'Swein would not help you, and he is your cousin. Why should I help you, who cannot help yourself?'

He nodded, and sighed. 'So, it seems no one will help me.'

I could not stand self-pity. 'Grow a backbone, lad,' I told him.

I did not think about Tostig much for the next week or so. I had other things to care about – Maria's wedding primarily. 'Let us do it after the harvest,' I said to Tora. The barley heads were already large. It looked like being a blessed year to stay home and see the simple gold of Christ's bounty, falling to the threshing floor.

She nodded, and said nothing.

The summer nights barely end in Norway. We lit fires under the stars, and drank wine and ale, and mead, like the old gods.

I had not spoken of my youth for many years. The stories had seemed dull to me, from over-use. When I had come back to Norway, I had locked them away, like my treasure, and left them in their dark chests.

But now, as I opened up the lid, they seemed to sparkle with light. They sucked it in, and threw it back in a wondrous glory of wealth and colour and detail, and I told them differently now. I was an old man, and I could see the pattern and weave of my life, and as I wove the tapestry for them, I began to have that feeling once more, that my story was not yet ended. A thought occurred to me. What *if* I conquered England?

It was like the tree root that snags your foot.

Harold was Knut's kinsman. And Knut had brought all my long exile about. Knut, and the men of Lathe like Thore Hund and Kalv Arnasson. Was conquering England my destiny?

I sat in silence, surprised by this notion. I had not thought of England much at all, but as I stared into the flames the boy in me awoke. The ten-year-old who wanted to follow Olaf's path, and take the Western Road to the England of Ethelred, where a hard warrior could milk the English, as Knut had done, in the year that I was born.

Knut, I thought, was no great warrior. If he could take England, then what could a man not do, who had seen the world and conquered all? I stood up, and walked a few paces forward. Flames licked up at the night. The evening sky was pale with summer light. From the hillside came the sound of a woodsman's axe, using the long hours to get work done. I heard the musical clang of cowbells as they grazed the meadows. A maid called out to another for a bucket.

I felt as though the mists cleared for a moment, and revealed the rocky heights.

This would be the crowning achievement. Glory and conquest of all the North. To be greater than Knut the Great. I closed my fist upon itself, and took a deep breath.

'Eystein,' I said. 'Come. Walk with me a while.'

Maria's eyes flashed with pleasure that I should pick out her betrothed for personal counsel.

We strode out into the half-night, the skies blue and pale above us, the fjords flat with reflected mountains, and behind us the light of the fire, throwing warmth onto our backs.

'I have a mind to help this Tostig,' I said. 'What do you think of this?'

I had spent the last dozen days arguing against it, but he did not look surprised, but beamed with pleasure. 'May I come with you? That way I can tell my sons that I fought with King Harald when I was young.'

I laughed to hear such a thought. 'Of course,' I told him.

For two seasons our war-gear – our mail and shields and spears and helms – had hung on our hall walls, gathering dust. Now they were brought down and rubbed clean, spear-shafts oiled, buckles and fittings rubbed with sweet beeswax.

The young who had not been tried before looked forward to their first battle with an eager joy. Which of a young man's pleasures can compare to that of looking forward to his first battle? They had that eager light in their eyes, and you could see them gathered about in bands, watching the older men spar, imagining themselves in the shieldwall, trying out little moves and feints and practising them on each other.

The old among us knew what we were going back to, and we walked with square shoulders, heavy footsteps, eyes that sucked in the world about us, knowing that these could be our final hours upon this earth. Knowing that the winter and spring and summer that we had just enjoyed might be our last.

I thought of Elizaveta, and how she had passed her last seasons with quiet courage. It is the manner of friendships, loves, reigns of kings, ages of man, even, that we do not see endings until they have already passed by.

CHAPTER EIGHT

The Ship Levy

There were many things to do before I left, and all the time I was thinking of the autumn storms that close the sea-lanes, and how much I had to get done before then if I was to conquer England.

I had my son Magnus declared king before I left Uppland, and sailed north through all the districts and gathered the great men of the country to come with me to Trondelag Fjord, where Harald Finehair had been declared king.

It was a fine summer evening. The fires were yellow in the pale blue evenings, and the skies were streaked with wild sweeps of cloud, like horses' tails.

I sailed into Nidaros, where I had built the cathedral over Olaf's tomb, and all came out to greet me.

I took Eystein and my sons with me to Stiklestad and recounted the battle to them all: our camp high in the valley; the route our Upplanders had taken from the south; the way we came down to the battle; the stone where Olaf was killed.

I asked men about the mountain hut where I had been brought after the battle, but no one knew, and I had no idea how I had got from battlefield to bed. There was no one alive who could tell me.

So I could not find the pass I had taken over the Keelbacks, and

I felt thwarted, and wasted three days in the effort, and only Eystein kept his humour up.

The mountains were blue in the sunlight, but I knew them still: Blackcrag, Whitespear, Old Grumpy. They looked less threatening in the summer, but Whitespear still kept her cap of ice. I raised a hand to them, and closed my eyes for a moment, and saw myself, a figure, faint with the years that had passed between us, standing on the path before the antlered elk, asking to pass through.

I was quiet on the way back down to Nidaros.

I could see the ships' square sails as they came in twos and threes and tens, according to the wealth of each chieftain.

I had called out half my levy, so that Norway should be defended in case any pirates took it into their minds to attack while I was gone. The country was abuzz with the thought of another war, against a country as great as England.

I felt alive again, alert to every detail. The fearless flight of the swallows, the circling of three hawks high in the air, the rustle of spirits in the trees.

I did all that a Norse king should do. I gave gifts, I feasted the men, I gave prizes to the best poets who could mark the occasion in words that would echo through halls for generations to come.

But I had learnt much in Micklegard, and I had clerks who drew up lists of men, their equipment, the competence of their commanders, and I sat with my Varangian retainers and we pored through the information as we had once done with detachments of Greeks and Armenians and Italians and Bulgars.

I was to leave Magnus behind, but Tora wanted to see her cousin in Orkney, and Maria and Ingegerd wanted to come as well, to see England. So, on the last morning I had said goodbye to all who needed a farewell, but there was one who I had been avoiding. And that last morning I went to see him.

*

The summer light was bright behind me as I strode into the church with my sons in tow. The lay brothers were still painting the west of the nave as I entered. 'Out,' the abbot told the men, and I waited while the oldest of them climbed down the wooden ladder, bowed and hurried after the others.

When they were gone the abbot led the four monks forward.

'This way, Lord,' he said, as if I didn't know.

I paced down the aisle. They had done fine work with the land and coin I'd given them, but it was just a start. They needed more books. They needed a scriptorium. I bowed at the altar and followed the abbot to the back, under the unshuttered window. Magnus had built a simple shrine of wood. I had encased it with a hogsbacked shrine with panels of silver and jewels, intricately worked with miniature figures and inlays of walrus ivory. The key was brought: a great brass thing that lay heavy in the open palm and was as long as an Armenian knife. I took it and unlocked the miniature front gates. The silver hinges creaked as one door was opened and then the other, and from the dark interior came the scent of Spanish cedar and frankincense.

It had been thirty-six years since Olaf had been killed; as long as he had lived upon the world, I thought. His coffin was a plain wooden thing, the planks stained with old wax drips and oil stains on them, from the earliest days when men could come and touch the coffin itself.

One of the monks pulled a face. 'It's so light,' he said as we slid it out onto the trestle table they kept for the holy days. The abbot hushed him, but he was right. The weight of a man leaves the corpse once he is long dead. The bones and muscles dry out and stretch. The soul is long gone.

They lit incense, sang Kyrie Eleison, and I ritually washed my hands before I knelt at his coffin side, and closed my eyes and prayed in a loud voice, before gently slipping the crowbar under the edge and working the ship-nails free. The church was so still you could hear the nails drop onto the earthen floor. As I lifted the lid, the scent of sainthood came with it. Oils, herbs, spices, purple. I placed the lid carefully to the side, drew back the cloths, and looked down at the cadaver within.

Olaf's corpse lay still, the eye sockets sunken, the teeth long and crooked and clenched shut against death. The skin had split about his nose and pulled back from his teeth, giving his face a grin of pain. I touched the leather of his cheek, just where the beard failed; put my fingers into the wound in his neck, and felt the bone within; found the wound in his gut that Thore Hund gave him; the wound in his thigh that had thrown him back against the stone.

I closed my eyes, and willed that memory back, and my flesh goosed as a cloud passed across the sun outside and the air was chill for a moment as the world went dark.

Last time I had come was after Kalv Arnasson died, and I had described the moment for his ghost. Then, as now, his body had lain unmoving and still, without a twitch or response. 'You said that your vision told you that you would always be king of Norway, and now you are the Saint-King, until Doomsday.'

I looked for a sign, and thought I saw one in the stillness of his face.

I cared for him as I had seen my mother do when he yet lived, took out the clippers I had brought, and gently trimmed his beard. When that was done, I lifted each hand from the swaddling cloth and trimmed his brown nails, and kept them all within a silken pouch about my neck.

I was the last of his family alive. It was fitting I should do this for him.

Now I beckoned my sons forward. They approached the body slowly, and with a little fear, but they knelt and touched his corpse, and called on his aid in formulaic prayers.

When all was done I wrapped Olaf in a silken cloth embroidered with silver and gold thread. His body was light and stiff, not much heavier than a child's. I laid his head back gently, eased the lid back in place, picked up the nails and tapped each one back into new holes. I paused a while, to take the moment in, then locked the silver shrine and hung the key about my neck. It weighed on me.

I did not need to drink that night at the leaving feast. There were great fires all along the strand, their yellow beards trailing up into the blue night air. In the yellow light, dark against the bright glow, men were standing, laughing, talking.

There was a fine air. Pitch-fires were burning all day long, a market sprang up, with women selling salted fish and barley bannocks, while potters and leather crafters and weaponsmiths moved through the camp, doing brisk business.

CHAPTER NINE
Scarborough

What sight can compare to a host of longships, sails swelling with the following wind and loping over the waves like a vast pack of brightly coloured hounds, each vying to outdo the other?

I had nearly three hundred in my fleet, the finest that ever sailed from Norway. The crossing was fair. We had a following wind all the way, and while the wind was cool, the sun shone brightly and kept us warm during the long September days.

Maria's face was as bright as the young men's. I could see that she wished that she could be a man, and come to war with us.

'Must I stay in Orkney?' she said.

'Yes,' I told her, for the tenth time at least, and she sighed.

'I would like to come with you. Who will look after you?'

'Don't worry. I was fighting wars long before you were born.'

'It is my part to worry,' she said. She was close to womanhood. I would have delayed her for a little longer, as fathers often want, but loved her for that, and I kissed her brow.

It was two days crossing the open seas to the Isles of Shetland. We did not pause there, as traders do, but turned due south, passed the rock of Fair Isle on our right, under a little crown of clouds, and then as the sun began to wester on the third day we saw the green of Orkney on the southern horizon, rimmed with the gold of sunset.

As the light failed and our shadows grew long, and then faded, we ploughed the waves southwards. All children who sit and listen to the saltbeards know the waymarkers: Fair Isle, Ronaldsay, round the dark rocks of Auskerry, which stand guard upon the harbour, and then due west, till you see the wide golden sands.

The sun had set by the time our boats rode up onto the beaching sands.

The days were already shortening. It was September already, what we call the Kornskurðarmánuður – the 'Corn-Cutting Month'.

Thorfinn, Earl of Orkney, had died, leaving his two sons, Paul and Erling, in the care of his widow, Ingibiorg.

She had a great welcome for us in her hall. Fire, food and foaming mead to fill our horns. She gave me gifts and begged me to take her son Paul, even though he was younger than my own, so that they might learn from me, and so I took them, and thirty ship crews joined us there. No man wants to be left behind.

Rognvald had come back to Orkney while I was with the Varangians, and he had been made earl. An old man was brought who had seen him killed, and could tell me the tale. 'He was surprised by his enemies, and hid from them in a hollow, but his lapdog would not stop barking, and it would not leave him, and so they found him and killed him.'

I remembered Rognvald's dog as it sat content upon his lap. 'Well, I am glad he saw Orkney again,' I said. 'When we were in Kiev together, he spoke long of this place. He was the best of men, handsome and brave and warlike. Before we leave I should like to visit his grave.'

After the feast with Earl Paul, I brought my youngest son, Olaf. He was fourteen, and had much to learn, and I was conscious that my days for teaching him were short. 'Rognvald was retainer to Olaf, my brother, the saint. He dragged me wounded from the battlefield of Stiklestad. I owe him my life, and you do too.' He nodded dutifully, and took it all in.

I left Tora and Maria and Ingegerd in Orkney. I shall summon them when the last battle is won, I thought. It cannot be long now. And then I embraced each one, but I held Maria a little tighter and for a little longer that the others, and watched her say her farewells to Eystein, her betrothed, and remembered how it was to be young and in love.

'Come, Eystein!' I said as the two lingered together, awkward before us all. 'Enough of making eyes! Kiss her and be done. The seas wait for no man.'

Maria laughed and kissed him, and then gave him a shove.

We swung up over the painted bulwark, rowed out into the sea, raised the sail, which stiffened the broad stripes with a stout flap – and behind us the women we loved fell away as the north wind blew us steadily southwards to new lands, new countries, new conquests.

We sailed down Scotland, being feasted by every two-field thane. Every man wanted to see me, to feel my hand's grip, to join in our expedition.

I turned away any who were not well-provided with mail and helm. We did not need any more men taking a share of the booty. We had plenty of brave warriors already, and as we sighted the cliffs of Northumbria I grew quiet with battle-thoughts, and the mood of the men turned from gaiety to the oncoming battle.

It is always good to blood an army before the main battle comes. It lets you test the mettle of your men, and a few deaths weed out the foolish and the luckless, and give the others something to revenge themselves upon when the real test comes.

I wanted a place that appeared well defended, so that word would spread across the countryside and fill our foes with fear, and so I picked the fort of Scarborough, which lies high on the rocks above the half-moon beaches.

We filled the curving beach with longships, and burnt the town as I sent the men of Orkney and the young bloods up to the fortress.

They were tentative at first as they looked up at the earthen ramparts and ditches and the helmed faces of the defenders, but as they gathered their numbers and their courage, so I spoke to them, calling on them to strike like the hawk that plunges from the sky, and promised rewards for the bravest. They felt my eyes on each of them, and in an hour the job was done. We had lost only twenty-three men, and we feasted and were stronger for it.

As we sailed down the long cliffs of Holderness words and details my brother had told me began to return, and I dreamt that night I was a boy again, sitting on the hall floor with the hounds, knees drawn up to my chin, listening to other men's tales.

The feeling was so lasting that it took a few minutes of waking to remember who I was, what stage my life had come to. As to recalling all the scars that covered me, I could not tell you who had given them to me, or even which country they might have come from.

We came up the Humber ten days ago. At the pools of Riccall, where the river makes its great slow bend, I left the ships in the marshes there, with a strong guard of warriors, and then led the army northwards, along a low, flat plain towards York. You'll remember how cool and bright the morning was. The grass was worn through in patches, and the earth was pale as old bones, and a haze of dust rose up as we set out, marching from dawn, each one like a workman carrying his tools: mail, sword, spear and shield.

I do not fear battle, but I am quiet when I feel it coming. Tense, taut as a bow that is slowly drawn back. I do not like the unexpected. My mind feels out the vague contours of the future, and assesses them, counters them, thinks what I might do if the enemy pull off such and such a trick.

Tostig has long since told me all he knows of Edwin and Morcar. How they are young and proud, and have much to prove. I let every

Northumbrian tell me what little they know. How the English earls have bands of huscarls, each one with mail and helm and bearded axe. How these warriors are the match of my own retainers. How bravely they fight. How harsh will be the meeting.

We see the glint of steel across the last bend of the river. The morning fires are being lit in York. They hang blue above the city. The river is high, and the morning tide has reached its height. A hawk hovers across the river, and then plunges into the reeds by the banks. It comes out moments later, carrying a frog its claws.

I draw in a breath, and have my banner, Landwaster, unfurled. It catches the wind.

CHAPTER TEN

Battle of Fulford Gate

You know the battlefield, Bishop. It is just across the river from your hawking lodge. You'll be familiar with how the river curves up from the south through flat summer meadows, and turns at last, west, towards the city.

It lay to our left as we approached York, the marshy ings to the right. We took the narrow high ground along which the path runs, and stopped within sight of the city ramparts, where the beck was swollen with high tide and the way before us blocked, and we watched the Northumbrians file the half-mile out of York towards us.

I counted their banners, gave my orders to each company as they tramped along the path behind us. The men were tense. They took their mood from me. I am not the man who laughs and jokes before battle. I never have been. I am who I am, and my way has seldom failed.

My retainers waved our companies into position as I strode down from the riverbank into the bed of the beck. The water was high enough to drown a man. Brown eddies swirled through the reeds and ferns, the water so dark that I could see nothing through it. It seemed to have stopped rising, but there would be no battle for an hour at least.

A bowshot away, along the far side of the beck, the foremost English companies were already forming. They were well armed and numerous, but their steps were short and hesitant and they clustered like sheep, looking for a leader to follow.

'Harald, King,' Eystein called to me. He fretted lest an Englishman might spy me out and feather me with an arrow.

I did not fear. I had survived so many battles, and I knew in my bones that this was not my day to die. I turned and made my way back up the bank. As each company filed past me they reached out their hands to mine. They all wanted to feel my grip. Each man took strength from it. Company by company I made my way along the line. I exchanged words with their captains. The land in the meadows was sodden. The water brimmed about my foot. 'Is this earth worth fighting for?' an Orkneyman joked.

I looked away from the battle and across the meadows, which had been cut for hay. Only here, in the marsh, were the plants still green. There were no mountains here. No fjord. The land was flat, the trees dark with late-summer, the skies wide and blue, the clouds like sheep, knitted by the gods and pushed out from the horizons. They barely moved. Even the sheep here were fat.

For a moment I felt as though I was back in Kiev, looking out across the steppes.

'The soil is dark and deep,' I said. 'The ploughmen must be happy here.'

The farmers there laughed and joked. They'd been thinking the same, but they did not expect me to know about such things. They expected fire and war and poetry. There was so much they didn't know. I had not told them about the years I helped my father in the fields, helping with the plough, like a thrall's lad.

Some truths will die with me.

The mud squelched as I trudged back to the dry bank. It sucked at my feet. I felt as though it was trying to draw me into it.

Some men would think this was a bad omen, but I've felt it

before. The land welcomed me. It took me as its king. I thought, Battle today will show whether I am right. It is the surest judge. It has always favoured me.

'Stand firm,' I told the Orkneymen as I waved them along our side of the flooded beck. 'Strike hard. Fight well.'

Across the beck the Northumbrians had already formed their shieldwall. They started forward, even though the beck's brown water was still waist-deep. The round shields walked towards us, our foemen's heads and faces showing dark, their helms gleaming in the mid-morning light.

A blackbird called. Its song was lost in the warning blast of horns. My companies were still moving along the bank of the beck. The Northumbrians could not resist the chance to attack.

'Form up!' I called, as slower companies kept tramping up behind us. They'd heard the horns and moved at a jog. The tide was draining fast away from the trees along the river banks. The reed beds seemed to rise from the muddy water. It ebbed down the reed shafts, leaving them stained and wet and gleaming. The Fates had chosen this moment. A few rams led the Northumbrians forward. They shuffled into place. They were about to charge. You could see it in the nervous shifting of their feet.

The men facing them were Earl Paul's Orcadians. I saw Paul shouting over the heads of his men. They drew about him like a fist, their shields raised together, throwing hands ready with their spears.

I felt a shudder. It was not fear, but something close, an exhilaration and a horror of what was about to come. War-cries flew, and then the Northumbrians, all as one, started to chant, and I laughed to hear their chorus. It was like facing Swein again. 'They're speaking Danish!' I said, and my men laughed and my words were repeated, and as the Northumbrians chanted 'Ut! Ut! Ut!' laughter rang out along our lines.

It goaded the enemy into charging too soon. They plunged down into the beck, shields held high, and the water foamed and splashed, it seethed; it seemed to lift out of the ditch as they waded up towards us, and then came the crunch as shieldwalls clashed one against the other, as when children bang two stones together and wonder which of them will break.

I let my breath sigh out. The Orkney line had held. Neither stone had broken. The Fates were feeding men into the millstones as they started to grind one against the other.

'Stand firm!' I called, though surely they could not hear me.

The Orkney line took a step backwards, and then another. They were drawing the English into the trap that Hannibal set at Cannae.

'Stand firm,' I told the men about me. Some of them were eager to charge. They turned to look at me. I saw it in all their faces. They wanted to fight. They wanted it all to be over.

'Hold,' I told them. I was watching. Just a word soothed them, a touch, as a stroke and a word from a mother will calm a sick child.

The Orkney line took two steps back. They were fighting fiercely, but the wet ground had funnelled so many of the English into the middle that it seemed as though Earl Paul's Orcadians were holding the entire army back.

The middle of the line swelled like a starving hound's belly, or a snake that has swallowed a rabbit whole. Orkneymen looked towards my banner. They were wondering why I did not strike, looking towards me for aid. I showed myself. I was watching.

The English poured into the centre. They thought they had won. You could hear it in their war-cries. Ut! the rear companies were still calling. Ut!

The words rose up again and again in waves of fury with curses and cries of pain and hatred.

The spear-din sounded, the sword-meeting, the thunder of shields, the chants of steel ringing hard against each other.

Eystein was standing beside me. We could see the banners of the Orkneymen being driven back, step by step. 'Will they hold?' he said. He feared defeat. He feared that I was too old. He feared that something was going wrong before our eyes, that he did not know.

'They will hold,' I told him. They had to. They could not run.

The marshes would slow them down and English spears would have run them through. I let the English crush down into the beck. They pushed past the line where I was standing. I let the Orkney lines strain backwards and turned to check. My household troops were all about me. Their faces were grim. They were ready. They were steel, hardened by years of war and service. The Varangians among them stood out, like me, with beards shot through with white and grey. I knew them as well as the fingers of my own hand.

'Raise my banner.'

They swung Landwaster in the air. The silk sounded like the flap of ravens' wings in the air above us. There were distant cheers. My mail shirt hung down to my knees. I hitched it up one last time, tightened my belt to take the weight upon my legs, and rolled my shoulders. I would use the axe that day. It did not need to cut through mail, it would smash the bones beneath. I felt the tight-bound thongs of the handle. It was the one that Olaf used. *Hel*, he called, it. I have set the blade onto a longer haft. *Hel* was coming to the English.

'Ready,' I called out.

The voices answered me, and I knew that all was set. The pattern had been woven. Time for the Fates to wield their shears.

All were waiting for me. The world seemed poised. I saw the world beyond the battle, the green towers of summer trees, the sedge and reeds and uncombed tangle of bramble, the distant shapes of women, standing to watch, the black carrion birds sitting on the dead crown of the distant oak. I held the world in balance, like a market trader with his scales, and then I took a step.

'Forward!' I called out and my men followed me. In a moment we were jogging forward into the flanks of the English bulge.

Astonished faces turned and I saw their fear and they saw me as I gripped *Hel* in both my hands, and I saw in their wild eyes that they knew that their death was upon them.

CHAPTER ELEVEN

King in the North

The English fought for over an hour before they broke. One earl fled back along the river, the other left his banner and fled east, stumbling through the marsh, searching for the dry land on the far side.

In the middle they left half their army trapped in the sucking mud. It held them tight, and we fell upon them like wolves upon a tethered horse. That was where I found you, Bishop, and led you back to safety across the stepping stones of dead men.

You spent the rest of that day, riding back and forth between me and your earls. I summoned Tostig to me.

'I am going to meet the earls,' I told him. 'I will do the talking.'

Tostig does not argue. He could not even raid the North. His force of sixty longships was crushed by the Mercians in the summer of this year. I have just stacked Mercia and Northumbria together, like a pair of wooden staves, and broken them both upon my knee. I can see that he is just starting to understand that he has been chained to the back of my chariot. I am the one who leads him now.

'They have offered you more silver if you will leave this land,' you said to me, Bishop, and I lost patience in the end, and banged my palm down on the table. 'Tell them to come and meet me.'

*

You could see that they were brothers, even though one was fair and the other dark. The two earls had the same square brow, the same way of swinging their arms, and the same wilful set of the jaw.

Edwin was the elder. His left arm was in a sling. His teeth were set against the pain.

Morcar stepped half a pace behind. This was the lad who had driven Tostig out last year. He had a mischievous look about him, like a naughty novice who is summoned by the abbot.

I took their hands and gave them the Harald handshake. No man expected a man of fifty to have a grip of iron, but I'd been a warrior all my life. Kingship did not come to me served on a carved wooden platter. In a moment's handshake they were cowed. Their hostile look had gone. I ushered them to the side of the fire that my men had lit.

There were stools there, brought from a farmhouse, the seats worn smooth with many years of backsides. I gestured to them. They sat. I smiled as I took my place. The three of us, like the Fates: Past, Present and Undecided.

We were about to weave the future.

'You fought well,' I said.

They forced out smiles, but I was honest and they felt respected.

It was for me to tell them what I wanted, but I kept chatting, until the young one said, 'So. What do you want?'

'Edward, your king, was Knut's heir, and he died this year without an heir.'

'And?'

'I want the kingship,' I told them. 'I am the heir of Knut.'

They argued for a while, but it was clear. Who else could possibly control the North?

'So what do you want from us?' Morcar, the young one, spoke.

'I want your oaths not to fight against me. I want your oaths that you will come with me, south, to fight Harold Godwinson.'

'And then?'

'I will give you back your earldoms.'

'What about Tostig?'

341

'I will deal with Tostig.'

It was all decided in the length of time it takes for a man to walk a mile. They were my men now. In five days they would bring me a hundred hostages, as tokens of their good faith. They would bring me horses to carry my army south. They would provide us with food and ale.

They stood and made oaths before all their retainers. 'What happened to the arm?' I said at the end.

Edwin held it up for a moment. It was his shield arm. 'An axe,' he said. He had barely spoken. He looked a little sick with the pain.

'Is it broken?'

He nodded. 'They think so.'

'Here,' I said, 'let me see,' and he looked wary, but held out his arm.

'I learnt a little medicine in Micklegard,' I assured him. The finest medicine-men in the world are there. I took the two halves of his arm in my hands, and felt along the bones, probing for the two in the forearm. He ground his teeth as my fingers found the break. I had it between my fingers, and I could have killed him with pain, but I was gentle. I treated him like one of my own men. The break was clean.

'Lay your arm here,' I said, and lifted my knee.

'Get me some cloth.' I spoke to no one in particular. A hand proffered a length of wood, cut from a broken spear-shaft, and a length of red cloth. It was weather-stained at one end. It looked as though it had been cut from a dead man's cloak.

I started at the wrist, wrapping the red cloth round and round to bind it tight to the spear-shaft. 'This will hurt,' I told him, as I swaddled the break. He flinched, but he did not make a sound.

When I had bound his whole arm, I stood. His retainers had gathered close to watch. I saw wonder in their eyes, as well as fear.

'There,' I said at the end, clapping him on his good shoulder. 'It will mend.'

*

The burghers of the town wanted to meet me separately. The little alliance that had driven Tostig out had already fractured. Defeat does that to men. They feel that God has judged them harshly.

I rode to meet them at the city gates: the burghers of York, in a great crowd. The wooden palisades were dark with the people of the city. As I approached on horseback, my retainers behind me, I heard the note of their talk change to the same buzz that bees make when you cut down their tree.

They walked out to greet me. I swung down from my horse. I did not need a mount to overshadow men, and I liked to stand on the same ground as men before me.

They introduced themselves. I shook hands with each

They were subdued before we even started to speak.

They pushed one of their number forward, a stout man named Hardwulf son of Dunstan. He ran through a string of compliments, and I saw through his words, and held up my hand to still him. I lifted my voice so that they all could hear me. We spoke the same tongue, they and I. We were all Norsemen once.

'Brothers!' I called out. 'It was not so long ago that Northumbria was a kingdom ruled from York, and your kings were brought over from Norway. From the sons of Harald Finehair, who was my forefather. How long has the South oppressed you all? Demanding taxes. Demanding tribute. Eroding the laws of the Northumbrians, who have always looked to Norway for their leaders. I have come among you, I who rule Norway and the isles of Orkney. I have brought you back under the care of the Norse king. I shall not demand hostages from you, as a conqueror. I offer to exchange men with you, as befits a fellowship.'

Whatever they had expected, it was not this. I had their attention now. Even on the walls people were silent, so silent that I could hear a dog bark inside the city walls, a woman's shout, a door slam shut.

'I am not here to raid,' I called out. 'I am not here to demand a Danegeld from you all. My treasure is famous. I am here to free you, the Northumbrians, from the oppression of the Saxon kings.

As a demonstration of my good feeling towards you all, I offer you a hundred and fifty of my men as hostages, on condition that you put into my care a hundred and fifty of your own, and then together we shall march south, and claim the freedoms that are rightfully yours.'

They were too surprised to answer at first, but it was not long before I was shaking their hands and slapping backs, and from the walls a chant started up, 'Harald! Harald!' and I lifted my hands to them, and men whose faces I could not make out waved back.

I spared the city. I took oaths from Morcar and Edwin. I took oaths from the burghers of the city, and the chief men of the country, who had not yet submitted to me.

It was agreed that we would exchange hostages in five days' time.

Until then I would not allow any of my men into the city, lest they harm the people there. And so I departed, in peace, having made myself king of the North.

I saw your father again that evening in the ponds at Riccall. Your father had left his ships in the mere there. The city sent out a great store of meat and ale and wine, and I had brought much of it loaded upon my own boat.

It was late afternoon. The day had clouded over, but the sun broke through as it was setting, lighting the cloud's soft underbellies up like coals. A heron was disturbed. It flapped up from the water and disappeared in the reeds on the other side of the river. My servants were nervous.

The Norse had spread their tents out into the fields. We saw the fires through the reed beds as we approached the bend. They were not watchfires. They did not need to stand guard. No one would dare come against them tonight.

The mere was clotted with longships. 'Go in,' I said, but my men did not know where to go.

'Here!' a man shouted, and signalled us into the side. He was a Norseman. He grinned as he saw the hams we had loaded. 'Pass them ashore,' he called out, wading waist-deep into the water and holding on to the side of our boat. Then he looked at me, crouching nervously at the side of the boat. 'Do you want to come ashore?' He did not wait for an answer. 'Come, hop on my back!' The man carried me a little unsteadily to the shore, and I found your father walking among them. This was his hour of victory. The firelight shone on his face. His eyes gleamed like garnets.

'Bishop!' he called out and took my hand, and it was like gripping steel. He wrapped an arm about me, 'Come! I have a tent made up for you.'

The Norsemen were telling and retelling their tales of battle. How they had seen friends die, how they had killed, how they had escaped death.

The world was all cooling blues, and greens, and the sky was pale as winter. I shivered and fancied I could hear the bells of the city ringing from six miles away. It was the Eve of the Feast of St Matthew the Apostle. I felt overcome with all that I had seen that day. I knelt to pray to the winged martyr; the Evangelist; the writer of the Gospel, the teacher, the proclaimer of the Truth.

He had faced greater difficulties than I. He had seen his Lord crucified upon the cross, had seen him rise again, had faced the best of all deaths: martyrdom, the chance to die for one's beliefs. Give me strength, I prayed, when the Devil tempted me; give me courage to face my own death with a calm face; and give me wisdom to know which of my beliefs were worth dying for.

The fire failed. Night fell about me. I was calm. It was as if the afterworld had thrown a comforting cloak over me, as if to say, hush, my child, the long dark is not so grim.

I was still praying when your father found the tent where I was lodging. He threw the door-flap open like a drunken groom searching for his wife's bed. The torch flames flickered like a serpent's tongue. They threw a fearsome and devilish light up onto his face. I crossed myself as your father strode towards me, and he laughed.

'Otli,' he called the man with him, the one who had carried me on his back from my boat. 'Why did we leave our Bishop here? Have you cared for him? He has no wine or ale. Otli's grandfather was a famous witch. Look at him, there's a heathen in there somewhere!'

He sat across from me and put his feet up on the table. I saw damp stains on his shoes. 'Sssh,' he said, though I had not spoken. 'Listen! Hear that? Men are still dying. Even here, miles away, we can hear their voices.

'I had a man who said that such groans were like the groans

of women giving birth. But instead of babies being born, these are souls passing free of worldly cares. Some souls go easily. Others linger on. The night after a battle it is always like this. The silence fills with moaning men who die too slowly. It would be a blessing to go about cutting their throats, I guess. I will give you my knife if you want. No, I thought not. Nor I. I am tired. I am not as young as I once was.

'Otli! Light the candles,' he shouted, and then took his feet off the table and leant forward. 'I grew up listening to tales of York's market. My father sent a ship each summer. Some years we would send furs. Other times salt cod. Those were poor years, and the ship came home with little to delight my mother. She loved York-red wool. I remember one year the captain had made a lot of money on some bear cubs we had found.

'They brought back a whole bolt, wrapped in linen and still dry despite the rough crossing. My mother carried it to the door and unwound a little and draped it over her arm, as I have seen the Greek traders do, held it up to the light of the noon sun. She did not weave but she loved fine cloth. There was a softness to her face, like lamb's wool. "Look at that!" she said. "The weave. The colour."

'I don't think she ever made anything out of that bolt. It stayed wrapped in linen, but she would take it out at times to stroke it. It was too good to use, I suppose. My mother hoarding cloth against hard times. And look at me! I am dressed in silks and wool of twice the quality!

'Halfdan gave the bolt to Budli's daughter in order to woo her. She was wearing a dress that colour when I met her. This was when I had come back from the East. Budli's daughter was tall like her father. She was big with child and the gown had ridden up over the bump, and I recognised the York-red cloth and thought of my mother standing by the hall door with the cloth draped over her arm, and wanted to slap her for daring to wear my mother's cloth.'

Your father broke off.

There was a long silence. Night had fallen at last on that sad day.

He yawned suddenly. He did not cover his mouth when he yawned, and then fell to talking of his childhood.

'When we were sick she would break little bits off and boil them in beer and give it to us. Each year after that she asked the captain to bring cinnamon home. One year he brought home a loaf of sugar. We had never seen such a thing! Do they still sell them here?'

I ended that night talking spices. Harald asked me to accompany me to where he slept, which was a short distance away. Men's feet had already worn muddy tracks through the camp. His tent was of dyed felt, with patterns woven about the door. Inside was a pair of stools, a barrel as a table, a stand for his mail-shirt, and a simple camp bed set on low trestles. His spears were leaning against the barrel, and his shield leant against the barrel. It was unmarked. He had not brought it to battle that day.

He lay down on his bed, fully dressed, and asked me to pray with him. I sang the Agnus Dei, and I could not help but think of my brothers, that morning, singing as we carried the relics to the battlefield, our hearts swelling with hope.

He reached out and patted my shoulder. 'Tomorrow you will be my guide,' he said. 'I shall send word to my wife and daughters. They are waiting in Orkney. You will meet them soon enough. I should have found husbands for them long ago, I know, but I am not the first father to put that day off a little too long. You should see Maria. She is my youngest. Young. Slender. Gentle. Her mother was like that when she was young. Ah!' he sighed. 'She would tempt a saint.'

He closed his eyes and I understood that I was dismissed and crossed myself and bowed and made my way to the door.

*

348

Otli was sitting outside the tent, turning over a golden ring in his hand. It had been cut off a corpse that afternoon. I could see the dark stains under Otli's nails. It was a thick gold band with a red garnet. He sniffed and yawned and said simply, 'Asleep?'

I nodded.

'I'll go and put a blanket on him.'

'Yes,' I said, 'a good idea.'

All this happened on the fifth day before your father was killed.

CHAPTER TWELVE

Thor's Day, 21st September 1066

The tent kept off rain and chill, but it did little to keep out the noise of an army.

The young men had not slept. All night they had been telling tales of battle, laughing, speaking of lost friends in low voices, singing songs, wondering who would bring the bad news back to the womenfolk.

No man can forget his first victory. His first woman. His first defeat.

Their humour seeped into my dreams. Today we set out for one of Tostig's old manors. He was keen on a place named Tadcaster, but I picked this one – it was nearer the coast. There was a river there, I was told, good roads east and west, north and south.

Many men had assured me that the locals would come to our cause.

I found Eystein and left Magnus with him. I thought perhaps I would stay in England, after the country was won. Eystein could go back and help Olaf rule. England would need a strong hand. It was a big country. Autumn was almost here. The trees – towers of dark late-summer green – were spent. A few leaves had already fallen, like hair at the foot of the barber's stool.

*

It was a morning's ride through farm and field.

The short-beards were still talking, but we – the old men, who had survived many battles – were running through the battle in our mind's eye, wondering when our luck would run out. It dwells in the hands of the Fates, who sit at the foot of Ygdrasil, the great ash tree that holds up the world, and they are jealous old ladies, and do not tell.

The sheep had all been driven up onto the higher fields. They bleated as we passed by. Dogs barked from the farmstead on the left, across the nodding barley. The soil was dark and rich down here in the valley. This was good land. Norway had none to compare with it.

We crossed at the ford, our horses knee-deep in the water.

'That's Scoresby,' someone told me. Here the vale rose to gentle slopes that looked south and west, and to fields already cut. At the foot of the hill a river threaded its way between the low-spreading ash trees. A few sheaves still stood in the fields, but I could hear the thud of threshing and every so often a puff of golden chaff lifted into the wind. The stay-at-homes would be harvesting as well. Better to be here than getting husks down your neck.

The first companies had already spread out along the banks of the river. Two men were pitching a tent where it met the York road. I could hear the tap-tap of a mallet on wooden pegs as one man knelt – it sounded like a distant woodpecker. Then he stood and did it again and they pulled the ropes tight.

Then one man told the other that I was here. I saw it in their movements. The tapper turned and shielded his eyes, and waved. I nodded towards him.

You could see in their manner how happy they were to have been noticed by the king, just the day after his victory. He will tell his wife, I thought. How King Harald noticed me just the day after his great victory over the English. How I was briefly picked out from the crowd. The mass of the unremembered, the undistinguished, the unnoticed, and then we passed on to where the four roads met

351

in a dusty, summer-cracked field, and a wooden bridge crossed the Derwent river, which flowed fast and clear from the chalky hillsides, and looked deep enough to drown a man.

I took the place in: the crossroads, the weir, the watermill, the wooden bridge wide enough for three cows to cross abreast. I thought of Maria and Ingegerd, and how they would love to see this land. It seemed a good and generous place, with rich soil and gentle hills. A place where you could rear livestock, raise children, enjoy the older years. It was less harsh than home. Did it breed weaker men, I wondered, and worried about my sons if they were raised here. Would they be weak men too?

The dusty harvest track led up to the longhouse that I was going to use. It was Danish, from the build and the wooden horns of the hall's doorposts. A row of horses were hobbled outside, heads lowered to the trough. The locals were ready to petition their new king. I will spend the day listening to a mix of flattery and complaint, I thought. I will find a cushion, or a cloak that can be folded up. I will tell each man how I shall uphold their Northumbrian laws.

I was not here to break and burn. I had come to build, and to grow. I was, I laughed, here to bring back the old ways: when Norse kings ruled north of the Humber.

I spent the day talking. Each man left with a slap on the back, a firm handshake, and a promise of fellowship. After the feast, I strolled out to the slopes above the manor. Half of my army was here, half were staying with the boats, in case enemies sneaked north to burn them.

I watched the last companies as they trudged north. They'd left their war-gear behind with the boats. They did not need mail shirts and helm and shield. It was good to leave the weight of them all behind for a few days, and feel the lightness of an unburdened man's stride. A man cannot live on war alone.

The heat of the day still lifted from the earth. The note of the blackbird lilted from the stubble-strip fields. A pale bird swooped low over the field. An owl, I thought, and waited for the call, but it did not come.

Not yet.

Dusk was not quite settled.

As the sun set, it lit columns of gnats down by the river. I looked about. Voices, places, memories, were milling in my head. Helen surprised me. She was young still, and beautiful. She put her arm to the back of mine and leant her head against my shoulder. 'My,' she said in Greek, and the thrill of that tongue – that world – ran through me again, unrecalled for too long. 'So now you are here, at the very end of the world. How green it is. How blue the sky. This is a place where we could raise children.'

And then I remembered. I would have had children here, with you, I thought.

Can ghosts read thoughts?

'Don't worry,' she told me. 'Our fates are all decided. You were not to blame.'

Of all the people I'd killed, I thought, I would have brought Helen back. 'So what now?' her ghost asked me. Her words came into my mind like thoughts. She saw the white of my beard, and it startled her. I slipped an arm about her. I tried to see her as she would have been, had Death not intervened. Her question hung in my mind, but for a moment I was content not to answer. I stood and looked down over this field, where the fires were already lit against the coming night, and felt the gentle English breeze upon my back, and the long-desired weight of Helen's head upon my side.

That night the curtains of the world were drawn back. So many ghosts clustered in the door of dreams, each one wanting to be picked out from the crowd, so thick that a single face could not be made out.

I dreamed that I was standing again in the shallows of Piraeus, with my ships in the water behind me. Halldor was glowering down at me.

'I'm coming!' I called up. He was fretting about the tide. I felt the lap of waves about my ankles and lifted my gaze from the shallows for one last look at the ruins of the citadel there, high up on the rock over the town. The air was cool in the mouth, like water. I paused to see the first light of the rising sun turn the white of the Parthenon of Athens to gold.

My heart wanted to climb those rocks again, to look out over the harbour from the giant-built hall of white marble, drink sweet red wine, carve our runes into the summer-warm marble. But the blue waters of the Aegean Sea were lapping at me, reminding me that it was time to go, that there were battles and honour and glory laid out before me, and Olaf Redbeard swung the last wicker baskets of chickens up onto the decks, and used the anchor rope to haul himself up. 'It's time,' Halldor called down.

An old man with bushy white eyebrows told us tales of ancient warriors, as the fire throws back the black of night. The old man was all eyebrows and no teeth. Those of us with Greek translate for the others. 'They wandered for ten years,' I told Halldor.

'This evening feels like ten years,' Halldor said. He was in a twist about something.

Next morning we climbed through sunrise in search of an ancient warrior's tomb. We kept going till the sun was hot on my back and I shed my cloak and threw it over one shoulder. The guide unwrapped a piece of cheese. No, I gestured, but he smiled at me, and spoke to me with the tone you would use to a child, and took another piece out of his belt. Below us in the bay my ships were moored: three on the beach, which was so small that there was no room for any more, and two further out in the shelter of a rocky finger of land that curved gently round the bay.

He pointed to a marble tomb and said a name. It meant nothing to me but it sounded a little like Odin. 'Odin is my ancestor,' I told him. He had nothing better to do than tell old tales and eat cheese.

'He walks about in a hooded cloak, and he is the wisest of all the old heroes.'

In the Holy Land: we had been baptised in the Jordan river, and were returning to Jerusalem. The sun was bright. I strode out into the yard and found the man the Caliph gave us as a guide. He was a small man with a red silk turban and bright blue eyes. 'Mohammed!' I shouted. 'Why does your Caliph not do something about these goat herders?'

He opened his mouth to speak, but I did not have the time to listen. We were at the city gates, and Mohammed was arguing with the guards there, and it took a long and heated debate before their commander, a hook-nosed lad with an ugly curl to his lips and scraggly beard, shrugged as if he did not care, and let us out.

'I think he is in league with these bandits,' Mohammed told me.

'Should we kill them?' my dream shape asked.

I looked to Helen. Her face was Maria's. That made me pause.

Earl Tostig took us hunting.

Scoresby had been one of Tostig's manors when he was earl here, and the servants – fearful at first – welcomed him warmly. The headman especially made a great show. I forget his name. He was a diligent young man, with a spade of a beard, a little foxy in colour, and small, bright, intelligent eyes. He had that way about him, that when he looked at you, you knew that he was listening. He reminded me a little of a gloved hawk. His name was Agmund and he brought out hams and malt that they said they had not given to Earl Morcar, because his men had murdered the huscarl here. Apparently my scribe, Julianus, knows the man. He is still alive, apparently, which is a blessing.

'I will take you out, Earl Tostig,' he said. 'And your king.'

Your father took offence at this. 'This man is a village dweller. He does not stray from his fields often. In Norway you are familiar with the type, I am sure. They think their local ponds are large bodies of water. Imagine if they ever saw the sea!'

Your father patted my back. 'Settle down, Bishop,' he said. 'When I want you to speak I will ask you a question.'

The weather was fine. Sunlight dappled the slopes of the Wolds. We took a gentle way up and the hounds had a scent of boar, though we did not catch any, but your father was in a fine mood.

'That was a good chase!' he said, as we turned our horses towards our home. As we came down through a vineyard, the grapes were almost ripe. Your father seemed amazed and jumped down. 'I dreamt of grapes last night.'

The whole company had been hunting since dawn, and it was already long past noon. We were all dusty, dry-mouthed, parched. 'Didn't I, Bishop?'

I nodded. The faces that turned towards me were full of

accusation, as if I had caused this delay. I smiled wanly. It was not my fault, my look said.

Your father paused for a moment, as if he was a man amazed, or scrambling for a memory. 'My! We used to eat so many of these that our turds smelt of grapes.' He looked about, and found an old red-nosed fellow and called him up. 'Snorri!' he said. 'You remember, don't you?'

Snorri had the manner of a man who acts the part. 'Yes,' he said. 'Yes, of course.'

Then your father stopped. 'No, you weren't in Micklegard. You were in Kiev.' He turned away, and I can't remember what Snorri said, but your father picked a grape, and popped it in his mouth and pulled a slow face, like a man with toothache. 'Sour,' he said, and spat it out, and picked another. The second wasn't much better.

'Tostig, these grapes are all sour.'

Tostig had no idea, bless his soul. He had no idea about so many things.

I put myself forward, as St Jerome did, when the lion came.

'My king,' I said in a firm and resolute voice, 'the monks use the sour grapes to make a juice. "Omphacium" it is in the Latin tongue. I suppose in the common language it would be something like "sour water". The cooks use it. And it has some medical properties, so the brothers tell me.'

'What uses?'

I looked about. Snorri kept his head down.

'I will ask. I know they put it on sores, with mouldy bread.'

Your father picked a few bunches, and the grapes were passed from horseback to horseback and each man tasted of the fruit. Some of them were a little ripe. I remember watching one young Norseman, who must have been on his first campaign, holding up one of the small red spheres, admiring the translucent light within them and laughing.

I remember that image very clearly. Ah! Julianus is laughing at me because tears come so easily these days. He is young and does not have enough things to weep about yet, but time will teach him. There, I have wiped my eyes, and the tears will not come again. They come when they surprise me, like the thought of that young warrior holding a grape up to the sun, and laughing at the light and veins of grape within.

Perhaps we should pause there, and think of him, surprised, amused, delighted by one of the many small wonders of Creation.

I was struck by how often your father would turn to one of his old Varangian companions and ask him to confirm a memory. I have seen it in other men who outlive those who were with them in former times, and begin to doubt the facts of their own lives. 'Did I really do that?' they seem to wonder. 'Was I really there?'

And they turn to other old men on the benches, who sit all day, sucking their gums, and say, 'Do you remember . . .' And the other man might nod and nod, or at other times, which always seem a little sad to me, the other will shake his head.

By the time we got back to the hall, your father's poets had been drinking, and they were competing with each other with skaldic verses about your father's victory at Fulford Gate. How the Northumbrian dead filled the ditches and how men could walk like St Peter, over the mere, without getting their feet wet, such was the carpet of English dead.

I was there, remember, under Brother Cuthbert, plucked like a fish from the water.

But the afternoon soon degenerated into drunken men belting out skaldic lines. You will know them all I'm sure. Many of them were lines composed about your father's remaining time in Micklegard. They were all composed by men who served with him as a commander of the Varangian Guard. He seemed to enjoy them. Many of them he had composed himself, and while he had aged, the words themselves had not.

'Bishop!' your father called to me. 'I have a question for you. When Jesus steps out of the water and the clouds open and the sun shines down and a dove sits on his shoulder. Why a dove? What use is a dove, except for eating? Odin had two ravens. At least ravens can talk.'

I explained it as best I could and he grew bored. Kings like to talk, not listen.

'I asked my brother something similar, and do you know what he told me?'

I did not.

'He said, "It's not a dove. It's a raven that God coloured white."'

CHAPTER TWELVE
Bath Day, 23rd September 1066

The mists of night chill over us as we sleep, and then the dawn breaks grey and blue and green and purple, which is the Emperor's colour. Each day is like a jewel, held up to autumn light. I have not seen such dawns for years. Norway's are lost behind the black troll mountains that sit guard over us.

I watch the colours slowly brighten and then fade as the sun breaks free from under the world. It is bathing day. A few men are already standing in the shallows, splashing water up to their chests. I will wait till the sun is up. I've never quite got used to the cold water. Not after the warmth of the Middle Sea. Cold has too much of the Keelbacks about it. Given a choice, I'd rather be warm.

Last night Eystein and Magnus rode up to feast with me.

Eystein has found men all along the Humber who want to join us. They say we can take ships halfway down the country, if we take the Trent. It is the way that Swein Forkbeard went, they tell us. In the time when their fathers were born.

'Is that a good omen?' I laugh.

Eystein does so want to please. 'He conquered England,' he says, a little defensively.

'He did, but did he get to enjoy it?'

My words silence him. I could say something kind, but it is good to keep your hounds a little hungry. I could remind him that poor Forkbeard died at Candlemas, barely weeks into his reign. English soil won the battle over him. It held his bones, Knut took his victory.

No, I think, as I sip wine. A conqueror should rule, should build, should govern, should bring peace. I am a warrior. I know how little a battle means. It is just a gateway for what comes after.

My bishop has been telling me about the south. England has been floundering from one poor king to the next. She needs a strong hand. One that will govern her earls, and bring them in line, one who will allow the common folk to live and grow and prosper. A builder. A churchman. A man who has seen something of the world.

'What manner of man is Harold Godwinson?' your father asked me once.

'He is a great man,' I said. I felt a little daring for speaking like that, to a man who also claimed the kingship.

Your father laughed at me.

'Harold's brother is over there. You know him of course.'

I nodded. There was Tostig. I had loved him like a son, once.

I blamed it all on him. The whole disaster. Though maybe it is all chance. If Macbeth had not killed Earl Siward's son then Tostig would never have been earl in Northumbria. And he would not have brought your father here. And York would not have been burnt. And many who are dead would still be living. And the library of Alcuin would not have been consumed by all-devouring flames.

'Travellers have come to my hall. They speak highly of him,' your father said.

'You will meet him soon. I am sure of that,' I said. It was a little bold, but your father looked at me and winked.

'So I shall!' he said.

There was no fear within him. Not even as he breathed his last.

CHAPTER THIRTEEN

Sun Day, 24th September 1066

This morning I watched Eystein and Magnus head back to the ships as the sun lifted over the mists. The dew was already burning off as I walked back to my hall. Men, up earlier than I, had left trails through the dew. The lines trail off to the outhouse, to the river, to the hall.

I stand to see them off. My shoes were soaked through already. A few bands set off with them, crossing a company of Scots who were sick of the river-damp and were heading back to the ships. All they had brought with them was their banner, a blue cross on a field of white. It hung lazily from the end of the angled pole.

One of my retainers showed them to a place, but they wanted a dryer spot on the other side of the river, and filed over the bridge, and made their way towards it.

Along the side of my hall a retainer was sitting on the log pile, repairing his shoe with twine. He did not know who strode towards him, whose shadow it was that was about to cross his.

'Maybe it is time to get some new shoes,' I told him, and he squinted up into the light, then gave me a sheepish look. 'We have a long march ahead of us.'

'This'll just get me to York,' he said.

I had passed him by already. If he said more I did not hear it.

The air of the hall was cool and damp. Pleasantly so, like walking into a Greek house in the middle of summer, and feeling the heat subside.

A few hostages had come along the roads that lead north and east and south. On the next day my hostages would be brought from York and the wider shire, by Morcar and Edwin, and to feast with me and seal my plan to take the whole country.

We would march south while the weather held. Lincoln would open her gates to me. Then Nottingham, Derby, Leicester, Stamford. The Danelaw would not resist, not as long as I held their earl, Morcar, in my grip. I should hold two-thirds of England in my grasp, and then King Harold Godwinson would have to fight. And in fighting he would lose.

When he came to me Tostig had been like a stray hound, whipped and hungry. In the time here he had changed the most. I had watched him, this traitor to his own kin. I was his last throw. When we plundered Scarborough, he was tense. If this should fail, you could see his mind working, then I am doomed.

The night of Fulford Gate he was cocksure. He had settled many personal debts that day, and picked through the dead men, pointing out many of them by name. Lifting a banner, and saying, 'Good that he died.'

I did not listen. I was not here for him to kill the men who wronged him.

But now that the battle at Fulford was won, he saw that he had set in motion something far bigger than himself. He was like the clod of snow that falls from the high mountain tree, that sets off a tumble of light winter snow, that starts an avalanche that a man can see from miles down the valley. It plunges out of the cloud-cap and fills the dale with the dull roar of approaching thunder.

He saw me and was fearful. What breed of wolf had he brought to his country? He watched me talk to my men about tomorrow's feast. The alewife had taken every grain of malt from twenty miles distant, the vats smelt of bubbling yeast. He saw something in me he did not have. Would never have, being one of life's losers.

It was the Lord's Day.

In the hall, someone gave a mouse to a dog. It held the limp thing in its mouth, the bare tail hanging out. The dog lay down, front paws first, and threw the mouse about, and jumped to catch it.

It was dead, I think. When next I looked the mouse was eaten, the dog asleep, the fun was over.

It was the Lord's Day. I must have Eucharist, with or without yeast.

Archbishop Ealdred

On the morning of 25th September I performed morning mass
for you father. He knelt for a long time, and prayed silently, his
lips moving, forehead pressed hard into clenched fists.

Amen, he said at last. He stood up and stretched as he
yawned, and his outflung fingers reached the hall-rafters. I
have heard that men still remark on this, that they saw King
Harald Sigurdsson casually touch the wood which other men
must jump to finger.

It was a bright, hot morning. The army was taking its leisure,
camped out along the river meadows. Some were sitting on
moss-covered rocks. Other shook off the night dew, and were
drying in the sunlight. It was a peaceful scene. There were
bees and butterflies thick in the meadow flowers. All had their
spears and shields. They had left their mail coats behind at the
ships, because they had fought a battle, and were not expecting
more warfare.

It was halfway through the morning when lookouts saw
horsemen riding along the road from York. Your father put his
dice away and walked over the grass to see who they might be.
Earl Tostig walked with him.

'Whose banners are those?'

No one knew. One of his men said, 'Well, they are either
friend or foe.'

Your father shook his head. He summoned Tostig. Tostig
put his hand to his eyes, and went very still.

'What is it?' your father asked.

Tostig kept staring. It was as if he could not believe his eyes.

'What?' your father said. There was a long silence.

'It might be some of the men who were loyal to me coming
to pay their respects to you.'

Your father nodded. He did not bring the men to battle

order in case it was disrespectful to those who would be his people, but he stood and watched, and as the horsemen kept coming the force of them seemed to multiply and they raised a great dust cloud over them.

'Tostig!' Your father shouted for him now. 'Those men are not friendly.'

Tostig swallowed. 'No,' he said. 'I think my brother has come.'

Your father cursed. 'You three!' he said, picking three good men. 'Take horses, and tell Eystein to come with all speed! Bring mail! Bring shields! Bring men!'

CHAPTER FOURTEEN
The Battle of Stamford Bridge

They looked to me. All of them, like lost sheep. I seized a wood-axe from the pile outside. The head was loose. I hammered it back with the flat of my fist and beat it against the hall planks, ringing the building like a vast bell.

The sound was low, but it carried, like far-off thunder. 'Come back!' I shouted to the men on the other side of the river. 'Back!'

They stood up. They had not seen. 'Back!' I shouted once more.

The road from York was wooded, and where the trees failed the riders came at pace. They wore mail and helm. They carried spears. All brightly polished. All gleaming and glittering, silver in the sunlight. It was like a river of ice in my gut.

Men were not friendly, I remembered Halldor once saying, who came to a meeting in mail and with shield.

'Back!' I roared. I brought these men across the seas with me. Some of them were sons and grandsons of warriors I once admired. When the English came they were watching a cock-fight. They were drying river water off their legs. They were lying on their backs, soaking up the sunlight. They were playing dice, tossing daisies back into the grass, they were sleeping, they were dreaming, they were yawning wide and slow like lazy hounds. They would be slaughtered if they do not . . .

'Back!' I shouted, and this time they heard and saw, and someone on the far side pointed.

Group by group they looked up and saw and understood. You could see the alarm in the movements of the men. Some plunged down into the water like landing ducks. Others ran for the bridge. Others started, and then doubled back to grab some favourite item. A cloak, a sword, their shoes.

Quick! I willed them. Quick!

The first horsemen were already plunging down the slope towards the meadows. I could feel the hoofs through the summer-dry soil. I felt it all in the thrill of my fingertips and in the veins of my neck. The fear of the men, the exhilaration of the hunters, the wild joy of the horses, the tautness of the king who saw and whose mind played out all the futures, and started to plan against them.

We had left our war-gear with the ships. We had no mail, no shields, only the weapons we brought with us. Spears had been left behind by any who had swords or axes. Almost all of us had swords, now that we had taken our pick from the fields of Fulford dead.

We went to battle like the men of old, who wore nothing but wool, and faced death without fear.

My men streamed up from the bridge. They were running hard. 'Into companies,' I bellowed. The men pushed past each other, found their fjord-neighbours and shipmates. My retainers rushed up about me. One of them held Landwaster.

The English were streaming down towards the river.

On the bridge three Norse warriors stood. One of them had a barrel-lid as a shield. The other two stood at his side.

The English dismounted to come against them. They could only come three wide. The first was knocked off the bridge. The second hesitated and was driven off it. The fight held our attention as I led my army away from the hall, to a field of open ground.

Everyone was talking. Some urged me to flee south to the ships to Eystein, to our mail and armour. Others were pointing to a higher place. 'Lord!' they gesticulated.

The English had crossed the river at the ford, their horsemen were galloping up. There was no fleeing now. 'This way,' I called, and we took the high ground, and my men formed up about me in a wide circle.

One man was left on the bridge. There was a heap of bodies before him. He had seized an English axe, and swung it about his head, two-handed.

'Who is that man?' I shouted.

'Jokull of Lathe,' one of his fellows shouted.

'Magnificent,' I said as he held the line. The English bunched up on the bridge mouth. Some of them waded down into the water. One had a long spear. He braced his legs as we shouted warnings.

'Jokull!' Some men cupped their hands.

'Beneath!' shouted others.

The thrown spear caught him in the side. He swung his axe once, twice, three more times, and then the English rushed and he was lost to us, and the enemy streamed over the bridge and their horsemen rode hard to catch our stragglers.

'Here!' we called, and brought the whole herd into our ring-fold, looked out as the wolves circled.

They hemmed us in with horsemen.

I started the chant:

> *Stand firm my friends!*
> *Foremost athelings of Hrólf!*
> *Awake not to wine nor to wives' sweet talk,*
> *but wake to the Valkyrie's game of war*

The whole company, five thousand voices, lifted with me chanting the *Bjarkamál* together. I never felt so brave, never felt so much part of a greater whole, never stood with finer men. The best men that ever stood on soil. The English cavalry thundered in circles, their faces grim, and one of them rode out towards the place where Tostig's banner stood.

The rider called out to Tostig, I stood and tried to hear what was happening, but it was impossible.

Archbishop Ealdred

King Harold rode right to the edge of the ring of men. He called out to Tostig.

'Brother! Do not stand with our foes. Leave these men and I will restore you to your former title.'

'Why should I believe you?' Tostig called back.

'I am your brother.'

'So?' Tostig's voice was charged with passion. His pride would not let him join his brother.

'Come,' Harold tried once more.

'I shall not,' Tostig called back. 'I have found a better lord. A worthier man who values my own worth.'

'I ask you a third time,' Harold Godwinson called back, but this time Tostig would not answer, but turned his back and did not speak.

'So be it,' Harold called, and turned his horse away. And the battle began.

The English crossed at ford and bridge. I did not believe it until I saw the banner of the Fighting Man, white on a field of blue, and knew that the English king had come. Where did they keep all these armed warriors?.

'Is Morcar there, or Edwin?'

'I do not see them, Lord,' the man next to me shouted.

Some of the English dismounted and came towards us on foot, but others rode round and round, stabbing at the shieldless men, turning away our missiles on their kite shields.

There was no time for thought or silence. All was noise and fear and command. I was everywhere, shouting, calling, jeering with my men. I did not want to lose a single soul like this. It was an unfair fight. How had we been caught? There was no time to look back or forwards, there was only now. The Northumbrians had deceived us. Instead of bringing hostages they brought our enemies. If we had to beat them twice, then so we should, but this time we would be less generous. Less kind. More harsh. More judgemental. We should lay down the law, and it would not all be Northumbrian.

There was a roar as the English foot charged in from the bridge. My warriors met them and threw them back, like two waves at the black rock's foot, clashing against each other.

There was another roar as horsemen wheeled in from the north. Another roar as they wheeled off. A few brave men rushed out to grab a shield or helm from a fallen Englishman. One man paused to drag at a suit of mail, and did not see the danger till he felt the horse shadow over him, and turned in time to see his death descend in a flash of steel.

We were like a shipwrecked crew clinging to a rock in the midst of a stormy sea. From all sides the surf crashed in, running back through rivulets, and over rock-pools, dragging a few of us off to the sea-goddess's embrace.

We clung together. We would not break. 'Any sign of Eystein?' I called out.

A man sat on another's shoulders, but he could see over the horses of our foes. More of them were coming over the river. All of them mailed, dressed to make war.

The waves crashed in again, from all sides. The waters receded, and the circle of warriors was growing thin.

'Where is Eystein?' I cursed, but really I wanted to see Hope over the hillside.

Olaf's words came to me now. Never fear, never flee.

I wheeled about. We were beset with foes.

It could not be long now.

I stopped. The heavens were blue. Great clouds floated like sails. I half expected the sun to go dark, but it shone as bright as it did in my youth. I shall not end like this. I have faced Death before and lived.

I fetched a bearded axe from a dead man. I felt the weight and balance.

'Who is with me?' I called out. 'Who wants to make an end of this that men will remember?'

I cannot tell you how many came, but come they did, and in coming they raised themselves above the rest.

'Make way,' I told the men in the circle. There was the banner of the Fighting Man. There was Harold, the English king. If I could just reach him and kill him then this battle was won. What a song that should be.

'Boar's snout!' I shouted. Those that knew fell into place. The men behind me even had shields. I had done this a hundred times before, it felt, though never without armour. 'Forward!' I shouted, and the shieldwall before me opened and I led the charge, that gathered speed with the slope before us.

Archbishop Ealdred

I stood on the crest of the hill and watched your father make his final charge. Landwaster flew out behind him, and he had nothing but a woollen shirt and a wood axe that he had picked up that morning.

He swung it two-handed, outpaced younger men, drove all before him; furious and unstoppable.

I watched Harold's huscarls ride towards him, spears held at their shoulders, ready for the strike. But none it seemed could hit or hurt him. He cut one spear blade off at the haft. Drove his shoulder into the ribs of a horse, and tipped it over, cut the legs from the next, his white beard flowing over his shoulder with the wind of his own passing.

The battle stopped to see him charge. Men say an arrow hit King Harald in the throat. It took the words as he was shouting them. His left leg tripped, and he stumbled, overwhelmed at last, fell hard upon his back as his lifeblood leaked out of the wound with each remaining beat of his heart, arms outstretched, just ten paces from the English king.

CHAPTER FIFTEEN

The Last Viking

I lie in the grass.

Above me is blue and cloud and the bright sun shining. About me silence. If the battle still rages I do not hear it. I have not lost yet, I am not dead. There is still hope. Eystein may yet come and help us win this day. I have been in harder spots.

I can feel the ghosts call out to me. Harald! they sing, like the sirens that lure men onto treacherous rocks. Harald!

I can feel their hands pushing my shoulders up. They are willing me to stand. Helen, Halldor, Elizaveta, Olaf, my mother, Guttorm even. Halfdan, too, stands over me and puts out a hand.

Stand, they urge me. Stand, Harald, and win this day.

I cannot move. My body is the lead that holds my spirit down, arms outstretched upon the grass.

I try to speak but I cannot. I cannot speak or breathe, and the only sound is the gurgle of blood in my throat. I taste it. It is mine. It is not rain, it is a river.

I told you so, Halldor says to me. Someone takes my hand. He lifts me up, and holds me under my armpits, and below I see the foaming water, silver herring, and the black and white of killer whales moving through the water in a knotwork of death.

I smell oysters. I smell seawater, whale-breath. Olaf lifts me up. I do not know what this life will bring for me. I am joyful, I am clapping, I am not afraid.

I am hopeful that it will be a good life for a man to live.

The sky above me is so bright. It could be Greece in the height of summer, the light dazzles, and then the ground thunders with approaching horses, and the shadow falls over me.

So ended the life of your father, Harald Sigurdsson.

The rest of the day was spent in caring for the dying and preparing a great pyre upon which they could burn the dead. The fire was lit only at sunset, and for a moment its light and heat held off the lengthening night. I watched the sparks lifting up on the smoke and it seemed that an age had ended with your father's death. Something proud and noble, wild and free, and I felt a deep sadness for all the lives that had been lost.

The next day, Harold met with Earl Paul of Orkney and your brother Magnus, and pardoned them, and allowed them to depart after swearing oaths of peace to him. Of the three hundred boats that had carried your father's army south, only enough men had survived to sail twenty-six of them back. I oversaw the burial of the dead, but with so many, I fear the graves were not dug deep, and farm-folk who pass that way tell me that each year the plough turns up more and more bones, and also that the crops that grow there are especially bountiful.

On the night after the battle, the English held their victory feast in the earl's manor in York. The wind that had been in the north turned southerly once more, and as King Harold of the English led the toasts at his victory feast, Duke William set sail from Normandy.

You will know, of course, what happened after. Your father defeated Earls Morcar and Edwin; Harold defeated your father; and William defeated Harold at Hastings. Each of the three claimants won his first battle. It was William's luck that he did not have to fight twice.

Your father never told me why he named his mail shirt Emma. Though, as the only Emma of note was the wife of Knut, I think he must have had some private joke.

A man in the market told me that before each battle your

father would call out, 'Bring me Emma!' Another man, with no link to the first, repeated the same joke, but this time the wording was a little more coarse. I have refrained from repeating it here. I never heard it said, and surely there are some in Norway who will be able to testify more reliably than we.

What I can tell you about is his stay here, in the space by the altar of our Minster.

There have been no miracles at your father's tomb, though we do get a trickle of Norse pilgrims who come to lay offerings there. Warriors, mostly.

Julianus says there was one such last week, a young lad with a fair beard who had sailed down from Orkney and stood there silently, then recited some lines – Julianus did not understand what he said – and then left. Julianus says that he does not think the man was a heathen.

I heard a line of poetry a week or so ago, and it made me think of your father.

Now we know which ones are brave,
When the war-walls crash the time of trial
Fated men fall as they must.

It was the poem, I think, that your father chanted before he charged. A poem of his own composition.

It seems fitting in many ways that your father's story should end with his own verse.

I would have written this letter to you with my own hand, but my eyesight fails, and so I have dictated this letter to my scribe, Julianus. He is a patient fellow. I am easily distracted, and at times the leaves of my memory are missing, and he helps fill them in for me. There are many poor souls who come to our abbey to beg for alms, and there is much suffering to alleviate.

I must see they are all tended to. I hope that this book brings some comfort. Your father was the most famous man of his age.

Forgive this book's poor binding. Times are not what they once were in York. If you find consolation in your grief, good Queen, and if this work is to your liking, then remember kindly the poor monks here, who labour to restore glory to Christ. Generosity should not be begrudged. We all leave the world naked and alone, as God sent us, but we all can do a little to honour God the Maker, before we pass away.

Remember us in your prayers. And remember the poor church of St Peter, and the many repairs that we must undertake in Christ's name and for the Lord's Glory.

I dedicate this work to Christ. In the name of Him who hung upon the gibbet for our sake, with the eternal Father and Holy Spirit, world without end. AMEN.

Ealdred, Archbishop of York
York, August 1069

Justin Hill was born in the Bahamas, and grew up in York, attending St Peter's School. He studied Old England and Medieval Literature at Durham University, and spent most of his twenties on postings with Voluntary Service Overseas in rural China and East Africa.

He has written poetry, non-fiction and fiction, which spans eras as distant from one another as Anglo Saxon England, in *Shieldwall*, to Tang Dynasty China, in *Passing Under Heaven*. His work has won numerous awards, including the Geoffrey Faber Memorial Prize, the Somerset Maugham Award and a Betty Trask Award, as well as being selected as a *Sunday Times* Book of the Year (*Shieldwall*) and a *Washington Post* Book of the Year (*The Drink and Dream Teahouse*).

In 2014 he was selected to write the sequel to the Oscar-winning film *Crouching Tiger, Hidden Dragon*.

He lives near York.